TRUST

Margaret Leroy studied music at St Hilda's College, Oxford, and social work at Leicester University, after which she spent fifteen years as a social worker and counsellor. She is the author of *Aristotle Sludge*, a story for children, and three non-fiction titles, *Miscarriage, Pleasure* and *Some Girls Do*. She has written widely for magazines and newspapers. She lives in Kingston-upon-Thames with her husband and two daughters. This is her first novel.

Miscarriage
Pleasure: The Truth About Female Sexuality
Some Girls Do: Why Women Do – and Don't – Make the First Move

For children

Aristotle Sludge

Trust

MARGARET LEROY

HarperCollins*Publishers*

HarperCollins*Publishers*
77–85 Fulham Palace Road,
Hammersmith, London W6 8JB

Published by HarperCollins*Publishers* 1999
1 3 5 7 9 8 6 4 2

This library edition 1999

A catalogue record for this book
is available from the British Library

ISBN 0 00 225881 1

Set in Plantin Light by
Palimpsest Book Production Limited,
Polmont, Sterlingshire

Printed in Great Britain by
Caledonian International Book Manufacturing Limited, Glasgow

ACKNOWLEDGEMENTS

These people provided vital information, advice or hospitality when I was writing this book: C. J. Goodwin, Jane Taylor, Richard Taylor, Gretta Mulrooney, Madeleine Fullerton, Roy Umney, Vicki Tippet, Martin Shaw, David Shaw, Jeremy Cameron and Jeremy Wakefield. My thanks to them all. Hugh Brayne's advice on legal procedure was invaluable. And thanks especially to Lucy Floyd for her wisdom and generosity.

Mick, Becky and Isabel were as supportive and loving as always, even when I was at my most preoccupied.

I am also indebted to Michael Fishwick for so much inspiration and encouragement, to Rebecca Lloyd for her thoughtful and intelligent editing, to Phyllis Richardson for her meticulous work on the text, and to my agent Lisa Eveleigh for her energy and commitment.

But those to whom I owe the most cannot be named. I am profoundly grateful for what they gave me.

PROLOGUE

A woman and a man. They stood on my doorstep, smiling but not with their eyes. The woman was smart and stylish, in a wholesome, head girl kind of way. Her glossy brown hair was cut in a neat bob: the skirt of her navy suit finished modestly at the knee. She had a faint, clean smell, of deodorant, perhaps, or fabric conditioner. The man was younger – tall, gangly, with his hair slicked back like Elvis.

'Mrs Langdon?' said the woman.

'Yes,' I said.

They showed me their identification.

'We're sorry to disturb you like this,' said the woman. 'We did try to phone, but no one answered.'

'You'd better come in,' I said.

They followed me past the door to the sitting room. Lucy was in there, settled in front of Tots TV as though entranced, her chest heaving with slow sleepy breaths, her comforter, an old cardigan, pressed to her cheek. She looked appealingly scruffy after her day at infant school, her face a little smudged, pale fronds of hair escaped from her scrunchie straggling down over her shoulders. She didn't turn her head as we passed: she wouldn't get up for an hour or so. This mattered to me: I wanted desperately to protect her from what was about to happen.

My kitchen was full of syrupy autumn sunlight. Geraniums flared red on my windowsill. Outside in the garden, the shadow of the apple tree fell sharp and dark across the bright grass. A bee buzzed opulently at the window, unnervingly loud in the stillness. I was acutely aware of all these things, as though all my senses were sharpened. Everything was precise and loud and clear.

The man and the woman stood either side of my big oak table. They seemed to take up a lot of space. It was the moment when you expect a visitor to express some sort of approbation – 'What a fabulous old fireplace' or 'I love your children's drawings'. They just stood there – not hostile, but not friendly either. A shaft of

3

sunlight fell on the table between us. Dust motes danced in it, casually beautiful.

'We want to talk to you about Daniel Whitmore,' they said.

'Yes,' I said. 'Why don't you sit down.'

They sat. The man had very long legs: he shifted around, trying to work out where to put his feet. They opened their briefcases, took out pens and notepads. The man had something else too, a blue official-looking folder. He put the folder down, opened it to reveal some handwritten pages inside, straightened it between his palms so it was neatly parallel to the edge of the table. What I saw there between those exact and unfamiliar hands appalled me. The writing was my own.

'Would you like coffee?' I said.

'Yes please,' they said. I felt a surge of relief that they'd accepted. I remembered Dan saying they'd refused his offer of coffee, and how that had panicked him.

I put on the kettle, took some mugs from the dresser, opened a cupboard to get out the biscuits. The cupboard was crammed full and a bit of a mess as usual: a packet of alphabet pasta and several stray puy lentils fell out onto the work surface. 'Sorry,' I said, irrelevantly. I had a fleeting fantasy that they might note down the dire state of my kitchen cupboards in their little books.

I found the gingernuts and put five of them on a plate, arranging them in a perfect semi-circle. This felt important, as though somehow I could make everything alright if only I put the biscuits in the right places. When I handed the woman her coffee, I saw that my hand was shaking.

'Mrs Langdon, let me assure you that there's nothing to worry about,' she said soothingly. 'We're just going to have a little conversation – we won't be taking a statement.'

'You haven't done anything wrong,' said the man. 'We just need your help. You mustn't worry about it.'

I sat down, clutching my coffee cup in both hands, holding it to me tightly, as Lucy would clutch her comforter whenever she was scared.

'Your name is Chloe Langdon?'

'Yes,' I said.

'And where do you work, Mrs Langdon?'

'At the Cambridge Centre. I'm a social worker. Part-time.'

'What kind of social worker?'

'Child protection,' I said.

The woman asked the questions. The man wrote my answers down in his little book. If they weren't taking a statement, why was he writing it down? I wondered for a moment if I was being unbelievably naive, if I should refuse to talk.

'This must be very difficult for you,' said the woman, rather surprisingly.

'Yes,' I said. In that state of heightened emotion, I was disproportionately moved by this attempt at empathy. I felt my eyes fill with tears.

'And do you have children, Mrs Langdon?' she said.

I nodded. 'Lucy's five and Alice is twelve.'

I realized they were asking me questions to which they already knew the answers. This made me very afraid. But what could I do, except tell what had happened exactly as I remembered it?

'And I believe you know Daniel Whitmore?'

'Yes,' I said. Yes, I knew Daniel Whitmore.

Part I

I

I'd hoped to have the party in the garden, with tea on the table under the apple tree: children are so much easier to manage with lots of room to move. But at the very last moment, big purple clouds had shut off the sun. 'It can't rain at *my* party,' said Lucy, outraged, as the first fat drops bounced off the patio. It was a classic June storm, noisy and extravagant. As we played the usual games, sang the songs, blew out the candles, I kept glancing out through the misted window, and saw how the rain was lashing at the pale briar roses in the hedge I never prune at the bottom of the garden, covering the lawn in drifts of sodden papery petals. It made me sad: they're so delicate, so fragile, hedgerow flowers really, and that year they'd had so little time to bloom.

The bit I remember best was when we played 'Tommy'. It's a game Jude taught me – Jude's good with children, endlessly inventive: I tell her – tactlessly perhaps – that it's because she doesn't have any herself. You get heaps of sweets – Smarties and refreshers and sticks of liquorice and what Lucy calls 'those little jelly lump things' – and you pile them all on a plate, a rainbow mountain, irresistible. One child gets sent outside and the other children whisper, happily conspiring, choosing Tommy. The child who went out comes back and takes a paper bag and picks sweets up one by one and puts them in her bag – till she touches the chosen sweet. Then everyone shrieks 'Tommy' and it's the next child's turn.

It's a cruel game. With luck you can make quite a killing, but of course it's totally random, exposing children to the lawlessness of things – something we usually go to great lengths to protect them from. I like to watch how they handle this, the way they behave as though it can all be controlled. That year, the first little girl went for sleight of hand, snatching her sweets with sudden bird-like darting movements. Lucy just shovelled hers in cheerfully, trusting in sheer energy and the beneficence of the universe. And Alice drove everyone crazy with her slowness, pausing, head on one side, before each choice: she's heavily into *feng shui* and likes astrological explanations for things – 'Well, Mum, you *are* a Cancer, and Cancers are full of fears' – and I suspected she was hoping for psychic guidance.

It all went well till Fred's turn. I'd rather fallen for Fred, Lucy's newest, most passionate playmate, her best friend since Wednesday, a beautiful elf of a child with a silky fringe that fell into his eyes. He sat down proudly and reached out one finger and touched his first jelly bean – and all the children shrieked 'Tommy'. He clutched his empty paper bag to his chest, smiled a carefully brave smile. I couldn't bear it. I scooped up a handful of sweets, tipped them into his bag. 'To make up,' I said. But it only helped a little. He turned away, his face translucent with imminent tears.

The parents came. I found anoraks and shoes, made the usual quips about having to call in the cleansing department, gave each child a bag of presents – lollipops, plastic aeroplanes, Japanese water flowers. Soon only Fred was left. I wondered what had happened to his parents: there's an unspoken rule you should never be late to pick up your child from a party. I left him playing with Alice and Lucy, though he still looked rather fragile, and retreated to the kitchen.

The table was littered with the remains of tea – paper cups, half-burnt candles smudged with soot, bits of Barbie cake with toothmarks in the icing, an untouched plate of the healthy wholemeal sandwiches I make each year so dutifully, then bin after the party. It could all wait. I kicked off my shoes, pulled a streamer out of my hair, poured wine.

There's a special silence that follows children's noise, a silence with a thick, soft texture that you can almost touch. I sat and sipped my wine and let the silence settle around me. Peace seemed to seep from the walls of my house like warmth from brick after a long day of sunshine. I love this kitchen of mine: the pots of flowering plants, the blue and white china jumbled on the dresser, the walls as yellow as butter, and everywhere the children's drawings – 'A Cow with a Bicycle', 'Lots of Magic Heather', 'Mummy Being Fierce' – Lucy's picture of me with long nails and teeth and witchy glittery earrings.

When Adam left, I repainted everywhere. Painting was all about taking possession – making it properly mine, as it somehow hadn't been when Adam lived here. And I really know it now, I could tell you all sorts of things about this house – its cracks and scars and the lines pencilled in by the damp, and the old anaglypta that soaked up the paint so thirstily, and the way it's all sinking slightly sideways. They're both intimate and banal, those things you learn as you work on your house, stripping, sanding, prying into corners – in a way rather like the things you know about the bodies of your children, the indelible white mark where they scratched a chickenpox spot, the thin crusts of cradle cap hidden under their hair, the scented curvy places in the backs of their necks. And now my house looks so much nicer than when Adam was here, though some people, I guess, might find it all a bit eccentric: my muslin curtains are tied back with string, and none of the china matches, and there are far too many candles. Alice certainly doesn't approve: 'Mum, what's that scarf thing doing there? Why can't we have *lampshades* like everybody else?' But to my eye it all works beautifully, especially the kitchen. This is the oldest part of the house, which was just a little Victorian two-up two-down before it was extended in the thirties: and sitting quite still in this warm old room in the peace after the party, I could almost sense those other lives lived out here, like friendly presences.

Lucy came stomping in, luscious in her orange linen dress and little canvas boots. Five is perfect: I've felt that with both of them. At five their bodies elongate a little, acquire that grace of the middle childhood years, yet they still have the baby roundness in their faces, the fat cheeks and dimples. Lucy at five was utterly succulent, like an apricot.

She stood in front of me now, clenching her fists, her plump face poignant with a sudden memory of deprivation. 'Mummy, why didn't you let me win anything? Why couldn't *I* win the Ugly Face competition?'

Alice came trailing behind her. 'Silly Lu. Mum never lets you win anything at your own party,' she said, with the world-weary sophistication of the almost-teenager who already has two piercings in either ear.

'*You* got all the presents,' I said to Lucy. 'Just think of those presents. A fire-engine and felt tips and a shaker maker – all that lovely stuff.'

I folded her into my lap. She resisted stiffly for a second, then relented, snuggling in. She pursed up her lips, plugged in her thumb. I buried my face in her hair.

'You smell yummy,' I said.

'*You* smell of *alcohol*,' said Lucy disapprovingly. She wriggled down and, still sucking her thumb, scampered off to the sitting room where the toys were. Alice followed.

I poured more wine and watched the rain. My window boxes, stuffed with lobelias and alyssum, were turning into puddles. Honeysuckle drooped against the window, its complicated flowers heavy with water. A couple of snails eased themselves up the pane: you could see their glossy undersides. There are hundreds of snails in my garden, huge ones with tiger-striped shells, and they always come out in the wet. The girls follow their silver trails across the patio, collect and abuse them, make snail hospitals and snail graveyards, but still their numbers grow, and I have to put Vaseline round the tops of my flowerpots to stop them eating my lilies. Yet I feel an obscure fondness for them. Like the fat white worms in the flowerbeds and the tiny grey frogs that flicker in the long grass, they seem to fit with the general lushness of my garden, where everything is a little excessive and overdone.

There was a sudden wail from the living room. I rushed in. Fred was crying. He'd managed to cut himself on Lucy's new fire-engine – a present from Jude, which Lucy hadn't yet looked at. I knelt to hug him. A bright drop of blood welled up from his finger. He turned his head away, sobbing, appalled. Lucy, whose Barbies are always suffering from unspeakable mutilations and lacerations, watched fascinated.

'I think this calls for a really big plaster,' I said.

I was sticking it on his finger, his cries quieting now to big shuddery breaths, when the doorbell rang. 'There – that must be your Dad,' I said, biting back the urge to say, And about time too.

But it wasn't. It was a man I'd never seen before – tall, dark, rather solid, soaked to the skin. The sight of him standing there confused me: it wasn't what I was expecting.

'I've come for Fred,' he said, as Fred hurled himself into his arms. 'Well, I guess you could work that one out.' There was a trace of Manchester in his voice. He smiled a self-deprecating smile, a little like Fred's. He was badly in need of a shave. 'Their car broke down. What can I say?'

I couldn't resist this very deliberate charm. 'It's absolutely fine,' I said. 'These things happen. You'd better come in and get Fred's things.'

The children drifted back to their games, Fred happy now that someone was here for him.

We told each other our names: he was Dan, Fred's uncle, he said. He followed me into the kitchen. He wasn't particularly good-looking – his face was rather asymmetrical, a heavy jaw, heavy eyebrows – but there was something pleasing about his tall, broad-shouldered body that seemed to fill my gaze, and the casual way his clothes hung from him. The stubble gave him a nicely dissolute air, where most men would just have looked seedy.

The shoulders of his shirt were dark with rain, his hair was stuck to his head. I gave him a towel. He put his head down and rubbed his hair. There was a strong smell of wet denim.

'Sorry about this,' he said.

'That's okay,' I said politely.

And then, not because I wanted to particularly, but because I felt I should – with my bottle of Chardonnay open on the table, and outside the rain tipping down – I offered him a drink.

'That sounds delightful,' he said. He put down the towel and smoothed his hair back. He had the kind of coarse hair that never looks neat. It was greying a bit: I guessed he was forty-something, more or less like me.

I poured him some wine. He stayed standing for a moment, looking at the drawings on the pinboard.

'Mummy Being Fierce. Are you?'

'Sometimes,' I said. 'Not often enough, probably.'

He looked me up and down very thoroughly. I was hotly aware that my shirt was rather tight and that there was a button missing between my breasts because I hate sewing and hadn't bothered to replace it.

'You've got the same earrings on,' he said.

'Yes. They're my favourites.'

'They don't match,' he said. 'A moon and a star. I like that.'

Lucy, curious, peered round the door.

Dan sat down at the table and smiled at her. 'You must be the birthday girl.'

She flounced in, very aware of this special status, waving her swagbag in one hand. She went right up to him and touched his sleeve. 'Yuk. You're everso wet.'

'It's pouring out there,' he said. 'Cats and dogs.'

'Look what I got in my swagbag,' she said. She tipped the little presents out onto the table – the aeroplane, the lollipop, the Japanese flower. She held the flower out to me. 'What's this for, Mummy? What does it do?'

'You put it in water, see it open out,' I told her. 'I'll show you.'

'No, let me,' said Lucy.

There was a cup with some dregs of lemonade in it. Lucy dropped the flower into the cup. The scrunched-up wizened colourless thing started to ease apart in the wetness, opening out into loose, exuberant curls and coils. Its dull colours deepened, sang out – scarlet, purple, acid yellow. Dan leaned across to watch. I could feel the warmth of his breath on my face.

Lucy gave a little sigh of pleasure. 'It's pretty. A real live paper flower.'

'So, birthday girl,' said Dan, 'was it a good party?'

Lucy frowned so that her nose wrinkled, not looking at him or me, watching her flower unfold. 'I wish Daddy could have come.'

I felt myself flush. I put out a hand, stroked her hair, soothing her. 'Sweetheart, you'll be seeing Daddy tomorrow. Straight after school. And he's taking you to Pizza Hut, remember.'

'Can I have every topping at the Ice Cream Factory? Can I have the red sauce and the marshmallows and hundreds and millions and thousands of Smarties?'

'Of course you can. It's your special day, you can do exactly what you want.'

Suddenly the light seemed to go out in her face. 'What if Daddy's mobile rings before we get to the pudding?'

'It won't. He won't have his mobile. He'll leave his mobile at home.'

'Tell him.'

'I will.'

She went out, then stopped and poked her head back round the door. 'Will Simone be there?'

'I expect so.'

'I hate Simone.'

And leaving no time for an answer, she marched off.

Dan shrugged, half-smiled. 'That's family life in the nineties for you,' he said.

'It's fine,' I said. 'Really, we get along just fine. We're all very used to it now. Really.'

My face felt hot: I knew I'd gone red. There was a little pause. The rain banged on the windowsill: summer smells washed in – pollen, wet grass, the sugary scent of honeysuckle.

Sensing my embarrassment, Dan started to talk about himself, trying to smooth things over. He told me about his work: I guess it seemed a safe sort of topic. He was a psychologist who worked in schools, he said. He made recommendations about schooling for children with disabilities, advised teachers, wrote reports for statements of special educational need. He seemed passionate about it all: he was, I suspected, the kind of man who'd get close to his clients – who'd be sent Christmas cards and asked to Diwali meals. He mentioned he was learning Urdu, and that particularly impressed me. He was based at an office very near the Cambridge Centre. Then I told him about my own job. He pointed out how much we had in common: his wife was a social worker too, he said, and he'd recently joined a working party on child protection. We talked about his working party.

Afterwards, from the perspective of everything that happened later, I would often muse on the timing of it – on his arrival there at my kitchen table almost exactly two years after Adam left. The timing was immaculate: the grief was mostly behind me, I was ready at last to be woken from my safe domestic dream, yearning deep down for some interesting male intrusion into my life – in spite of all my protestations about the pleasures of independence. And in my wilder moments, pondering on this surprising synchronicity, I'd wonder if in some sense I drew him to me, made it happen: if, witch-like, I summoned him with the birthday spells, the candles and incantations.

Not quite able to meet his eyes, I watched as he curved his hand round the base of the wine-glass, noting the square male shape of his palm, the fine black hairs on the backs of his fingers. What I felt wasn't yet straightforward lust, more a sense that there was a boundary missing between us – that some kind of physical and emotional cordon that usually marks one stranger off from another just wasn't there. It was a feeling perhaps that nothing further needed to be negotiated. As though it would have been perfectly natural – almost expected in fact – to reach across the table and insinuate my fingers gently and insistently between his.

Fred came in, dive-bombing his plastic aeroplane. Dan finished his wine.

'Party's over, Fred. Say goodbye.'

'Thank you for having me,' said Fred.

I bent to him, gave him a hug. The gesture went beyond what I'd normally do, said rather shamelessly, See how warm and womanly I am.

'Look,' said Dan, 'if you're in child protection, perhaps we could have a drink sometime. I'm always interested in people's points of view.' He smiled, a lovely crooked smile like a little boy's, as though acknowledging the tenuousness of the excuse. 'You can get me on this number during the day.' He tipped some cake remains off a Barbie plate and wrote his name and number. 'If you want to,' he said. 'I hope you can read my writing.'

'Yes,' I said, though I didn't yet know which bit I was saying yes to.

I led the way to the hall, pushed aside the ivies that trail from hanging baskets by the front door, said goodbye. He took Fred's hand and went off into the rain, which was falling more quietly now. I watched them for a moment through the glass panel beside the door. The sun was coming out through the cloud: the wet road shone. It was only then, as they walked away and vanished in the tentative sunlight, that the sense of sexual longing really opened out in me, so sudden, so startling, it made me catch my breath.

'Mum, you're not going to go out with him, are you?' said Alice, as I turned away.

'Who's Mum going out with?' said Lucy eagerly, scampering up, her face distorted with the lollipop she'd tucked in her cheek.

'That man,' said Alice. 'Mum really fancied him. You can always tell.'

'Honestly, Alice.'

'Well, are you?'

I laughed. 'I don't suppose so . . . There's 50p for each of you if we get the tidying finished in half an hour.'

And I went to get the rubbish sacks and set about the seemingly impossible task of restoring my house to the way it had been before.

2

Jude was in before me, on the phone, placating somebody, her flamboyant fingernails – navy-blue that morning – tapping furiously on her desk. The kettle had just boiled. I made two coffees in our Amnesty mugs and took one to her.

It was already hot. Traffic noise and exhaust fumes surged in through the open windows. Pigeons slumped in a feathery heap on the windowsill, murmuring softly and peering round with hostile little eyes. High above the mess and noise of the street, the sky was a miraculous blue, as though washed pure and clean by yesterday's rain.

She put the phone down, turned to me. 'God, I hate that woman.' She screwed up her face, put on a whiney voice. '"It's nothing to do with me, *I* didn't know . . ." I mean, it was going on for five years, twice a week for five years, in the next bedroom. How could she not have known?'

'I've often had mothers say that,' I said. 'You never know what to think.'

'It's only a three-bed semi, for God's sake,' said Jude, shaking her head. She raised her cup to her lips. 'Jesus, this coffee's like engine oil. You have a seriously addictive personality, Chloe.'

I sipped my coffee and shuddered pleasantly. 'It tastes fine to me.'

'Nice party?'

'Yeah. It all went well. Nobody cried. Nobody puked. Lucy loved the fire-engine. Thanks.'

'She's adorable.' She leaned back in her chair, stretched luxuriantly, her long arms muscly and very tanned. Jude likes it hot: she comes from Chicago, where the winters are white and the summers sweltering. Sometimes she gets quite nostalgic for those extremes.

I was aware of clearing my throat, which had suddenly clogged up. 'Jude – d'you know Dan Whitmore?'

A tanker passing in the street below drowned my words. I had to repeat them. Shit, I thought: I sound about thirteen.

Jude folded her arms abruptly and frowned at me.

I laughed. 'You look so *ferocious!*'

'Chloe, what is this?'

'Just tell me.'

She plucked a dead leaf from the begonia on her desk: the whole plant shook. 'Dan Whitmore. Yeah, I do know him a bit. We ran a group together a few years ago. He put a lot of work in . . . Nice-looking. Well, you've obviously noticed that.'

'I just wondered,' I said.

'Oh yes?'

'He came to pick one of the kids up from Lucy's party, that's all.'

Jude opened her mouth, then shut it again, trying to decide whether to say something.

The door crashed back. Nat, our team leader, rushed in, late as usual, and dumped his briefcase on Jude's desk.

'Hi there. Good weekends?'

We made inconclusive noises. He poured coffee.

Nat is a clever and dedicated worker who could have gone far if only he'd been able to give up his habit of relentless self-deprecation. He's got a kind of dissolute look, his face trenched with lines by years of cynicism and an addiction to Camel cigarettes: his suits could have come from Oxfam. Once I came on him eating chips from a paper bag in an underpass, and thought that you might be moved to slip him a coin as you passed. Jude and I depend on him utterly.

Now Jude jumped up. 'Nat, I need to see you about that new case. Right this minute.'

They went into his office, which opens out of ours.

I had a review in a children's home that morning. Amber McNaughton, a case like so many others, a thirteen-year-old girl who kept running away, had sex in car parks for money, sometimes cut her wrists with a Stanley knife, the incisions neatly arranged at approximately half-inch intervals. I went to get her file, which was fat and full as a triple-decker sandwich: this is always a bad sign. I flicked through without undoing the clasp, though a strip of typing down the edge of every page was obscured. When a file is very full, I worry that if I undo it bits of paper will spew out all over the place and I'll never get them back in.

My car was hot and smelt, as usual, of stale crisps. People sometimes helpfully remark that I ought to organize rubbish bags for the girls, but I never seem to get round to it. The air through the ventilation system was warm, the steering wheel was already painful to touch, the backs of my knees stuck to the seat. I listened to Jazz FM, a woman's voice that made you think of a bolt of silk being shaken out, and thought, of course, about Dan, not Amber McNaughton. I was still at the point where you feel you have a choice. You think: I could walk away, I only have to decide. Sometimes for a second I saw him – his fingers curving round the stem of the wine glass or pushing his wet hair back – and a thin bright line of sensation seared through me.

The children's home was on the edge of a high-rise estate. I parked and went in, through a room with a sagging sofa and table football, where a woman was mopping the vinyl floor. The place smelt of Jeyes Fluid and last night's curry, the wallpaper was peeling. For all the efforts of the woman with the mop, there was so much that looked messy and broken and uncared-for. Since doing this kind of work, I often dream about places like this – impersonal rooms with broken sofas and random radios blaring and nowhere to feel safe. In the dreams, I know I have come here to find something I want or need, something infinitely important to me, but of course I wake before I find what I'm looking for – or even remember what it might be.

It was the usual kind of thing. We sat round a big veneered table that smelt faintly of dishcloth: me and the Head of Home and Amber's care worker, and a child psychiatrist with a mid-European accent and dangly jewellery. Amber's mother Trish was there too, showing lots of freckled cleavage. She's a difficult, angry woman, but I came to like her when I asked that staple question of therapists: If I could wave a magic wand and make one wish come true, what would you ask for? 'I'll show you, Chloe, love,' she said, and she took me to her fridge door where she'd stuck up a newspaper clipping, a picture advertising a cruise on Russia's inland waterways: white minarets, star-painted, against a pale blue sky. That moved me – a yearning that was so specific: the way it suggested a whole life lived in the longing to be anywhere but here.

We drank a lot of tepid coffee and expressed scepticism about the future. A clock ticked intrusively in the barren room: there was a smell of warm vinyl. Amber came in, wearing a T-shirt that said, 'I get it every Sunday,' and cried a bit, dabbing at her face with scrunched-up bits of loo roll. I tried to concentrate, but kept thinking about Jude, trying to remember her expression, wondering about her hesitancy as she opened her mouth to speak. I felt desperately impatient to find out what she knew. We ended with some vague and over-optimistic recommendations – to work on Amber's social skills, to set up some sessions for Trish and Amber together – and I gave Trish a lift home then drove back to the office. It was clouding over, threatening a downpour like yesterday's. I bought an undemanding egg mayonnaise roll.

I finally caught up with Jude in the loo, where she was flossing her teeth before a Failure To Thrive case conference. She grinned as my reflection joined hers in the mirror. The harsh lighting emphasized the deepening lines and little saggy patches on our faces.

'So tell me,' I said.

She took the floss out of her mouth. 'Dan?'

I nodded.

'He gets around, Chloe,' she said. 'Someone I know was involved with him.' She shut the floss with a loud snap, dropped it in her bag, hunted for her lip-pencil. 'The usual shit. Talks a good line, wouldn't leave his wife. Sara threw a toaster at him.'

'D'you know his wife?' I said to her face in the mirror.

'I've met her. She works with the elderly: a Care Manager, I think.'

Curiosity flooded me like nausea. 'What does she – well – look like – roughly?'

'Oh, Chloe.' She grinned at me. She took the lid off her lip-pencil and drew extravagant lines just outside the edge of her lips. 'God, I've got some new wrinkles. Time for collagen implants, perhaps. I hate these ones between my mouth and my chin. They make me think of my mother.'

'Go on. Tell me.'

'Kind of attractive. Slim.'

'How slim?'

'Very slim.'

I frowned at my reflection, at the weight I'd put on since having the girls. On my better days I think of nice words like voluptuous.

'Hair pulled back, brown lipstick, tailored trousers – you know that kind of thing.' Jude took out her own very red lipstick and pursed up her lips to apply it. I waited impatiently. She pressed her lips together to even the lipstick out. 'They have this wonderful house in Wimpole Avenue. Their kitchen's gorgeous. Smallbone. I went there to a party once. Very classy. Limed oak and these yummy dark blue tiles.'

'Oh,' I said, discouraged. I thought of my blocked drains and messy cupboards and general air of mildly glamorous disorder. How could a couple of candlesticks made of old French banisters possibly compete with a Smallbone kitchen?

She turned to face me, smelling of freshly-applied Opium.

'Chloe, are you sure that this is what you really want? I'm starting to think that married men are totally over-rated.'

'Well, you should know,' I said.

'Bitch,' said Jude amiably. 'I mean it, Chloe. Seriously. It's all the anxiety, it really gets to me. I mean, one day one of these guys is going to have some dreadful cardiac event in my bed and lumber me with a helluva lot of explaining.' She snapped the top on her lipstick, dropped it into her huge handbag. 'Have you slept together?'

'Of course not.'

'Are you seeing him?'

'I don't know.'

She brushed her hand tenderly against my cheek. 'Chloe, just take care, okay? I've got a brilliant book on sex addiction. I've got all the symptoms, but I'm working on it. I'll give it to you when I've finished.'

'Alright.'

'Don't do a thing till you've read it. Promise me.'

I went to my desk and peeled the clingfilm off my roll. There wasn't enough mayonnaise in it, and the bread stuck to the roof of my mouth. Outside the brightness had all gone out of the day, the sky was the colour of a bruise.

It was quiet in the office that afternoon, with Nat and Jude at the conference and the others all out on visits. The silence, in this room that usually simmered with activity, was somehow troubling – like the uneasy feeling you get, the tiny stirring of panic, if everyone at a party stops talking at once. I dictated some notes on the review. My voice echoed in the emptiness: it sounded mournful, full of downward intonations. And in a way I was mourning, I suppose – grieving for the loss of my twenty-four-hour fantasy of sweetly empathic and hugely significant sex with this man whose face I could scarcely remember. Because Jude was absolutely right to warn me off. I knew my own limitations: I knew that a physical closeness that was transitory and lacked some deeper meaning for him held no interest for me, however pleasant it might be: I'd done enough of that kind of thing when I was younger.

In the end I took the scrap of envelope onto which I'd copied his number out of my bag and scrunched it up and dropped it in the bin – hoping the gesture would put a line under the whole episode and free me to get on.

Instantly, the phone rang. It's Dan, something squealed like a child inside me. But it was only Trish, wanting to know if she'd left her cigarette lighter in my car.

I don't know exactly what it was that made me change my mind. Maybe it was something to do with the grey ordinariness of the afternoon, the way it was just like so many other afternoons, sitting there at my desk between the filing cabinets, with a distant ice-cream van blurting out 'The Teddy Bears' Picnic' and the phones shrilling down the corridor. Maybe it was simply the intensity of the sexual feeling, which of course wouldn't go away however often I told myself that Jude was undoubtedly right. But most likely it was that idiot surge of hope I'd felt at the sound of the phone. Weird, really, to think that if Trish hadn't mislaid her cigarette lighter it might all have turned out differently. Because as I sat there dictating my notes, something shifted inside me and a decision formed, with disconcerting clarity, as decisions sometimes do, and I knew what I wanted. I fished the scrap of envelope out of the waste-bin and smoothed out the creases. As my finger moved towards the keypad, I was irresistibly reminded of the game at Lucy's party, and the heap of scented shiny sweets, the sherbet and liquorice and jelly bears, and the way the children had reached out their hands so hopefully.

3

I grew up on the edge of the New Forest, on the cusp between the farmland and the wood. You go down a gravel track that winds between high hedges creamy with meadowsweet in summer, past a field of white cows and some barns roofed with rusting corrugated iron. You cross a cattle-grid and come to a little hamlet of brick houses with antlers over their porches and hollyhocks in their gardens. That's where I grew up, an only child, happy enough, in an unexceptional kind of way, till the first real loss of my life – the death of my father when I was thirteen.

Beyond the cluster of houses there was a patch of common land before you got to the wood. The grass was cropped short by cattle and Forest ponies, littered with pale rotting turds, criss-crossed with muddy tracks that sucked at your feet in the wet. Yellow potentilla grew there, and twisted crab-apple trees, their tiny jewelled fruit irresistible to a child, but, when you chewed, all bitter pith, and gorse smelling of coconut, and frail blue harebells nodding in the wind. The only sounds were the tiniest fizzings and rustlings – hidden grasshoppers, the wind in the birch leaves – and on damp days the crackling and spitting of the power lines where the pylons stalked through the fields behind the houses.

From my bedroom window you could see eastward across the farmland to the chemical works and the oil refinery on the edge of the Solent, the chimneys stark and ugly, spiking the sky. At night the flares from the refinery lit the sky to that side of the house with an apricot glow: there was always light in my bedroom. It was darker – though never completely dark – on the other side of the house, where the windows looked across the common and down to the wood. We went walking in that wood sometimes, on Sunday afternoons. The old oakwood had been partially felled by the Forestry Commission, and replanted with spindly conifers for making telegraph poles. It was a silent and confusing place, where paths seemed to shift and change, where you never quite knew where you were.

My mother's father had been a forester. For a bit of extra cash, he'd sold Christmas trees that he grew on his own land, and when my mother married my father and they moved into the house down the gravel track, she brought thirty-two of them with her, and planted them in the garden. Conifers grow quickly: soon our garden was like a little outpost of the wood. My father occasionally muttered that he'd have some of them cut down, but she wouldn't hear of it. She could never bear to fell or uproot anything. Any seedling she found in the gravel driveway she'd plant out and nurture: natural selection was anathema to my mother. It's an odd trait, perhaps, in a forester's daughter: for surely forestry is all about control – pruning, thinning, taking over from nature. She still lives there: the trees are huge now, their highest branches skeletal, dying from acid rain. I think about them sometimes when I look at my own untamed garden, at the overhanging hedge, the laurel that badly needs pruning. I ought to have learnt, I suppose.

My father taught English at the local grammar school. We were very close. I think of him now in fragments, precious chunks of memory, physical things mostly, the safe smell of his tweed jacket and its reassuring roughness against my cheek, the bristliness of his face in the evening, the gravelly tones in his voice when we sat together at the formica-top table in the kitchen drinking tea and talking. He was a clever man, but with a perpetual sense of failure, a deeply held belief that he'd taken a wrong path, and his talents were unused and wasted. His depressions made me sad. There's a look in the face of someone with a depressive temperament – eyes a little full, eyebrows permanently raised, like his, in a sort of upward frown – I can recognize it immediately. It scares me, that look: I've never let myself be drawn to a man who has it. In fact, I've always gone for men who are if anything rather arrogant, who know and enjoy their own strength. Not in a violent or excessive way, though I suspect that, like many women, I have a masochistic streak, and certainly the men who haunt my fantasies tend to be rather cold-eyed and unrelenting. In real life, of course, I like them altruistic and politically aware and all those good things. But they only ever turn me on if they're pretty self-confident too: the kind of men who don't need or want my compassion, who are not prone to regret. Which is one of the reasons, of course, why what happened with Dan was so intolerable for me.

My mother stayed at home, as middle-class women did then. Pictures of her in her twenties before she got married show a lithe, pretty woman, always laughing. I guess it was that brightness that had drawn my father to her: he'd felt perhaps that she had some secret, that she might save him from his sadness. But marriage and motherhood had blurred her edges, dulled her. She wore thick stockings and blouses with bows; she obsessed about germs. When her weekly delivery of groceries arrived, she'd scald the tops of the tins with boiling water before lining them up on the larder shelves next to the cream crockery with the green rim that we used when we didn't have visitors. Fear was the great motivator, I think, in my mother's life. She specialized in health scares – radioactive brazil nuts, X-ray machines in shoe shops, fluoride in drinking water. In a way, she was well ahead of her time.

I was happy enough – yet, like so many children, or like Trish with the Russian minarets stuck to her fridge, I always longed to be somewhere else. My dreams were urban dreams, fuelled by occasional shopping trips to Southampton, where my mother would buy me a Bri-nylon blouse or a tartan miniskirt from C & A and we'd have a lunch of plaice and boiled potatoes in Mayes department store, and I'd thrill to the rich smell of exhaust, the gleaming of the neon on the Gaumont cinema, the litter blowing casually in the streets. This was what I wanted from adult life, I thought – to live somewhere vivid and bright and urgent, where men rushed by in important overcoats, where women sat in scented cafés and drank wine from glittery glasses and ate sugary ice-creams with long silver spoons. And I've kept to my childhood vow: since leaving home, I've never lived in the country. Sure, I've always had something to cultivate – a windowbox or a yard with fruit trees in pots – and now, best of all, this garden between its heavy hedges, like a little womb, so safe. But I've never lived away from the sound of traffic. Never in the middle of farmland, where darkness spreads like smoke through the fields, obscuring everything, or on the edge of a wood, where saplings in the undergrowth struggle towards the light and the crunch of your footsteps is swallowed up by the silence.

One dark evening my father set out in his Ford Cortina for the parents' evening at the school where he worked. A truck had been parked in a bend on one of those twisting unlit forest roads, where the branches of the trees meet in the middle and keep out the moonlight. The driver had gone off to pee behind a bush and neglected to leave on the lights. Death had been instantaneous, the doctor told me and my mother, as we sat on tubular steel and canvas chairs in a little white room in the casualty department at the General Hospital, a room with a desk and a basin and a paper towel dispenser: even now the sight of those harsh grey-green towels and the smell of antiseptic soap can fill me with desolation. 'Really, you mustn't torture yourselves,' the doctor went on. 'It was all over so quickly. I'm sure he didn't know what was happening.' I thought about this a lot as I lay in bed, staring into the apricot glow in the sky through the gap in the curtains, and came miserably to the conclusion that the doctor had got it wrong, that there'd been a long long moment when the truck had loomed in the headlights and he knew. I lived that moment with him again and again, wondering how it had been, fearing so much that in that moment of perfect clarity he had felt a kind of joy.

My social worker friends think this explains everything, of course. It's what we're always looking for, I suppose, as we listen to our clients' life stories – the Rosetta Stone, the defining event – a death, a rape, a meeting with a monster, an angel impregnation – the one event in the light of which all the rest can be read. Jude loves this way of looking at things. When I have some sexual disaster – when Adam left, or at the end of my brief, rather frenzied affair with the solicitor who handled my divorce – she'll shake her head and say, 'There you go again, Chloe. It's the same old story. You're convinced they'll leave you, so sooner or later they do. It's all to do with your father, don't you see?' It's not as though Jude's the expert exactly, in spite of all those books she's read about women who love too much and men who can't commit: the marriage that brought her over here, to a duplicitous West Hampstead psychotherapist called Gregory Rosen, was pretty catastrophic, and one of her more recent lovers landed her in Casualty with a broken finger – but that doesn't stop her enjoying the analysis over some nice Pinot Grigio. I don't mind: I quite enjoy it too, this attempt to make sense of things. Anyway, it's all a long time ago now.

Yet I still dream about him sometimes. In the dreams he's alive again. He sits at the formica-top kitchen table, drinking tea from the cream cup with the green rim. He's utterly ordinary, utterly without numinosity. He explains patiently that death isn't quite what people imagine. It was true he died in a way – but look, here he is again, sitting as large as life at the kitchen table. Why is it, Chloe, you won't believe the evidence of your eyes? And I laugh in the dream, and say I can see what he means, that I've obviously been mistaken. When I dream this dream, I sometimes wake up crying.

After my father's death, my mother retreated into herself. Grief etched sharp lines on her face, as she struggled harder than ever to protect the house from germs and decay and dirt. She put down old carpet runners to save the carpets from wear, poured Dettol down the sink every day, spread dust-sheets to stop the furniture from fading. And she never threw anything out. Boxes of old shoes and clothes piled up, sorted and labelled against the day when they might come back into use. The trees she'd planted when she got married were now great heavy things, weighing the house down with dense shadow even in the brightest time of the year.

I worked hard at school. I knew this was the way out. I was stick thin, all knees and elbows: I didn't yet menstruate, didn't have boyfriends. I just studied with a passion, earning my parole.

I went to London University, read English like my father. College was a culture shock, full of golden girls from private schools who swore insouciantly in a way that would have appalled my mother, and had weird table manners. I tried to be like them. I bought some high white boots and some sticky white lipstick, I ate with my fork in my right hand, I smoothed out the frizz in my hair with an iron and brown paper. I learnt to flirt – to smile enigmatically, push my hand through my hair, turn my head away a little and look up through my lashes. It seemed to work beautifully. The men I chose were always clever and confident, with slightly carnivorous smiles – men to whom everything was simple, who weren't going to make me sad like my father had done. They had a lot of opinions about what I needed: You need to stop analysing . . . to let go . . . to lose those inhibitions . . . to make love with your feet sticking out the back of my van . . . I didn't take much notice – except to wonder what it was in me that inspired such a torrent of advice-giving.

I had plenty of reasonably nice sex: I gave the men precise instructions, and supported their efforts with rather rigid little fantasies – a scene from *Last Tango in Paris*, one of the less painful bits of *The Story of O*. Yet somehow I never felt satisfied: whatever I was looking for in the beds of these tense and eager young men I certainly never found it. It was as though my own sexuality existed somewhere at the periphery of all this frenetic activity. I'd see a man in the street in the rain – someone I didn't know, leaning against a car, his sleeves rolled up: his eyes would rest on me for a moment, appraisingly, and I'd feel a quick dry thrill of desire, something promised that was never realized as my current lover pushed into me yet again, in a pleasant enough way. There's a story by Anaïs Nin I liked a lot then: an artist is painting a young woman, and while she sits there naked, he talks, apparently oblivious of her, tells outrageous stories of men with huge cocks and tubercular women of ineffable lasciviousness, and the girl just sits there naked, tangential yet essential. Much later in the story she gets into bed with him, of course – but the erotic bit, the bit that you remember, is the innocent, hungry, troubled bit at the beginning.

It was at college that I met Adam – though we didn't get together properly till years later. He was a man I drank with, slept with intermittently. A medical student, a bit wild like they usually are. Tall, rather gangly then, with unflattering wire-rimmed glasses that made him look even thinner, but very public school and self-confident. Nice enough: just one of my crowd. Then in the summer term of my second year I started to feel very tired, to weep over my essays, and woke one morning to find a great big lump in the side of my neck. I struggled to the surgery, and the air pressed down on me so heavily I thought I might die with the weight of it. The doctor diagnosed glandular fever. I sat in bed in my college room, white and exhausted, and the men drifted off, leaving no sign of their previously noisy and ubiquitous presence in my life – causing me to reflect lugubriously on the fragility of human connections as I drank endless cups of Lemsip and struggled to walk to the loo. Only Adam hung around, bringing me books from the library, and vitamins and Mars Bars. I was deeply grateful: I clung to him. The fact that he was a medical student made his solicitousness especially impressive.

There's a moment from those days that sticks in my mind with peculiar vividness. I was still ill, but Adam had decided I needed to get out, and took me to a play in a college garden, a wooded place, rather magical on that hazy summer afternoon with its thin acidic sunshine. There were glasses of port to drink and strawberries, and I wore a very short dress from C & A, a dress in some silky synthetic material patterned with pale blue poppies. My tights were almost white, and I remember noticing how the blonde hair on my thighs gleamed through the pale nylon, and wondering vaguely if I should have shaved it off. My throat scraped like a raw wound every time I swallowed, and my body felt as though it wasn't mine. Adam ran one finger slowly up my thigh: 'The iller you get,' he said, 'the more I want to fuck you.' This sounds kind of sexy when you're well, but then it just made me feel tired. The play was *The Hunting of the Snark*: it seemed weighted with significance, as things do when you're feverish, this story of hunting for something so ill-defined and elusive, something that was never found. A man in a top hat ran off into the distance, disappeared in the haze between the trees. In that strange hallucinatory light, you felt he had actually vanished, dissolved into the brightness. I wanted to weep, I felt such incompleteness. I started to fear then that I had an inbuilt flaw – some hunger that would never be assuaged.

Adam and I eventually drifted apart. It was me who finally finished it, with the usual little speech about wanting some space. The truth is that I didn't need him so much once I was better – I'm aware this doesn't show me up in a particularly good light. We didn't meet again for ten years. Those were years when I carried on much as before – work I enjoyed, lots of men, a vague sense of something eluding me. Then I moved to this job I still have on the edge of London. I was lonely, and fed up with my succession of relationships. I felt there was nothing in my life that grounded or anchored me – the classic turning-thirty thing at root, I guess, the predictable ache for a child. I arrived at the local hospital for a child abuse case conference – and there was Adam, now a senior registrar in paediatrics, and terribly pleased to see me. Before he'd been a wild student who'd put ethyl alcohol in the punch at parties, who'd been wheeled naked through the streets on a hospital trolley: now he did heart operations on babies while their parents paced the waiting room. He'd filled out a little, got squarer and more solid, he looked good in suits: a man of substance, I thought. He had the kind of self-assurance that makes scared people feel safe. He took me to a quietly expensive restaurant and spent £60 on a bottle of marvellous Bordeaux. I told him I wanted a child and he wasn't deterred. And he earned a lot of money, and he seemed to love me, and the sex was fine really.

We married: I flushed my pills down the loo. Pregnancy and childbirth thrilled me. I adored breast-feeding especially, my breasts so swollen and useful, the veins blue as if drawn with ballpoint – and Adam muttering like new fathers everywhere, 'They look so wonderful: why won't you let me *touch* them?' From the moment Alice was born, in a furious temper and smeared with white guck, I was consumed with passion for this raging little person, a passion that left no room for anyone else. Looking back, it's as though I was drugged or entranced. The world contracted: I built invisible walls around me and her, and the part of my life that really mattered was contained within those walls – with the cot and the musical mobile and the packets of Milupa – and Alice, trying to kiss my face with a soft fierce wide-open mouth, a kiss that felt like the most sensuous thing in the world. Everything outside those walls I'd built filled me with fear. Confused by lack of sleep, haunted by appalling fantasies in which she fell down a hole or drowned or was eaten by beasts, I saw threats all around – in pesticides in apple juice, in global warming and flood and fire, in young men who drove their cars too fast – even in whooping-cough injections, which I refused to let her have, though Adam said I was a deluded and petulant female and refused to speak to me for days. When you have a child, you learn what it means to be afraid. I came to understand my mother better: I could empathize with her compulsion to scald the tops of tins.

My fear made my work harder to tolerate. I read the files, with their accounts of rape and violence and neglect, and thought of these terrible words being written on the sweet, soft body of my child. At my first case conference after going back to work – on a little girl who'd been sexually abused and horribly neglected, who obsessively wrote lists of people who liked her, very short lists that always started with My Little Pony – my eyes filled with tears. When I got back to the office I went to the loo and cried. Jude found me there, and told me I was being totally weak and held me close in a healing Opium-scented hug.

31

It was easier with Lucy. I wasn't quite so fearful. Yet with her too I was entranced, oblivious, utterly preoccupied.

Adam worked hard and did well. Around the time that Lucy turned two, he started putting in longer and longer hours. Eventually I noticed. I started to wonder a little, though I wasn't really worried. One day he said, 'I don't think we're communicating any more.' I looked up briefly from the Play-Doh: I was trying to make a cat for Lucy, and its tail kept falling off. I was surprised but on reflection I could see what he meant. 'Maybe you're right,' I said.

I talked to Jude about it: she already knew we hardly ever had sex.

'D'you think he might be having an affair?' I said.

We looked at each other over our glasses of wine. We were in one of those trendy re-fitted pubs with a stripped floor and candles and copies of *Vogue*, sitting very close. And as our eyes met we burst out laughing.

'Adam? Nah . . . He worships you, Chloe.'

It was unimaginable. He was always so devoted, conscientious, reliable. A week later, over a glass of wine on a scented summer evening on our patio, he said he was leaving to live with Simone, a nurse on the Intensive Care Unit.

He left politely, closing a door in my life with quiet decorousness and absolute finality. The girls had their own ways of coping. Lucy had six months of horrendous tantrums, then it was over. With Alice it seemed to go deeper: she started chewing bits of herself – her hair, her fingernails, the tips of her fingers – and getting bad grades at school, and sometimes I caught her staring into space with a look of such sadness it panicked me. Adam, it has to be said, has done all he can to make it easier for them. He is a conscientious parent still. He pays me a lot of maintenance. He pays Alice's school fees. He sees the girls every other weekend. He takes them to Pizza Hut or Planet Hollywood for their birthdays. He buys them appropriate presents.

For two years I had no sexual relationships at all – apart from my brief fling with Felix the solicitor. Felix was an inventive lover: he gave me a key to his office, and sometimes I'd let myself in at lunchtime and he'd find me there and we'd make love furtively, Felix with his hand over my mouth so as not to disturb the secretaries at their Ryvitas. It was fun for a while. But I was very aware of being just one of a series and I hated the way he could never remember the names and ages of my children, so when he finished it, I didn't really mind. After that there was no one. I was doing something else – painting my kitchen, teaching Lucy to read, taking sick guinea-pigs to the vet, mulching my camellias – putting it all together, making it work. Like anyone with something big to cope with – a disease, a bereavement, a birth – I guess I seemed to be somewhere else. Men sensed that and left me alone.

I cried quite a lot at first. It wasn't that I really wanted Adam back, though I did feel intense irritation around Simone, who has that air of self-confident bossiness that little girls have when they play at nurses. I just felt in a general non-specific way rather lonely and abandoned. I felt this most in the middle of the night, when I'd drink scotch and cook a greasy snack in an attempt to woo sleep and wonder if I'd be on my own for ever. It's in the early hours of the morning, Adam once told me, that our metabolism is slowest and we're most likely to die: there are even some orders of nuns who get up at three every morning to pray for the dying. I find the thought of those nuns an infinite comfort – and sometimes I've wondered if they spare a thought for those whose sufferings, like their sins, are really pretty venal – who go to cook fried eggs and weep a little and feel that their future is meaningless: I'd like to think they do. But gradually it got better: I slept through the night, I achieved a kind of contentment that was quite new to me, a sense of repletion almost, as I pottered round in my cosy picture-book house with the flowery plates on the dresser and the cat curled up on the hearthrug.

I can see now that I was living out a fantasy then, a fantasy as romantic in its way as the dream of perfect sexual love: the earth-mother bringing up her children alone, nurturing but powerful, totally autonomous except in a few minor practical ways – blocked drains, for instance, and fuse boxes and those fiddly bits on anchovy tins – for it has to be said I'm better at the spiritual than the practical aspects of self-sufficiency. The other day Lucy took an empty shoe box and filled it with her special things – some glittery beads of my mother's, shells we'd found on Brighton beach, a stone shaped like a turtle. She called it her Me Moi Myself box: 'I love the sound of that, Mummy,' she said. 'Me Moi Myself.' I lived in a box like Lucy's for

two and a half years. And it was good, in its way, it was enough –
till Dan came and sat at my kitchen table and wrote his number out
for me and pushed his wet hair back with his beautiful long brown
fingers and turned everything inside out and upside down.

4

Alice was sprawled on the sofa, chewing her hair, poring over tales of spontaneous human combustion in the *Fortean Times*. She took one look at me – the short silk dress, the lipstick, the high-heeled sandals.

'You're going out,' she said accusingly.

I nodded. 'Hannah's coming round. I should have told you before. It was all a bit last minutish.' Why do I have to sound so apologetic? I wondered.

Usually there were protests about the babysitter. God, Mum, Hannah's only three years older than me. And why's it called a *baby*sitter anyway? Tonight she just stared. Her eyes are blue as the remote distance on a clear summer's day. Even I can't always hold her gaze. 'It's that man who came to pick Fred up from the party, isn't it?' she said.

'You don't miss a thing,' I said.

'So when exactly are you going to help me with my True Vine for RE?'

'I'm sorry, sweetheart. I thought it wasn't due in till Monday. We'll do it tomorrow, okay?'

'She'll slaughter me if I don't get it finished.'

'Won't tomorrow do?'

'But tomorrow's Friday – and I hate having homework to do at the weekend. You know that, Mum.'

'Friday isn't exactly the weekend,' I said.

She said nothing. I put a hand on her shoulder. She leaned over sideways, away from my touch, shielding her face with her magazine as though I might turn violent. The deliberate pose emphasized her adolescent ungainliness: some bits of her were growing faster than others, her legs seemed too long for her body, her feet too big. I felt a rush of anger with her, an infantile, Lucy-like anger – Why don't you ever let me do what I want?

35

I was ready far too early, but I couldn't sit still. I looked out some *Marie Claires* for Hannah to read, straightened a picture, swiped at the dust on the writing desk where I kept my old letters and diaries. Balloons left from the party moved round like animals in eddies of air, making unnerving hollow bumping noises. I wondered what to do with them: leave them for a day or two, perhaps, then puncture them when Lucy was asleep, to avoid the protests.

Suddenly Alice put down her magazine. 'We get on okay, don't we, Mum? It's fine living like this, isn't it?'

'Alice, you're jumping ahead a bit, aren't you? I'm only going out for a drink. I do need a bit of a social life.'

'Oh yeah? This isn't just a bit of a social life, though, is it?'

'I don't know,' I said. I sat down beside her, making a huge effort to reach her. Her hair was wet and sleek where she'd sucked it. She tucked the damp strand behind an ear. 'Look, nothing's going to change,' I said.

She seemed to soften a little. She touched my skirt. 'Actually, you look really nice,' she said. 'You ought to wear that dress more often.'

I dropped a kiss on the top of her head.

I went to put out coffee-making things for Hannah. Some roses I'd stuck in a jam-jar on the kitchen table were at the point of disintegration, petals falling everywhere. I picked up a petal, held it to my cheek. It was cool and thick and soft, still faintly scented but browning as though someone had shaded the edges with pencil. I thought briefly and deliciously of cool insistent unequivocal fingers easing apart the buttons down the front of my dress.

Yet when he did arrive, closely followed by Hannah, and looking good – dark trousers, a baggy cream linen shirt with the sleeves rolled up, just the kind of thing I like – I felt a rush of uncertainty. I took him into the living room, we smiled tentatively at one another, remarked how hot it was – and I hoped the shock I felt didn't show in my face, for I scarcely recognized him. The lover I'd had in my head for five whole days and nights had been completely different, a stranger from a fantasy. With the real man standing so close, the thought of the things I'd done so hopefully before he came – clean sheets on the bed, putting in my diaphragm – made me flush.

36

Alice said hello with icy politeness and went up to her room, refusing out of principle to be on the same floor as the babysitter. But Lucy came bouncing in, her face bright with the expectation that everyone would be pleased to see her.

Dan bent to her. 'Hi, Lu.' He poked the front of her nightshirt with one finger. 'Hey, love this bear.'

'That's not a bear, that's *Barney*,' she said, in a teasingly outraged but best-mates sort of way. She shrugged, her hands turned out, an expressive little gesture that said, Grownups don't know *anything*, then giggled. 'Are you looking after us?' she asked, her face glowing, almost translucent with pleasure, like one of those ceramic candle-holders when you light the candle.

'Not tonight,' he said carefully, sensitive to the riskiness of this. 'Hannah's looking after you tonight. Your Mum and me are going out to dinner.'

The light in her face went out. She aimed a kick at a balloon on the floor near her feet, but it skittered away and she stubbed her toe on the sofa. Tears shone in her eyes.

'Mum, why don't you take us out when you go?' she said. 'It's everso everso selfish.'

'Hannah will read you a story,' I said quickly.

'Lots of stories,' said Hannah. She grabbed a book, pulled Lucy on to her lap. I went to the front door quickly. Dan followed.

Warmth from the pavement washed over us. It was a perfect summer evening, the air heavy with the scent of the tobacco flowers that glimmered in pots outside my neighbour's front door.

'There's a Chinese restaurant by the railway bridge,' he said. 'It's a bit scruffy. The food's great though. Will that be okay?'

I nodded.

He had a small blue inconsequential car. When I leaned back against the seat, the silk of my dress stuck wetly to my back. My body felt awkward, too big, not sleek or neat at all: I remembered how it had felt to be Alice's age – when you suddenly grow hips and keep banging into things, how nothing flows, how you feel you don't quite fit in your skin any more.

I couldn't work out how to wind the window down. He leaned across me to do it. I sat very still. I was intensely aware of his separateness and strangeness, that I knew almost nothing about

37

him. The smell of his skin filled me with an indefinable emotion halfway between pleasure and fear.

He parked near the railway bridge, just outside the restaurant. It was called The Water Margin. Caramelized ducks hung in the window, brown and glossy as chestnuts, the shapes of their heads and beaks unnervingly specific. It had, as he'd said, quite a downmarket air. There were plastic fruit hanging round the bar and plastic roses on the tables, and to decorate the plain walls someone had stuck up sheets of dragon-and-peony wrapping paper: you could see the Sellotape at the corners. When a train went over the bridge at the side of the restaurant, you sensed it more as a vibration than a noise, like something stirring deep inside yourself.

I felt horribly overdressed for the place, my heels too high, my dress too short and shiny, my lips too sharply defined. I didn't know what to do with my hands, I clasped them in front of my mouth.

The tables were small. He leaned towards me, resting on his elbows. He was so close I could see the reddish flecks in his eyes, the sheen of sweat on his forehead.

'Do they mind you coming out?' he said.

'Lucy doesn't. Not really. She'll be fine by now. She loves having someone different to read to her. Alice is more suspicious.'

'Suspicious of me?'

'A little, I think. She's very close to her father,' I said, then wondered if the implications of this were too intimate, so early in the evening.

He nodded questioningly, waiting. I was very aware that his eyes never left my face. There was something compelling about his gaze, but I only let my eyes meet his for a moment, then glanced down and away, wanting to savour it all, not wanting to rush.

'They see him a lot,' I said. 'It's been okay since he left. It was tough for a while. Now I don't quite know what he did any more. We get on just fine without him. They miss him, of course, but not too much. I hope.'

'And what about you?'

'I'm fine,' I said. 'I grow things. I love my garden. I love to scrabble about in the earth.' And then, responding to the question in his face, 'There hasn't been anyone really. I guess I've quite liked being on my own.' I felt a little surge of embarrassment at the past tense I'd used so unthinkingly.

He poured the wine. I liked the definite gesture, the way he took charge. The wine felt velvety on my tongue. My mouth was dry with nerves and I drank greedily.

'And you?' I said. 'How have you managed to come out? I mean . . .'

'Helena and I lead very separate lives,' he said. 'It isn't a problem. Well, maybe I'm kidding myself. But that's how we live.'

It was framed almost as a question. I fiddled with the pot of toothpicks on the table, didn't really know how to respond.

'So tell me how you got into social work,' he said.

'Perhaps I'm just a terrible voyeur,' I said.

'You like to hear stories.'

'Yeah. And I like it being so difficult, in a way. Mostly I thrash around. Sometimes I think, that's good, I've done something useful.'

I asked how he'd become a psychologist. He said he'd left school with two GCEs and worked as a lorry driver: then eventually he'd gone to FE college and got some qualifications and made it to university. 'I did a politics degree to start with,' he said. 'I didn't do well – I was always out on picket lines – never did any work.'

This made me smile. It fitted with the way he'd talked at Lucy's party, the political passion that was still there: I liked that. In my twenties, I'd often been out with men who wanted to change the world. Sometimes I wondered if it reflected some deep failing or apathy in me – a hope, perhaps, that they'd do it so I wouldn't have to.

'In my first summer holiday,' he went on, 'I got a job on an adventure playground. We built it from scratch. They were inner city kids like I'd been, they'd had so little that was theirs. We built towers, a huge slide, a walkway where you could step from rung to rung high up above everybody. In your twenties you feel so powerful.'

He paused for a moment while the waiter brought a hotplate warmed with a candle, and dishes of spare ribs with a shiny sauce and a plate of something green and intricate and cabbagey. It all smelt subtle and sweet, but it intimidated me. I had no appetite, I just wanted to drink.

'The day we finished the building, we had a party to celebrate,' he said. 'I went home thoroughly pleased with myself. I felt I'd done something worthwhile. The police rang me at three in the morning. It had been torched. I went and watched it burning.'

I tried to picture it – the crashing structures edged with flame. In some perverse way it aroused me, this tale of devastation, made me long to lean across the table, to touch the strong planes of his face, to explore his mouth with mine.

'It was one of the kids who'd helped build it, of course,' he said. 'That seems obvious now: at the time it seemed so awful. He'd set fire to things before.'

'And then?'

'We started again, but it wasn't the same. The kids drifted off. When I went back to college, I changed course. It was connected somehow.'

He asked where I'd grown up. I told him about my childhood in the forest, and my mother living alone in the shadow of the trees. He asked me a lot of questions. I liked his searching questions, and the urge I felt to open myself up to him.

The main course was pale and complicated, lots of glossy vegetables and huge translucent prawns smelling of the sea. As I picked up one of the dishes I burnt myself on the candle. I stuck my finger in my mouth, sucked it to soothe it. He watched in an interested appraising kind of way. I felt myself flush.

He told me about his own childhood then. He sketched it out quite lightly – but his story still shocked me. He'd grown up in Manchester, an only child like me: his father had been a plasterer, a violent man who'd sometimes beaten Dan with his belt. His earliest memory, he said, was of his father's face, vast, threatening, thrust towards him, filling up all his vision. I sensed as he talked how he'd distanced himself from all that long-ago misery, saw too that this distancing was something he still worked at, only achieved by a conscious effort of will.

'I got in trouble a lot at school for fighting,' he said. 'But I'm afraid I always found fighting to be very effective.'

'I can imagine that,' I said. 'That you would fight for things.'

His mother was dead now, he told me, his father in a home. He didn't visit him any more. 'He's pathetic,' he said. 'I guess in the end you always win the war with your parents.'

I told him about my own father then, and how he'd died, and how I still dream about him. Dan reached out a hand and touched me as I talked, just the tip of his finger on my wrist. The warmth of his touch seemed to suffuse right through me, warming me everywhere.

He left his finger there a moment, then leaned back, filled our glasses to the brim again.

'Helena and I don't sleep together,' he said. 'Not since we had Sally – scarcely at all. I've had other relationships.' It wasn't very original, I guess, but it did what was necessary. He looked across at me, and I held his gaze then, I think I nodded slightly. I knew I was giving my assent.

I got up to go to the loo. The tables were all full now, the room fizzing with noise and laughter. This amazed me – I'd been quite unaware of the other people coming in, of the crescendo of chatter. Next to us, two tables had been pushed together, to accommodate what looked like an entire Chinese family celebrating something. A man was bending over a tiny perfect boy with blue-black hair, feeding him noodles, gently solicitous. Suddenly seeing these things, it was as though I'd stepped outside a circle we'd drawn around ourselves, that magically contained us – a circle in which we saw and heard only one another as we told the stories that defined us.

To get to the loo you went out the front door, past the succulent dead ducks, and down a side alley. The door to the kitchen was half-open: steamy heat brushed against me as I passed. I went in the loo but found I was too turned on to pee. I lingered in front of the mirror, running a comb rather pointlessly through my hair. The glass was spattered with silvery flaws like waterdrops, yet my reflection seemed clearer, more vivid than usual: most of my makeup had worn off, my skin was pink, my eyes big and bright.

I went back to the table.

'I'd better warn you the coffee's rather dismal here,' he said.

'You could come back to me for coffee,' I said.

'I'd like that very much,' he said.

We finished the wine and got the bill. He tried to pay for me, I wouldn't let him.

Outside, it was getting dark, purplish shadows thickening where the shop fronts weren't lit up. A warm wind that smelt of flowers ruffled the rubbish on the pavements. Above us a train passed over the railway bridge. You could see the passengers framed in squares of brightness above our heads, every detail clear, every book, frown, earring. We got into the car, carefully not touching.

Hannah was watching some frenetic hospital soap.

'Were they okay?'

'No problem. Lucy's tucked up. We had lots of stories. I just went to turn off her light.'

'Will you get home alright? D'you need a lift?'

'Nah, thanks.'

'Are you sure?' I said, then smiled inside at the sudden nervousness that had made me say it.

Hannah looked at me indulgently, fifteen years old and very knowing. 'I'll be fine, Chloe, really. Bye.' And she drifted off into the night.

I closed the door. 'I'd rather have more wine than coffee. Would you?'

'Yes,' he said.

He followed me into the kitchen, didn't sit down. There was some Chilean red I'd started yesterday. I found some glasses, took out the cork. As I poured, my back to him, I could feel his gaze like a warmth between my shoulder blades. Poised on that knife-edge between one kind of existence and another, I felt a brief, embarrassed urge to say something inconsequential, to chatter brightly, push the moment away. But I just stood there, turned away from him, pouring the wine. He came over and took the bottle from my hand and put it down and put out his hands to pull my face towards him. There was nothing but the sound, shockingly loud, of our intermingled breathing.

He started to unbutton my dress.

'No,' I said. 'Not here.' We went upstairs.

That first time we made love amazed me. It wasn't that it was a particularly accomplished performance, or that everything flowed or that we always knew just what to do without asking: first time sex is never like that for me, never easily empathic. But as he ran his hands over me, explored and investigated me with his fingers and lips and tongue, I found myself responding in a new way, a way I didn't recognize. I felt undone, as though every ligament had softened, as though everything that was normally knit together came unravelled at his touch. I scrabbled around briefly for the images that usually turned me on, but couldn't find them. My whole consciousness seemed taken up with him – the texture of his body, hard and springy and solid, filling my arms so beautifully, the warm musky smell of his sweat, the precise feel of the surface of his cock, hot and dry against my hand, silky against my tongue. These sensations filled my body and my mind: everything else was obliterated.

His hand on my clitoris was all wrong to start with, too fast and rough, as men often are at first. But once I'd shown him with my hand on his and the rhythm was right, I felt I was going to fall apart. The shuddering of my body unnerved me, scared me almost. I didn't know how to stay in control. I couldn't do the usual things – the physical focusing, the tensing of my thighs that would reliably tip me over into orgasm. My old routines didn't work anymore. And so, just like the first time I'd ever tried to come, furtively under the eiderdown in the apricot dark of my childhood bedroom, when I'd stopped on the edge, overwhelmed by sensations I couldn't name – so now too I stopped, and gently pushed his hand away.

'What's wrong?' he said.

'I won't come tonight. I can't kind of get it together. It's all too new.'

He shook his head a little.

'It doesn't matter. Really,' I said.

He gave a small shrug as though disappointed, kissed me, eased inside me.

'Why do you keep your eyes shut?' he said.

'I just do,' I said.

'Open them,' he said. 'Look at me.' So I did.

He came quickly. We lay together for a while, not speaking. His breathing slowed.

I propped myself up on one elbow and watched him sleeping, seeing new things in him – the smoky darkness of stubble showing through his sun-browned skin, the way he half-smiled in sleep. His unruly hair fell over his face: it reminded me of something that at first I couldn't place, then I realized it was Fred at Lucy's party, with the fringe falling into his eyes.

I reached out a hand, touched the side of his face. He opened his eyes lazily, put my fingers in his mouth for a moment, kissed me.

'When can I see you next?' he said.

'Whenever you like.'

'When would suit you?'

I laughed but wouldn't say. This was a delicate moment, fragile as eggshell: the moment when the rules would be fixed, the relationship defined. 'No. You decide.'

'Monday then?'

'Mmm.'

This was what I'd wanted – to have it all secure. I felt safe, happy. But now that I knew where I was with him, I also felt terribly frustrated and cross with myself that I'd chosen not to come.

He got up and pulled on his clothes. I didn't know what to put on to see him out. My dressing gown lay on the windowseat – but it was made of purple towelling and slightly stained with coffee and plastic animals were often to be found in its pockets: it belonged to a different kind of life. So I slipped my dress on again: it clung to me where I was damp.

He looked me up and down. 'I like that,' he said.

I went down to the front door with him, holding the dress together in front with my hand, aware that people passing in the street might be able to see in through the glass panel beside the front door. I reached up to kiss him. He brushed his lips against mine: I shivered. He sensed how turned on I still was, took my hand away from the front of my dress, put his hand inside, tracing out my breast with one finger. Standing there by the door, hidden from the street only by the trailing stems and leaves of the grape ivies that spilled from my hanging baskets, I pulled his hand down, moved my legs a little apart. I came almost at a touch, clinging to him.

He kissed me all over my face. He was pleased and somehow amused. He grinned. 'Goodnight then, Chloe.'

I nodded. I felt full of a light happiness like laughter, but was quite unable to speak.

I went to the kitchen and sat down shakily, I poured more wine, sipped it slowly, enjoying the rich taste of it, savouring an absurd huge hopefulness.

There was a clatter outside the kitchen door, then a thump as Lucy pushed the door open with her foot and almost fell into the room. She was fogged with sleep, her face bleary, soft, drooping, her eyes vast, the pupils dark as the petals of some dark flower, those sooty purple tulips perhaps. She sucked at her comforter and a little translucent line of dribble ran down her chin. I realised with a shock I'd completely forgotten about the girls, hadn't gone to check on them, hadn't given them a thought.

I scooped her up in my arms.

'I had a bad dream, Mummy. There was a horrible man and he sticked me down a drainpipe and I was just the right size to be sticked down a drainpipe. I was that little, itsy-bitsy. And there were spiders in the drainpipe and bugs and earwigs and things. And the bumble-bees tried to save me but the spiders just laughed at me.'

'It's all right, my love. It was only a dream.'

My body was so relaxed that she melted into me. Her breath was warm on my hand, her eyelids drooped. Then she opened her eyes suddenly.

'Charmaine squashed a big black bumble-bee today,' she said. 'It didn't have a very long life.' She put the ribbon edging of the cardigan against her mouth; there were sucking noises, and the snuffling sound of her breathing. 'I hate Charmaine,' she said.

'Never mind. Go to sleep.' I rocked her. Her breathing slowed.

'It hadn't hurt her. It was just staggering around,' she said. The words came out slowly, one at a time. 'It hadn't . . . even . . . touched . . . her.'

I carried her upstairs, carefully like something infinitely breakable. Asleep, she felt incredibly heavy. In the pool of light from her nightlight, I could see how she'd flung herself out of bed: her duvet was thrown back, the imprint of her head still on her pillow. I put her down carefully so as not to wake her, bending my knees as I'd learnt to do when she was a baby, letting the weight of her head press my hand deep into the pillow before I moved my hand away. She scarcely stirred.

Even when I'd tucked her up, it was as though I could still feel the soft heaviness of her body pressing down on me.

5

It all got very intense very quickly. We'd see each other two or three times a week – on Mondays and Wednesdays, and sometimes late on Fridays after his Urdu class. Hannah prospered, adding massively to her CD collection. We'd go out for a drink or a meal, come back early. I'd make sure the girls were asleep – after that first time, I always made quite sure of that. We'd make love, then around midnight he'd leave and go back to Helena.

I bought some new clothes – dresses and shirts in frail clingy fabrics, in colours I'd never worn before, pale blue, lemon yellow – happy colours. I had my eyelashes dyed and my legs waxed. I had highlights put in my hair in an intimidating salon where the stylist had black fingernails and a silver safety pin through her eyebrow.

When I was seeing Dan for lunch, I wore one of my new frocks in to work.

Jude looked me up and down. 'God, Chloe, I've never seen you show so much *skin*. It's the Real Thing, I take it.'

'Absolutely.'

'Shit. It's too late for my book on sex addiction then?'

'Afraid so,' I said.

'Actually,' she said, 'I'm jealous as hell. You've got that kind of glow. It looks so *nice*.'

Everything pleased me in those early days. The world looked different, as though a light had been switched on. When I walked Lucy home from school, past the Victorian houses behind the hospital, past the florist's and the funeral parlour and down by the Blue Moon store where we sometimes stopped to buy a KitKat, the edges of things seemed sharper and clearer than usual, their colours more intense. I was dazzled by the fiery brightness of the red carnations in buckets outside the florist's, by the watery shimmer and glint of the silver birch in the little patch of garden next to the coroner's office. I relished Lucy's company on those walks. I was more available to her than usual, I think, more willing to go at her pace, delighting in her conversation, the delicious way she was always focused on something very big or very little – on issues of origins – 'Mummy, if people catch a disease, who gets it *first*?' – or on the detail of our walk and the shifting intricate surfaces of things – insects, toadstools, a hub cap that had fallen off a car, the paw-prints that some dog had left in the cement round a lamp-post. She basked in my pleasure in her: we grew very close. And people everywhere were warm to me. The man in the Blue Moon always looked pleased to see me and everyone at the school gate smiled and the scrum of mothers opened out like arms and drew me in.

Adam found out immediately, of course.

'Lucy tells me you've got a boyfriend,' he said, when he dropped the girls off after their weekend together. 'He's very nice and has big eyebrows, she says.'

'Yes,' I said.

'Hence the posh new hair?' He put out a hand and touched the hair that fell at the side of my face: it was the first time he'd tried to touch me since he'd left. I moved a little away.

'I just felt like having it done,' I said.

'Is he married?'

'That is absolutely none of your business,' I said.

'That means yes. Well, don't go getting hurt now, will you, Chloe? I'd hate to see you getting hurt,' he said, with an air of genuine solicitousness that I found completely bizarre.

Even my clients noticed the change in me. Trish remarked on it when she came to the office to see me about a giro that hadn't come.

'You're looking well, Chloe, love,' she said, smiling at me. Her smile erased the angry lines from her face, and for a moment I glimpsed a different Trish – someone vivid and at ease, whose life fitted her like a well-tailored jacket instead of chafing against her.

'I'm feeling well,' I said, laughing a little.

'It must be the heat,' she said. And she gave me a knowing look, as though I was transparent to her. 'Here's hoping it lasts.'

The sex I had with Dan in those first weeks was a revelation to me. Where before I'd always struggled a bit, turned inward, been very aware that pleasure was something I worked for, that in some way I made it happen, now it seemed to happen to me, utterly overwhelming me. I didn't need my fantasies anymore, or the little physical sequences I'd always used to build up the tension in a deliberate way: I didn't need to think about what I was doing. I simply stopped trying, let myself be taken over. There was such tenderness between us too. Or maybe not tenderness exactly, for sex always has its hard, greedy edge, however gently you touch. It was more a kind of empathy perhaps, so that when we were completely physically enmeshed, like during the simplest kind of intercourse, with one of us stretched out on top of the other, so many surfaces pressed together, tongues, skin, everything, I'd get all mixed up about what was him and what was me, and his penis inside me felt like part of my body, and I felt a rush of excitement when he came.

My preoccupation with him was such a physical thing, it was almost as though I was living inside out. I guess we tend to think of our essence as existing somewhere deep within ourselves – well, introverts like me do anyway – but with Dan I felt that the most real and essential parts of me were the parts that he could touch and kiss and penetrate, as though my soul had seeped out onto the surface of my skin. When I wasn't with him, my thoughts of him had a hallucinatory immediacy, like a little psychosis. I couldn't summon up these remembered sensations deliberately – they came from nowhere, as if inserted in my head from outside. Sometimes during the day I'd be dictating notes on a review, or trying to get onto a roundabout, or observing some poor troubled child beating up a baby doll in a playroom, or concentrating on someone else's statement at a case conference, my attention all taken up with whatever it was I had to do – and I'd be startled by the thought of his mouth on me, that extreme sensation: I'd feel it as though it was happening. Or I'd try to remember what he looked like and I'd fail completely – then later, entirely unbidden, as I pottered in my kitchen, I'd suddenly smell the muskiness of his skin – and that scent would seem as present, as real to me as the honey scent of the alyssum in my window boxes. But I could never conjure him up by force of will: I couldn't recall his voice, and his face completely eluded me. There was always that slight shock of recognition when I saw him – oh yes, he's like that, that's it, that's what he looks like.

'Does Helena know?' I asked him once, feeling a sudden fear of her rage, and trepidation at the potential mess. I felt such curiosity about her – this woman whom I'd never met, who shared his life and his bed, who knew about him in ways I didn't and couldn't.

'No,' he said, 'she doesn't know.'

'What does she think is going on then? You're hardly ever there.'

'It's how we've lived for a long time,' he said.

'Does she have somebody too?'

'No. Well, to be honest, of course, I don't know. You can never really know, can you? About somebody else? But I don't think so.'

It was terribly fragile; I could see that, in my saner moments. It could all so easily fall apart. A moment's inattention, and our secret might be told.

And how could Helena not know? I wondered. Those close to us usually know, don't they? There are always signs, surely – secret smiles, an intimation of absence, an unfamiliar fragrance, a single yellow leaf clinging to a sleeve. Yet of course Adam had had his affair – and I hadn't known.

Sometimes I thought about him with other women. I thought about some woman at work, sitting on his desk in a dress that fitted like a bandage, a woman with sparrow-boned wrists and ankles, eyes the colour of ferns, hair that fell straight as water: a woman who could do astoundingly subtle things with her hands and her mouth, who had an uncanny talent for telephone sex. I imagined him looking at this woman the way he looked at me: it hurt like hell. Fidelity matters so much in adulterous affairs: you have the clearest possible evidence of your lover's capacity for duplicity. And I was of course intensely aware of Dan's attractiveness – his easy walk, his strong body, the casual way his clothes hung from him, the total attention with which he'd listen when you talked. I'm so good at torturing myself, at imagining the worst possible case in devastating detail, then believing my imagined scenarios to be the way things are. Yet for all the extravagance of my imaginings, I never for a moment envisaged what did happen.

My thoughts filled me with such fear. He had so rapidly become indispensable to me – like bread, like salt. If he was late, even by just a few minutes, I thought he would never come. I thought he'd changed his mind, gone back to Helena, gone off with someone else, that it was all over. I paced the house, drank too much scotch, was scratchy with the girls. Five minutes later he'd be there – though somehow I never quite learned to rely on it.

But just once he was really late, and I got very upset. He finally arrived on my doorstep, full of apology; they'd had a union meeting which had got a bit over-excited, he said, and he'd gone to the pub afterwards with the union rep, who went by the unnervingly exotic name of Paola Valente, and he hadn't realized the time.

'What does she look like?' I said.

'Perfectly acceptable,' he said, carefully.

I was cross for about half an hour, though with the saner part of myself I knew I was being unreasonable, knew in fact that this was just the kind of behaviour to make what I most feared happen and drive him away. Then I caught sight of my face in the mirror – a scowl like Lucy's on the edge of a tantrum. I felt ashamed, let myself be soothed by his touch. But I did sometimes find myself wondering about the exotic Paola in moments of doubt – grey days when I had period pain and things going wrong at work, nights when I couldn't sleep.

I wanted to know everything about him. He was my favourite subject. I loved to find out about his passions and fears and stories: his fear of heights and the edges of tube platforms, his flair for languages, his reverence for Miles Davis, his fondness for burnt toast, the fact that stairs in his dreams always led upwards, though in mine they always go down.

There were things he didn't much like to talk about – his childhood, his violent father in particular.

'Why don't you visit him?' I asked him once. It worried me somehow.

He didn't say anything.

'I mean, is it too depressing?' I said. 'Old people's homes are usually horrible.'

'It's not that,' he said. 'Though it's not very nice – it smells – I mean, they always do, I guess. No, I just decided really.'

He paused, his face turned away from me. I waited.

'The last time I was there,' he went on, 'he was in one of his moods: the mince for lunch had been watery, and he was ranting on about what he'd like to do to those half-arsed care assistants. Just ranting on, this pathetic old man.'

'Like when you were little?' I said, sounding horribly social-workerish.

He didn't mind. 'Yes,' he said. 'Like when I was little. I just sat there, in that room smelling of piss, listening to this pathetic old man going on and on, and I thought about the belt and the big buckle and the way his face had contorted when he'd hit me, and the fear I'd felt: I could remember the flavour of it. And I thought – I don't have to do this any more, I can just walk out. So I went, and I've never been back.'

He flushed as he told me: I could sense what an effort it was for him to say this. My eyes filled with tears.

He didn't say much about Helena either: he certainly never criticized her – and I liked him for that. I think their relationship was in most ways very close, but that all the sex had somehow got washed away in the maelstrom of parenting. It happens. I gleaned she'd done a lot for him – smoothed off the rough edges, got him to tone down the rages he felt with the absurdities of the education system, to stop going on about fascists and racists, to wear suits and prepare answers before job interviews.

But he loved to talk about Sally, his daughter, whom he obviously adored. He showed me pictures: wild hair, a pierced nostril, eyebrows like his, a deliciously sceptical expression.

'She's gorgeous,' I said.

'I'd love you to meet her,' he said.

I didn't know what to say, couldn't see how that could ever happen.

Sally had started a media studies course at Cardiff University the previous September – and it had clearly been a big rite of passage for him too. He and Helena had driven up with her, helped her carry her stuff into her room. 'She hugged us and then she just stood there,' he said. 'She was so pink and excited and itching to get on with it, dying for us to go. She absolutely didn't need us any more. It was one of those moments when everything suddenly shifts inside your head. I saw that things were going to be different from then on – for me and Helena too, not just for her.' So I knew there had been some rightness about the timing of my arrival in his life – as there had been about his arrival in mine.

He seemed less curious about me, more accepting. When I talked to him about some of the men in my past, mainly to catalogue their deficiencies, he put a finger on my lips. 'Does it matter? You're here with me now. That's what's important,' he said. But I wanted to know everything – even the daily textures of his life, what he had in his sandwiches for lunch, what music he listened to on his car radio.

'I've had a lousy day,' he said, one evening. We were in bed, lying back on the pillows drinking wine after making love. The wine had been in the freezer: there was moisture like sweat on the bottle, and the coldness of it chilled the glass and made a cold circle on my skin as I rested it between my breasts.

'So tell me,' I said.

He told me. I listened hungrily. And that was when I first heard about Northolt Primary and the Rainbow Room, when I first heard the name Carly Smithson.

He'd gone to Northolt Primary to assess a little boy called Nicky Atwood. Nicky had Downs and was being taught in a normal class-room, with a special support assistant always sitting beside him. The headmistress had told Dan that in September his class was going to be taught upstairs – but Nicky was scared stiff of stairs and might not be able to manage. Dan was furious: he felt the choice of classroom was a deliberate strategy by the headmistress to get Nicky moved to a special school.

'Why would she do that?' I said. 'Couldn't she just ask directly?'

'It wouldn't look good. Fiona Parker always wants to look good.'

'You don't like her,' I said.

'Too right,' he said.

It was break when he arrived, so he got a coffee and went out into the playground to watch how Nicky played. The other children accepted him, seemed fond of him, brought him sand toys. But Nicky was quite wrapped up in himself, and didn't seem to notice. He kept repeating a rather mad-looking little manoeuvre: he'd run a few steps, stop, turn his head, smile secretly to himself – he'd just discovered his shadow. As the children lined up to go back into class, it fell against the wall, stood upright beside him, black and immaculate, showing the feathery tuft of hair on his head, the lumpiness of his feet in their smart new trainers. He stopped, transfixed, and stared with wide-open eyes: the child behind had to push him into the class.

I lay there and listened as Dan talked. I liked the precision of all this – the way he noticed things, tried to get inside this little boy's head.

'Then I took him off to the Rainbow Room,' he said.

I asked him to explain.

'It's a little room that's used for one-to-one teaching,' he said. 'Mostly with children whose first language isn't English. There are piles of Spot books in Urdu and Korean, and one of those posters that say "Welcome" in lots of languages. It's way down the end of a corridor, and always gloomy – you have to put the lights on. I could just hear children singing hymns in the hall.'

I closed my eyes and pictured it – Dan and the little boy with the tufty hair sitting together in that secluded room that was shut off from the school, lit by harsh lighting even in bright summer – and I heard the children singing far away. Later, when that room filled my thoughts so much of the time, when I was obsessed with the mystery of what had once happened there, I often thought back to that lazy conversation as we lay in bed after making love – when, if I shivered, it was only because the wine I'd spilt on my stomach had just come out of the freezer.

Dan took out his tests. Nicky had to name some objects in pictures, to build blocks into a tower, to fit shapes into an inset tray. When Dan totted up the results, he was surprised: it was an unusually high score for a child with Downs; it made Dan still more convinced that Nicky shouldn't be moved. He took Nicky back to his classroom and went to see the headmistress.

'Tell me what she looks like,' I said.

'Far too much makeup and one of those silly headbands posh women often wear,' he said. 'She's got a really salacious streak: I hate it. I showed her Nicky's test results, said I couldn't see why his class had to be taught upstairs when he's so scared of stairs. She said, "I do have other children to think of, Dan. There are thirty-three other children in that class . . .'''

'Well, you can see her point,' I said tentatively – then rather wished I hadn't.

'It's total crap,' said Dan – so emphatically the surface of the wine in my wine-glass trembled. 'She just wants him out. She's got this pretty little middle-class school and she doesn't want any snotty-nosed thick kids cluttering it up.'

I thought guiltily of Alice's school – Connington House, a very pretty middle-class school indeed, with its panelling and smell of polish and vases of lilies – a school where all the girls have names like Claudia and Clarissa and none are thick or snotty-nosed. As Jude sometimes remarks, I'm entirely without principles where my children's education is concerned. Dan and I had agreed not to talk about it.

He told Fiona Parker he thought it was wrong to think of moving Nicky to a special school. 'I have to disagree with you there, Dan,' she said. 'I'm afraid we do consider Nicky's problems to be exceptionally severe.' And then added in her silkiest voice, 'Don't forget, Dan, that we've worked very successfully with other children with special needs in the past. Though frankly I do feel we haven't quite had the support from your service we might have hoped for.'

Here we go again, thought Dan. He was always getting into these conversations: there were so many children who needed help, so little money to help them. 'We've been very busy, I'm afraid,' he said.

She looked at him coldly. 'I do know what it's like to be busy, Dan,' she said. 'What I can't understand is why you feel Nicky deserves so much help when other children don't. We've certainly had others where it would have been nice to see the same degree of commitment you seem to feel towards Nicky. Little Carly Smithson, for instance. She has such potential, that little girl. She was really benefiting from the extra help she was getting from Mr Bradley, our support teacher, and his rapport with her was a joy to see. But then your service in its wisdom withdrew that support from her.'

Carly Smithson. Dan struggled to remember her – he saw over fifty children a year. He vaguely recalled a girl with a language disorder he'd seen a few times to assess several months before. A little waif in a Disney Shop sweatshirt, with fidgety restless fingers and white eyelashes and the speech patterns of a much younger child. She'd had some individual teaching for a while, but Dan had reluctantly concluded that the expense couldn't be justified. He had an inchoate memory of trying to help her with letter formation.

'I believe we failed that child, Dan, we failed her terribly,' Fiona

Parker went on. 'One of a number where a little more help from your service would have made her future a whole lot brighter.'

Dan had tried to get the conversation back on track. 'I made some remark about Nicky's mother, said she feels he's really benefiting from being in a mainstream school,' he told me. 'Fiona Parker launched into some ludicrously irrelevant story – how she's heard there are lots of different men in the house, how once she'd gone to the house at nine o'clock in the morning and Nicky's mother had opened the door in her dressing-gown and you could see quite plainly that under the dressing-gown she hadn't got anything on. Jesus.

'I lost it then,' he said. 'I was furious, said some stuff about how all she cared about was attracting middle-class parents to her cosy middle-class school. I think I shouted. She said, "Dan, I have nothing more to say to you," and she went and opened the door.'

I poured him more wine. He drank quickly, his movements were awkward, abrupt. 'Shit,' he said, after a while. 'I shouldn't have done it. I know I've made an enemy. She's a powerful woman.'

I wanted to soothe him, to make it all right. 'These things happen, surely,' I said. 'We all lose our tempers sometimes at work, don't we? Say things we shouldn't?'

'I don't know,' said Dan. 'I don't know. I've got a bad feeling about it. That kind of thing doesn't get you anywhere. And it's fuck-all use to Nicky. I don't understand what happened. I should have learnt to control my temper by now.'

He drank his wine quickly. 'I have to go.'

'I know you do. I don't have to like it, though.'

I moved across to kiss him, rolled on top of him. I could feel him hard against me. I reached down to encircle his penis in my hand. 'Well, maybe I don't have to go for ten minutes,' he said. We made love again: he was soothed, smiling, when he left.

But I lay awake for a long time that night – I suppose the anxiety he felt had got into me. When I finally slept I had a disconcerting dream, in which I went down a long flight of stairs and found myself in a big old empty building, shadowy and decaying, with grass growing through the floor. There were stained glass windows and vases of lilies like in the reception area at Alice's school, and the lilies and stained glass made it seem like a church or a chapel, though I knew in the dream it was actually a schoolroom. I stood on the edge of this great empty space and felt a kind of dread, though I didn't know why. Something caught my eye then down the other end of the room, a sudden slight movement, and I saw a weird little boy sitting there, wearing a velvet headband and one of Lucy's sweatshirts, his shadow falling darkly onto the floor in front of him. I knew he shouldn't be wearing Lucy's sweatshirt, I couldn't understand it, something awful must have happened, I knew I needed to go and see if my children were safe. But I couldn't move, couldn't do anything, stood there stuck to the spot, my body paralysed, just watching the boy and his shadow, watching how his shadow grew bigger and bigger, reaching out towards me, seeping across the grassy floor till it lapped at my feet like dark water.

6

The summer holidays. Adam and Simone took the girls away for two weeks, to a villa with a swimming pool near Assisi. For the rest of the holiday I'd booked them into a day camp. It was modelled on the kind of thing they have in the States – camp songs, camp jokes, camp T-shirts with special logos and matching baseball caps – and the girls adored it. They ate more and laughed more and slept longer than in term-time, and Lucy never had tantrums.

'They're so different in the holidays,' I said to Jude. 'School must be such a strain for them.'

'Poor little things, how they suffer. Perhaps you should educate them at home,' she said, then laughed out loud at my appalled expression.

The weeks had themes – the Middle Ages, Dinosaurs, Save the Animals. Saving the animals made them both thoughtful, edging Alice a little closer towards vegetarianism, inspiring Lucy with grandiose schemes of redemption. 'I'm going to be a zoo-keeper when I grow up,' she said. 'I'll give them all their favourite foods and make their cages bigger.' The house was full of delicate artefacts – knights and dragons and stegosauruses made of clay, whose feet, talons and swords fell off as they dried, huge exuberant paintings with a thick skin of vivid poster paint that flaked off like little scabs on the carpet.

The girls had that unkempt summer look that I love. Their skin smelt of suntan oil and their hair of sun. Alice's shoulders peeled monstrously and her hair bleached almost white: Lucy's knees were permanently muddy, her fingernails crammed with paint and sand and earth, her arms powdered with tiny red-brown freckles as though she'd brushed against some polleny flower.

In my garden, dusty now and tired with late summer, the briar roses were almost over, but the cultivated bushes in the rose bed were weighed down with blossoms, yellow and pink, full of bees. I can never quite decide whether I like them or whether they are too formal, too deliberate, those opulent whorls of plush petals. There were insects everywhere, wasps, gnats, loud intrusive irritating flies. One evening I opened Lucy's lunchbox, and found the crusts of her sandwiches and her fromage frais pot darkly seething with ants. The sight filled me with horror, made me think of that ghastly scene at the end of *A Hundred Years of Solitude* where the ants carry off the baby. There was no sign of a break in the weather, though the shadows were lengthening earlier in the evening. I thought summer would last for ever.

Then Dan went on holiday with Helena. They only went to Brittany: they never travelled far, she didn't much like flying. I hated them being away together. I was obsessed with the notion that he'd be reconciled to her and give me up. I thought of them sitting together in some Gitane-scented café with red check tablecloths, forgiving one another. I could see his face softening as he leaned towards her, as they laughed together over the chocolate crêpes, recalling something cute and funny their daughter had done way way back in their shared history. I lay awake for hours and ached for him.

He sent me postcards. They were all from the forest of Broceliande. The pictures were rather banal – spindly trees, unexceptional little lakes, a rather small megalith – but the names were full of magic: the Château of Compère, birthplace of Vivienne the enchantress; the Giants' Tomb; a pond called the Fairies' Mirror. The messages were simple, nothing to cause trouble if Alice or Lucy had seen them. I'm missing you so much; Love to the girls; All my love. I subjected the writing to scrupulous analysis: the 'Love' was satisfyingly big.

I wondered how he'd managed to send them. I thought of him making some excuse as he had so often all through his married life – going out to buy baguettes, perhaps, in some cluttered grocery store smelling of olives and yeast – then writing the postcard quickly and slipping it into the letterbox and thinking of me. The thought gave me a huge fat feeling of happiness.

He rang me the Saturday they came home. Helena was away the next day, he said. He wanted to come and spend some time with the girls. I liked him wanting this.

We were in the garden when he came: I didn't hear the doorbell. So he came in round the side, through the garden gate, which is usually on the latch. We kissed quickly and chastely, his cool lips just brushing mine. His skin was dark from the sun: the sight of him made me hungry.

I made the girls fancy drinks that looked like Pimms – lemonade with bits of strawberry and cucumber in, and curly straws and paper umbrellas, and poured chilled wine for Dan and me, and we sat on the lawn in my white-painted wicker armchairs. The grass was the colour of sand, the sky harshly, intensely blue. Some of the shrubs in my borders were dying, their leaves crinkled like brown paper, black as though scorched at the edges. I'd put the sprinkler on – it felt rather delinquent, as the council was threatening a hosepipe ban – and Lucy in her Esmeralda swimsuit jumped through it, giggling and shrieking, her thighs and upper arms goose-fleshed, the water on her skin glittering in the sun, while Alice lay on a towel in the shade of the apple-tree and sorted through the Tarot pack that had come with one of her magazines.

Dan had brought his camera. He took pictures of me and the girls. It felt very intimate – the kind of thing a proper family would do. I felt so happy.

But when I went in to top up the girls' drinks, Alice followed me. She stood close to me: she was getting tall now – soon she'd overtake me. I cut up some cucumber and sliced a few strawberries with a serrated knife, the red juice like blood stains on my hands. Alice watched. She started twisting a strand of hair round a finger, then stuck the end of it in her mouth.

'Don't do that,' I said. 'It's revolting.'

She pulled a face, let the hair fall back. 'Is Dan staying for tea?' she said.

'Yes,' I said.

'Oh.' Where the skin had peeled on her nose, you could see the new skin underneath, frail and pink and shiny like a baby's.

'Alice, what's the problem, exactly? We're having a nice afternoon, aren't we? I thought you were happy.'

'I like to have time with just us,' she said.

'We have masses of time with just us.'

'Do we? You're always doing something. You send us off to

playschemes and we're always having babysitters and you're always going out and you don't often meet me from school and Lizzie's mum does all the time and when I talk to you you're always thinking of something else.'

A child-like anger flared in me. All the things I do for you . . . I wanted to hit her, hard. I struggled to keep control, slicing neatly at the strawberries with precise careful strokes. The sweet juice ran freely, reddening the chopping board.

'Alice, you can be so bloody selfish,' I said, in the cold, critical voice I knew she hated. 'You expect life to revolve around you. You can be self-centred beyond belief. You think you're the centre of the universe.'

She said nothing. She just stood there frowning, chewing her hair.

I tipped the fruit into the glasses, poured on too much lemonade so it frothed over. I could feel her flinching away from me as though I'd touched a raw graze on her skin.

We went back out into the garden. Dan was in the sandpit with Lucy. They were sticking bits of grass and twigs into mounds of sand to make a forest, she was laughing at something he'd said. He looked up – I could tell he'd overheard.

He got up and went to get his camera and gave it to Alice and showed her how it worked. It was easy, he said: the viewfinder was in the top of the camera and showed you exactly what you'd get in the picture. She shrugged as though it didn't matter to her, but I could tell she was intrigued. She'd often asked me for a camera and I'd put it off, deterred by the cost of getting the films developed, but I didn't think I'd ever mentioned this to Dan. He was gentle, careful not to crowd her, not looking directly at her: I loved him so much for it. He told her a bit about composition and how to find a picture. 'You have to look at something quite ordinary and see it in a way that nobody's seen it before,' he said. 'You have to come at it from the other side.' Watching the two of them together, I was very aware how awkward she was, all knees and elbows and little mistimed bits of laughter, remembering how painful it is to be twelve. She flushed when his hand brushed against her wrist: she flushes so easily, with her pink and white colouring. But she was fascinated in spite of herself. She started to find things to photograph

– the hard green apples forming on the tree, a bucketful of snails and bits of snail that Lucy had collected, a bee lumbering around on the patio, a softly slumping yellow rose. She played around with things, putting them together, looking for new conjunctions. The results might be surprising, I thought. She could find a picture in an unexpected place.

Watching the growth of these tiny tendrils of connection between them, I began to hope that she might in time come to accept him. I'd been wrong to get cross with her, I should have tried to understand. It made me so happy to see them together, establishing this tentative friendship. I did feel a niggle of disquiet, though, about the photographs. I wondered what he planned to do with them when he'd got them developed. I must warn him, I thought, to keep them safe. I didn't want Helena to come across pictures of me or my children – especially my children. It was a kind of primitive thing – as though the photographs, like nail parings or hair clippings in cultures where magic is practised, would carry something of our essence and put us in her power, as though she might work some terrible spell on us, stitching up our limbs with cramps and filling our mouths with ashes. I feared her, I suppose – as we do fear those we have wronged.

That night, when the girls were in their rooms, we made love with the big windows that face onto the street wide open. I'd taken off the duvet and we lay on a sheet that I'd dried outside, that smelt of sunlight. My pale Indian cotton curtains blew a little apart: I love the way long curtains blow, the patterns they make in a summer breeze as they fill out and billow and swell. With the windows wide you felt very close to the street. As he traced me out with his fingers, opened me, slid inside me, you could hear noises from outside almost as though they were in the room: a couple of teenage girls talking and laughing as they sat and smoked on the steps of the church hall opposite, someone calling a dog, someone getting into a car – you could hear every sound in the sequence, the key clicking in the lock, the hinge groaning, the creaking of the seat, the engine starting up. It made what we were doing seem secret, almost illicit, like making love only half-concealed in a public place. When he came, flamboyantly, saying my name over and over, I wondered if the teenage girls could hear. But they went on talking and laughing quietly together.

Afterwards, I lay on my side facing him in the wet bed, and he stroked my face with fingers that smelt of me. I wanted to ask him what he'd do with the photographs, to warn him to keep them safe. But I didn't know how to put it – and perhaps it was better to say nothing. I didn't want to imply that I didn't trust him to be careful.

Then he told me.

'Helena knows,' he said.

My heard started beating very fast. 'What d'you mean?' I said. I envisaged some dreadful scene of revelation – her smelling my scent on his hair, perhaps, or finding one of my earrings in his pocket.

'I've told her. She knows.'

'Was it awful?'

'Yeah. She wasn't surprised though. She'd suspected, of course.'

'Why did you tell her?'

'I wanted to. I'm sick of all this lying. But actually doing it felt cruel. Perhaps it's just selfish, really.'

'I don't know,' I said.

'I've been lying for years,' he said. 'I've had enough of that. I want to lead a different kind of life.'

Through the gap where the curtains moved apart, you could see the sky darkening to an incredibly rich blue. There was a freshness in the air now, as the shadows grew longer. We could hear the teenage girls get up and wander off down the street, giggling, telling stories. Their laughter faded in the distance.

I felt a surprising chill of panic. I didn't understand myself: this was what I wanted more than anything, wasn't it? To have him exclusively mine? It was a sense perhaps that the pace wasn't right – that things were moving forward with an inexorable rhythm that was out of my control. It was almost a superstitious thing – a fear of careering too fast towards the future. A sense that if you got the timing wrong, you could never go back and do it again.

'Can I stay all night?' he said.

'I'd love that,' I said. And then added, thinking of Alice, 'But could you go before breakfast? Because of the girls.'

'Why? Are you ashamed of me?' He said it half-jokingly, but I knew he was hurt. 'They know we sleep together.'

'No, of course it's not that. Just to make it easier in the morning. The girls are always awful in the morning. D'you mind?'

He did mind. There was a hard edge to him, something harsh in the set of his mouth – the look he always had when I mentioned something I'd done that he didn't agree with – bribing the girls to tidy their rooms, perhaps, or going along with some inane decision at work rather than taking a stand. But he did what I'd asked. He set the alarm and left early, before the girls were up.

7

I took Alice's accusations to heart: I resolved at least to pick her up
from school more often. The first Thursday of term seemed an ideal
opportunity: Lucy was staying late, to her French club, so Alice and
I could have some time together, just the two of us.

I love this time of year – all the September things, the crisp
unmarked exercise books, the flurry of new mad cow jokes from the
playground, the spiders' webs wet and glittery on my rose hedge in
the morning. It's odd how there's always a sense of promise about the
first hints of autumn – though rationally you know that soon there will
be frosts and bare branches and dying things. I suppose it's because
we associate it from childhood with the start of the school year, and
a chance to begin again.

This year it was Lucy who'd had the fresh start: she'd left nursery
and started at big school. She had a uniform now, stiffer and more
formal than the clothes she was used to, with tight cuffs and buttons
under the neck and a tie on a piece of elastic. It took her a long
time to get it all on, and everything had to be very precise. She'd
get upset if she let go of a shirt cuff while wriggling into her
sweatshirt: and once she had a major tantrum, a screaming fit
that lasted for ten minutes, because I insisted on helping as we
were late, and buttoned her shirt from bottom to top instead of
from top to bottom.

She did well from the beginning: she was always a popular child.
Her only complaint was about a little boy called Jake whom she
played with sometimes. 'He keeps playing kiss chase and I don't
want to,' she told me. I was busy cooking dinner at the time.

'Have you tried telling him not to?' I said.

'Of course I have,' she said. 'He still does it. I mean, if he'd been
sick and then he kissed me I could be sick. I mean, *yuk*.' The
hands went out in that little expressive gesture that I loved, her

face quizzical, screwed up. 'The trouble is, I do like Jake. I don't want him not to be my friend. If I told the dinner lady he'd be mad at me, and I don't want him to be mad at me.'

'I know it's hard,' I said, falling back on cheap social work-style empathy because I didn't know how to help. I was a bit preoccupied, juggling pans on the hob, draining pasta, frying tomatoes and peppers for ratatouille, and it smelt as though the oil was over-heating. 'Look, my love, we must sit down some time and talk about this properly.'

'Mummy, you always say that. And you never do,' she said, leaving me with a vague sense of failure. I resolved to bring the subject up again but somehow it never happened. I couldn't really see a solution. I hoped the problem would just go away.

Alice was waiting alone on the grass verge under the chestnuts in front of the school. I was late: most of the other parents had come and gone. She had a messy, end-of-the-day look, her blouse hanging out of her waistband, her hair waving crookedly, still damp from swimming. She came over to the car, tipped her bags onto the back seat, got in, looking worried. In her hand she had an apple, shiny and acid green, with a bitemark going brown.

'We're not allowed to pick them. I found it in the grass,' she said, as though pre-empting a telling-off.

'Can I have a bite?'

'Please do, Mum. Finish it. I thought it would be nice but it's not.'

I bit. It smelt wonderfully, nostalgically, of childhood orchards, of long ago afternoons crawling with wasps and suffused with golden light – but the smell dissipated with the first crunch and the flesh was woolly.

I put it down on the dashboard. 'It needed longer on the tree. It's not really ripe,' I said. We drove in silence for a while.

'An awful thing happened to me today,' she said.

'Poor love. Tell me.'

'I was sitting having lunch at Suzie's table, and Claudia and Kate came up and when they saw me they went away again.'

'You don't know it was anything to do with you,' I said.

'It was, though. They went over to Hester and I heard them laughing together.'

'Oh sweetheart. Girls can be so horrid. You just have to ignore it, not mind too much. Next week you might all be friends again.'

It sounded so inadequate. I ached with the pain of being twelve, remembering it so vividly – being excluded, and the terrible shame you felt, the sense that there was something profoundly wrong with you, like a bad smell or a contagion.

'I used to go round with Kate's gang,' said Alice. 'I started to think they didn't like me when they put salt in my Pepsi.'

'You've just got to decide that if they don't like you, that's their loss,' I said. 'You've got to think, Stuff you.'

'But I *do* mind.'

I patted her knee. 'I hated school,' I said. 'It gets so much better when you're grown up.'

'That's rather a long time to wait, though, isn't it, Mum?'

We turned the corner towards home down the back of the hospital, past the florist's where pots of pink cyclamens dazzled in the lavish autumn light, past the funeral parlour, recently refurbished with smart Café Rouge-style lamps and tab-top curtains, where a man in a serious suit was caressing a hearse with a chamois leather.

'What's for tea?'

'Lasagne.'

'Well, I hope you're not expecting me to eat the meat, Mum. I don't know how you can eat all those animals. Anyway,' she added suspiciously, 'why exactly are we having lasagne in the middle of the week?'

'Dan's coming.'

Out of the corner of my eye, I saw how her face twisted up. She was still on the edge of tears. 'I don't like Dan,' she said.

Here we go again, I thought. But this time I resolved to handle it right – to be all warm and understanding.

'Why don't you like him?' I said, as gently as I could.

'I just don't. I hope you don't mind me saying this, Mum.'

I was touched by that: she was trying, too.

'I can't stand those jeans and leather jackets he wears. He's nearly *fifty*, Mum. It's *gross*. I mean, shouldn't someone of his age wear grey suits and those lace-up shoes with lots of little holes in?'

'Oh Alice.' I laughed.

'Really, Mum, I'm serious.' But she relaxed a little, smiled. 'I can see that he tries to be nice,' she went on, struggling to reach out to me. 'He just doesn't belong to us, though, does he?'

'I know it's difficult for you,' I said, thinking carefully, wondering how to put it. 'You must feel like it's an intrusion.'

'I hate it when you say things like that.'

'Like what?'

'When you say what it feels like to be me. You don't know how I feel. Nobody knows how I feel except me.'

'No.' I had to fight the urge to apologize profusely.

'We won't ever have to call him Dad or anything, will we?'

'Of course not. Your Dad will always be your only dad.'

'Lauren wants to come round to hear my new tape. He won't be there when Lauren comes round, will he?'

'We'll arrange it just how you want it, sweetheart. But please try, Alice,' I said. 'Could you do that for me, d'you think?' I sounded pleading. She said nothing. I wondered if it would have been better not to ask.

Dan came straight from work, wearing formal clothes for once, but not in a way Alice would approve of, with his tie at half-mast and his sleeves rolled up, so you could see the smooth skin on the insides of his forearms and the warm hollow at the base of his throat: I loved that casual way he wore his clothes, as though he hadn't quite finished dressing. He always brought something for the girls – gelatine-free jelly sweets, favourite magazines, real bandages for Lucy's endlessly-suffering dolls. This time he'd brought the latest *Sugar* for Alice, and a load of computer paper for Lucy to draw on.

But after the bandages the computer paper was a bit of a disappointment. Lucy was more interested in the contents of the briefcase he'd dumped in the hall.

'That's what I keep my tests in,' he said. 'I'll show you.'

He opened up the case, took out a picture of a teddy bear, a little yellow box of plastic animals, some spiral-bound books with pictures and puzzles in. She was intrigued by one of them – a fat shiny book with three patterns on each page and a space where you had to fill in the fourth. He asked if she'd like to try it and she said yes, so they did it together, very solemnly. She adored it. Everything about it made her feel important – the pompous words on the title page, the complexity of the patterns, the way Dan had to use a calculator to work out her score. When Alice asked me for help with her geography, Lucy told her off. 'Ssh,' she said, very melodramatic. 'No one can talk. Dan and me are doing a test. We have to concentrate.'

Then she drew a picture of a cat with various injuries, while Dan and I cut up vegetables for the salad. I liked him helping me cook – as I liked it when he sorted out practical things for me – unblocked the drains, put up smoke alarms. His latest project was my shed – which had a marked sideways list from the weight of the clematis that clambered over it: he'd promised to retrain the clematis into the apple tree and put up a new shed for me. The very ordinariness of these things somehow made our relationship feel more solid, more complete.

The lasagne took a long time to cook. Lucy demanded a chocolate biscuit. I said she could have a yoghurt. She went to the fridge and stamped her foot. 'Oh! I can't reach. Why do people always put things on top of my yoghurt?'

'I don't think they do it deliberately,' I said.

'They do,' she said. 'I *see* them do it deliberately. On top of my yoghurt.'

I gave her the yoghurt. She ripped the top off.

'Yuk,' she said. 'It's got that water stuff on.' She never ate a yoghurt if it had separated. She hurled it into the bin. Her head jutted forward fiercely: this always meant trouble.

Dan took a piece of the computer paper, made a fold in it. Lucy watched warily, still frowning. The paper became a snapping mouth. 'She's called Fearsome Fangs,' he said, nipping Lucy's hand with the mouth. 'She lives on fromage frais and it's a real mistake to get on the wrong side of her.' Lucy giggled, made the mouth go round biting things.

Alice watched. I thought she'd say something satirical, but she didn't. 'Could you make something for me?' she said.

'I can't do anything more complicated,' he said. 'Not from memory, anyway.'

'I've got a book on origami,' said Alice. She went to fetch it from the living room, opened it up on the table. They pored over it together, his dark head, her fair one, almost touching.

She chose the crane.

Dan groaned. 'Trust you,' he said. 'It's the trickiest one in the book.'

It was the sort of thing I could never do. I abhorred that whole side of parenting – the cutting and sticking and all those clever things you're meant to do with kidney beans and the insides of loo rolls – and trying to follow a diagram could reduce me to inchoate rage and Quentin Tarantino-style swearing. But Dan was good: he didn't have to keep turning the page upside down to work out which way the folds went. I watched his quick clever fingers, twisting, sculpting. He made the final fold and put his fingers inside.

The bird swooped and dipped over the table. It was rather beautiful, its fragility somehow moving. The wings seemed to curve and droop like feathers, as though, by some mysterious alchemy, Dan had transmuted the physical properties of the paper. There was an illusion of floatiness about it, you felt it might defy gravity, soar away.

'Ah, cool,' said Alice.

He gave it to her, showed her where to put her fingers to make it fly.

'It'll bring you luck,' he said.

'How d'you know?' said Alice.

'It says so in your book. It says cranes are lucky. In Japan anyway.'

'D'you believe in luck?' she asked, very serious, fiddling with the bird, tracing the line of its wing with her finger.

'I think you make your own luck,' said Dan. 'You make it happen. If you believe in yourself, you can make anything happen.'

'I don't believe in luck,' said Lucy. 'That's for little children. That's like magic and stuff. I mean, Jake thinks the tooth fairy really exists. I ask you.'

'I bet your Mum thinks there's such a thing as luck,' said Dan.

'I do,' I said. Then, feeling Alice required something more precise, 'Well, I at least believe that some people go on being lucky throughout their lives – that there's a kind of pattern – and for other people nothing seems to go right.' It sounded rather lame. I tried to work out what I really thought. 'That perhaps we all have some kind of life script that we live out. Perhaps that's what the luck is –

it's an illusion because we're acting out a life script we're given by our parents.'

'Really, Mum,' said Alice. 'You're not in the office now. She's awful, isn't she?' she said, teasingly to Dan. 'She's always going on about life scripts. It's all those workshops she goes to: Understanding Your Personal Mythology and How to Rewrite Your Life Script and Boost Your Self-Esteem.'

It was the first time she'd ever done this – siding with him against me, wanting to make him laugh. He said nothing, just grinned, a teasing, slightly triumphant grin.

'She has campaigns sometimes,' Alice went on, 'when she's been to a really good workshop.' She played around with the bird, making it swoop and dip and hover over the table. 'When we were little, she went to this workshop on star charts, and she gave us stars for good behaviour, and when we had enough stars we were meant to get a chocolate orange. Only Lucy made such a fuss, Mum gave her the chocolate anyway, before she'd got any stars.'

Dan laughed. Alice flushed with pleasure.

Lucy looked a little hurt, tried to attack Alice's bird with her biting mouth.

'Don't,' said Alice. 'It's very fragile.' She brought the bird to rest on her book. When she went to bed, she took it upstairs with her.

8

One evening, when I got in his car, before we went to The Water Margin, he said, 'There's something I want to show you.'

He drove me down an unfamiliar street, rather rundown, with big Victorian houses mostly divided into flats or bedsits. He stopped by a three-storey house opposite a park, and motioned me to get out. A cherry tree in a front garden had dropped its fruit on the pavement: some were still a sickly pink, some mashed to a bruised brown pulp where people had trodden on them. Further down the street a child was playing the piano with the window open, stumbling through 'Für Elise' with its endless repetitions.

We passed the window of a downstairs flat in the corner house. The ornaments on the windowsill – china cups and velvet-framed photos of children – were the kind of thing old ladies collect. There were several doorbells, but he had a key. We went in, past a bureau with a dried flower arrangement, past some prints of Swiss landscapes. The hallway smelt of fried onions.

We went upstairs. Another key, a Yale this time. I followed him into a big, high-ceilinged room, with a bay window looking out over the park. There was a bed with a gaudy taffeta spread and a bookcase and a gas fire and some awful wallpaper with a shiny embossed pattern, and a mirror with a gilt frame opposite the bed. Boxes were scattered on the floor, one opened up, full of books: pictures were propped against the wall.

I stared at him.

'I've left Helena,' he said. As I opened my mouth to say something he put a finger on my lips. 'No,' he said. 'This is just about me and Helena – okay? I don't want you to feel I'm asking for anything. My life with her is over, that's all. It's been inevitable for a long time. That's what this is about.'

A little kitchen opened off the side of the room. I poked around in it – an old gas cooker, a sink with a new washing-up bowl, a geyser, a fridge.

'It's so simple,' I said, coming back into the main room. 'It's like a monk's cell.'

'Scarcely,' he said. 'Not with you in it.' He pulled me down on the bed beside him. 'Look,' he said, pointing to the mirror opposite the bed. 'We could watch ourselves. I'd like that.'

We kissed, but I didn't feel in the least like making love. I got up again and went to look out of the window, resting my hands on the low sill.

It was a neat rectangular park, a very conventional municipal open space: a gravel path round the perimeter, children's swings in one corner, borders full of hydrangeas with heavy dead flowerheads, wrought iron gates – rather pretentiously big and ornate, given the size of the park. In the dim light the grass looked grey. A young man was pushing a pram out through the gates, walking too fast along the gravel path, shoving the pram roughly across the stones as though it held groceries or a load of free papers to deliver, though I could see from my vantage point that there was a baby inside. I feared briefly for the baby.

'We'll take it very slowly,' said Dan, 'as slowly as you want. I know there's the Alice thing.'

'Yes,' I said, though I didn't quite like him putting it like that. 'But it's not just Alice,' I went on. 'I want us to be . . . solid, somehow. To really know each other. To feel that the future's predictable, reliable – I mean, I know it can't be – but to feel we've done all we can to make it like that . . .'

A sudden feeling of misery pressed down on me. The room had that bleakness you always find in places where lots of people have lived in a transitory way. You could sense all the light imprints of other people's lives, like graffiti scratched on the walls. They'd been lonely people, perhaps, with only the most tenuous connections. It made me think of the rooms of men I'd been out with at university and in my twenties – rooms with sheets pinned up at the windows, and scummy basins, and bits of car strewn around, and a vague smell of socks. Rooms I'd sometimes left unsatisfied in the morning, after a cup of grey instant coffee, with casual thanks and a vague promise to see you around. Rooms you hope to move on from. I feared that the fact of his living here in this bleak place might make him less attractive to me – and I hated what that seemed to say about me.

He sensed my depression, of course.

'Hey, I know it's kind of dreary now,' he said. 'But it'll be fine when I've got my things organized.'

I went to look in the box of books. Well-thumbed psychology books, some Urdu textbooks on cheap thin paper, a few novels – *G*, *A Suitable Boy*, some thrillers – and his comprehensive collection of Miles Davis tapes. On top was a diary, quite thick, not his usual appointments diary. 'I didn't know you kept a diary,' I said.

'It's a new thing,' he said. 'You can look if you like. There's lots of you in it.'

'No,' I said. 'Of course I won't look.'

Under the diary was a paperback copy of Dante's *Inferno*, on the cover a painting from Orvieto Cathedral – damned souls as naked writhing bodies being thrown down into Hell by wonderfully camp angels with great wide wings blue as woodsmoke. I turned to the start of the text: it was in Italian.

'Can you read this?' I said.

'Kind of. It was last year's evening class.'

'Go on then: show off,' I said.

He read me a stanza or two. I scarcely know enough Italian to order a cappuccino, but I could tell it was the bit that always gets quoted – those very first lines of the poem, where Dante wakes to find himself in a dark wood where the straight way is lost. Lines I've always loved – that sense of the wood as a bitter, confusing place, with nothing pretty or safe or obvious about it, like the woods where I grew up, where the undergrowth was spiky with brambles, and the spindly conifers jostled one another, struggling towards the light, and the paths were so hard to learn.

'That's beautiful,' I said. His voice sounded different speaking Italian, less Manchester and measured, a little extravagant, with more light and shade in it, more music. 'I like you reading that,' I told him.

But the depression still clung to me. At the end of the evening, when I was back home and Dan had gone, I went slowly round my kitchen, enjoying its richness, touching things – the mismatched flowery cups and saucers on my dresser, the hanging baskets of flowering plants, the photographs and children's paintings and dismembered clay dinosaurs – as though these multifarious and evocative things could restore me to myself, make me whole again.

Yet the next time I went there, it was fine, just as he'd predicted. He'd hung his pictures and put his books on a shelf, and I saw then that it was a pleasant room – airy, pleasantly proportioned, with the big bay window letting in lots of light. We made love on the bed with the taffeta cover, and were startled and pleased by the explicitness of our entangled bodies reflected in the mirror on the wall.

Now he was living alone, it changed things. Once I'd got over the sense of panic and knew that he meant what he said – that we could take things at my pace – it was very freeing. I realized how scared I'd been of Helena, how I'd lived in fear of some kind of dreadful showdown, but now I could put that fear at least behind me.

Sometimes during the day I'd go by a different route on a visit to a client so I would pass Dan's flat. I'd write little notes and leave them for him. I wrote about the things I'd specially liked in our love-making – the touches that made me shiver, the positions where I felt him most deeply inside me: and I told him how I loved the feel of his fingers tracing me out and the subtle musky taste of him in my mouth and the catch in his voice when he came. It was bold for me: it was something I'd never done before. I liked to think of my letters lying there on the doormat, in that prim and rather anonymous place, and the old lady who lived downstairs perhaps picking them up and putting them on the bureau in front of the dried flower arrangement, not knowing what was inside, and Dan coming home in the evening and seeing my writing and wondering what was waiting there for him. It was strangely arousing to spell out my feelings so nakedly, to leave my words lying there for him to find. I felt for the first time in my life as though sex was something I could play around with, be creative with, even. I seemed to be changing so fast – turning into a different person, someone bolder and freer, the lover I'd never quite managed to be till Dan entered my life.

Those were good days for me, perhaps the happiest we had. I wasn't exactly content, though. I worried ceaselessly about the girls and how they were handling it all. Alice got an unexpected D in geography: I fretted about its significance. Lucy's teacher cornered me after school: I panicked, expecting her to say, 'She seems to have something on her mind, Mrs Langdon. Is everything alright at home?' But it was only to say that Lucy's wobbly tooth had come out in PE and she was sending it home in a little plastic envelope. And always there was the fear of loss, that he'd lose interest, withdraw, start looking at someone else. I was in so deep with Dan: I knew I'd made myself utterly open, utterly vulnerable.

I still slept erratically. The nights he wasn't there – and I insisted I had plenty of evenings with just me and the girls – on those nights I'd sometimes wake at four o'clock in the morning. If then I managed with the help of a fried egg and a lot of scotch and a few pages of John Le Carré to get back to sleep, I'd always have vividly sexual dreams: I've read somewhere that our sex hormones peak in the hour or two before we wake, so maybe this is a common dream pattern, though Jude, the only person I've asked about it, says wistfully that it's never happened to her. The dreams were often cruel, dreams of women whose legs were forced apart, whose mouths when not in use were harshly gagged, whose perfect bodies were soon exquisitely bruised, who were penetrated through every opening. I guess I only ever slept lightly at that time of night, they were invariably half-conscious or lucid dreams in which I always seemed to be aware that carrying on sleeping was at some level a choice, something I had control over, that I could have woken up if I'd wanted to, but I didn't quite want to. Then finally I'd wake when the milkman came round, just before my alarm went off, still full of the sexual feeling but with my conscious mind rejecting the anonymous men, the cruel images, and I'd float into a waking dream of Dan and me together, feel him slide inside me, hear him speaking my name.

9

I woke one Sunday in early September to a startlingly beautiful day –
a day so golden and perfect it simply had to be celebrated. The girls
were with me – it wasn't Adam's weekend. On a sudden impulse, I
rang Jude and asked if she'd take them for the day, and I put on a
nice short skirt and a T-shirt in summery colours and dropped the
girls off and went to pick him up. Then we drove round London
and headed off up the M1.

'It's a really strange place we're going to,' I said. 'I went there
once before a long time ago. The house has got the Magnificat in
stone letters all round the edge of the roof.'

He was happy. He liked me doing all the planning and driving
for once. And though he would never say it, I knew he loved me
packing the girls off, putting him first.

We left the motorway at last and drove through the empty
Northamptonshire countryside, past flat fields where quiet cattle
grazed, through villages of squat little factories and modern brick
houses where women in floral dresses moved slowly along the
pavements. We parked on the edge of a recreation ground, where
a rusted swing and slide stood empty in the sleepy mid-day sun.

A gravel path wound between some cottages. We turned a corner
and came suddenly into the open – on one side the manor house with
its flamboyant balustrade – on the other, a great bowl of silky grass
where swallows dipped and wheeled, a cedar, a vast green drive that
stretched to the horizon.

'There's an orangery,' I said. 'We'll go there first. That's the bit
I like best.'

It was tucked away at the side of the house, shaded by tall trees,
an elegant Edwardian building of yellow Northamptonshire stone.

'Weird,' said Dan, as we pushed open the heavy door. 'It feels as
though no one ever comes here.'

It had been recently watered: the floor was wet. It smelt of damp soil, rotting vegetation, mingled Mediterranean pollens. There were exuberant hibiscuses, their poised flowers reaching out like dancers, and orange trees with little oily fruit shining like suns or moons among the dark leaves, and gardenias, my favourite – some flowers still pleated into buds, some open and white and perfect, decadently scented. There were lilies too, and jasmine, and formal agapanthus with lush blue flowers, and among the plants in the flowerbeds there were statues of women with complicated hair, their breasts spilling out of their clothes, all encrusted with grey-green lichen.

'I can see why you like it,' he said. 'It feels really old, kind of untouched – like the twentieth century swept past it up north on the motorway. It's rather beautiful.' I felt hugely happy.

At the heart of the place was an octagonal pool, choked up with waterlilies with great white waxy flowers, their fibrous stems all knotted together. The water was murky and still, thick with decay. Here the bad smell was stronger, drowning out the honeyed scents of the flowers – that smell of stagnant water that's the same wherever you come across it – on the steps of some rotting Venetian palazzo, or in a gunged-up ditch where you stop to pee on a journey.

Automatically I felt in my bag for a coin. It was what the girls always did whenever they came to a pond or pool in a wood or garden or shopping centre, anywhere with a ring of water: they'd always make a wish. They knew of course the rule about wishing – that it should be secret – but found it hard to comply – especially Lucy, whose wish would always be told to me in a sibilant stage whisper, her breath warm on my ear, the minute the coin was flung: 'I wished for everyone to be happy and no one to hurt the animals. Was that a good wish, Mummy?'

I tossed my 20p into the pool. Dan watched, amused. My wish was very like Lucy's – vague, over-inclusive, excessively optimistic – a wish for things to stay just as they were, all of us healthy and happy and Dan and me together.

My 20p had landed on a lilypad. 'D'you think that means it won't come true?' I said. 'I mean, doesn't it have to really get under the water?'

He looked at me as though I was mad. I giggled, a bit embarrassed at my excessive superstitiousness.

'I think you understand the mechanics of all this better than me,' he said. 'But I hope it works for you . . . What was it anyway?'

'No. It's a secret,' I said.

'D'you have many secrets from me?'

'Only a few.'

'So tell me one.'

I shook my head, laughing a little.

We walked on slowly, past more hibiscuses flaming with reddish flowers, under a fig with big ornate leaves that brushed our heads as we passed.

'Go on,' he said. 'Something you've hidden from me.'

'Well – fantasies perhaps,' I said. 'I wouldn't tell you some of those.'

'Why not?'

'They're mostly kind of cruel. I don't like them.'

'But they make you come?'

'Mmm.'

'Is that what you think about when we make love?'

'No. I don't think about anything with you. Well, just about what we're doing . . . Sometimes I see things – floaty shapes, colours . . . So what do you hide from me?'

He stopped and thought about this, seriously, standing under a fig-tree, a fretwork of shadow falling across his face. 'It's not a question of hiding, exactly. But there are things I wouldn't tell you about because there'd be no point – and anyway I suppose you wouldn't want to know really. Like fancying other women. In that transitory kind of way one does.'

I turned away, bent down, buried my nose in a gardenia. Suddenly, this conversation, so lightly entered into, felt a little dangerous.

'I'd get so jealous if I was with you all the time. I think I'd hate that about living with you. You'd make me so jealous because I want you so much,' I said, then wished I hadn't. It all sounded far too intense.

'How did we get into this, Chloe?' He took my hand and pulled me up. 'Let's go and look at the garden.'

'No, I want to know really.'

'But you're the same too, surely.'

'Maybe not. I don't fancy many people. It's a rare event with me

. . . You hid a lot from Helena,' I went on. 'Not just thoughts.' I could hear the edge of accusation in my voice. I knew it was unfair, but I couldn't make it go.

'Okay, so it's not very admirable,' he said. 'I have to say it was very easy, though. I'd be with some other woman, a woman I was having a relationship with, and I'd only be thinking of her. Then it would be over – I mean, the sexual part – and instantly I'd just switch, I'd find myself worrying whether Sally had remembered her clarinet lesson or whether I'd defrosted the chicken for supper. It was as though when I was in one world the other didn't exist. So it was easy to hide things, to keep the worlds apart.'

'Is it ever like that with me? Do I sometimes not exist?'

'Never. You're always with me . . . Why are we talking about this anyway?'

'It's interesting.'

'Is it? I think you're just making yourself miserable. It's my fault. I shouldn't have started it. It's like picking at a scab or something.'

He turned towards me, trailed his fingers all over my face. I wrapped myself round him: we kissed for a long time.

'You complicate things,' he said, as we finally moved breathlessly apart. 'You see, it's all very simple really.'

On the other side of the orangery there were gardens – sleek immaculate lawns, and stone urns planted with friendly, cheerful flowers, petunias, geraniums, lobelias. We walked down the neat gravel path between the lawns and the flowers. Here it was sheltered and very hot – I pushed the sleeves of my T-shirt up onto my shoulders so I could feel the sun all the way up my arms. The drive ran for a hundred yards or so through the gardens. Then suddenly it stopped, at a padlocked gate in a stone wall, an old wrought iron gate, beautifully made, the iron shaped into pointy gargoyle faces and the stamens and pistils and sepals of nameless flowers – and the other side of the gate a neglected field, grey and green and entangled, full of huge thistles gone to seed, and stinging nettles and a few broken beehives. Wisps of thistledown the colour of fog were caught on the spiky bits of the gate.

We stood there for a moment with our backs to the garden, looking at the overgrown field.

'That woman did make a complaint against me,' he said.

79

For a moment I didn't get it – then I recalled that conversation we'd had before the summer holiday about the little boy with Downs.

'The horrid headmistress?'

'Yes. She rang Brian on Friday and said she'd discussed it with her governors and she felt I'd been unprofessional and wasn't prepared to work with me anymore.'

'So what will happen?'

'Nothing much, probably. Brian asked me about it. He'll allocate the school to someone else. He said I'd been stupid, but he didn't think it warranted an official warning.'

'Still, what a pain.'

'It was my fault, really. I shouldn't have lost my temper like that.' He picked some bits of thistledown off the gate – they drifted away from the touch of his fingers. 'Anyway, I guess she's pretty stressed out at the moment. Brian said something else had happened there since – a child's made some kind of abuse allegation, apparently.'

'Will that involve you?'

'I don't see why. I suppose I could be asked to do an assessment. But it might explain why she was being so foul.'

'I expect it's just what she's like,' I said. I put my hand on his arm. 'Look, I'm sorry I was pestering you like that. It's all a bit overwhelming sometimes. I'm sorry.'

He smoothed my hair back from my face, made us happy again.

We were wandering back towards the car and lunch in a pub garden somewhere, when we passed a five-barred gate that led into the churchyard.

'I don't remember this bit,' I said. 'Shall we look?' He followed me.

It was a crowded churchyard, full of jumbled gravestones. Some were very old, crooked, stained with lichen and mosses, white or metallic green. There were some Victorian ones, too, imposing and deliciously sanctimonious: in one corner, four louche angels, beautiful boys, gazed heavenward round a grave planted with succulent crassulas with fat fleshy leaves. Over by the fence there were newer, more poignant graves, neat and well-tended: on some the earth was freshly-turned and raw. Moths like scraps of shadow flitted on the periphery of vision.

We went in the church. Much of it was empty floor without pews, an airless place, smelling of damp and dry rot treatment. It had once catered for a large estate but was now presumably little used, except for funerals. It spoke of absences: it felt dead, not numinous, a place where nothing happened any more. The prayer books piled on a table at the back were speckled with velvety mould.

There were elaborate carvings on the tombs – more swooning Pre-Raphaelite angels with complicated drapery, and on one memorial, a carving of Mary and Ann with their children. Dan read the inscription: 'Elizabeth Beloved Daughter of James and Emily. Born June 19 1882. Died January 7 1884.' I put out my hand, touched the face of one of the children. The marble was so cold it made the little hairs on my arms stand on end.

'When the girls were tiny I used to think a lot about them dying,' I said. 'Especially Alice, because she was the first: I was so terrified that something would happen and she'd be snatched away. Once I dreamt she was drowning and I was struggling to reach her and I woke up and found myself on the bedroom carpet scrabbling around . . . I hate this church. I don't know why I wanted to come in here.'

He slipped his hand up the back of my T-shirt. 'You're so cold,' he said. 'You're shivering.'

'I want to be warmed up,' I said.

He wrapped his arm round me, steered me to the door. Outside it seemed so bright and fresh. We breathed deeply. He took my hand and pulled me after him.

Past the new graves there was a hidden place beyond the fence where a clump of yew-trees cast deep shadows. We climbed over the fence.

Under the yews it was cool, but not the dry airless cold of the church – cool like water, like a premonition of winter. He kissed me hungrily, pushed up my T-shirt. I felt a bit reluctant at first. I've never much liked making love outside – there are all those twigs and nettles and things, and it's awkward with half your clothes still on – and there was something inhibiting, too, about the nearness of the church, the newly-dug graves. But my doubts dissolved as he undid my skirt and let it slide off, ran his hands over me, pushing his fingers into me, my mouth, my cunt, as I started to respond to him in that shaky abandoned way I had. And, though we could perhaps be seen from the churchyard, it was surely perfectly safe: there was no one about, no one would ever know.

I knelt down, felt the narrow sinewy roots of the yews dig into my knees. As I sketched him out with my hand, my mouth, tracing out the thin urgent veins with my tongue, the sense of deathliness left me: the way he moved at my touch made me feel vivid and powerful again.

He took my head gently in his hands, pulled me up, tried to move inside me. I couldn't work this out at all, I seemed to be at quite the wrong height.

'It's too difficult,' I said.

'No, it's not,' he said.

He moved me round so my back was against one of the trees, put his hands under my hips, went in just an inch or two, moving slowly and gently so the sensation on my clitoris was very full and complete: it felt amazingly good. I felt terribly opened up to him somehow, very exposed, there in that almost public place. The shapes and colours around me blurred. I closed my eyes and the dark behind my lids was full of brightness like flame: as the heat seared through me, I thought I was going to fall over, I dug my hands into his shoulders. He leaned forward into me, resting one forearm against the tree trunk beside me, moved very suddenly inside me, so deeply it was on the edge of hurting, and came quickly. With his orgasm so soon after mine, I felt a sense of absolute confusion about where he stopped and I began.

Afterwards I felt dazzled, as though I'd spent a whole day in Mediterranean sunlight. I couldn't tell if minutes had passed, or hours. We went back to the car, and found a pub that felt like a pub from twenty years ago, with red lino and hunting prints, and drank some wonderfully hoppy beer and ate chicken in the basket. When I crossed my legs, I saw there were bits of leaf mould on the toes of my shoes and the imprints of roots on my knees. For once we didn't talk much. I spent a lot of time just looking at him. Then, full of a peaceful happiness like a smile deep inside, we headed home, down the narrow Northamptonshire roads where the shadows were long and some of the leaves were already edged with yellow, hinting of their turning.

Part II

10

Next morning I rang him at his office. I could still taste him faintly on my fingers, smell him on my hair. I wanted to tell him how I'd loved our day together: and if there was no one to overhear I was going to be so open and precise, to talk about the kinds of things I put in my notes to him but could never normally say. The thought was pleasing: I liked this freer, more passionate person I seemed to have become.

'He's not in,' said the receptionist.

'D'you know when he'll be back?'

'I don't, I'm afraid.'

'Well – will it be later this morning or this afternoon?'

'Sorry, I really can't say.'

'Could you tell him I've phoned?'

'I'll leave him the message,' she said. 'I can't guarantee he'll get it, though.'

I was irritated. I briefly cursed the woman's lack of efficiency, wondering in a rather unsisterly way if she was one of those women who only get appointed because of their nice long legs and skill with eyelash curlers.

I went to see Amber in the children's home – she'd had a row with another girl and cut herself with a Stanley knife; I went to a long and horribly heated conference on Kyle Marston, my new physical abuse case; I had a desultory lunch of quiche and alcohol-free lager in the pub with Jude; I caught up with my dictation. He didn't ring, he left no message. I wondered if the receptionist, out of some oversight or deliberate perversity, had failed to pass my message on. I was reluctant to ring again, it would look too clingy, too insistent. After all, it wasn't as though there was anything I really needed to say. But I did start to feel the crossness that always niggles away at you when you're waiting for a call that doesn't come – though I also knew my irritation to be unfair. Something must have held him up, some drama at work. A special needs tribunal perhaps? He went to quite a few of them: more and more parents of disabled children were appealing against the local authority's decisions if they didn't get the help they knew they needed. But surely the receptionist would have told me?

It was after six, and I was home and scraping the remains of tea off the plates and stacking the dishwasher while the girls watched a video, when the call finally came.

'Is that you, Chloe?'

'Of course it is. I tried to ring you.'

'Chloe. I must see you now.'

There was something in his voice that alarmed me – it was quick, harsh, high. My first thought was that somebody had died.

'What is it?' I said.

'I'll tell you when I come,' he said.

I switched on the dishwasher, boiled the kettle. I felt a bit scared already, I think, wondering what had happened. I decided it was almost certainly a death. I ran down a mental list of all the people who were close to him, seeking for the most terrible thing, the death of a child, perhaps.

He was on my doorstep in a few minutes. He looked white, ill: there were lines in his face I hadn't seen before. I didn't put my arms round him: something held me back, and anyway I felt he wouldn't have noticed. I took him into the kitchen. This is what he told me, as we sat quite still at my kitchen table, while the dishwasher chuntered right through its programme, and the cold evening air seeped in through the open window, and the blue light drained from the sky till the room was all darkness and shadow, and panic rose in me like nausea.

The phone had rung that morning, just before he left the flat for his first school visit. He'd thought it was me.

A woman's voice, clipped, business-like.

'Mr Daniel Whitmore?'

'Speaking.'

'It's Detective Sergeant Griggs from the Child Protection Unit. We'd like to speak to you.'

'That's fine,' he said. 'Just hold on a minute while I get my diary.'

86

He found his diary in his briefcase, thumbed through it. 'Any time tomorrow morning would be fine,' he said. 'Today I've got appointments all day.'

'You'll have to cancel them, I'm afraid,' she said. 'We're coming round now.'

Dan was irritated. He had a long list of children to see at a school – he knew the headmaster would be angry if he cancelled. Still, it must be something fairly urgent – some child in trouble, presumably. He ran through his current cases in his head: he only had two or three where there was a possible child abuse issue, where the police might be involved.

'Would you mind telling me what it's about?' he said.

'It's a delicate matter,' said the woman, and put down the phone.

My mind was churning away as he told me this, trying to make sense of it, as he talked on in that quick harsh voice, leaving no time for me to respond. But I still didn't get it.

Dan rang the school he'd been due to visit. 'Oh *dear*,' said the secretary. 'I know the head wanted to see you most particularly. He *will* be disappointed.'

Pious cow, thought Dan. He felt a surge of rage – after all, none of this was his fault – but bit his anger down. 'I'm sorry,' he said. 'Something urgent's come up. I'll ring later today to rearrange it.'

He tidied a bit, piled up the sections of yesterday's *Observer* that were scattered on the floor, pulled chairs round so they could talk in comfort, started to percolate coffee. The bell rang, he went downstairs. There were two of them waiting there, an efficient-looking woman in her twenties, a man with lots of gel on his hair.

'Mr Daniel Whitmore?' said the woman.

He nodded, led the way up to his flat, pushed the door open. They followed without speaking.

'I'll make some coffee,' he said.

'We won't have coffee,' said the woman.

'Well, do sit down,' he said.

They stayed standing. He felt a little afraid then. It was mainly a physical thing, he told me, a tightening in his stomach. It was something to do with their refusal to sit down or have coffee.

'We're here about Carly Smithson,' said the woman. 'It's alleged that you've committed indecent assault against her.'

I sat there quite still as he told me this, and felt the cold that came in through the open window get right inside me, felt how it crept right through me. It was as if I seized up deep inside: as if something died in me.

Dan had said nothing. He'd been unable to respond or reply or protest. Then he'd felt that brief hysterical urge to smile you can get when you have to pass on bad news. Someone's made a terrible mistake, he thought, but it will all be sorted out, all resolved: it's just a matter of waiting. Someone will rescue me.

The woman cautioned him, and told him they needed to interview him, that they were going to arrest him and take him to the police station to be interviewed.

'Can I ring my boss?' he said.

'Why?' she said.

'I must speak to him,' he said.

They let him ring.

'Brian's at the Civic Centre,' said his PA. 'Can I take a message?'

He didn't know what message to give. 'Tell him it's about Carly Smithson,' he said. He put the phone down.

'We're going to search your flat,' said the man.

They had big clear self-sealing plastic bags. They went through everything in his flat, scooping it into the bags, with quick, efficient gestures. They worked in turn, one of them searching, the other watching the search, moving steadily round the room. They looked through his desk, methodically, first the top and then the drawers. They took his books from the shelves, held them up, shook them to see if anything fell out. They thumbed through the Sunday paper, looking for things that might be concealed. He watched as his room, so recently put together, was undone again. They took all his letters. They took his work diary, his personal diary. They took the homework from his Urdu evening class. 'I almost tried to stop them taking that,' he told me. 'I'd only just finished it. I kept thinking how all that work would be wasted.'

I knew all about this, of course – the search for evidence of the use of child pornography that would help to back up a case in court. Paedophiles in cases I'd been involved with had often had stacks of it – magazines and videos imported illegally, and really sick stuff downloaded from the Internet.

'What did you do?' I said.

'I sort of walked round after them,' he said. 'I kept saying, "This is crazy, I can't believe this is happening." They ignored me. I guess they're used to it: I guess it's what people say.'

They found the battered briefcase in which he kept the intelligence tests that Lucy had so loved doing. They told him to unlock the case.

The man took out some building blocks, piled three of them into a tower. 'Well,' he said, 'I could play with these for hours.'

There was a large photograph of a teddy bear, part of an object recognition test. The woman picked it up, held it at arm's length, put her head on one side. 'Aah,' she said. 'Cute or what?'

The man added more blocks to his tower. 'I guess children would really like these,' he said. 'Children would love to come and play with these toys. Fond of playing with children, are you, Mr Whitmore?'

'They're intelligence tests,' said Dan.

'Are they now?' said the man. 'And what else do you use them for exactly?' His voice was thin with menace. 'You use them to win children over, don't you, Mr Whitmore? You use them to entice children to your flat, to win their confidence.'

Dan was seized by rage. He called the man a bastard under his breath, felt a crazy urge to hit him. The man and the woman looked at one another and shrugged. The man flicked the tower of blocks over casually with one finger, left them where they fell.

Dan's camera was on the bookshelf. The woman clicked it open, tipped out the film. They took all his videos. They stripped the bed, pulling off the duvet cover and the pillow cases, flinging them down, leaving them where they were flung. They looked behind the pictures.

'Quite a poky flat, this,' remarked the woman to no one in particular, in the conversational tone you might use when appraising an empty property.

'A bit of a comedown from Wimpole Avenue,' said the man. Dan knew then that they'd already been there, that they'd seen Helena: it was still his official address, the one on his driving licence. 'Rather posh kitchen, I thought, at Wimpole Avenue,' the man went on.

'Still,' said the woman, 'I guess this is nice and convenient for Mrs Langdon.'

I gasped when Dan told me that. Stupidly, it wasn't till I heard that the woman had said my name that the implications of all this really started to open up before me, like a huge hole in front of my feet. They knew about me: they knew, or would know very soon, about my children.

They asked him where the bathroom was. They looked in the toilet cistern, under the lagging round the water tank.

'We need to search your car,' said the man.

Dan nodded.

The man waited. 'Well? The keys? I imagine you do keep it locked, Mr Whitmore.'

He handed them over. The man went out. The woman continued her search in the kitchen, poking around in the fridge and the breadbin.

'I let them get on with it,' he told me. 'There was nothing I could do. I sat there and tried to remember Carly Smithson. It was quite a while ago. I could just see this fidgety little girl with white eyelashes: she was so pale, like she'd never been out in the sun. All I could remember doing was sitting beside her and helping her write a Y – I'd put my hand on hers to help her do that. I kept thinking – Had that been misinterpreted somehow? Had someone misread it?'

And of course he'd thought of me, he said. He'd worried that I'd be frightened, that I'd put the worst possible interpretation on it.

'How d'you mean?' I said sharply. 'What interpretation?'

'That you'd worry that it was serious, like these cases you read about where men lose their jobs and everything after allegations like this. That it might go all the way,' he said.

I said nothing, sitting there in the dark. I was so cold that the little hairs stood up on my arms, but I couldn't move, couldn't get up to shut the window.

He'd clung to the thought of Brian, he said. Surely Brian would sort it all out. He worried that the PA would forget to hand on the message. He asked if he could try ringing Brian again.

'No,' said the man. 'We're taking you to the police station now.'

Dan grabbed two books from the bookshelf – the latest John Grisham and his Urdu textbook.

'It's funny what you think,' he told me. 'On the way to the police station in the car, I was obsessed with the idea that I'd left my percolator on. I thought it would start a fire and my flat would burn down. I kept imagining it going up in smoke, how it would all be destroyed and I'd be left with nothing. I wanted to ask them to go back so I could check but I knew they wouldn't.'

They went in round the back. It smelt of disinfectant. At the desk he emptied his pockets for the custody sergeant. There was nothing much – his cheque cards, some money, some peppermints, a biro. He watched himself handing them over as though it was somebody else. The custody sergeant recorded them on the property sheet and gave them back to him and read him his rights.

'I want to ring for a lawyer now,' he said.

He was given a list of solicitors and taken to a phone.

There was only one firm he recognized – Gannon and Lacey, the firm that had done the conveyancing on the house in Wimpole Avenue. They'd been inefficient: they'd kept postponing the date for exchange of contracts, and Dan had got angry with them. The sight of the name still evoked a feeling of irritation in him. But he didn't know anyone else.

'I'm afraid Mr Gannon is in court this morning, Mr Whitmore,' said the woman on the other end of the line.

'Look, could you tell him I must have a solicitor,' said Dan. 'I'm in the police station.'

'We'll send you Mr Dyball,' she said.

They put him in the custody suite – a cell with a narrow bed with a single grey blanket neatly folded, and in the centre of the floor a stainless steel toilet without a seat. The door clanged shut, the key was turned. Dan felt very cold. He sat on the bed and wrapped himself in the blanket. He tried to read the John Grisham but it didn't seem to make sense, so he opened his Urdu textbook, looked through the vocabulary he'd been meant to learn for his evening class.

And as his eye fell on the pages, he told me, he kept revisiting the room where he'd seen Carly, the room with the 'Welcome' posters and picture books he'd described to me on that long-ago summer evening. He tried to recall the detail of what had happened there, but his memory was blurred: it was months since he'd seen her, there'd been so many other children in little rooms that looked much the same. And he puzzled over the precise meaning of indecent assault. Was it exposing yourself, touching the child's genitals, getting her to touch yours? He thought that at least when they interviewed him he'd be able to find out what it meant: that even if they didn't tell him directly, they'd talk about it and then he'd know.

Much later, Mr Dyball came. He was in his fifties – a pink scalp, fat white fingers, a smell of cologne. He sat on the bed beside Dan.

'They won't tell me the details of the charge,' he said.

'Don't they have to?'

'No. We just have to go on waiting.'

He went out again.

The custody sergeant asked Dan if he wanted to eat. Dan asked for coffee: the sergeant brought it. It was instant, weak, whitened with Marvel that left a powdery scum on top, but it warmed him up a little.

An hour later Mr Dyball came back.

'They still won't tell me what exactly you're charged with,' he said. 'We have a choice. We could go ahead with the interview today or we could hang on . . .'

Dan was desperate to get on with it, to be the other side of the cell door.

'Listen then, Mr Whitmore,' said the solicitor. 'You've got to be very clever. You must say "No comment" to everything they ask. They'll try and start the interview by getting you to talk, they'll be quite friendly and talk about anything – and once you begin to talk, that's when the investigation really starts – so you must say "No comment" to everything, right from the beginning. That's all we can do – because I don't know what I'm meant to be defending you against.'

They took Dan to an interview room. It was the same pair: the woman did most of the talking. She asked him his name, his interests, about his work. He said 'No comment' to everything.

I listened to this with a sense of mounting alarm. This surely was what people did when they had something to hide. If you were innocent you'd have nothing to fear, no reason to be silent. I pictured it: the bleak little room, the battered table and chairs, the panic button, the tape recorder on the table – and Dan sitting there next to the solicitor, shocked, exhausted, with that ill look, saying 'No comment' to everything. He must have looked guilty as hell.

'But didn't you say you hadn't done anything?' I said. 'How could you bear it? Didn't you want to shout at them?'

'I did what he told me to,' said Dan.

'But shouldn't you have protested? How could you bear not to say it was all a terrible mistake?'

'But I don't even know what I'm meant to have done,' he said.

'I don't see how you could bear to just keep saying "No comment",' I said.

The woman was getting impatient, he told me – pursing her lips, tapping on the table.

Then a man came and gave her a message. She turned to Dan. 'The Director of Education would like to speak to you,' she said. Her manner had changed: it was warmer, more conciliatory. 'You can take the call in here.' They gave him the phone.

He felt a rush of relief, he said: he was sure he was about to be rescued. He was surprised it wasn't Brian, though: he supposed it reflected the gravity of the allegation that had been made, that it had taken the Director to sort it out.

'I wasn't thinking straight,' he told me. 'The call was to say I'll be suspended from work while the investigation's going on – I've got to go to the Civic Centre tomorrow to be officially suspended.'

The woman told him the interview was over and bailed him: the man took him back to his flat.

Silence hemmed us in like fog: I couldn't find a way through. I wanted to speak, but my throat felt thick, choked up. I didn't know if I'd be able to get out the words. I coughed, tried to clear my throat.

'You didn't do it.' I tried to make it sound as if I was sure. But my voice was small and squeaky, like a child's.

He said nothing.

'Dan, you've got to tell me. I have to hear it from you.'

'Jesus.'

'Look, I've only known you since June.' My voice was louder now, harsh, ugly. 'Don't make this so difficult for me.'

'Chloe . . .'

'It's such a short time to know someone. We all have things we hide from one another.' I flinched at my words. It was a cruel thing to say to this man who the day before had felt like part of my body.

He looked across at me then. The only light in the room came from the thin moon that was rising over my garden. I sensed rather than saw the desperation in his face.

'For Chrissake, I don't even know what I'm meant to have done. What *is* indecent assault anyway? You'd know, I suppose – you're the expert.'

'It could be anything,' I said. 'Anything less than rape.'

'That's what I'm meant to have done, then,' said Dan. 'Anything less than rape.'

'You've got to help me,' I said. 'I have to hear you say you didn't do it.'

He was angry now. 'I don't see why the hell I should have to defend myself,' he said. 'My God. You can't believe me capable of this terrible thing.'

I rushed on. 'Dan. I must understand. I must be sure. I've trusted you with myself – with my children. I have to know. Did you do something? Did you touch her? Do children turn you on?' I didn't say, Do *my* children turn you on? – but the question was hanging there, echoing in the hollowness between us as clearly as if I'd said the words. 'Dan, I must know. Don't you see?' Tears inched silently down my face.

'I didn't do it, Chloe,' he said, more gently. 'Whatever it was, I didn't do it.'

I reached out, felt for his hand in the dark, put my hand on his.

'I just can't understand how you could bear to say "No comment",' I said.

I couldn't see his face, only the shape of him, the droop of his shoulders as he sat slumped at my table. I hated to see him like that – all his courage and certainty drained away. I hated him to be so utterly dependent on me, on my opinion of him. I didn't want this power.

'I did what the solicitor told me to,' he said. 'You're in their hands. You have to let them get on with it. They know what they're doing.'

'But didn't you want to scream at them that you hadn't done it?'

'Of course I did, but I couldn't. They arrest you and you're into a different world. It's different rules – you have to be so careful. Jesus, you just don't get it, do you?'

There was a rustling in the hall outside the kitchen door. I should have paid attention but I didn't.

'If you didn't do it, why is this little girl saying you did?'

'How do I know? Perhaps she made it up. Perhaps someone else did it and she said it was me. She's obviously a really mixed-up kid. How do I know?'

'But then why you? Why would she say it was you?'

'I don't know.'

'Did she name you?'

'I don't know. God, I don't know anything. I've told you everything they told me. I don't have the faintest idea why they think it was me.'

'How often did you see her?'

'I don't know.'

I jumped as the door swung back and Lucy came bouncing in.

'Hi, Dan. Alice, Dan's here,' she yelled down the hall. 'Why are you two sitting in the dark?' she asked, her voice lustrous with laughter, happy to catch grownups doing something so very silly.

She stood on tiptoe, turned on the light. 'There!' she said. 'That's better.' After being in the dark so long, the light was a shock, like a physical blow: my eyes hurt with it. Everything in the kitchen was suddenly sharp and clear, as though outlined with a fine black pen. It was a surprise to find the ordinary things still there, the candlesticks and pictures and plants, all orderly and in their places, just as they had been before.

'Lucy, we're busy,' I said. 'You must leave us alone for a while.'

'Why didn't you tell me Dan was here?' she said.

'Never mind,' I said. 'Just go off and play for a bit, will you?'

She was about to protest, then she grinned as an idea formed. She went up to Dan, touched his arm. 'I will if Dan comes with me,' she said triumphantly.

'He won't,' I said. 'He can't come now.'

'Yes he can,' she said, still grinning. 'Yes yes yes.' She tugged at his sleeve.

'For God's sake, Lucy,' I said, furious, 'can't we ever have a bit of peace?'

She seemed to fall apart. Her smiley face crumpled like Play-Doh scrunched between your palms. Tears streamed down her cheeks.

'You don't have to *shout*,' she sobbed. 'I haven't done anything. You hate me. Everyone hates me.' She went off – but not so far that we wouldn't hear her sobs. When I didn't go to her, her sobs got more strangled and desperate, till she seemed to be struggling for breath.

'You'd better deal with that,' said Dan.

She was crammed into a corner the other side of the kitchen door, her face to the wall, so you could only see the back of her head, which shuddered eloquently as she sobbed.

I put my arms round her. 'Oh come on, Lucy.'

'Why did you have to shout at me?' she wailed. 'I didn't do anything wrong.'

I found her some chocolate, took her on my lap, anxious to soothe her quickly. She stopped sobbing, munched hungrily. Chocolate dribbled down her chin. Her wet eyelashes stuck together in clumps, as though smeared with too much mascara.

I turned back to Dan. 'You must know how often you saw that child,' I went on.

'No.'

'But it must be in your diary.'

'They took my diary.'

'Well, the file notes then.'

'They took those too. I spoke to Brian before I rang you. They cleared my office. The others will have to pick up my work. God knows how, without any file notes.'

'Why did they clear his office, Mummy?' said Lucy through the chocolate, in a stage whisper charged with significance, a whisper that acknowledged the importance of this adult conversation, but also yearned to be part of it.

'They tidied it – it needed tidying. They threw the old things away,' I said. I noticed how evasive I was being. And I realized that it would be like that from now on with the children – that we had moved into a new world of lies and half-lies, a new kind of communication where so much would stay unsaid.

'Have you eaten?' I said to Dan.

He shook his head.

'There's a bit of casserole in the fridge. You could put on some pasta – I'll take Lucy to bed.'

It was nine o'clock. Alice was already in her room. I took Lucy upstairs and we had a much shortened bedtime routine – no bath, no story, just tooth-cleaning and vitamins and into her nightshirt. She'd recovered from her tearfulness now: she was being carefully, elaborately co-operative, as she usually is afterwards, on the rare occasions I've shouted at her.

'Mummy, why are you so sad?' she said as I tucked her up. 'Is it because I was cross?'

'No, sweetheart. It's nothing to do with you. Everyone's sad sometimes.' She seemed to accept that. I tucked her in. In the warm light cast by her bedside lamp, you could see the bloom of tiny hairs on her skin. 'Go to sleep now,' I said.

I stroked her back and her head. She was tired out with crying. She snuggled up to her comforter, her eyes rolled up, her eyelids flickered extravagantly and closed. The sight of her soothed me a little, her quiet breathing calming the dreadful restlessness inside me.

The food was ready, but neither of us wanted to eat. We tipped most of it into the bin. We drank some whisky.

'D'you want to stay?' I said, hoping so much he'd say no. But he said yes.

'Look, they'll want to see you,' he said as we undressed. 'You know that, don't you?'

'Yes,' I said. It was obvious: I just hadn't thought it through.

'They'll want you to tell them about me, about our relationship,' he said.

'Yes,' I said. But my mouth went dry. I was so cold I pulled on my old dressing gown, the purple towelling one he'd never seen me in before. I wrapped it round me like a blanket and went to the bathroom, but all the time I cleaned my teeth I couldn't stop shivering.

We got into bed and I turned off the light. A pulse I didn't know I had started twitching and snickering at the corner of my eye. We lay on our backs, staring into the dark.

'What happens next?' I said into the blackness.

'They try to get evidence. I guess they'll interview all the children I've worked with – that kind of thing. Then they'll call me in and interview me.'

'You'll need a good solicitor,' I said.

'Yes, I suppose so,' said Dan. 'I hate solicitors. Solicitors are toads.'

'I know somebody,' I said. 'Felix Floyd. He mainly takes legal aid clients. He's very good.' I didn't say how I knew him – and Dan didn't ask. I suspected that if I told Dan about the relationship I'd had with Felix, he wouldn't want to go to him. But the omission made me uncomfortable. It felt like another rip in the texture of the life we'd had together.

'He's not an easy man,' I said. 'He can be incredibly rude. I've heard him be quite insulting about clients in court if he thinks it might mitigate the sentence. "This man is a complete dolt, your worships . . ." He's not kind of *nice*. But he likes taking on the cases that nobody else wants – you know, people who are beyond the pale – the outcasts.' The whisky had made me a little expansive. I felt moved suddenly by a kind of nobility in Felix – how far he'd sometimes gone for people whom everyone else had rejected. 'He was the solicitor for a woman I worked with. She'd injured her child quite horribly – cigarette burns – and then she got pregnant again, and we took the baby away at birth. He sent her a huge bunch of flowers in hospital. He likes that kind of thing.' I gulped. I realized too late what I'd implied. 'Jesus, Dan, I didn't mean . . .'

He put his hand on mine. 'It's okay,' he said wearily.

'He's very clever,' I said. 'That's what matters. You'll need somebody clever. He'd take you on, I'm sure. If it comes to that . . .'

'If you think he's good, I'll go to him,' he said.

I lay with my head on his shoulder for a while. He smelt of sweat, not his usual warm musky scent that I loved, but the sharp sour smell of fear. I felt little flickers of desire, like a memory or shadow of lust, but he made no move to make love. I turned over and he curled into my back and held me. He was quite limp and soft. It was a relief in a way. In spite of everything, he went to sleep very quickly. I lay with my eyes open and stared into the dark. I lay like that for hours, as I'd done so often in childhood, in the house on the edge of the common, with the apricot light from the oil refinery on the ceiling, and the shadow of my wardrobe falling across my bed – and outside the dark silhouettes of the trees and beyond that the empty places, the woods, the winding treacherous forest roads. I lay there and felt rage, such bitter rage, at what had been taken from us.

II

I glanced through the memos on my desk. The words shifted and swam in front of my eyes, forming familiar patterns, but not quite making sense. The office smells – coffee, cardboard, photocopying toner – made me feel sick, as they had when I was pregnant.

Jude was late for once. I found her absence almost unbearable, I longed for her to come in so I could tell her everything. Holding it all inside felt physically difficult – as though there was an actual physical obstruction in my chest.

The door swung back. She was wearing a new jacket, rather trendy, the kind of thing Alice aspired to, in sleek green nylon with a zip up the front.

'So, Chloe, d'you like it? Is this a good colour for me?' She sashayed up to my desk, quite self-preoccupied, flaunting herself, then suddenly stopped. 'What the hell's happened? You look awful.'

I told her. It took a while: I found it surprisingly difficult. It was hard to express, hard to put into sentences. I knew I was going red, and didn't understand why. It felt messy and embarrassing, like confessing a sin or owning up to doing something really stupid.

'Oh my God, oh my God,' she kept saying. 'Oh you poor thing.' When I'd finished she hugged me. Her new coat had a synthetic chemical smell. The zip snagged my cheek.

Nat came in. He didn't crash into our conversation as he usually did, banging his briefcase down on a desk: he just stood there, looking at me warily as though trying to work me out.

Jude turned to him. 'Tell him,' she said.

'Dan?' said Nat.

I nodded.

'Yeah, I heard,' he said. 'A sex abuse allegation.'

I nodded.

99

'Perk of the job, isn't it?' he said.

'Nathaniel, you are *sick*,' said Jude. 'For Chrissake, it's not something to joke about.'

Nat looked sheepish: he flicked some lint from his sleeve, shook himself slightly. 'Okay, okay, I'm sorry,' he said. 'Seriously though, Chloe, it could have been any of us. Me, you, Little Miss PC here' – he poked Jude's arm – 'any of us. Poor bastard. He's been suspended?'

'Yes,' I said.

Nat shook his head. 'Poor poor bastard.' He shuffled into his office.

I put my hand on her arm. 'Jude, tell me what you think.'

She went to ring the switchboard, told them not to put any calls through for ten minutes. I was grateful that she took it so seriously, wanted to give me her total attention. She came and sat on my desk, still wearing her new coat. She leant towards me. 'Look, Chloe,' she said carefully, 'children are to be believed, aren't they?'

'We don't even know if she's identified him by name,' I said.

'Chloe, children don't lie about these things,' she said. 'We know that, surely: they don't lie. I mean, why would she say it if it wasn't true?' She put her hand on my arm. 'Jesus, it must be tough,' she added. The attempt at empathy annoyed me. It seemed out of place in our friendship: it felt as though she was talking to a client.

'Okay – so this little girl's been abused,' I said. 'That's pretty obvious. But mightn't she tell a fib about who it was? Because she was scared or threatened, say? That happens, doesn't it? We know that happens – I mean, there's been work done on it, you know, research papers . . .'

Jude said nothing, just went on looking at me with infinite compassion. The little lines from her mouth to her chin that she hates because they remind her of her mother were sharp and clear, as though shaded in with pencil. A sense of irritation nagged at me like an inaccessible itch.

'I mean,' I said, 'to suddenly turn into a paedophile in your forties – that seems pretty implausible. Most abusers start by about seventeen, don't they?'

'Look,' said Jude, 'just because it's unusual doesn't mean it doesn't happen . . .' She fiddled with the cuffs of her coat. There was a price tag she hadn't cut off: she tugged at it, but it wouldn't come. She went on fiddling: the fabric would surely tear. 'Nothing a man does can surprise me any more,' she said. 'I mean – isn't abuse the essence of male sexuality? The abuse of power. Given half a chance, I guess they'd all be at it.'

Everything about her was irritating me now – the exuberance of her gestures, the brightness of her lipstick, the absolute conviction with which she held her opinions. She took up too much space: she was so vivid and exhausting. With some detached part of myself, I could acknowledge that this irritation with my dearest friend was really very odd – but I had no control over it.

'Can't I claim to know him?' I said. My voice sounded high-pitched, girlish, somehow naive. 'I mean, we've made love scores of time, we've talked endlessly. Don't you think you can ever know someone?'

'Chloe, we all have secrets,' she said gently.

I shook my head. I didn't know what to say.

She leant towards me. 'You've got to believe this little girl. Hell, there's enough evidence they tell the truth, isn't there?'

I said nothing. My silence seemed to trouble her. The lines in her face deepened.

'Jesus, Chloe, we can't spend all these years listening to children – and then suddenly choose not to because it's *inconvenient*.'

'Well,' I said, getting up, 'I've got a conference to go to.' I picked up my bag and my notes and walked out quickly. My body felt weird. Gravity didn't seem to be working properly any more: I was dizzy and uncentred, as though all my proportions had changed, and I was all gangly limbs and no substance, tall enough to reach the ceiling yet with arms and legs as spindly and easily broken as twigs.

'Chloe, you did ask for my opinion,' she said softly, half to herself. Out of the corner of my eye as I went, I registered the hurt in her face.

Later she left flowers on my desk. I found them there that after-noon, when I went back to pick up some things I needed before I went home – her Amnesty coffee cup stuffed full of freesias, creamy-white and green, veined with the tenderest purple like a child's wrists, scenting the whole place. I'd never noticed before that freesias have such a strong smell. The note said, 'I've been really crass. I'm so sorry. Please forgive.'

'Crass'. I thought about that word a lot. It seemed to suggest that you'd used the wrong words or said something out of order, not that you'd been fundamentally mistaken. I did forgive her, of course: I wanted her back. But I knew too with a kind of prescient sadness that this would always be between us, something that had to be approached with care, like a lump of old scar tissue that you're careful not to touch. I wrapped the wet stems of the freesias in a paper towel, but the paper got instantly soggy and I left a trail of drips wherever I went.

12

I dropped the car and the flowers off at home. It was a bright afternoon, with a chill in the shadows. On my lawn, one side of every blade of grass gleamed silver. I decided to walk to pick up Lucy: I felt so anxious about the thing I knew I had to do, and walking might relax me a little, help me breathe.

I joined the other mothers at the classroom door, chatted about the usual things: the PTA line dancing evening, and did tea tree oil in the rinsing water really discourage headlice. The children came out, as always, one at a time. When Alice was five, they'd all surged out in a seething mass at the end of the day, but today the teacher only lets them go once she's spotted their parents, so anxious have we become about the safety of our children. Lucy was called and rushed out, kissed me, thrust her new reading book at me.

'*Amazing Spiders*,' I said. 'Wow.'

'*I'm* not scared,' she said. Fronds of pale hair straggled across her face. She smelt of school.

We walked down the avenue behind the hospital, her hand in mine. On the crab apple tree in the garden in front of the coroner's office, little red fruit were ripening, nursery rhyme fruit, berry bright.

Suddenly she squeezed my hand hard. 'Mummy, why aren't we talking?'

'Sorry, sweetheart. Sometimes I have things going on in my head.'

'What kind of things?'

'Conversations with people. Things I wish I'd said.'

'You could have a conversation with *me*,' she said.

So we talked about trees, and how they turn.

'That tree looks like it's had paint spilt down it,' she said, pointing to an elm in a front garden, which had a streak of yellow leaves all down one side. 'Is that how it happens in autumn, Mummy? Do trees go yellow in bits?'

'I don't know,' I said. 'I've never had a proper look.' It was odd not to know, I thought – to have been surrounded every year by all this changing, all this dying off, and to have been oblivious to the sequence of the thing. So we looked carefully at every tree we passed, and found that trees rarely change with an even wash of colour, that usually it's ragged, random – sometimes a leaf here, a leaf there, sometimes a whole side streaked yellow and the rest still green. Leaves die one by one, by a process of attrition – till one morning you pass and there's no green left at all.

She stopped to talk to a favourite long-haired cat that sat on a wall. The cat looked at her with blank, mysterious eyes, dull like scum on water. She murmured endearments, stroked it with infinite care. 'He's got the loveliest fur,' she said. I had to fight my urge to grab her hand, drag her along after me. Usually I'm charmed by her waywardness, her need to poke in puddles, count magpies, investigate caterpillars: but now I found it maddening. I wished I'd brought the car, I was desperate to get home.

The cat jumped down, sauntered off. We walked on.

'Why is fur soft when it's fur and stiff when it's paintbrushes?' she said.

As so often, I couldn't supply the precision she wanted. 'I think they use different kinds of fur for the bristles in paintbrushes,' I said, hazarding a guess. 'Like badgers. I think badgers have coarse hair and they use that for brushes.'

'Do they kill the badgers?'

'I don't know if they kill them.' How did I get into this? I thought. 'Well, perhaps they used to, long ago.'

'They didn't,' she said emphatically. 'They kept a badger as a pet and when it moulted they put the bits of fur in a basket.'

I squeezed her hand. 'That's a lovely idea,' I said.

'It's not an idea, Mummy.' She was hurt. 'It's *true*.'

'Well, maybe . . .'

'It *is* true, Mummy.' She was getting cross, her forehead creased with frown-lines, her voice emphatic. 'That's what they did. They never killed the badgers.'

With Lucy, I usually end up acquiescing in her truth, however outrageous. It's easier that way.

At the Blue Moon store, I bought her a Kinder Surprise. It was a rather big treat for a weekday, I wanted to be sure she was in a good mood. 'It's to eat when we get home,' I said. She was pleased at this unexpected bounty, clasped it tightly. When she stopped for a moment to do up her shoe-lace and gave it to me to hold, I could feel the indentation where the warmth of her finger had softened the chocolate. I felt a huge rush of love for her.

We got home and unwrapped the Kinder Surprise. Inside the chocolate egg there was a tiny red car that had to be put together. She munched her way through the chocolate.

'I've got something new for you to do,' I said. My mouth was so dry I could scarcely speak. The smell of Jude's freesias thickened the air, made it hard to breathe. I took some pictures I'd brought from work out of my bag. 'I thought you could have a go at this while I make up your car.'

'I want to read my spider book,' she said.

I couldn't bear to put it off. 'Look, it's fun,' I said. I showed her the pictures of a boy and a girl. 'There's some colouring to do.'

'Mummy, why's your voice gone funny?' she said.

I rushed on. 'It's all about parts of the body where we don't mind being touched, and parts that are private. D'you think you could colour in the parts of the little girl where she wouldn't want anyone to touch her?'

But Lucy was more interested in the boy. 'Yuk, that's gross. You can see his *willy*.'

'I'll fix your car and you can colour the picture in and then we'll watch *Pet Rescue*,' I said.

'Okay,' she said. She started to colour, holding the crayon loosely, not very interested, putting a haphazard bikini of crayon on the girl.

I tried to fit the car together, but the instructions were in tiny hieroglyphics on a little scroll of paper, and I couldn't work them out.

'We did this at school,' she said.

'Did what?'

'Colouring in the private bits. And two policemen came specially to see us. They were Policeman Geoff and Policeman Frank, and they took our fingerprints and they told us not to talk to strangers and all that.'

'Sometimes people do touch children where they don't want to be touched – not just strangers, sometimes it's people you know,' I said. 'Has anyone ever touched you in any of those private places?'

'Nope,' she said. 'It's Jake that's the problem. He keeps kissing me and I don't want to be kissed. I tell you and I tell you and you never listen.'

'Lucy,' I said, 'what about Dan? Has Dan ever done anything you didn't want him to do?'

She put down her crayon and looked across at me, with a fierce disapproving frown like when she plays teachers. 'That's not a very nice thing to say, Mummy. Dan wouldn't. He's my *friend*. Honestly, Mummy. You haven't been listening. It's Jake who does, but you never do anything about it.'

I felt as though I'd been holding my breath for hours, and suddenly I could let it out. The pieces of car snapped into place with a fat, happy click. I pushed it along the table towards her with the tip of my finger. She laughed, steered it round the edge of the page of pictures.

'They said my fingerprints were boring,' she said. 'I thought that was rather rude – saying someone's fingerprints are boring.'

'Never mind,' I said. 'It's not the end of the world to have boring fingerprints. It would make it harder to catch you if you robbed a bank.'

She giggled. I put on the television and we curled up on the sofa together, Lucy warmly wrapped in the curve of my arm.

Alice came home rather late, with a carrier bag full of other people's throw-outs she'd bought for a few pence – Devon Violets scent, a *Bunty* annual, twenty-five stickers of the Norwegian flag: it was Charity Week at school. I made dinner, washed up, tidied a bit. The evening seemed to last for ever, minutes stretching out like hours.

When I'd finally got Lucy bathed and tucked up in bed, I went into Alice's bedroom. She was sprawled on the bed, reading the *Bunty* annual. Her room, as always, was the tidiest in the house, her precious eyeshadows and blushers and the bottles of ear care solution from her latest pair of piercings lovingly arranged in symmetrical patterns on top of her chest of drawers. Her bedside lamp with its terracotta shade cast a circle of light, reddish like firelight.

I sat down. The bed was warm where her body had been.

'Hi, Mum.' She was pleased to see me – hungry as always to have time with me on her own. She let the book slip from her fingers. 'This is *so* sexist,' she said.

'Alice, I need to talk to you,' I said.

She was surprised at the formality of this. 'Okay,' she said, a question mark in her voice.

'Something's happened with Dan,' I said. 'A little girl has said he sexually abused her.'

Her eyes snapped wide open. She sat upright on the bed, as though this warranted her serious attention. 'That's dreadful,' she said. 'Poor Dan. How awful for him.'

Her sympathy for him made it easier to go on. I looked away from her, finding some kind of solace in the dailiness of her room, the pop star posters, Body Shop soaps, Tarot packs, seeking somehow to ground myself in this familiar clutter, as I tried to frame my question.

'I need to know, Alice – has Dan ever done anything that's made you feel uncomfortable?'

'What? Like touched me on the boobs, that sort of thing?'

'Yes. That sort of thing.'

'No, of course not, Mum.' She was totally calm about it, a grownup soothing a highly-strung child. 'You don't think I'd let something like that happen, anyway, do you?'

'It can be terribly hard for a child to stop an adult,' I said.

'For goodness sake, I'm nearly thirteen,' she said. 'Children today do know about these things. Anyway, Mum, d'you really think Dan could do something like that?'

'I don't know,' I said again.

She frowned, like when she was tackling some difficult algebraic problem. 'But I thought you were dead keen on him,' she said.

I didn't say anything. There in Alice's room, on the warm bed in the warm light, with this child to whom it all seemed so simple, I felt accused, as though I'd failed Dan or somehow betrayed him.

'Dan's okay,' she said. 'I mean, I don't like him. But he'd never do a thing like that. But . . .' She looked down, let her hair swing across her face, suddenly retreating, hiding in the shadow of her hair. 'I don't know if I should say this. No, I shouldn't really.'

'Go on,' I said, all my pulses jumping.

'Well, it's just that I do know what you're on about. I mean, there *are* people who make me uncomfortable in that kind of way.'

'Who?' I said carefully.

'You know when I went to that after school club at junior school? There was one of the helpers that I didn't like. He wanted the girls to sit on his lap and he called us all darling. And he kept taking pictures, but just of the girls. I think he was probably a pervert.'

'God, Alice, why didn't you tell me at the time?'

'There was nothing to tell, really. Nothing happened, I just didn't like him touching me.' She fixed me with that steady gaze of hers, bluey-grey like the distance. 'I guess I didn't want to worry you, Mum. I mean, it would have worried you, wouldn't it?'

I swallowed hard. 'Next time, tell me, okay? And now you should go to sleep.'

I went downstairs, poured a scotch, drank it quickly. I went through the conversations again, step by step, word by word, checking out everything they'd said. Then just to be on the safe side I wrote it all down and locked the notes away in my writing desk: I knew the time might come when I would need them.

I went back to the kitchen, poured another drink, put on some music, lit candles: in a way, it was a kind of celebration. I poured another drink and another. Relief flooded through me in great warm waves, permeating every cell of my body with a heat like fever. My daughters were unharmed, everything was well. I wondered how I could ever have doubted him. I felt so sure now that it would be alright, that we could pick up our relationship again, that we could carry on. He must come and live with me, I thought, I'd been silly to be so hesitant. This terrible interruption, this rip in the fabric of our love, had at least made me see sense, realize that it was stupid to wait till the moment felt absolutely right, as though we had all the time in the world. My tentativeness seemed incomprehensible to me now. I swilled the scented alcohol round my mouth and thought how it would be when he came to live here, and the future seemed as full of promise as a present wrapped in silver paper or a bowl of rising dough covered with clean gingham. I saw us sitting and laughing together in a room full of light, where my walls were coloured like honey in the sunset and my hanging baskets ran over with milky campanulas. The image was very precise and clear and lovely, as though these things were actually happening in front of me. I saw Alice puzzling over her geometry and Dan and me sipping Chardonnay and smiling at one another and Lucy, flower-like in a coloured frock, humming to herself as she drew – and my house was all as orderly, as safe and content and contained, as a house in one of Lucy's pictures – with a tabby cat and an apple tree and a row of trim tulips standing up like soldiers. And as I sat and drank – rather fast – and thought about this sweetly ordered life we'd lead together, all the sexual feelings that had been switched off in an instant the day before came flooding back: my stomach hardened, flipped over, and I thought how we'd go up and make love hungrily as soon as the girls had gone to bed, and later, in the night, how he'd wake me with his mouth and I'd reach for him and our bodies would melt into one another, moist and tender and languid at first with sleep.

I almost rang him then. But something stopped me when I'd already dialled half his number – the awareness perhaps that I was rather drunk and not quite in control, that though I wanted to comfort him, to soothe him with my certainty, to say it would all be okay, in the event I might well get all weepy and emotional and be absolutely no use. I knew I had to plan, to be prepared, to know what I wanted to say, to make sure it came out right.

I checked on the girls before I went to bed, as I'd done when they were babies. Alice was restless as always, shifting, whispering words I couldn't quite catch. But Lucy is a peaceful sleeper. She lay sprawled on her back as though dropped from a great height, her face round and soft like a baby's. The sight of her asleep on her pillow is like hot milk in the stomach, it makes you feel quiet and full.

I went to bed so peacefully. But when I woke it was only three o'clock. I went downstairs to get another scotch and a cheese sandwich. From the kitchen window you can see beyond my high hedge to a tower block on a rundown estate half a mile away. As usual at night, it was randomly speckled with lights, like an autumn tree with a few yellow leaves. There too people were out of bed – some sick, perhaps, or getting up to start shifts, but some, like me, just unable to sleep. I wondered about them, these unknown insomniacs. Did they too drink whisky and look to the future and feel afraid?

It was then that the fact of the allegation really came back to me.

And I knew then that nothing I had discovered – neither Lucy's careless lack of interest nor Alice's blithe assurances – actually changed anything. They were unharmed, and for that I was hugely grateful. But the allegation was still there: it couldn't be circumvented or overlooked. Everything had shifted round in my head while I had been asleep. My dream of the life we might lead together now seemed flimsy, manic – the allegation hard, solid, substantial. What had happened could not so easily be undone.

13

The next day the police came, just as Dan had said they would. When the doorbell went, I thought at first it was my new shed being delivered from Homebase. But there they were on my doorstep, the head-girlish woman smelling of deodorant, the gangly man with the Elvis hair. That was when they came and sat at my table and got out their pens and notebooks, while Lucy sat half-entranced in front of the television, and a bee buzzed opulently at the window, and the gorgeous autumn sunlight flooded in over everything, the coffee mugs and the plate with the gingernuts I'd superstitiously placed in a perfect semi-circle, and the woman's hair that swung so sleek and shiny, and the folder in which I could see the words that I had written.

They drank my coffee, ate my biscuits. The woman asked briefly about my work and how long I'd known Dan, and the man wrote my answers down. I found myself wondering how they'd found out about our affair – and realized with a surge of alarm that it must have been from Helena. Then the woman put down her cup with a clear little click and shifted in her chair. It was a paragraph break or a change of gear. There was a different tone to her voice: the questions were more detailed, intent, purposeful. This, I sensed, was where the interview proper began.

'So, tell me, Mrs Langdon, how do your children get on with Mr Whitmore?'

'They like him really,' I said. 'Well, Alice is quite suspicious of him.'

She looked at me with an expression of the mildest curiosity, just the tiniest flicker of something, carefully controlled. 'When you say suspicious, what d'you mean exactly?'

'I guess she wants to keep me to herself. She was quite upset when we got divorced – well, children always are, I suppose.'

'And your little one? Lucy?'

'Oh, Lucy loves him. He's really good with children.'

The woman said nothing, frowned very slightly. My words hung in the air between us, freighted with meanings I hadn't intended.

She leant forward, her hands clasped in front of her on the table. Her nails were palely varnished, immaculate, her wedding ring gleamed. 'As I'm sure you're aware from your work, Mrs Langdon, these men are often very good with children. They can seem very charming people – and they'll go to great lengths to endear themselves to a child they intend to abuse.'

My shock at her assumption that Dan was one of 'these men' threw me off balance, almost made me laugh out loud. 'But the fact that someone's nice with children doesn't mean they must have ulterior motives,' I said.

'An allegation has been made, Mrs Langdon. We mustn't lose sight of that,' she said, rather primly. She flicked back her hair. I wondered briefly how she got it so straight and orderly, suspected it always did just what she wanted. 'So tell us,' she went on, 'do you have any reason to believe he might have touched them inappropriately? Anything at all you can recall?'

'No – I've tried to think. But really, there's nothing. Nothing that comes to mind.'

'Did he ever seem especially interested in them, in an inappropriate way? Did he ever offer to bath Lucy, for instance?'

'No. But if he had I wouldn't see that as inappropriate particularly.'

'Have there been any behaviour changes in them since your relationship with him began?'

'No.'

'Any unexpected crying? Bedwetting? Refusal to eat?' put in the man. The side of his face stuck out, distorted by a mouthful of gingernut. I felt he was reciting from a list in a manual.

'No.'

'Any tantrums?'

'No. Well – no more than usual,' I said.

The woman smiled at me. 'I've got one like that,' she said. Emotional as I was, I felt stupidly grateful for this display of warmth, felt a brief tearful urge to confide in her, to go and sit beside her and rest my head on her shoulder and confess; but there was nothing to confess. I swallowed hard.

'Look, I've asked them directly,' I went on. 'As soon as I heard about the allegation. I mean, I've made notes of what they said. And I really don't think anything has happened.'

I studied their faces to see what they thought of this, tried to read them, as people long ago read auguries in the movement of birds in the sky and omens in entrails. But I couldn't make any sense of what I saw. The man's face stayed impassive, the woman's brow just puckered a little at everything I said. 'I trust him,' I said. 'I've never had any reason not to.'

The woman rested her fingertips together, like a child praying. 'You realize of course that we'll have to interview Alice and Lucy about this,' she said.

I was suddenly furious. 'No,' I said, 'you can't.'

'I'm sorry, Mrs Langdon, but we have to.'

'No. Surely if I've asked them, that ought to be enough.'

'Why is it you don't want us to talk to them?' said the man. There was a sliver of steel in his voice. The change in his manner chilled me. All this friendliness, I thought, this manner that said, Confide in us, we're on your side: it was all just a front, a means to an end.

'They've never had to go through anything like that,' I said, faltering a bit. 'I want to protect them from it all, keep them separate.'

'Mrs Langdon,' said the woman, 'if anything *has* happened to your children, I'm sure you'd want to know. Any responsible parent would. And as a social worker, you must know better than anyone the terrible damage that sexual abuse can cause. It's all done very tactfully. We have training in talking to children and I can assure you we do know what we're doing.'

'I don't doubt that,' I said. 'I just don't see that it's necessary.'

'We've got to do a thorough job,' said the man. 'We've got to do it properly. We owe it to all children, to do it properly.'

'And surely, Mrs Langdon,' said the woman, 'with your background and concerns, you wouldn't want to stand in the way of an investigation?'

I shrugged. My anger seeped away as quickly as it had come. My eye fell on the blue folder, and I knew I had no power at all.

When I didn't say anything, the woman made a quick sideways gesture with her hand, as though pushing something away. There was a sense that my objection had been disposed of.

'Okay,' she said. 'Now, I'd like to talk some more about your relationship with Mr Whitmore.'

I felt a kind of pressure on my chest, a soft dull heavy pressure, as though someone was pushing down on me through a pillow or cushion, making it hard to breathe. We were moving on, I realized, to the bit I dreaded most.

'You've already told us you had a sexual relationship with Mr Whitmore,' she said.

'Yes,' I said.

'Could you tell us when your sexual relationship began?'

I told them. Images of that evening flashed randomly into my head – the little flame under the hotplate, the plastic roses, Dan putting out his hands to pull my face towards him, seeking out my mouth with his. But the images were tiny and distant and hemmed in by darkness, like looking down the wrong end of a telescope.

'And he was still living with Mrs Whitmore then, I believe?'

'Yes.'

'And since then he's left her?'

'Yes,' I said, unnerved by these questions to which they already knew the answers.

'I wonder if you could explain something to us,' she said, with the air of someone who's thoroughly puzzled, who sincerely wants to be enlightened. 'I mean, isn't it odd that he hasn't moved in with you?'

There was a clatter and slam from the hall, as though someone had been flung in off the street: Alice coming home. Buying me time.

'Just a moment,' I said. I went to her.

Everything was flung down, her jacket and jumper and a bag spewing books and Doritos wrappers and sports socks and a grubby knitted rabbit she must have bought for Lucy from Charity Week. It was somehow a surprise to see her standing there, absolutely herself, all pink and shiny with the effort of walking from the bus stop. She seemed to have brought the light and fresh air from the street in with her.

'I'm busy, Alice,' I said. 'I've got some people with me in the kitchen. I need you to stay in the living room till we've finished.'

'That's okay,' she said. 'I want to watch Ricki Lake.'

'What about your homework?'

'I've got some really gross French, but I'll do it later.'

She went into the sitting room, collapsed on the sofa next to Lucy. I wanted so much to stay there with them, to cuddle up on the sofa, pretend that everything was as it should be. I went back to the kitchen.

'As I was saying,' said the woman, as I sat down again, 'this rather surprising fact that Mr Whitmore hasn't moved in with you. Does that mean you had some doubts about the relationship, perhaps – a feeling that something wasn't quite right?'

'Not at all,' I said.

But had I? I wondered. Was this what my hesitancy had been about? My reasons, which had felt so rational, started to seem strange – like when you stare at a word, unsure if you've spelt it right, and it suddenly looks as though it's written in a foreign language.

She waited. When I didn't say anything more, she fixed me with her clear untroubled gaze.

'Now, Mrs Langdon,' she said, 'I wonder if you could tell us what your sexual relationship with Mr Whitmore was like?'

I had a mouthful of coffee: I tried to swallow it and started coughing. I was cross with myself: I'd meant to be cool and controlled and I just looked silly.

'Sorry we have to ask you these personal questions,' she said, with the briskly optimistic air of a nurse about to do a smear test. 'Just tell us in general for now.'

I focused carefully on the plate of biscuits.

'It's been good,' I said. She waited, obviously expecting more. I couldn't work out what she was expecting, what she wanted to hear. 'It was a very happy time for me.' There was a little pause. My words seemed to resonate in the silence. I was acutely aware of that past tense I'd used so automatically. It filled me with a terrible sadness. I wanted to say more, to reclaim or reassert my feelings for him in some way. 'We've been very close,' I said.

'Yes,' she said quite gently. 'But as I'm sure you know, Mrs Langdon, these men do sometimes form sexual relationships with women in order to gain access to the woman's children. We know that. There have been studies done in the States. Sometimes if there's a child they want, they'll pursue the woman for years in order to get access to the child.'

I sat quite still. The bee rattled around in the honeysuckle, intrusive in the quiet room. My senses were so acute I felt I could hear the tiniest things – the fall of a leaf, the slide of a snail across a paving-stone.

'Now, some men do have unusual tastes in what they like,' she said. She made it sound like something essentially culinary – an unfashionable fondness for suet pudding, perhaps. 'Can you tell us if Mr Whitmore has any unusual tastes?'

I hesitated.

'Please don't be embarrassed,' she said. 'It's nothing to us.'

'But I don't know what you mean.'

'Well.' She shrugged, as though saying, We're all adults here, after all. 'Some men like sex to be quite rough, for instance.'

'No. Nothing like that. We just do normal things. Intercourse, oral sex sometimes – well, most of the time, I suppose. What everybody does, don't they?'

She sat there, quite calm and bright, with her sleek hair and her faint wholesome smell: she seemed so pure.

'Does he have any rituals,' she went on, 'anything he might do just before or after sex?'

'What kind of thing?'

'Any rituals,' she said again. 'Any ritualistic behaviour.'

I shook my head. 'No, not really.'

'Please think. Anything at all: any little gesture even.'

I couldn't imagine what she meant. I could only think of foot fetishists and some man I'd read about in a magazine who'd found the touch of saucepan lids a turn-on. 'No. There's nothing.'

'Right. Thank you,' said the woman. 'That's all I wanted to ask.' She leant back in her chair, picked up her pen and notepad.

It was the man who leaned forward now. He flicked through the folder in front of him, his fingers moving quickly and deftly, in the light but careful way you'd touch something sticky or greasy that might adhere to your fingers. I was sitting quite close, just the other side of the table: because it was my writing, I could read it upside down. I watched as he rifled through the letters I'd written to Dan, all the fumblingly intimate things I'd scrawled on scrappy bits of paper and posted through his letterbox. Some phrases had been highlighted in pink highlighter pen.

'There are one or two things in your letters that we need to clear up,' he said. 'You write to Mr Whitmore on September the 7th. I gather from your letter that you'd had sex with him the day before – that would be the 6th of September. Now, we can find no reference to that in Mr Whitmore's diary. But he writes in his diary that he had sex on the 7th.'

'Was the 7th a Sunday?' I said.

He nodded.

'I must have got the date wrong,' I said.

'I think that clears that one up,' he said. 'Now, you write something here about having his fingers inside you. I assume that means in your vagina?'

'Yes,' I said.

'Is that a particularly important part of sex for him, would you say?'

'Not especially,' I said.

'Okay. And here you've written about liking to be quite passive and wanting to be "taken over" during sex – I think that was the expression you used – "taken over".' He glanced down the page, pointed to it with his pen. 'I'd like to know whether you think it was important for Mr Whitmore to be dominant during sex?'

I shook my head. 'That thing I wrote was more about me than him,' I said.

'I understand,' he said. 'Okay. And could you tell us please whether on September the 14th you had sex with Mr Whitmore in a churchyard?'

The feeling of pressure in my chest sharpened to pain. I misunderstood for a moment: in a way that seems quite ludicrous to me now, I thought he was accusing me in some way, saying this was something we shouldn't have done. 'It wasn't exactly in the churchyard,' I said. 'There was a fence round the churchyard. We climbed over the fence. It was more like a little wood. It does seem rather irreverent, I suppose.'

'And this was definitely on September the 14th? Could you check for us, please?'

My calendar hangs beside the fridge. I went to look. On the 14th it said 'A and L to Jude's – 10.15.' And underneath, 'Dan' in capitals, in fat red letters – one of the children's felt-tips. 'Yes, it was the 14th,' I said. The woman wrote it down.

I tried to remember it. I tried to think of that place under the yews and how we'd made love there, to tell myself that was all still real, that it couldn't be erased, it was part of my life, tender, intense and irrevocable, whatever was happening now. But I couldn't picture it at all. All I could remember was the church where it had been so hard to breathe, and the prayer books speckled with mould, and the place where the little girl who'd died so young was buried.

They closed their things up then, their files and notebooks and briefcases. They pushed their coffee cups away. The man stretched his legs.

'I think that's all we need to ask you for now,' said the woman.

They stood up, ready to go. There was a slight sense of relaxation about them that I recognized from the ends of my own interviews with clients. Often this is when people tell you their secrets – as you turn to leave. The man caught sight of his reflection in the mirror above my fireplace and skimmed a hand quickly over his hair.

I didn't get up. I took a deep breath. I had such a need to assert myself in some way – to take something back from them. 'Why do you need to know these things?' I said. 'Like about the churchyard. Why does that matter?'

They looked at one another. Then the woman turned to me. 'There's an entry in his diary,' she said. 'It only gives the person's initial. We needed to be sure it was you.'

This was an opening, a concession. I charged on, though my throat was clogged up. 'Can you tell me what this child is saying?' I asked.

'Not in detail,' said the woman. 'All we can tell you is that it's an allegation of indecent assault, a very serious allegation.'

'Did she name him?'

'We can't answer that either, I'm afraid.'

'How long will it take, this whole thing?'

'Several months, I should think,' said the woman. 'We'll collect the evidence and it'll go to court. Unfortunately, it's very hard to get a conviction in these cases.'

That was when I saw that they were quite convinced of his guilt, that what Carly Smithson had said made them sure it was him, that their whole concern was not his guilt or innocence, but building up a case to convince the court.

'Do remember that these men can be very charming and very cunning,' said the man. 'They're very good at concealing their intentions. You should be aware of this in the decisions you make about your children.'

I said nothing.

The woman handed me her card. 'You must get in touch if you think of anything else,' she said.

'What kind of thing?' I said.

'Something might cross your mind. Anything. Don't worry if it seems trivial – give me a ring anyway.'

I took them to the front door. Lucy didn't stir as we passed the living room, but Alice looked up thoughtfully, then turned back to Ricki Lake. I showed them out.

I went back into the kitchen and looked at the woman's card. 'DS Victoria Griggs.' Victoria: it suited her, a wholesome name, a bar shoes and French pleats sort of name. I put the card on the dresser behind a pot plant. I opened the big window wide and leaned out, breathing deeply, thirstily, stood there for a long time, just breathing.

'Mum, what's wrong with you?' It was Alice, shaking my arm. 'Didn't you hear the doorbell? It's the man with the shed.'

'I didn't hear it,' I said.

'Well, don't you have to sign for it?'

I went into the hall. She followed.

'They were policemen, weren't they?' she said. 'Did they come about Dan?'

I nodded.

'Will we have to see them?'

'Yes,' I said. 'I didn't want them to see you, but they say they have to.'

'Really, Mum, there's no need to get so worked up about it,' she said. 'I don't mind. And Lu will love it. She'll feel dead important . . .'

The doorbell rang again.

'Mum, I really think you should let that man in.' She opened the door, and gave me a little push out into the sunlight.

14

Among the things that Alice had bought during Charity Week was a wind chime made from twelve bits of shell suspended on strings. It was pretty in its way, the shell translucent and warmly white like fresh milk. It had cost her seven pence. On Sunday afternoon, as Dan and I cleared all the stuff out of the old shed before we knocked it down, she came outside and hung the wind chime from a branch of the apple tree. The wind was getting up: the bits of shell rattled together, percussive like water dripping on metal, like gamelan music, exotic and anachronistic in an English garden.

Lucy stood and looked up at it.

'That's cool,' she said. Her hair, hanging loose because I don't usually bother to tie it back at weekends, was blown into loose swirly shapes, like the beautiful random patterns wind makes on water.

We hauled out half-empty paint cans, tatty old kitchen chairs, broken sand toys, and piled them all on the lawn.

'You look so tired,' I said to Dan. I held him for a moment, looking into his face. His appearance worried me. He looked muted, dulled, all his brightness and sharpness gone, like metal when it tarnishes, and there was a lack of focus in his eyes, as though he was always looking at something that wasn't there. 'Are you sure you should be doing this?'

He shrugged, kissed me lightly. 'It's good to have something to do. It takes your mind off things. Really, I'm glad to.'

Lucy came to help, struggling bravely with things that were far too heavy for her. She helped Dan drag a big stack'n'store box out of the shed. 'What's this?' she said. 'Mummy, what's inside?'

'Oh, I don't know,' I said, carefully casual, suspecting it was some old toys I'd packed away and planned to take to Oxfam. 'Nothing very interesting. A load of old rubbish, probably.'

I'd protested too much. Lucy levered off the lid. Inside there was a gaggle of Alice's discarded Barbies, all glitter and spangles and pert breasts and tough shiny nylon hair like the hair you find on sweetcorn cobs. They'd looked wonderful in their boxes, at birthdays or Christmas, with their flouncy skirts fanning out like overblown flowers: now, sprawled together, with bits of their outfits missing, limbs casually disarranged, blonde hair tangled, they looked ugly, slightly pornographic.

'I *knew* it was toys,' said Lucy triumphantly. She got them out and arranged them on upturned flowerpots. When they wouldn't sit up, she decided they'd all stepped on landmines and needed lots of nursing. Alice came out and drifted over, still lured by them a little though she knew she was really too old.

'Okay, girls, stand well back,' said Dan.

He took a hammer to my shed. It came apart very easily: the thin planks splintered and fell. It must have been terribly fragile, a flimsy structure with just a few rusty nails to hold it together: I couldn't understand how it had supported the weight of the clematis that had sagged there all summer, a heavy waterfall of foam-coloured flowers. Just a few precise hits with the hammer, and it was gone. Jagged bits of wood with old nails sticking out piled up on the lawn. I sat on the patio steps and watched.

It was a cold afternoon for September: the wind had a keen edge to it. The flowers in my window boxes were dying: the alyssum that had smelt of honey all summer would be gone with the first hint of frost. In my elderly neighbour's garden, the sumac that some people call the Judas tree had its autumn colours – the strange scrunched-up purple fruit like pine-cones and the fringes of reddish leaves. The purple clashed with the red: the colours seemed wrong in Dorothy's garden, harsh, synthetic, more like cheap fabric dyes than the colours of fruit or leaves.

As I watched the shed come down, I suddenly felt my eyes fill with tears. I wasn't aware of feeling sad – in fact, I didn't feel anything. It was as though I'd left out part of the sequence: the emotion was missing, there was just the physical manifestation of grief, tears welling up in me, uncontrollable. I went in and scrubbed my face with kitchen paper.

In about ten minutes, the shed was completely flattened. I went to help Dan then, and we piled the old planks together in the corner of the garden.

'Can we have a bonfire?' said Lucy.

'We'll wait for Bonfire Night,' I said.

'Please, Mummy. Just a little one. *Please.*'

'No, sweetheart. Not today. It's not so long till Bonfire Night.'

You had to pick the wood up carefully, delicately between finger and thumb – it was full of sharp splinters and broken nails: it was easy to snag yourself. Thick dust, dark and soft as soot, clung to it: we got very dirty.

Dan was breathing heavily and there was a sheen of sweat on his forehead.

'You look like you could do with a break,' I said.

He nodded gratefully.

Lucy followed us in, hungry as ever to join in a grown-up conversation, but I found her some Elastoplasts and Savlon for the Barbies and sent her out again. I made coffee.

'The police came,' I said, as we sat and sipped our coffee, our grimy hands fingerprinting the cups with sooty smudges.

'Yes,' he said. 'I thought they would.'

'They'll have to interview the girls,' I said.

'Didn't you realize?'

'No,' I said.

'Chloe, I'm so sorry, I'm so sorry.'

'Why are you so sorry?' I said sharply. 'It's not your fault. Is it?'

'I didn't mean that,' he said. 'You're always reading things into what I say. It doesn't help. It's just that if we weren't involved, you wouldn't be part of this, you wouldn't have to go through it all.'

I didn't know what to say: it was true.

Dan went to rinse his cup in the sink. 'Did they say anything about the allegation?' he said.

'No. I asked them if she'd named you: they said they couldn't tell me. They just said – an allegation of indecent assault.'

He banged the cup down on the draining board. As he struggled with his anger, clenching his fists, his face flushing, the forcefulness in him frightened me for a moment. The veins stuck out like wire on the backs of his hands. 'I can't stand it,' he said. 'Being accused of something but not knowing what it is I'm meant to have done.'

'You'll find out soon, surely,' I said.

'I didn't know this happened,' he said. 'I didn't know you could be accused of a crime and investigated for it and still kept in the dark about it. Jesus. Where's the justice in that?' He turned away from me abruptly, like someone in the middle of a quarrel, and went back outside.

Some fence posts had come with the shed, to make a foundation. First they had to be damp-proofed. We laid them in place and Dan got out the creosote and started to paint it on. The smell of it, that rich male smell, made me think of my father, who was always pottering in the garden, mending the garage, putting up new bits of fence, trying to preserve things. I've always loved those male smells – pipe tobacco, tweed, turps, engine oil: I find them so much friendlier than the smells of women – the pastel, rather febrile scents of cosmetic counters. The creosote fumes gave me a sudden sharp sense of my father's physical presence – of the gravelly tones in his voice and his rare laughter.

Lucy came over.

'What's that stuff for?' she said.

'It stops the wood from rotting,' Dan told her. 'Otherwise water would get in and your smart new shed could go crooked again.'

She stood and watched. She loves watching people building and painting and fixing, loves workmen's things – tools, paints, plans, careful measurements. She's a scientist at heart, like her father. The books she most values are the ones with facts in: once, on learning that a child at Alice's school had been told off for damaging a book, she said with horror, 'I hope it wasn't a *finding-out* book.'

Dan noticed how engaged she was. He mopped his brow extravagantly. 'It's tough, this job,' he said. 'If only I had someone to help me.'

Lucy jumped up and down. '*I* could help you. Let *me* help you.'

He held the brush out to her. She flushed with excitement.

'Hang on, Lucy,' I called. 'You'll get that stuff on your sweatshirt and it doesn't come off. You need something to wear on top. You need workmen's clothes.'

Lucy showed no sign of coming. She started to paint on the creosote, very precise and careful.

I went to her. 'If you don't change, you can't do it,' I said in my firmest voice.

She was cross. She came in reluctantly, arms folded petulantly across her body. I found her an old shirt of mine that came down to her ankles, helped her put it on, rolled up the cuffs. As I knelt, her head was just on a level with mine. I nuzzled her hair.

'You smell of the wind,' I said.

'How can I smell of the wind?' she said.

'It's how your hair always smells when the wind gets in it,' I said. 'I don't know what makes the smell. I love it.'

'That's silly, Mummy,' she said.

The oversized shirt emphasized her smallness. Her skin had that translucent look, like light shining through pale china.

'You're a real workman now,' I said.

She wasn't mollified. She fidgeted as I tried to do up the top button. 'Do hurry up, Mummy. I've got to get back to Dan. Dan *needs* me.'

I watched them through the open kitchen door. She painted the creosote on so meticulously, tremendously self-conscious and proud. And Dan looked happier now, finding some kind of relief or distraction in the work, and perhaps in Lucy's cheerful presence too. 'That's wonderful,' he said to her. 'That's a really professional job.'

She glowed. Her long blonde hair blew back from her face. There was a splodge of creosote on her cheek.

I stood and sipped the cold coffee in the bottom of my cup and looked at them working together. I was watching, always watching. I knew it and hated it. I felt ugly and intrusive, like some big brooding insect sitting on the edge of a web, waiting to pounce. Watching this man who so recently had felt like part of my body, and whom I now studied as you might study a man you don't know. Like late at night on the tube, when you try to suss men out, alert to any hint of danger, anything to make you move further down the carriage – a druggy glazed look, a lack of inhibition, a reluctance to look away if your eye meets his. I knew I was looking at Dan now in that wary, appraising way, looking for clues, for evidence – how he touched her, looked at her, leaned towards her, showed her how to move the brush with his hand on hers. He sensed my eyes on him, turned and looked at me. I moved my gaze away, felt ashamed, felt I'd betrayed someone – though I didn't yet know if it was him or me.

When the creosoting was finished, I went out to him. 'Shouldn't you leave it there?' I said. 'You'll be knackered tomorrow.'

'What the hell,' said Dan. 'It's not as though I'm doing anything tomorrow.'

'No,' I said. For a moment I'd forgotten about his suspension. I felt ashamed.

So we put up the shed together, with the aid of the diagram that had come with it. It was surprisingly straightforward. Lucy and I held the panels of red-stained cedarwood in place and Dan hammered in the nails.

'If we at least get the roof up, we can put the things back in,' he said. 'It won't be perfect, but it'll keep your stuff out of the weather. I can do the windows and roofing felt some other time.'

The light was thickening already, the shadows dark as ripe damsons. In September, the evenings close in and the temperature drops so early: by six o'clock, you find yourself thinking of winter, however fine the day's been. The wind was blowing more strongly now. The wind chime made a loud noise, bits of shell dashing against one another like some frenzied percussion band, leaderless and disorderly. It would only have to blow a little harder and the bits of shell would surely shatter.

I sent the girls up to bed straight after dinner: it was pretty late by then. I poured red wine, lit candles and turned out most of the lights, moved a jug of late roses onto the table. Making the room look special, a little romantic, was a secret act of contrition, an attempt to make up for that moment when Dan had seen me looking at him as though he was a stranger. We sat there drinking quietly, almost at peace for a while. Then we stacked the plates in the dishwasher, and I scrubbed the saucepans and Dan dried them. He'd showered, he smelt of my soap.

'I've seen Felix,' he said.

'Good,' I said. 'Was he okay?'

'Kind of. You're right. He's not exactly – how did you put it? – not *nice*. I can see he'd be good, though. He put me through it rather. It was like an interrogation.'

'But he'll take you on?'

'Yes.' He put the teatowel down for a moment, turned away, picked up his wine. 'I said it was you who'd recommended him.

He said, "Ah – *Chloe*" – he seemed amused. He's fond of you, isn't he?'

I shrugged.

'It made me wonder if you'd had a relationship with him,' he said.

I wasn't looking at him. 'Just a flirtation,' I said. I scrubbed at the casserole dish: the scourer was clogged up with bits of burnt carrot. 'You can see the kind of man he is – he'd probably try it on with anyone. It was only ever a flirtation.' I didn't understand why I'd started to lie to Dan. It was as though I'd become a double agent – keeping my options open, not quite knowing which side I was on. I scrubbed away, though the dish was already clean. Dan said nothing.

The candles on the table flickered: shadows on the wall came together then shimmied apart, in an intricate choreography. There was the softest thud as a petal fell from a rose.

'They seem so sure you did it, the police,' I said. I had my back to him. I turned on the tap to rinse the casserole, but I wasn't concentrating and the running water splashed in the bowl of a spoon and spattered all over me. I swore, dabbed at myself with a J-cloth. 'Shall I tell you about it?' I said. 'What they asked and what I said – so you'll be prepared when they interview you?'

'Why do I need to be prepared?' he said sharply. The way his voice had quickened and hardened unnerved me – but I charged on.

'For when they ask you all about us and your sex life and everything,' I said.

He went very still, said nothing. I couldn't understand why he didn't get it, why he seemed to need to have it spelled out to him.

'So your story matches mine,' I said.

He threw his wine glass across the room. It smashed against the fridge door. The sound of breaking glass seemed to go on for ever. Red wine spurted everywhere, blood pulsing from an artery. He grabbed my shoulders, twisted me round to face him. His fingers dug deep into me, hurt me.

He shouted into my face. 'Why the fuck should it matter what you said?'

He pushed me away from him, too hard. I steadied myself against the door of the fridge. I was shaking.

'For Chrissake, Chloe,' he shouted, 'I don't give a fuck what you said.'

'I was only trying to help,' I whispered stupidly. My hands pressed against the fridge behind me were wet with the spilt wine. Tears fell down my face. I reached out my hand towards him.

He shuddered, rubbed his hand across his eyes, as you do when a mood passes as suddenly as it came. 'Jesus,' he said. He blinked as though he couldn't see, came towards me. We held one another, carefully as though something might break. His eyes were wet too. 'When you say things like that,' he said, 'about our stories matching, it's as though you think I did it, as though you think I'm lying to you.'

He let go of me, very gently, and sat down at the table. He moved heavily. The movement shook the table and made more rose petals fall.

'Surely I only need to tell the truth,' he said.

I swept up the broken glass and wrapped it in some newspaper and put it in the bin. I wiped the fridge down with the J-cloth. I didn't mind that he didn't offer to help: I felt he was far away in some private world, unaware of what I was doing.

'Can I stay?' he said.

'Of course,' I said.

As we got into bed, we could hear the rising wind rattling things – dustbin lids, milk bottles, the wind chime in the garden. Then the rain started, just whispering at the window at first, soon banging down.

'It's a good thing we got the roof on,' he said.

He made love to me with a kind of desperation that night – as though he felt it would heal everything. But I couldn't get into it somehow. I was easily distracted: the noise of the storm kept getting in the way. And though the working of his mouth on me was as sweet as ever, I didn't have that sense that I'd always had with him before, of being overwhelmed, flooded with feeling: there were no colours, no shifting flickering lights – I knew I had to make it happen, in my familiar old way. It was a struggle, an uphill thing, like it had been in my twenties sometimes, like when you think, If I take much longer he'll get fed up, and with the thought the excitement seeps away. And as I lay there, tense, wanting to come and not quite able to, nearing the moment, then slipping back again, I reached for the sexual images I rely on to ease me towards orgasm, and found instead a scared little girl in a room full of Spot books in Urdu and Korean, and a man who relished his power over her, who hurt her and enjoyed it, and who had the face and the probing fingers of the man who touched me now. The image didn't – thank God – turn me on – but it didn't slow me down either. It was just there, it was part of me, imprinted in my head – it couldn't be got rid of.

Afterwards I cried, quietly, turned away, hoping he wouldn't hear, that the noise of the storm would mask the sound of my broken breathing. I guess he realized, though, but he didn't try to comfort me, just lay there on his back beside me, knowing, I suppose, that there was nothing he could do.

'Will we get through this together?' he said, after a while.

'Of course,' I said, and turned and rested my head on his shoulder. Yet knew there was something in me that resisted that 'together', made me want to move a little away.

15

Next morning, as Dan left, it was quiet again, though still overcast. There were snails everywhere in my garden, oozing out of their shells, translucent and rather nauseating, and lots of leaves had been torn off the trees by the wind, some still green. They lay like saucers on the patio, holding pools of clear rainwater.

Lucy still smelt of creosote. I scrubbed her face and hands before I took her to school, but I couldn't get rid of the smell. It seemed to cling to her hair. The smell I'd liked so much the day before irritated me now. It seemed stale and somehow inappropriate on a child.

I spent the morning supervising an access visit to a foster home. Kyle Marston, my new physical abuse case. He was just four. The abuse had come to light when his mother had taken him to Casualty with a broken leg, and the casualty doctor, worried by unexplained bruising, had given him general X-rays that had showed up several old fractures. Kyle had been taken straight into care and his mother was only allowed to see him under supervision. It was a foster home we used a lot: dedicated foster parents, rabbits, picture books, teatimes when the children ate chocolate crispie cakes they'd made themselves. Kyle's mother smoked her way through the session – ill at ease, already haggard at nineteen, her badly bleached hair falling all over her face. She rarely touched him, and needed a lot of help to play with him: as she lit her cigarettes, her thin fingers shook. But he was utterly distraught when the time came for her to go. 'No no no no,' he screamed, desperate, clinging to her. I had to peel his fingers off her arms one at a time, like bits of Elastoplast. 'No no no no.' I drove her home. She sat quite silent in the car, smoking.

I dictated my notes on the session while I waited in the queue for a place in the office car park, and once I'd parked I went to the secretaries' office to drop off the tape so it could be typed up.

Maureen my typist looked up. 'Oh, I was just writing you a note,' she said. 'Your friend Vicky rang.'

Vicky? I thought.

She handed me the slip of paper.

'Thanks.' I glanced at it, recognized the number.

She must have read something in my face, because she said, 'Nothing's wrong, I hope? She sounded quite cheerful. If anything, a bit concerned about you, I'd say.' She looked at me expectantly, hoping for some interesting nugget of information to liven up her day.

'No, nothing's wrong,' I said.

Jude was just rushing out: we almost collided in the office doorway. She looked at me, her face a question.

'The flowers were lovely, thanks, they really helped,' I said.

We hugged briefly, carefully.

'You okay?' she said.

'I'm fine,' I said.

Nat was out. I went into his office where I wouldn't be overheard, and rang the number.

'Detective Sergeant Griggs, please.'

'Speaking.'

'Oh. It's Chloe Langdon.'

'Hello, Chloe.' We were now on first-name terms, it seemed. 'Thanks for ringing back.'

'That's okay.'

'Chloe, I have something I want you to see.'

'What is it?'

'It's best if I show you.'

We arranged to meet at my house after lunch. I had some time in lieu owing and nothing in my diary.

She was waiting in her car when I got there. As I pulled up she got out, waving and smiling. For a brief crazy moment, I felt flattered that she seemed so pleased to see me. She looked particularly stylish today: she could have stepped straight out of a Sunday supplement piece on how to wear the new softer trouser-suit.

I took her into the kitchen. It was a dark dreary day, I had to put on the light. Against the brown and black and grey of my dank September garden, my new shed was a harsh red, like a cut that's only just scabbed over. I wiped the breakfast crumbs from the table, made coffee.

She opened her briefcase and took out a pack of photographs.

'This film was in Mr Whitmore's camera – we've had it developed,' she said. 'I'd like you to look through the pictures, please.'

'What for?' I said. 'I mean, what do you want to know?'

'Just have a look for me, Chloe,' she said. 'Tell me what you think.'

I took the pack from her hand. I felt the sequence of stress reactions, as familiar to me now as the physical sequence of desire – the lurch in my stomach, the dry mouth, the rapid pulse in my ears.

Yet the photos looked perfectly straightforward. They were the ones that Dan had taken in my garden on that hot August afternoon. Lucy in her Esmeralda swimsuit, playing in the sprinkler, rushing out of the frame, moving so fast that bits of her were blurred, her skin glittering with waterdrops. The camera or the developing hadn't been able to cope with the brightness of her hair in the sunshine: it looked white like the sky, you couldn't tell where her hair stopped and the sky began. Alice lying under the apple tree, pulling funny faces, too embarrassed to pose. Lucy piggyback on Alice, the two of them anarchically poking out their tongues at the camera. And the ones that Alice had taken under Dan's direction, self-consciously arty shots – a rose, a bucket of snails – and some that Dan had taken of me – the straps of my dress pushed down so I'd get an even tan, my eyes narrowed against the sun, my face scrunched up with laughter.

The grass was a little high and bleached by the sun and crammed with daisies, and the clematis was foaming with creamy flowers, and there were roses everywhere – a few pale briar roses still in the hedge, and in the rose bed the opulent cultivated blooms, red and sulphur yellow, spilling lavish petals on the lawn. The colours dazzled me, on this damp dark September day. I'd forgotten how full of flowers my garden was in summer.

I flicked through. 'This is all perfectly ordinary, isn't it?' I said. 'I mean – Lucy in her swimsuit – there's nothing wrong with that, surely.'

'Just go on looking,' she said.

Then I came to it. This photograph had been taken indoors without flash: it was rather dark and blurry. It was a photograph of a reflection in a mirror. The mirror was steamed up, and the steaming gave it a soft focus look, as though there'd been gauze across the lens.

'Do you know this room?' she said.

'It's my bathroom,' I said.

On the shelf below the mirror you could see bits of bathroom clutter – a box of tissues, Lucy's strawberry toothpaste, my Frizz-ease hair conditioner.

I looked at the picture – at my bathroom mirror and at the girl in the mirror, who stared straight at her reflection, her arms by her sides. She was naked at least to the navel, though the bottom of the mirror frame cut off her reflection there. Her outline was blurred by the steam, but you could make out the slim torso, the small white definite breasts.

'This is your daughter Alice?'

'Yes,' I said.

'Did you take this photo?'

'No,' I said. My voice sounded strange, half-strangled.

'Do you know who took this photo?'

'I don't,' I said.

There was an insistent high-pitched sound in my ears – so real it seemed to be outside my head though I knew it wasn't. It was the little boy's screaming cry that I'd heard that morning echoing in my head – No no no no. The sound went on and on, like some screeching bird that has only one note. No no no no.

It was the last photo in the pack. I left it on top, pushed the photos across the table back to her.

'Does Dan often take photos of your children?' she said, in that brisk matter-of-fact way she had.

'Only that afternoon in the garden,' I said.

'Did he take any nude pictures or undressed pictures?'

'No, not that I know of.' The photo of Alice lay on the table between us, refuting what I'd said. 'Well, not if I'd known. I mean, I had no idea. Jesus.' Suddenly I couldn't talk anymore. I hid my face in my hands.

She waited. I suppose she was used to this sort of thing – these moments of revelation, the worlds turned upside down: this was what she traded in. She sat there quietly till I opened my eyes.

I looked across at her, waiting like a child for her to take control, to tell me what to do. In some way she was coming into focus for me. I was aware of things I hadn't noticed before – the friendly crows' feet round her eyes, the way you could just see the line where her foundation ended. She seemed more real, more human. I didn't exactly like her – but she was all I had.

She asked if I would show her the bathroom. We went upstairs – Vicky with the photograph in her hand. The landing was dark: it has no windows. I had to put on the light. I opened the door, showed the tangle and smudge of my bathroom, the clutter of embarrassing things – tampons, nit combs, hairs in the plughole. I didn't care. I was becoming hardened to these little revelations of bits of bad housekeeping. I showed her how the door was opposite the mirror, we worked out how you could photograph someone in the mirror from the open door.

'Would she have known the picture was being taken?' I said.

'Not necessarily. Not if someone was very quick and quiet. It's dark on the landing. If you were looking in the mirror, you couldn't really see someone outside the door if the landing light was off.'

I tried it: you couldn't.

'And the picture's slightly crooked,' she went on. 'I would guess it was taken in a hurry.'

'So for Alice it's as though this never happened?'

'There's certainly no obvious reason why she'd have known it was happening,' she said.

And she never would know, I resolved. Never. She would never find out that someone had stolen an image of her and planned to use that image for their own pleasure. I would keep her absolutely protected from that. My resolve gave me a sense almost of relief: it was something to rest in. It was as though for days I'd been falling, falling down a rock face – scrabbling at earth and stones, grabbing pieces of root that held for a moment or two then gave way – and now at least I'd fallen as far as I could. I had solid ground under my feet. I was hurt but I knew where I was.

We went back downstairs. I sipped mechanically at my coffee: it was cold. 'That afternoon when he brought his camera round and took those pictures, I was so happy,' I said. 'I thought he was just

134

being friendly, just getting her to like him. She'd always resented him a bit: she liked it best when it was just us, she said.'

'Yes, you told me,' said Vicky.

'I thought it was his way of reaching out to her,' I said.

'If Dan did take that picture, Chloe, then there's no avoiding the fact that he's had some quite other intention than reaching out to her.' She put the pictures back in their envelope. 'Ring me if you think of anything,' she said. 'Anything at all. You know where I am.'

I showed her to the door.

I went back and sat down at my table. I knew I needed to think, to plan what to do, to start from scratch again, but I found I couldn't sit still. It was like the twitchy inability to stay in one place you get if you've had far too much coffee. Everything was moving too fast inside me, my heart, my pulses, and my body had to respond with action.

I went out into the garden. The limbs and trunks of the trees were black with rain, all the colours darkening and fading: it was the time of year when everything goes underground. Brown leaves from the laurel, heavy as leather with wet, littered the lawn.

I walked up and down, across the patio onto the grass, down to the rose hedge at the bottom of the garden, where the wood from the old shed was protected by a tarpaulin, waiting for Bonfire Night, then back up the other side past the apple tree and the rose-bed and onto the patio again.

As I walked, I picked things up, then let them slip from my hands – green apples now maggoty and decaying underneath that had fallen on the lawn, a few dead flowerheads that crumbled like dust in my fingers. There was a lot that needed doing. I saw how I had let it all go, I had been a bad gardener, it had got horribly out of hand. My garden, I realized, no longer pleased me. I simply couldn't see why I'd loved it so much, all this overhang and green shade, all this lushness and excess. Even now, with the flowers over and the leaves falling as the garden thinned out and sifted down towards winter, it was terribly muddled and disorganized. The shrubs were competing with one another in the flowerbed, taking each other's light and shade, the briar hedge was leaching all the goodness out of the lawn, some weeds that I hadn't uprooted because I rather liked their careless yellow flowers now threatened to take over the herb patch. My fondness for things that creep and climb seemed especially peculiar to me – the ivy that wrapped itself round the prunus, the passion flower creeping through the lilac, the clematis that now clambered into the apple tree. Wherever there was a trunk or a stem, I had something growing up it, embracing it, clutching at it, draining the life out of it.

I had started out from the wrong assumptions. From now on, I would approach it quite differently: it would all be orderly and restrained, everything would have its own little plot, nothing would encroach on anything else. I would begin now, I thought, do something definite about these suckers and creepers and entanglements. I went to get the spade from the shed, and started to turn over the earth in the rosebed. It was extraordinarily heavy, but I felt strong, full of energy.

The garden still smelt faintly of creosote. I saw myself the day before, when he'd put up my shed, when I'd still believed him to be the victim of an injustice, believed that a troubled little girl had been unable to remember or identify her abuser clearly, or had been threatened by the real abuser so she didn't dare to tell the whole truth. The woman I'd been then felt like somebody else: I was shocked by that woman's naivety. As I worked there in the garden, that belief that after a few weeks of fucking you could know somebody seemed as blindly innocent as believing in smart bombs or tooth fairies.

I dug and dug – turning over huge puddingy clods of soil, bringing up last year's daffodil bulbs and fat white earthworms, thinning out the border, trying to get up the docks, though their roots went deep and sometimes they wouldn't come up however hard you pulled. I worked for a long time. It was some kind of new start.

When the alarm on my watch went, to remind me that it was time to pick up Lucy, I flinched as though someone had hit me. I was amazed to see that an hour and a half had gone.

I went inside. I felt unutterably tired and very wet: it had been raining steadily, though I'd been quite unaware of it. I looked at myself in the mirror over the mantelpiece. I had a rather wild look: my hair had frizzed, raindrops clung to it, my face was red. I changed, put on some makeup to calm down the colour in my face. My eye fell on the cup that Vicky had drunk from: I dumped it quickly in the sink.

I drove to school somehow, though another driver hooted at me and I realized I'd turned right without signalling. Lucy came rushing out grinning. I hugged her hard. She shook me off, she didn't want to be hugged, she wanted to show me the 10 out of 10 she'd got for her spelling test. She slipped her warm hand into mine: it felt real – more real than anything. 'Mummy, you're *pinching*,' she said, and pulled her hand away.

We went home. I watched anxiously for Alice. When she crashed through the door, flinging her bags down, I was somehow surprised to find her just fine, just the same as ever – inky, raggety, grouchy about her German homework.

I went to hug her.

She hugged me back but gave me a rather suspicious look. 'What's this all about, Mum? You're not in some kind of state, are you?'

'Not really,' I said.

'It's Dan, isn't it?'

'No, it's not Dan,' I said.

She went to do her homework and Lucy watched television. I sat at the kitchen table and took some deep breaths, reaching down into myself, seeking for some core of strength, a hard clear place deep inside. I talked to myself like a parent to a child, told myself I would cope: I had my daughters, my house, my friends – my life was built on solid foundations, I would survive.

I realized I had to make a meal. I opened the fridge to find something for tea, and my hand knocked against a jug of yesterday's chicken gravy. The jug was plastic, not very stable – it tipped and gravy slurped everywhere, all over the fridge and me and my only clean shirt, all over the floor.

'Shit.'

Lucy came running. 'Mummy, I heard you swear,' she said triumphantly.

'Just go away. Just stay out of here,' I screamed at her. She stormed off, outraged.

I finally sat down and cried then, vast sobs that sucked my chest in, tears spilling everywhere: I felt I would never stop. I sat at the kitchen table and just gave in to it, absolutely taken over by it. Then after a while, when the worst of the sobbing was over, I got up, all muddled and drunk with tears, and spread newspaper to soak up the gravy, newspaper that formed a heavy dark mat, impregnated with grease. Then I put the newspaper in a rubbish sack and got out the mop. The gravy was thick and sticky: however often you rinsed the mop, you couldn't get rid of it. I scrubbed and swilled, but the grease just wouldn't go. There was a strong meaty smell, with an undertone of bile. I mopped and mopped and I couldn't get the floor clean and I couldn't stop crying.

Alice came down, hovered nervously in the doorway, seeing my tears. 'Mum, I'm starving,' she said tentatively.

'Oh God,' I said. 'I'll make you some sandwiches.' I wiped my face, gave up on the mopping though the floor still sucked at my feet. I found a packet of ham in the fridge and made some kind of a meal.

I picked up my keys.

'Where are you going?' said Alice.

'Round to Dan's. I won't be long.'

'I want to come,' said Lucy, thickly through a mouthful of sand-wich.

'You can't,' I said.

'Why not? He's my friend too.'

'Christ. Why does there always have to be a reason?'

'I *am* coming,' said Lucy. 'It's boring here.' She went to get her coat. She pulled it down too sharply from the peg and ripped the fabric loop it hangs from.

'You stupid stupid little girl. Now look what you've done,' I said.

'I didn't mean to.' Her face crumpled. She was torn between shame at tearing her coat and rage because she felt my anger to be unjust.

'I don't care,' I said. I grabbed her head between my hands, spoke right into her face. 'You listen to me. You are staying here. For once in your life you are going to do exactly what you're told.'

'I hate you,' said Lucy. She twisted free of my grasp, tried to kick me. 'I'd rather be dead than live with you.' I could see her struggling for curses that were big and bad enough to encom-pass her feelings. 'You're the worst mother in the whole wide world.' Her grubby afternoon face was streaked with the pale tracks of tears.

I slammed the door on the sound of her sobbing and banging the radiator and Alice trying to calm her.

I realized I hadn't changed my grease-spotted shirt. It didn't matter. I got in the car.

He opened the door quickly. 'Chloe . . .' The pleasure in his face hurt me, and that way he had of saying my name that felt like a caress.

He moved to hold me. I pushed him away, pushed past him up the stairs and into his flat.

He came in after me. The flat smelt of something he'd cooked for supper. His Urdu textbooks were scattered around.

'I'm afraid it's a bit of a mess,' he said uncertainly. 'I haven't tidied, I wasn't expecting you.'

With only the overhead light on and the day darkening into night outside, the room had that bleakness, that transitory unconnected quality, that I'd originally sensed in it.

I couldn't face him. I went to the window, looked out over the park. You could just make out the complicated shapes of the park gates, the papery dead hydrangeas. No one was walking there tonight.

'I can't make love with you anymore,' I said.

There was a moment of utter stillness. I wondered if either of us would say anything ever again.

Then he shifted slightly. 'You could tell me why,' he said coldly.

I turned to him. 'There's a photograph.'

'What photograph?'

'The police have it. Vicky came to see me.'

'Vicky?'

'DS Griggs.'

'Oh.' He pulled a face, as though there was a rancid taste in his mouth. 'It's Vicky now, is it? You're cosying up to them, are you?'

I said nothing.

'Well?' he said.

'She calls me Chloe,' I said, not understanding.

'No,' he said. 'I mean the photograph. What's in this photograph that your Vicky's got so worked up about?'

'You should know. You took it, for Christ's sake.'

He moved away from me. His fists were clenched. I could see him struggling to keep control. 'Chloe, I don't have the faintest fucking idea what you're talking about,' he said. 'Why won't you believe me?'

'Why should I believe you?' I said. 'The police don't believe you.'

The shadow of the unlit standard lamp fell across his face. He seemed to have aged, as he stood there in the harsh light, the lines on his face etched in shadow. I saw how much grey there was in his hair. He's old, I thought: we are both old. 'Jesus, Chloe, you've got to tell me,' he said. He wasn't shouting. His voice was quite quiet, breaking a bit. I wished he would shout. 'You're throwing away everything we had. Don't I at least have the right to know why?'

I shook my head. 'I trusted you,' I said. There seemed nothing else to say. I turned to go.

'Felix says there's a video of the girl's disclosure,' he said quickly, with an edge of desperation in his voice. 'You know – what she said when she was interviewed. They pass it over to him at some point.'

There was a video. I longed to ask more, but I said nothing. I could feel how he was trying to make me stay and talk, trying to hold me there.

'At least then we'll know what I'm meant to have done,' he said bitterly.

I got to the door. He came to me. 'Can I still see you?' he said. The pleading in his voice appalled me, and my sense of my absolute power over him. I could bear his anger, I forgave that quickly: but I hated, hated his distress – the misery in his face, that broken look he had.

'I don't know,' I said.

'Chloe . . .' I was intensely aware of the smell of his skin. He touched my shoulder, a touch like a question, gentle, tentative. I felt how very very easy it would be to lose my resolve, to slip back into the old pattern. I shook him off. The door clicked shut behind me.

16

I lay awake for what seemed like hours that night. I felt I would never sleep again. I was very afraid, for I knew it was all only just beginning, that my life would be opened out to them, that everything that was precious to me might be taken away. Fear, I learnt that night, fills you with a relentless energy: I felt I could run for miles. I had such a need for action, for some simple emphatic deed that couldn't be undone, that would make me and my children safe, and let me sleep at last.

I went to the landing window, looked out into the garden. It was a clear cold night – a moon, big glittery stars. I could make out the heap of wood that had once been my shed, a denser black in the darkness under the hedge, waiting for Bonfire Night.

I went down to the living room. In the writing desk there was a drawer I kept locked because I didn't want the girls rummaging in it. They knew where the key was kept, so it was a largely symbolic gesture, an expression of that need that is often felt by mothers to have a space that is ours alone – a room, a table-top – something for me.

I took the key from its place, unlocked the drawer, pulled it out, tipped everything in it onto the floor: diaries, letters, notebooks, photographs. I got a black rubbish sack from the kitchen: it smelt synthetic, sickly. I sorted through these pieces of my past.

There were my teenage diaries, three plump notebooks with Pre-Raphaelite covers and nice thick faintly purplish pages: I'd started when I was sixteen and kept them going till I left college. I flicked through – recalling briefly the many men, the morning-after post-mortems, the phones that didn't ring. I felt weirdly moved by this encounter with my younger self: I wanted to take her in my arms and comfort her, to tell her that none of it mattered that much. My eye fell on my notes on the start of a romance that had seemed at the time like the answer to everything. 'Dear diary, I've never felt like this before. Well, I know it's not the first time I've written that but this time it's really true. I can't eat, I can't sleep, I keep walking into walls.' I couldn't now remember the name of the man, or the colour of his eyes, or whether we'd slept together – we probably had, I usually did. My writing had been smaller then, so many words, so much emotion, crammed on a single purple page. I tipped the diaries into the rubbish sack.

There was stuff I'd collected on holiday – menus, concert programmes, Venetian sugarlumps. There was an empty packet of French bicarbonate of soda, a souvenir of a brief affair with a man I'd met in Provence before I was married. The sight of it brought back that week of absolute innocence, and all the Mediterranean things – figs, absinthe, olives, sex in the drowsy afternoon behind closed shutters, the way time slows in the heat. He'd been rather large and very enthusiastic and I'd got a bad bout of cystitis, hence the bicarb: in an act of uncharacteristic sentimentality I'd kept the packet.

Under the holiday stuff, some photographs, pictures of me that Adam had taken when I was heavily pregnant. It was the only time I'd let anyone photograph me naked: but at eight months pregnant I simply hadn't cared. I looked in amazement at the images, they seemed quite sexless yet somehow blatant, the huge stomach with strong blue veins, an awful lot more pubic hair than usual, and that terribly smug air you usually have when you're pregnant – the one time in life when you know for sure what you're meant to be doing. I certainly didn't want anyone else to see these pictures. They went out too.

Then there were mementos of Alice and Lucy's babyhoods – locks of hair, their pink plastic wristbands from the maternity ward, the notebook where I'd written all about them. Utterly wrapped up in them as I'd been, I'd loved to note down the tiny changes, the little everyday miracles. As other people use photographs, I'd used words: it was my way of holding on to it all. 'Lucy is frightened of the very smallest spiders and pictures of men with teeth – Pavarotti, a caricature of Bill Clinton ... Today she brushed her hair with a dustpan and brush, and pretended to eat a raw potato, giggling loudly at my cries of Yuk!' Scanning through, I kept coming on things I'd forgotten: it would be good to read it all through properly one day, to remember all the details. Yet as I turned the pages, I saw how much there was about the warmth of their bodies, the softness of their skin, the scent of their hair. This too had to go. The rubbish sack was clingy with plasticizer, it closed round the notebook. Tears welled briefly in my eyes.

Last I came to the postcards that Dan had sent me from Brittany – the postcards that had filled me with such a huge sense of happiness. Before I threw them away, I spread them out on the floor like a hand in a game of cards and looked at them, those pictures of the old forest of Broceliande, of spindly trees with pale leaves, tussocks of grass, muddy paths that didn't seem to lead anywhere, ugly little conifers with summer sunshine streaking their trunks with silver, matted undergrowth of bramble and fern, all very like the forest where I grew up. Then I turned them over. On the back, his handwriting, self-assured, using up lots of space. His writing, as surely as his voice or his touch or the sight of his leather jacket thrown down on a chair, sent a shiver of desire through me. 'I miss you horribly. Love to the girls.' That second phrase now appalled me.

I put on my plimsolls and pulled on my winter coat over my dressing-gown. I put some matches in my pocket and drew back the curtains in the living-room, so the light from indoors lit up part of the garden.

I picked up the sack of stuff – it was surprisingly light really, all those little bits of my history didn't add up to much – and I went out into the darkness. My breath was cloudy, my hands already so cold that I couldn't at first work the catch on the shed door. I took a rake, went down to the woodpile, threw back the tarpaulin. There at the bottom of the garden, behind the apple tree so the scar on the grass wouldn't look too unsightly from the house, I built a neat little bonfire out of the ruins of my old shed. I cut my finger on a nail, sucked the cut. It tasted of rust, I wondered vaguely if it was a tetanus risk, but didn't really care.

My hands were so stiff with cold that I broke several matches. But even when I managed to light one, the fire burned only reluctantly, a pale, tentative, emaciated flame. I got some petrol from the shed, threw a little on the fire. It smelt of danger: it worked beautifully. The fire flared up, startling in the darkness. I fed it with bits of wood, careful not to put on too much and damp it down again.

Turning, I saw Dorothy my neighbour come to her bedroom window and look out – I paid no attention, though I knew I must look thoroughly mad, with my dressing-gown hanging down below my coat, and my hair everywhere, silhouetted against the flames in the night.

When the fire was going well, I emptied the rubbish sack onto the flames. Like stepping off a high building, it was appallingly easy to do. I threw on too many things at once – they didn't burn at first, I had a moment of crazy hope that the fire would simply refuse them. But then a little wind came, and the fire stirred and reared up. It turned the pages of my diaries one at a time, like an unseen hand. The flames leapt and flickered, and the words I'd written faded as the pages they were written on darkened and dried. The photos of my pregnant body went brown, crumbled to pale ash. The wood made mysterious caverns, small illuminated rooms that collapsed in on themselves, sending up showers of red sparks, and then opened out somewhere else. The fire was noisy: it hissed and spat. The flames licked at the wood like the tongues of animals: they were greedy, they ate away at my things – they took my words, my pictures, my past tense.

I was bitterly cold, standing there, feeding the flames. The heat from the fire hurt my face, but somehow it didn't penetrate, it stayed on the surface of my skin, I couldn't stop shivering. The sack was empty now. I stood and watched for a long time as it all burned. I felt purified, pared down to something fine and thin and skeletal, reduced to the essence, all skin and bone, no flesh. There was nothing extraneous or superfluous about me any more – nothing excessive or frivolous, nothing that anyone could take and use and expose.

The fire shuffled softly, dying quietly. I raked over the remains. Charred scraps of paper fluttered up, like black moths, pieces of the night, their wings tipped with fire. Now the fire had died down, I was very aware of the glittering of the stars – so bright, so far away. I went inside and fell instantly asleep.

Part III

17

He tried to talk to me, of course. He rang the next day.

'Chloe, I must see you.' He sounded distraught, his voice hard, high-pitched.

'No,' I said. 'It's completely impossible. Surely you realize that. No, I can't see you.' I put down the phone. My throat felt tight and sore, as though talking to him had hurt me.

That week I kept bursting into tears at work. The first time was when I told Jude what had happened – so that was understandable, I suppose. Then on Thursday morning Kyle Marston's natural father turned up from Corby and came into the office and started abusing me for taking Kyle into care. He was pretty nasty – I was a fucking slag and I didn't know what the fuck I was doing and I was fucking lucky he was such a peaceable man, 'know what I mean'. But I kept the door of the interview room open and I never felt physically threatened, and if a purely verbal tirade like that upsets you, you'd never last in this line of work. It was the kind of thing that normally warrants a raised eyebrow, perhaps a sardonic remark to Nat or Jude – yet it left me shaky and tearful.

Jude plied me with tissues and coffee, while I sat there apologizing and feeling thoroughly feeble.

'Chloe, what about the weekend?' she said, scratching her head thoughtfully with one purple fingernail. 'D'you have any plans?'

'I haven't thought that far ahead,' I said.

'I'm taking you out for the day, then,' she said. 'You and those girls. We'll go to Brighton, get away for a bit.'

'You're so good to me,' I said.

We drove there in her dreadful old Alfa Romeo, that's still quite quick off the mark but lets in lots of rainwater: the carpet on the passenger side is permanently soggy. At Brighton she headed straight for the front, past the tall thin terraced houses that are all in pale quiet colours like wild flowers, blue and yellow and cream. She parked, we went down to the stony beach between the piers and sat at the edge of the water, Jude bending down rather carefully because she was wearing very louche leather trousers that didn't have much give. The sun was out, everything was blue and white, the colours in the sky all running together, streaky as though painted on wet paper by a child.

She'd brought a picnic – strictly vegetarian in deference to Alice, with lots of chocolate fudge brownies for Lucy. The girls ate quickly, then rushed down to the sea. Lucy jumped around shrieking, her bright hair blowing everywhere: Alice paddled more contempla-tively, her jeans rolled up, caught between pleasure in the movement of the waves and the need to project an almost-teenage cool, posing a bit, turning so her face would catch the sun. I went to join them but the pebbles were too painful: they don't hurt children nearly as much, I guess they can step quite lightly on top, they don't sink in like we do. So I gave up trying to paddle and sat on the beach with Jude.

'Perhaps I should top up my tan,' she said: she loves sunbathing, seems oblivious to the health warnings. She pulled off her sweater to reveal a micro T-shirt. But really it was too cold.

I folded my arms on my bunched-up knees, rested my head on my forearms, closed my eyes. The salt gets into everything, your hair, skin, fingernails: everything smells, tastes of it. I remembered how, as a child, I'd liked the subtle secret tastes of my body – knuckles, knees, the insides of my elbows. The sea was very noisy, the waves crashing down, the undertow hissing on the shingle. It was soothing in a way, there on the white beach, with the girls playing happily and Jude sitting beside me, not saying much, and the pounding of the surf that filled up my head, didn't leave room for anything else.

'This was such a nice idea,' I said. 'Thank you.'

'I just wanted you to have a good day,' she said.

Eventually we called the girls in – they were getting too cold, I thought – but Lucy didn't want to leave, she wanted to sit on the beach and dig with her fingers in the shingle, seeking out perfect pebbles – the white ones she likes best, scoured and cleaned by the tides, with a faint texture of salt on them, drying your fingers. She kept finding stones that she simply had to keep, till my pockets were bulging and heavy, weighing me down.

We wandered along the front, past the ice-cream and popcorn stalls and the little shops selling rather lovely things made from beachcombings – driftwood pictures, suncatchers made from fragments of coloured glass – and I bought the girls some candy pebbles.

Lucy needed to go to the loo. I went in reluctantly: it was cavernous and sour-smelling. Alice couldn't face it and waited outside with Jude. As we washed our hands in the little dribble of water, a girl came out of one of the cubicles with a dog on a piece of string and tied the dog to a waterpipe. She was maybe sixteen, her long hair matted, with cheap plimsolls and a grubby, old-fashioned coat like old women sometimes wear that had obviously come from a charity shop. She tried to drink from the tap, put her head right into the basin but still couldn't quite get her mouth to the water, so she picked up a Coke can someone had left there, held it under the tap to fill it, drank from it, taking big, grateful gulps. Lucy watched fascinated. The girl untied the dog, spoke to it. The dog lurched off, stopped suddenly to sniff at something: the girl stood quietly, the leash slack in her hand, waiting.

'Mummy.' Lucy tugged at me. I bent down. 'Look,' she hissed in my ear. 'She's waiting for him. She must really love him. Some people just pull them along. She must love that dog a lot.' I was still so over-emotional: my eyes filled with tears.

There are always lots of fortune tellers along the seafront. Jude and I lingered in front of one of their stalls. It had a bead curtain across the doorway, a painted notice in extravagant red lettering: 'Consult Madame Suzanna about Any Problem you may have'.

We looked at one another, laughed a bit.

'I've got a problem,' I said.

There was a long list of endorsements. 'She read my past as though she had lived it with me . . . Her palm reading is better than all the pills in the world . . .' I felt an absolute longing to do it, felt for a brief, crazy moment that all the answers were waiting behind that bead curtain.

'Hell, you've nothing to lose,' said Jude.

'She might see an awful illness: cancer cells or something.'

149

'They don't tell you the bad stuff,' said Jude.

'How do you know?' I said.

She smiled rather furtively. 'It was when it was all going wrong with that bastard Gregory Rosen,' she said.

'I'd hate Alice to find out,' I said. 'She's far too superstitious as it is.'

'I'll get them out of your hair,' said Jude. 'There's a café I know in the Lanes, opposite Jaeger. We'll meet there.'

I regretted it almost immediately. It was a dark little room, lit by dim light bulbs that strove to be atmospheric, smelling of joss sticks and noisy with unremitting metallic music from the roundabout just outside on the beach. The psychic looked like a rather downmarket hairdresser – big bleached hairdo, too much makeup, predictable dangly earrings. I handed over my ten pound note and wondered why I was there. She gave me a Tarot pack, asked me to shuffle it: I said I wasn't any good at shuffling cards, and she said how we limit ourselves by thinking we can't do things – like in those books that Jude's always reading, how you can get a great sex life and a house with a jacuzzi by thinking the right thoughts.

She took the pack, dealt the cards out on the table. The symbols of the Tarot are so rich, so resonant, they seem to promise a kind of truth: I felt a shiver of anticipation, between fascination and fear. But when she started to talk it was all vague platitudes, as predictable as a taxi-driver railing against the impotence of the criminal justice system. She said I'd been hurt. Well, you could say that to anyone. She said that I had challenges to face, but I might find help in unexpected places. 'You worry, darling,' she said. 'You're a terrible worrier. You think you can change things by worrying about them.' This was accurate enough – but not so very impressive, given that my nails were gnawed to the quick.

I felt oppressed, claustrophobic, itching to be out in the clean sea air again. I realised I'd gone there with a sudden naive faith or hope that she'd give me the answers, tell me what I needed to know, and of course she couldn't. I started to think of all the nice things I could have bought with ten pounds: a bottle of whisky, a small but luscious gardenia.

She looked at my palm, said I'd have a long life, that I wouldn't end my days alone. I picked up my bag, ready to go.

But suddenly she looked rather sharply across at me. 'There's something else, isn't there, my darling?' she said. 'But I feel it's a delicate matter.'

It was the phrase that Vicky Griggs had used in that very first phone call to Dan. All the little hairs on my arms and legs went suddenly stiff.

'You're going to have to be very brave,' she said.

I'd come to hear something specific, something about Dan and me – but now it was happening I didn't want to know. I got up quickly and went.

I climbed the steps to the promenade and crossed the road and wound my way down through the Lanes. There were lots of food smells, grilling meat, garlic dressing, slightly nauseating after the freshness of the beach. A fat man sitting on a wall tried to sell me his poems. There were buskers and performance artists. Outside Next a man was being a statue. He was dressed in a toga and sitting on a stool and all covered in white paint or powder, the pupils of his eyes exotically dark against the white, like glossy black grapes. People gathered round, hushed, staring. It seemed vaguely perverse, such elaborate self-discipline just to suggest life's absence, to make flesh look like stone.

I had a kind of grubby feeling about the fortune-teller: embarrassed, a little ashamed. Yet, given the unnerving precision of her final words to me, I couldn't entirely dismiss the things she'd told me. I thought about what she'd said, how I had to be brave. And I thought how I didn't really know what courage was – not for me now anyway. Perhaps it meant to cut loose, to put the past behind me – to come and live here with my daughters in a thin terraced house pale as wildflowers, to sit on a balcony with a wide view of the water, to wear a skirt made from bright scraps of patchwork and tie up my hair with string and wake to the sound of the sea. To cut off the past completely, to make a new future: self-contained, inviolate. Yet the fantasy seemed rather bleak and lonely somehow, for all it was so pretty.

I found the café, bought a cappuccino, sat at a table on the pavement. The girls soon came rushing up, pink and excited, clutching at me, followed by Jude, who was turning heads in her leather trousers.

151

'Look, look, Mummy!'

Jude had bought them presents: Alice had a turquoise T-shirt that said 'Shopaholic', and Lucy a little marionette, an indeterminate creature made of wooden balls joined by bits of red wool.

'I hope you won't have trouble with the puppet,' said Jude. 'Tangled strings can be hell. But it was that or the mutant finger ball, and I thought the puppet was more kind of human.'

'You're very lucky girls,' I said. 'I hope you've thanked Jude nicely.'

'Really, Mum,' hissed Alice. 'You are *so* embarrassing.'

They pulled up chairs. Lucy crashed into my lap, cradling her puppet like a baby. I breathed in the saltiness of her hair.

Alice nudged Jude. 'Tell her,' she said.

'Oh, and Alice wants her belly button pierced,' said Jude. 'She found a sleazy place that does it cheap. It's okay, don't freak,' she added, seeing my expression. 'I told her that if she ever had it done it would be in the beauty salon at Debenhams and in the presence of several high-ranking members of the St John's ambulance service. I hope that was right.'

'Absolutely,' I said.

Alice shrugged, resigned.

'What did you get, Mummy?' said Lucy.

'I didn't get anything exactly,' I said. 'I just had a look around. I saw a statue man. You can go and look if you like. Just don't get lost,' I added, never able to resist giving pointless good advice.

They went off, clutching their presents, holding hands.

'You've been very sweet to them,' I said.

'They're so lovely,' said Jude. 'I envy you, you know. I really get an ache for a baby sometimes.'

'I didn't know,' I said.

'I get this dream that I've actually had a baby and I've lost it, left it somewhere,' she said. 'Last time, it was on a shelf in Waitrose with the strawberry jam. D'you think it might have meant the placenta? You know, the strawberry jam?'

'For God's sake,' I said, 'why don't you just go ahead and have one?'

'Oh, I don't know. I'm not sure I'm really strong enough to bring up a child on my own. I'm not like you,' she said.

'It doesn't feel strong, being me,' I said.

She put her hand on my arm. 'I'll get you another coffee,' she said. 'And a cake. You definitely need a cake.'

I sat at the table, watched the people go past. I usually love this place, the colour, the gentle craziness. But today I felt irritated and overwhelmed by it all – the smells of frying, the raucous music, the pigeons that fluttered in too close, all pink claws, hard greedy beaks.

She brought me a huge wedge of chocolate gateau. 'Just what the doctor ordered,' she said. 'Chocolate's got magnesium in. Good for PMT and losses in love.'

'I believe you,' I said.

'So what was she like, this psychic?'

I told her. And then, deciding I'd be brave, as the fortune teller had urged me to be, I said, 'I was so angry with you, you know. When I told you about it first, and you were sure he'd done it.'

'I know,' she said.

We sipped our coffee. A little froth clung to her lip.

'Has he tried to speak to you?' she said.

'Yes,' I said. 'I put the phone down.'

She put her hand on mine. 'I really admire you,' she said, 'just walking away like this. You're a survivor, Chloe.'

I shrugged. I've never much liked that word 'survivor'. It limits you somehow. A survivor is a scrubby plant that clings to a bare hillside, that puts down thin roots into the stony earth, sprouts just a few pale leaves. No fruit, no blossom.

'So he's gone to Felix Floyd?'

I nodded.

'I could never stand Felix.'

'No. You said.'

'There was a rumour he kept a piranha in his office,' she said.

'Actually it was a Siamese Swordfish,' I said. 'It was so fierce it had to have its own tank.'

'Typical,' she said. 'I've always thought he's a bit of a psychopath. Not that he goes round flaying virgins exactly, just that he lives by a different set of rules from the rest of us. He looks so innocent with those baby-blue eyes of his, but really . . . I have to say,' she added, 'your affair with Felix was one of life's great mysteries.'

'I guess I was feeling vulnerable after Adam walked out,' I said, falling back on cliché.

'Sure. Anyone would. But I can't help finding him a sleaze. I've sometimes wondered if he's bi.'

'He seemed thoroughly heterosexual to me,' I said.

'Well, maybe it's something deeper than sex. A kind of ambiguity. But then perhaps you need to be weird to be a good solicitor,' she said. 'And Felix is good, you can't deny that. He usually gets what he wants.'

'Yes,' I said.

She put down her coffee cup with an emphatic click, looked across at me, an earnest searching look.

'Felix could get Dan off,' she said.

I felt accused by this – as though I'd been somehow colluding in Dan's guilt by sending him to Felix. 'That's up to him,' I said.

'I wonder what Felix thinks of him,' she said.

The palms of my hands felt suddenly wet. 'I'd give anything to know what Felix knows,' I said. 'What the evidence is – what this child is saying Dan's done.' I heard how my voice came suddenly to life, animated, emphatic. Embarrassed, I fiddled with my cake.

Jude put her hand on my arm, her face creased, the little lines beside her mouth deepening.

'You've walked away,' she said. 'I'm sure that's right, that's got to be right. You've just got to keep on walking.'

I turned away from her a little, disconcerted by the intensity of her gaze, looked past her to the next table. A man and a girl were sitting there, the girl pretty in a careless, unglossy kind of way – full lips, uncombed Rapunzel hair – the man very young, a bit spotty, with an unlit cigarette hanging from his lips. They sat there quite still and stared at one another, just staring into each other's eyes, not saying anything: it was like their eyes were locked together, that they couldn't pull apart even if they'd wanted to. Then she picked up her lighter from the table and lit his cigarette, never taking her eyes from his. It was like a caress, the way she did it – the flick of her wrist, the sudden flare reflecting in her dilated pupils, the assurance with which her hand moved to his mouth.

Jude was talking again.

'Of course, Dan's finished anyway,' she said. 'Even if he does get off, they're never going to give him back his job. I mean, who would employ him now?'

We could see the girls approaching, holding hands, crossing the road, which had very little traffic, with pantomimic care because they knew I was watching.

'Chloe,' said Jude hurriedly, 'have you told them you're not seeing Dan any more? I need to know what to say.'

'Not exactly,' I said.

I saw Jude's concerned face, the sharp lines of her frown.

The girls came up to the table, Lucy's eyes very wide.

'Did you see the statue man?' I said.

Lucy nodded. She grabbed my arm and wrapped it round her. 'If I was four I would be frightened,' she said.

I bought them drinks and cakes. They were both very taken with a blackboard that listed the café's attractions: Gourmet Sandwiches, Grilled Ciabatta, Friendly Staff. Alice said she'd like some friendly staff on toast and they both found this very funny and laughed so much that all the pigeons on the ground around us took off in a flurry and scatter of grey feathers: while I glanced past them, watched as the man and the girl got up and wandered off, curving into one another, his hand on her hipbone, the fingers splayed possessively, rucking up the thin fabric of her frock, so you felt like a voyeur just watching.

Lucy wanted another paddle, so we went briefly back to the beach. It was after five and getting colder. The sea was already darkening, the horizon a deep blue line drawn with dazzling exactness. Brighton always makes me feel sad in the evening, when all the poor lost kids come out like moths as the shadows lengthen and sit on the beach, and too many of them look like they live in bleak boarding-houses and drink from other people's discarded Coke cans, for all the casual glamour of their rainbow hair and piercings. I wanted to go home.

I told Lucy it was time to leave. She came reluctantly. She was plainly tired out by the wind and the sun and all the new things she'd seen: she seemed fractious and easily upset. Her clothes irritated her, sticking to her damp skin: the stones that had been getting in her shoes all afternoon were suddenly intolerable. As we went back to the car she hung heavily on my hand, weighing me down like the dozens of special pebbles she'd crammed into my pockets.

I gave the girls crisps and Jude put on Alice's favourite tape and we headed off, past the tatty terraced houses that glimmered pale in the dusk, out into the darkening countryside, where the ploughed fields were turning the precise blue-purple of lavender flowers as the sun set.

Lucy took out her puppet and started to play.

'Mummy, he's got his legs crossed,' she said, almost immediately. 'Sort him out.'

I tried but I couldn't. I kept thinking I saw the solution but every move I made just seemed to pull the knot tighter.

'Shit,' muttered Jude. 'I should have seen this coming.'

Lucy was impatient. 'Mummy, you've got to do it,' she said, her voice sharp, brittle, threatening to break.

'I don't think I can,' I said. 'Maybe when we get home, when the light's better . . .'

The puppet was now in a complete tangle. I turned to her. Her face was set, fierce.

'Dan could do it,' she said suddenly. 'Dan's good at things. Why didn't Dan come, Mummy? You should have brought Dan.'

Jude took a hand off the steering-wheel, patted my arm. I said nothing.

'Mummy, why aren't you talking to me?' said Lucy.

But I didn't know what to say.

'Say something, Mummy. *Say something.*'

When I didn't, she started crying, hot angry tired tears.

'No one notices me,' she said through the sobs. 'No one cares about me. Dan listens to me. I want Dan.'

Her sobs got louder.

'Oh shut up, Lucy,' said Alice. 'Stop being such a baby. I can't hear the track.'

Lucy licked her hand lavishly and, just as I turned but too quick for me to stop her, smeared saliva on Alice's sleeve.

'You little bitch,' said Alice, and hit her. Not hard, just to let her know she'd gone too far.

But Lucy was outraged, started wailing, huge wails of absolute fury.

'Oh God,' I said to Jude. 'I'm sorry.'

'Don't be,' said Jude, turning the tape up a little. 'She's just tired. She'll crash out in a minute.'

It didn't take long. She stopped with absolute precision in mid-wail and slumped to the side, deeply sweetly asleep. Jude grinned at me.

We drove on quietly, listening to Alice's music. After a while, I turned, checking on Lucy over my shoulder. She was slumped right over, the seat belt pulled taut against her throat, her face hot and shiny, her fringe plastered wetly to her forehead where she was sweating from pressing against the child-seat. I never like it when the belt catches across her neck like that. She seemed so still: in the dim light I couldn't see for sure if she was breathing. A little impulse of fear shivered down my spine. I reached a hand awkwardly back, touched the nearest part of her, a bit of warm leg: she stirred, sighed a little, swung over so her head was resting back against the seat, still sleeping.

'Really, Mum,' said Alice. 'You don't need to worry. She's still alive, worse luck.' She chewed on her candy pebbles contentedly.

But that moment of fear had triggered something in me, and all the time we drove on through the lavender dusk towards London, I couldn't stop feeling afraid.

18

We walked home down the back of the hospital, where the pavement was littered with yellow leaves and a few fallen plums from a tree in the hospital grounds: the plums had left black tarry smudges where they'd been trampled, with here and there a luscious lick of rich golden flesh. Lucy was sucking a lollipop, red and shiny as lip gloss: a little boy in her class had handed them out to celebrate his birthday.

'There's a policewoman who wants to talk to you,' I said. 'Her name's Vicky and she seems very nice.'

Lucy's eyes opened wide. She took the lollipop out of her mouth. 'They don't send children to prison, Mummy,' she said. 'Not ever ever.'

'No, of course they don't,' I said.

'Not even if they do really really bad things,' she said.

'Of course not,' I said.

I'd been mulling this conversation over in my head since nine o'clock that morning, when Vicky had rung to fix the interviews with the girls. I simply hadn't known how much to tell them. But now, walking home from school through the clear bright afternoon, it didn't seem so difficult. Lucy accepted my reassurance, didn't ask any more questions. In fact she was far more interested in some balloons that were hanging from the door of the children's unit at the hospital. We decided that there too it must be someone's birthday. Intrigued by this synchronicity of birthdays, she forgot about the policewoman. A faint smell of cooking hung around on the pavement outside the unit, the musty mince-and-cabbage smell of institutional cooking everywhere. The sky was dazzling and it was very cold.

When we got back to the house, I went to fetch her comforter, which normally she grabs the minute she's home.

'You can have this with you,' I said. 'Vicky won't mind.'

She was appalled. 'No I can't,' she said. 'She'll think it's baby-ish.'

She hid the comforter under one of the sofa cushions, tucking it in neatly so no one would guess it was there. I put on the television and she curled up in front of it, her eyes glazed, unblinking, her breathing slow. She kept putting her thumb in her mouth, then taking it out: it obviously wasn't quite satisfactory.

Alice was home on time, her coat unzipped in spite of the weather, in a little act of defiance against the adult world and its platitudes and precautions. None of the girls at her school ever do up their coats.

'Alice,' I said, 'Detective Sergeant Griggs is coming today, like we said she would. She wants to talk to both of you.'

'Oh,' she said. She shrugged a little, very matter-of-fact. 'I suppose it's about that sex abuse thingy.'

'Yes,' I said.

I'd been puzzling all day over whether I should talk to her about the photograph. I knew Vicky might well tell her, might want to know if she'd heard anything, seen anything, and the thought appalled me. It would surely be easier for her to hear about it from me. But if I was going to do it, I had to do it now.

She pre-empted me.

'God, when will she be here, Mum?' she said, raising her eyebrows in camped-up drama-lesson alarm.

'Any minute,' I said.

'Well, I'm not going to see her wearing all this skanky stuff,' she said, gesturing at her school clothes. 'No way.'

She rushed upstairs and I didn't call her back: I let the decision be made for me.

'Be quick then,' I called.

She was still in her bedroom when the doorbell rang.

This time Vicky had a social worker with her, Bernadette O'Connor from the duty team. She was a pleasant woman, younger than me but experienced, with bad skin and a beguiling Irish accent.

'Hi, Chloe,' said Bernadette. 'This feels kind of weird.'

'Yes,' I said. It helped, her saying that.

'Chloe'll be getting really fed up with me soon,' said Vicky cheerfully. 'I seem to be a bit of a fixture round here.'

I laughed politely. Through the closed door of the sitting room we could hear Lucy's television programme, a lively young presenter saying something, then a youth jazz band bursting into 'The Way You Look Tonight', gorgeously ebullient and a tiny bit out of tune. I offered them coffee.

'Let's have it after we've had our little chat,' said Vicky, smiling, with that air of eminent reasonableness she's good at. 'We'd like to see them one at a time, without you. Would that be okay?'

I was getting used to these questions which give you only a semblance of choice. I knew 'Would that be okay' was just for politeness, a concession perhaps to the protest I'd made before about the girls being interviewed.

I nodded.

'You know what we do,' she said. 'I don't have to tell you, I'm sure. We'll talk about places children don't like to be touched and people who make you promise not to tell and good secrets and bad secrets.'

'Yes,' I said.

Then, almost as an afterthought. 'Oh – and I'd better get this straight,' she said. 'Are you seeing him at all?'

'No,' I said. 'It's over.'

'Good,' she said. 'That's good. So the girls know that? You'll have told them that?'

'Sort of,' I said. 'I mean, not quite in so many words.'

'But they do know?'

I thought of Lucy sobbing on the way back from Brighton, wanting Dan. 'I guess so,' I said.

'Good. Okay. I just wanted to get it clear,' she said.

I had a sudden uneasy feeling that it wasn't clear at all. I wanted to pause for a moment, to rewind, to sort it all out. But she was a very definite person, and you tended to move at her pace, to do what she said.

Alice came down, in jeans and Reeboks and her new 'Shopaholic' T-shirt. I showed them into the study. They shut the door.

I went to the kitchen. I thought I'd make something special for supper, something warm and filling: toad in the hole perhaps, it seemed just what was needed, with lots of nutritious milk and eggs and that cosy nursery name. The sort of meal good mothers cook

– the mothers who make fairy cakes sprinkled with hundreds and thousands for the PTA cake sale and sew elaborate angel outfits stuck with sequins and bits of tinfoil for the school Nativity play. Mothers who'd never let their kids go to bed without brushing their teeth, or get them to clean their rooms with bribes of peppermint Aero.

I'd left the kitchen door open – I could see through to the shut door of the study as I stood there and mixed the batter. There was something about that door that made me feel so guilty: my daughter in there without me, so young, so fragile, being quizzed about things that even adults will flinch from. And it was because of my failure that it had come to this, I thought, as I beat at the mixture, beat at it with more than usual ferocity, so it slipped off the spoon in fat glossy dollops: I wished I could go back and do it all again, could find a way to protect her and keep her safe. If I stood very still and concentrated I could just hear the drone of voices, but I couldn't make out the words. I felt a brief crazy urge to slip off my shoes and creep up to the door, to skulk in the corner behind the velvet curtain, to put my ear to the hinge of the door and peep in at the keyhole.

But it was all over very quickly. The door opened and Alice came out.

'Was it all right?' I said.

She shrugged, didn't say anything.

I went to fetch Lucy – who came along happily, rather dignified and self-important. She sat down neatly between Vicky and Bernadette, her hands folded decorously in her lap.

Alice was waiting for me in the kitchen. She was chewing the ends of her fingers, something I hadn't seen her do for months. I was suddenly afraid: they must have told her about the photograph. I put my arm round her. She stiffened, withdrew a little.

'Alice, what on earth's the matter?' I said.

'I didn't tell them about that man at the after school club,' she said. 'I was going to – but there wasn't a chance. D'you think I should have done?'

'No, sweetheart. That wasn't what they came about.'

'But that's what they do, isn't it? Catch perverts? I mean, he might hurt a child – and it would be my fault.'

It was like she felt all guilty and in the wrong. The police often have this effect on people, I guess. They only have to get out their little notepads and you find yourself suddenly recalling all the yellow lines you've parked on, the speeding restrictions you've exceeded, the discreet acts of indecency you've committed in public places.

'Alice, that's not for you to deal with,' I said. 'You told me – that's what matters. Whatever he did could never ever be your fault.'

'I wasn't quite brave enough, really,' she said. 'It felt too difficult.'

'You mustn't worry,' I said. 'I'll think about what to do.'

'Please remember. You will, won't you, Mum? Sometimes you say you're going to do things and then you don't,' she said.

She went off to her room to do some drawings of volcanoes.

I went outside to get the herbs for the gravy. A squirrel rattled along the fence behind my overgrown border: the sudden loud sound in that quiet place made me jump and let out a brief undignified scream. There was a wonderful wintry sky, huge and wide and clear, all in that Disney-princess peachy-pink colour that presages frosty weather. Everything was black against the brightness – the birds, the branches of the trees, the steep roof of my new shed, the gable end of Dorothy's extension.

I went over to the herb patch, where there was a faint lingering acrid smell of cat piss. It's the time of year when you recognize that everything has its limits, that some of the things you'd hoped for will never happen: that the Indian Shot you grew so lovingly from seed will never flower, and the grapes on your vine will never swell and sweeten, though you put the pot in the sunniest place on the patio: that the only fruit you'll get from your mulberry tree is that single perfect berry you ate so unthinkingly in August, with its tiny crunch of seeds, its slick of richness like Burgundy on your tongue, and even the roses that looked like they'd last for ever will soon be over. I looked round my garden, noting all these little losses and disappointments. Rooks circled slowly in the pink sky and my clothes felt far too thin.

Soon it would get really cold, I thought, and as usual I wasn't properly prepared. This happens every year. Winter kicks in: the first frosts come, whitening our breath, glazing over the puddles on the patio, and I find I haven't got any woolly tights for the girls or their last year's gloves have holes in the fingertips or I've forgotten that their thermal vests got tumble-dried by mistake and have shrunk to the size of dolls' clothes. Sometimes I worry that I don't quite look after them properly – at least on the material level. We talk and hug and read stories a lot – but I'm not very good at sewing back buttons or rationing Mars Bars or getting them all the right gear.

I picked some sage, routinely crushing a leaf between my fingers to release its smoky scent, went back into the warmth.

I'd only just got the toad into the oven when the study door opened and Vicky and Bernadette came cheerily into the kitchen.

'Okay. All over,' said Vicky, smiling brightly, like a dentist who's just performed a rather tricky extraction.

Lucy was in the hall.

'There, that was all right, wasn't it?' I said to her. Silence. No smile. I stepped towards her but she ignored me, turned, went into the living room. When she came back she had her comforter clasped to her face. She went slowly upstairs, pressing the ribbon edging of it against her nose and mouth, which meant she had to walk slowly, both feet together on each step like someone carrying a coffin. You couldn't see her expression, her mouth was hidden in the folds of the cardigan. I longed to follow her, but knew I couldn't for now.

'They're lovely kids,' said Bernadette. 'So articulate.'

She and Vicky sat down and I made them coffee.

'So was there anything?' I said.

Vicky smiled. 'I think Lucy was a teeny bit disappointed I wasn't in uniform,' she said. 'She might have liked me to come with some CS gas and perhaps an extendible baton.'

'They see it all on *The Bill* of course,' I said.

'Like in court,' said Bernadette. 'Everyone worries about being too formal and intimidating kids – but the kids have seen the telly and expect the judge to have his wig on.'

We nodded, smiled, sipped our coffee – professionals together, sharing the things we all knew.

But then Vicky pushed away her mug and put her hands together, the fingertips touching like somebody praying. I'd learnt to dread that gesture, I knew it meant business. 'There *was* one thing we wondered about,' she said. 'Lucy does seem terribly attached to Dan. Perhaps a little unusually so.'

'She's a very affectionate child,' I said.

'Sure,' said Vicky. 'I was just wondering if you thought he worked a little too hard to make her like him – if you were aware of that?'

'Not really,' I said.

'You know these men will do that,' she said. 'They'll groom a child they want – sometimes for years.'

Of course I knew. The policeman who'd come with Vicky that first time had said it, the books said it, Jude had said it, everyone said it: I just wished they wouldn't all keep repeating it, because I couldn't bear it.

'That was all, though,' said Vicky soothingly, responding to the distress that must have shown in my face. 'Really, you mustn't worry. I don't think there's anything to fret about with those two at the moment.' I didn't like the way she phrased it – the implication that in the future there might be something to fret about. 'But maybe it's as well we caught up with Daniel Whitmore when we did,' she added briskly.

There was a little pause. No one knew what to say.

Bernadette finished her coffee, picked up her bag. 'You're in Nat Williams's team, aren't you?' she said.

'Yes,' I said.

'He's nice, Nat,' she said. 'I was on placement with him on my course.' I knew it was quite deliberate, this social work small talk. She wanted to give me my status back, make me a proper person again, not just the mother of children who might have been abused. I was intensely grateful.

Vicky got up, stood for a moment in front of the window, the angle at the bottom of her haircut black and sharp against the wide pink sky. 'Chloe, I did just want to say – you do need to be very clear with them about what's happened. I know it's not always easy.'

I wasn't quite sure what she meant, but I nodded anyway.

'Say goodbye to the girls for us,' added Bernadette. She touched my arm. 'I hope it all turns out okay.'

They went.

I wondered what had happened to Lucy. I called. She didn't answer. I went upstairs to look for her. I glanced briefly in her bedroom, couldn't see her. I went to my own bedroom – she sometimes likes to lie across my bed and look at a book, luxuriating in all the space and the thickness of the duvet. But she wasn't there.

'Lucy,' I called. 'Don't hide. *Please.*'

No answer. Sudden panic chilled me, like a draught of cold air from a door kicked open. Panic like in those dreams all new mothers have when you think you've lost them, like in those appalling moments at Mums and Tots group when they're actually hiding in the Wendy house, like in my nightmare about my baby drowning. It's as though the circuits are there, ready and waiting, we're all wired up, and it takes so little to move the switch across, flip us into hysteria. I saw her going out the front door and straight under a truck, falling from an upstairs window, saw a man with a knife breaking in and abducting her. I shouted again but she didn't come.

I went back to her bedroom, realized then that she'd been there all the time. She was lying right under the duvet, absolutely unmoving so I hadn't seen her: she was still so little then, she'd looked like a hump in the bedding. I folded the duvet back. She was crying silently, her wet comforter clutched to her face.

'Go away,' she said, brittle.

'Lucy.' I sat down beside her. 'Sweetheart, what's happened? Did they frighten you?' I said. 'There's nothing to be frightened of.'

She started to sob. I tried to hug her, she pushed me away. She was very upset, very cross. I was flooded with rage against Vicky and Bernadette – that they'd reduced my child to this. They were meant to be so good with children and they'd made her so miserable. I wanted to annihilate them.

The sobbing gradually quietened, and I tried again.

'What is it, Lucy? Please tell me.'

She stared at me as though she wasn't quite sure who I was, her pupils dilated. 'Dan's not coming back,' she said.

'What did they say?' I said.

'They said Dan's not seeing us ever again,' she said. 'I hate you, Mummy. You're so selfish. You never think of anyone else but *you*. He was my friend too.' Her face collapsed and she started sobbing again.

I didn't know how to handle this – felt helpless, feeble, stupid, just knew I couldn't stay there to be accused by my child.

I got up. 'I'm going now,' I said. 'Come downstairs when you're feeling better and we'll have a big hug and make up.'

There was a smell of burning from the oven. The toad was black round the edges but mysteriously still slightly runny in the middle. I put out some for Alice and some for me.

'I'm not going to eat the pig bits,' said Alice, and lined all the sausages up round the edge of her plate.

'Alice, for goodness sake,' I said, 'you've got to have some protein, you can't live on batter and peas.'

'I'll have two chocolate mousses then,' she said.

'That's like eating nuclear waste,' I said. 'Those things aren't proper food.'

'Yes they are.' She got one from the fridge, thrust the list of ingredients in my face. 'Look, it's got skimmed milk in.'

She peeled off the top. There was a strong synthetic smell.

'I can't imagine why you like them anyway,' I said.

'I don't know why,' she said. 'Why do people always ask the reason for things? Sometimes things don't have a reason.'

Lucy came down eventually, white and poised and fragile with great big pupils, her lashes clotted with tears.

'Lucy,' I said carefully: I'd rehearsed in my head how to put it. 'I should have told you before: I'm sorry. But Dan's in trouble and the police think he's done something bad. And I'm afraid we can't see Dan while this is happening.'

'Why not?' said Lucy.

'We can't. We're meant not to.'

I knew I was being evasive – not making it clear that this was *my* choice, *my* decision. Afraid of my five-year-old's disapproval.

She still minded, but she didn't want to go on being cross with me. She sat on my lap and we had a qualified making-up. She said she wasn't feeling hungry but was persuaded to eat four sausages from which all traces of batter had been fastidiously removed.

Dan rang again that night, before the girls had gone to bed.

'Chloe,' he said, 'please don't put the phone down. I only want to talk – that's all I'm asking.'

'Dan, I really don't think I can talk to you,' I said.

But I just went on standing there with the phone in my hand, as though my arm wouldn't move, part of me wanting to hold him there, to listen to his voice for a minute more. He knew my hesitation, of course, even over the phone.

'I want to tell you what's happening,' he said. Careful, even-toned, as you talk to a skittish animal you don't want to frighten off. 'The police are trying to interview all the children I've seen over the past year. Imagine. Then they'll interview me. Felix reckons the end of October or so.'

'Yes,' I said.

'We still don't know what the allegation is exactly,' he said. 'Felix has found out that it's about some sort of touching.'

'Yes,' I said.

'But he doesn't know the details. I can't bear it, this not knowing.'

'No,' I said.

'Can I see you?' he said then. 'It could be anywhere you like. I mean, just for half-an-hour if you'd rather. Whatever you want.'

I was acutely aware of all the notes in his voice, the uncertainty in the upward intonation, the trace of Manchester that came through as he tried so hard not to plead. Just for a second or two I stood there, gripping the phone so hard it hurt, poised between yes and no. But I knew I had to be absolutely firm, absolutely clear. For myself, for my children.

'It's best just not to see you at all,' I said. I'd wanted to sound so strong and decisive, but my voice came out all wrong: it sounded pathetic, plaintive, almost a question, almost a whine, like a child. 'I'm sorry, Dan, I'm so sorry.' I put down the phone. My hands were shaking slightly, like after holding something heavy.

Lucy looked at me suspiciously when I went back into the living room, but said nothing.

Later, when I tucked her up for the night, she clung to me. I held her tight: it comforted me a little, the warmth of her body, the nutmeg smell of her hair that hadn't been washed for weeks. Then I found myself thinking how one day she wouldn't want me to do this any more – the fierce hugs, burying my face in her hair – as Alice already didn't much like being touched. The thought made me terribly sad, to the point almost of tears.

'That woman thought I didn't know what a fib was,' she said sleepily, burrowing down under her duvet. 'She said, "If I said there was a parrot sitting on my head, would that be the truth or a fib?" Well really.'

'I think she just needed to make quite sure you knew,' I said. 'I think that's part of her job.'

'I do know what the truth is,' she said. 'Everyone knows what the truth is. Even babies know.'

19

All through October it was like I was living in a police state – frightened by tiny clicks or thuds on the phone line, checking, when I got home at night, that everything was precisely as it had been when I left. I even looked at my mail to make sure it hadn't been tampered with – though I can't quite now recall what I imagined anyone might glean from the kinds of letters I got, the Greenpeace catalogues and Amnesty raffle tickets and extravagant offers from credit card companies. I didn't go as far as the protagonists in the spy stories I read to get me to sleep – the little block of wood wedged under the door – but I have to confess I considered it.

Everything scared me. I'd be startled by a sudden footfall behind me, turn sharply, only to find a perfectly unexceptional person going innocently about their business, yards away, or even just some dry leaves shuffling along the pavement. Once, walking home with Lucy, I heard someone following very close, started, looked round – but it was only Lucy's lunchbox inside her rucksack. The straps of the rucksack were loose, and the lunchbox inside drummed companionably against her back in time to our steps.

'Really, Mummy, you made me *jump*,' she said crossly.

It was almost as though there was some kind of short-circuit in my nervous system, my senses playing tricks on me. As I hurried to school one afternoon, I was shocked by a grey face in a window that seemed to stare malignantly at me – slack-jawed, hollow-cheeked, spectral, not quite human. It was all an illusion, of course, a coming together of images in the darkened pane, the reflections of great dead heads of hydrangeas in an overgrown front garden and a streak of sky white as bone. And once I heard someone calling my name. I was walking along Queen's Road at the time, in the middle of the afternoon, when it's quite trafficky and banal, with a beer lorry pulling into the pub and women with buggies on the pavement – not at all conducive, you'd think, to psychic intimations or anything surreal. The voice called *Chloe Chloe*, perfectly clear – a voice full of pleasure, as someone calls who greets a long-lost friend in an unexpected place. A man's voice, but I couldn't quite place it, though it sounded familiar. And when I turned there was no one there.

I became appallingly superstitious, a process that had begun with the fortune teller in Brighton and threatened to get quite out of control. I read my horoscope in Alice's magazines. I saw significance in everything, in the rainbow fluidities of spilt oil in the gutters, in troubling conjunctions of magpies in my garden, so rarely two for joy. When one morning I woke to find that a lovely old pear tree in Dorothy's flower border had been felled by a wind in the night – it was covered in Russian vine that had caught the wind like a spinnaker and toppled it over – I felt it as a terrible omen of loss or mutilation and my eyes filled with tears.

I'd told Adam all about it of course. I'd rung him up straight away – the day after Vicky had come to see me. I'd hated, absolutely hated, telling him: it felt so shaming somehow. He was pretty appalled to start with, as anyone would be. But when he'd got over his initial shock he was good to me, gentle, comforting. He was always good in a crisis.

I told him everything. I even gave him Vicky's phone number, though I very much hoped he'd never have occasion to use it. But I did beg him not to talk to Alice about the photo. I could see the temptation – to try and find out whether she'd been aware, whether she'd known there'd been someone there behind her – but I was sure for myself that she hadn't had the faintest idea, and I so terribly wanted to protect her from that knowledge, and Adam to my great relief agreed.

But he did quiz the girls about Dan, something a less conscientious parent might well have shirked – it's not easy to do. And when he dropped them off one Sunday night in October, he stayed for a coffee, to talk it through: it was the first time he'd stayed to sit and talk since we'd separated.

'It's not that I doubt you, of course,' he said. 'I'm sure you asked all the right questions. I just wanted to hear it from them for myself.'

'Of course,' I said. I rather wished he would get up and go. It felt weird having him sitting in my kitchen, which had once been his kitchen too. It brought out something very territorial in me.

'And really,' he said, 'I'm sure there's nothing to worry about – they seem quite unscathed, thank God.' He pushed his mug away, leaving half of it undrunk: he'd been put off coffee years before by some research linking it to pancreatic cancer. 'Simone got herself in a bit of a state about it, though,' he said.

'How d'you mean?' I said. 'What kind of state?'

He didn't answer directly.

'She can be a tiny bit paranoid at times,' he said. 'Well, I suppose it's understandable.' He wasn't looking at me. 'She's very fond of the girls, you know. Really, she'd like to see them a bit more often.'

My stomach contracted with a quick judder of anxiety. I could understand her, of course, and this yen she had to play a bigger role in the girls' lives – because that way she'd own Adam rather more completely. It was something I'd seen and feared in her since first they got together.

'Well, we've got our arrangement,' I said, my voice as light and casual as I could make it. 'And it works just fine, don't you think?'

'Sure, it works okay,' he said. He shifted a little, cleared his throat. I wondered what was coming. 'But Simone and I are absolutely agreed that if there was any risk of the girls having even the briefest contact with him . . .' He stopped. The words he hadn't spoken hung there in the space between us.

I lowered my head, fiddled with my cup. I didn't want him to see how very much he'd scared me.

'I'm not going to see him,' I said.

'No,' he said, more gently, almost conciliatory. 'No, of course you're not.' And then, perhaps because he felt rather contrite about being so threatening, 'You are all right, aren't you, Chloe? You're coping okay? You don't look at all well, you know.'

'It's probably just that I haven't put my makeup on,' I said.

'No, really. You're kind of pasty. You've got bags under your eyes.'

'Thanks a lot,' I said. 'That does sound appetizing.'

He stood up, patted my shoulder. He'd started to touch me again: I didn't much like it. 'You ought to get out more,' he said. He sounded like my very first social work senior, long ago now, a woman in her fifties, an old-style hospital almoner, who was fond of prescribing evening classes as the cure for any malaise of body, mind or soul. Abused? Bereaved? Broken-hearted? Take a pottery class. Try tap-dancing for beginners. 'You shouldn't just fester,' he went on. 'Get yourself a babysitter, go out and have some fun. You do brood, Chloe.'

'I'm fine,' I said. 'Really.'

I suspected he was being warmer with me because he was glad my affair with Dan was over. Perhaps there was even a secret triumph in him. I don't mean that as criticism particularly. He's not a bad man – it was scarcely surprising he felt it. Everyone's ambivalent about their ex-partner's love life – deep down, I suspect, you don't really want them to have one: and I guess that's almost as true for the one who did the leaving. Sexual jealousy has such weaselly ways, it sneaks up and insinuates itself into the most inappropriate places. I'm sure if you'd asked Adam directly he'd have said he wanted to see me settled – but I think deep inside he'd have liked it to be with someone safe and unthreatening: not in so overtly sexual a relationship as the one I'd had with Dan.

Jude, like Adam, kept urging me to go out.

'You need to *socialize,* Chloe,' she'd say, her face all creased and concerned.

Sometimes she took me out herself, to our favourite pub, with the candles and the copies of *Vogue.* We'd sit at one of the bleached wood tables drinking lager and she'd entertain me with tales of her current man, an orthodontist called Elliot who expected a full range of sexual services but never took her anywhere remotely glitzy.

'I'm not complaining,' she said. 'I mean, he's a good lover and all that. It's just that sometimes I'd like to go to a really posh bar and him to buy me one of those cocktails with cranberry in. A metropolitan. Like roadrunners.'

'I think you *are* complaining,' I said. 'And why like roadrunners exactly?'

'Before they mate, the male feeds the female a nice little lizard,' she said. 'I read it somewhere. Sometimes I really need a nice little lizard to get me in the mood. I just want him to spend some *money* on me, for God's sake.'

'Really,' I said, rather shocked that she should confess to such retrogressive yearnings. 'Anyone would think that we'd never done all that feminist stuff – you know, swapped vibrators and peed in the gents and worn those great big boots and gone to Greenham.'

'Aren't you getting a bit global about this?' said Jude. 'All I said was that I want this man to take me to a really cool bar and buy me a cocktail. It's not such a lot to ask. I don't see why you have to bring Trident into it.'

'It wasn't Trident.'

'Well, Polaris then. Whatever.'

And always towards the end of the second lager she'd get into advice mode.

'You've got to find someone else, Chloe. Pick someone up. Jump into bed with someone. There's this cute guy I know in Fostering and Adoption. Really rather a hunk. You should go and have a look. It doesn't have to be perfect, it would still really cheer you up. Well, that's what I always find anyway.'

'Whatever happened to the sex addiction programme?'

She shrugged. 'It's possible I didn't have the necessary motivation,' she said.

I spent a lot of time in my garden. It was the only place where I felt any kind of peace. It was all looking quite autumnal now – frailer, less substantial. The leaves of my nasturtiums had been nibbled by caterpillars and were full of holes, as one imagines bones crumbling with osteoporosis, and the trees were thinning out, the briar hedge with just a few dark leaves, so you could see through to the other gardens further down the street, and the branches of my apple all skeletal and delicate, black like finely worked iron against the sky. The only bright things were the autumn cyclamens, tiny sweet flowers in a bed of pebbles in a pot, like little wings, little pink moths poised for flight. After a wind, the lawn would be covered with leaves. The girls loved to sweep them away, rather ineffectually, fighting over the broomstick, to pick them up in their arms – huge rich-smelling heaps of damp chestnut-brown leaves, that fell in clumps, sodden, to the earth: loved to fling them on the compost heap next to the remains of the wood pile. Lucy still talked about the fire I'd made: she hadn't forgiven me yet for that morning when she'd woken to find a ring of ash on the lawn.

'What if there was a hedgehog underneath?' she said. 'You could have roasted it, Mummy. That would have been horrible. The poor little thing, all curled up for winter.'

'There wasn't a hedgehog,' I said. 'I promise.'

I replanted my window boxes. The summer flowers were mostly dead, brown and papery and a bit sticky with some kind of greenfly – I'd tried to keep them going far too long. The old soil was held together by a fine filigree of pale roots. I chucked most of it out: it smelt rich as I disturbed it, felt dry and warm and crumbly against my fingers, but I knew it was all used up now, all its nourishment gone.

I tried to involve Lucy, but she wasn't interested.

'You helped last year,' I said.

She shrugged. 'I was four then,' she said.

But she did come to look at the woodlice, scores of them wriggling shrimp-like in the bottom of the trough. She named them after the Animaniacs and poked them upright with a twig when they fell on their backs.

I put gravel and bits of old tile in the bottom of the troughs, filled them up with handfuls of potting compost, arranged the new plants I'd chosen from Homebase. Little pansies, blue and yellow. Pretty but a bit cautious perhaps. Neat obedient plants, each sitting precise and separate in its block of earth, its roots like cotton wool.

Afterwards, I washed my hands under the garden tap. I looked at them carefully, sluicing off all the earth, and saw how they were wrinkled as though soaked in water for too long, how the skin on the backs of my hands was rather loose, the elasticity all gone, how the knuckles crumpled if I straightened my fingers. In the fading late-afternoon light, with the traces of mud that lingered in the creases accentuating the lines in the skin like contour lines on a map, they looked like the hands of an old woman. I felt all creased up and dried out, as though some vital sap had sunk in me.

Sometimes I thought I saw him. It would always be a back view: someone driving round a roundabout, though never in the right car, my fevered imagination defying all logic: someone ahead of me in the queue for a cash machine. It would be something about the casual way the man's suit jacket hung from him, or the precise patterning of the hair in the nape of the neck – and I'd sit or stand there staring at this person, convinced it was him, getting intensely anxious, my eye caught, mesmerized, my pulse quickening. Then the man would turn, and the profile would be totally different of course – it would strike me as ugly, misshapen almost, suggesting a petty, trivial life – and though an instant before I'd been so afraid it was him, now I'd be flooded with disappointment, the colour and music all gone out of the day. And I'd have to go through it all again, remind myself who he was, what he'd done.

But there was nothing sexual in these moments, it was just the intense anxiety followed by the aching emptiness. My sex drive seemed to have gone underground, like the life in the plants in my garden. Nothing could move me, stir me. I had absolutely no interest in other men. I remained quite untouched by the sexiest bits of television, the most lingering kiss in some black and white forties Hollywood drama. I had no interest in what I looked like. I went to buy some new trousers, and tried on two pairs in Jigsaw and they were both quite nice and I simply couldn't see any point in choosing one pair rather than the other – so I left them both and went home again. I moved through my monthly cycle utterly unaware of the peaks and troughs so familiar to me for years, the sudden impulses and sensitivities.

It was only in my dreams that I became in any sense a sexual creature. The dreams I had were rather extraordinary, dreams that were lavishly sexual almost every night. I tried hard to make sense of these dreams, and what I worked out was that my unconscious mind somehow hadn't caught up with what had happened – was still in that sensuous haze, that state of intoxication. That the unconscious is about what you know with your body, perhaps – and what I had learnt about Dan since had all been learnt with the mind, it wasn't that kind of visceral knowing, the learning you do with skin and fingers and tongue – and my unconscious simply hadn't grasped that the sexual connection was now all undone, cancelled out.

They often had rather idyllic rustic settings, these dreams – forests, lakes, meadows – landscapes that were full of obvious, rather crude correspondences, fruiting trees, excessive waterfalls, swollen red flowers with fleshy petals that opened out under rain. And where before, even when my love life had been most vivid and tender, my sexual dreams had been stark, cruel, all about compulsion and control – now, when I had no sex life at all, when the very thought of my

175

lover was linked with the worst kind of corruption, my dreams were full of an almost innocent sexuality, that was all about nakedness, about gently probing touch and the scent and softness of skin. As though in dreams we do, as some analysts have thought, re-balance our waking selves, express something that's hidden or denied.

Sometimes the man, the lover, was nameless in these dreams – but more often he had something of Dan in him – the dark hair falling over the brow, the warmth and weight of him, filling my arms. And I'd wake from these dreams, my body remembering – his fingers investigating and exploring me everywhere, the touch of his penis against my lips, the taste of sex in my mouth – and I'd have to unlearn it all, cancel that knowledge out, push it away. In a way it was like after those dreams I sometimes have of my father alive and sitting at the kitchen table – where, on waking, his absence, the reality, the things that have indisputably happened, seem for a moment so much less real than the dream.

20

One Sunday evening towards the end of October, he rang again.

'Felix has got the disclosure video,' he said.

'Oh,' I said, the longing to know what was in that video surging through me.

'We're going to watch it tomorrow.'

'Right,' I said. I didn't hang up. It was like I'd worked out the parameters, the rules. That I'd let myself talk about certain things – practical stuff, facts and procedures, the progress of the case: but not about us.

But then he said, 'Chloe, when can I see you?' That pleading in his voice that I couldn't bear.

'Dan, how can I see you?' I said. 'Please don't ask me. You know it's not possible.'

'You can't do this, Chloe.' His voice hardening, an edge of anger to it. 'You can't just close the door like this – just end it without saying why.'

'But I told you why,' I said.

'That photograph you were going on about?'

'Yes,' I said.

'How the hell can I defend myself when you won't tell me what's in it? Jesus.' He was shouting now. 'That's what my whole fucking life's been about since all this started. Being accused of things and not being told what I'm accused of. Just that everyone thinks I'm guilty.'

His words pummelled into my head, and I felt it with him – that sense of being entrapped, of not being heard: then thought of the allegation, the powerless little girl. The two things jostling in my mind, thinking them both together.

I tried to speak. He talked over me. 'I tell you, it's like fucking Kafka,' he said. 'I didn't know this stuff could happen. And you doing it too, that's what I can't bear. I mean, we had something good, didn't we?'

There were big lumpy tears in my throat: I swallowed them down.

'Chloe, talk to me, for God's sake,' he said. 'Didn't we?'

'Yes,' I said. 'Yes, we did.'

There was a brief silence between us, tense and somehow shocking, like the moment of absolute quiet that follows a car crash.

'Shit. I'm sorry,' he said. Speaking more softly now, his voice undoing something deep inside me. 'I didn't mean to lose my rag, I was so determined not to.'

I mumbled some stuff about it being okay. And in some weird way meant it: it was almost a relief to have him rage at me. 'You were saying. About the video,' I said, trying to drag the conversation back to something I could cope with. 'You're going to watch it with Felix.'

'Yes. Tomorrow afternoon,' he said. 'They have these special videos that fade after twenty showings, so they can't ever be passed round as porn. Well, you'd know all about that, I guess.'

'Yes,' I said.

'At least we'll find out exactly what Carly is saying,' he said.

Carly. He'd never used her name before, he'd always called her 'the child' or 'the little girl'. Her name resonated in my head, I couldn't get rid of it all evening, it was like a snatch of tune – a jingle from a commercial or a phrase from a children's hymn that nags away at you. I thought, not for the first time, that it was somehow spooky that her name was so like mine.

When I got into work the next morning, Jude rang in to say she was ill – a bad attack of cystitis after an over-vigorous weekend with her orthodontist.

'It's my own damn fault,' she said. 'But there's no way I can come in. I've had tons of bicarb and I'm still crawling up the walls.'

'Oh Jude. How ghastly.'

'I'd go to the doctor, but really what's the point?' she said. Jude doesn't approve of British GPs and their tatty premises and conservative prescribing habits: they're among her favourite gripes about life in London, along with the grittiness of our peanut butter and why the hell do women here do their own ironing instead of sending it to the dry-cleaner's – I mean, is this some kind of Third World country?

'Poor you,' I said. 'I'll tell Nat.'

She had some appointments she needed me to cancel.

In my highly superstitious state of mind, Jude's absence seemed like an omen, a sign that I should act. I looked at my watch. I was due at a case conference at ten: it was just downstairs, in the conference suite. I had almost half an hour, which was masses of time.

We still keep basic client information in a card index system. They're always promising to computerize it, but they never have enough money, so we all spend ages hunting through these dog-eared bits of card. The system is kept in a recess in the secretaries' office.

I went along the corridor to see Maureen, gave her the details of Jude's cancellations. Then I went round the corner to the card index. I felt furtive, almost delinquent, like I was doing something I shouldn't: which was idiotic, because I consult the card index at least once a week. But I wasn't quite sure what I'd say if Maureen came over all friendly and helpful and asked what I was after.

I pulled out the Sc to Sm drawer. My hands felt big and clumsy and not quite under control, like when a fracture's healing, and they cut off your plaster-cast after weeks of forced inertia and finally you can use your fingers again.

There were several Smithsons, two of them – Gavin and Lee – at the same address as Carly. Carly's case had been opened then closed again several years before, and re-opened on 3 September this year, which was six days before the police had gone to see Dan. Somebody had presumably contacted the police and Social Services simultaneously. The card didn't give many details, just addresses and dates and the name of the social worker – Philippa Nicholls. I knew her by sight: she was fresh off a training course and her team worked on the floor below me.

I rang her. She was in.

'Hi. It's Chloe Langdon from the Manor team. Could I come down and see you for a moment?'

'Sure,' she said. 'I've got a foul social inquiry report to do and I'd love to be interrupted.'

'It's about Carly Smithson,' I said.

'Poor little scrap,' she said. 'I'll put the kettle on.'

The stairs smelt of disinfectant and everyone was rushing, as always on Monday mornings. I went slowly down to her room, my hand on the rail because I felt all ungainly and out of proportion, as though I could easily fall. I wondered how on earth I'd explain my interest in the case. Perhaps I could say I was planning some research on child witnesses. Since all this had started happening, my life was so full of lies.

The office was just like ours – the same wilting begonias and grey-green filing cabinets and cheerful coffee cups and air of imminent crisis. She was on the phone when I got there. She smiled at me, made an apologetic gesture with her free hand. I pulled a chair up to her desk.

She was one of those social workers who seek to express their empathy with the children they work with by dressing like the presenters on children's ITV, in stripey jumpers and elephant ear-rings and sweatshirts appliquéd with animals. In Philippa's case, with frogs.

She put down the phone. 'Hi,' she said. 'Call me Flip.'

'Right,' I said, with as much conviction as I could muster.

She made me coffee in a Garfield mug.

There was some literature about a child abuse course on her desk. I picked it up, skimmed through. 'Are you going on this?' I said. Just to make conversation, really.

'You bet. If they'll fund me,' she said. Her voice was even, sibilant, sensible. 'I went on a course those people ran last year. It was brilliant. We heard from abuse survivors, and then we divided into groups, and people started coming out about their own experiences. And there were three women in my group who'd been abused themselves. It was incredible.'

'There's a lot of it about,' I said.

'Telling me,' she said. 'In a way, I suppose, we've all been abused – if you include emotional abuse.'

'If you do, I suppose we have,' I said.

The coffee was milky and very weak.

'Right,' she said, sitting down. 'Carly Smithson. You know about this case then?'

'A bit,' I said. I saw that I needn't have bothered about my cover story: she wasn't going to probe. I was a level 3 worker and she was just off a course and she accepted that I had my reasons.

She had long brown hair. She tucked it crisply behind her ears. 'What can I tell you?' she said.

'About the family,' I said. 'A bit of background. I gather we've had involvement before?'

'Yep – four years ago,' she said. 'There were concerns about one of the older children. Nasty bruising. It was never really established if it was non-accidental. Mum's story didn't fit.'

'So who was suspected?' I said. 'The mother's cohab presumably?'

She nodded. 'He sounds like a nasty piece of work,' she said. 'The feeling was that she'd tried to cover up for him, but no one could ever pin anything on him. But then she kicked him out, and we closed the case.'

'Who's in the family?' I said.

'Three kids – Carly's the youngest. Carly's Dad's out of the picture. Various bits of extended family. It's the kind of house where you visit and there'll always be someone new – some auntie or best mate or rottweiler or something. There's a brother of Mum's who's quite a regular fixture, and a granddad who pops in a lot.'

'This granddad,' I said. 'Tell me about him.'

'He's partially sighted,' she said. 'Diabetic. Nice with the kids, I thought.'

'And the uncle?'

She smiled indulgently. 'A bit of a lad is Darren,' she said. I guessed she rather liked him. 'Big footie fan, lots of girlfriends. He lives just round the corner. Mum seems to depend on him – I don't know where she'd be without him, quite honestly.' She fiddled with her hair, teased a strand out between her fingers, scanning it absent-mindedly for split ends.

'And what do you make of the mother?' I said, very aware how I kept firing questions at her: but she seemed quite happy to demonstrate her knowledge of her case.

'Mum's physical care is good, I'd say. The children and the house are always very clean. Lots of little ornaments. It's incredible how people manage – I mean, I'm sure I couldn't, not on the money she gets.'

I looked away a little, let my eyes rest on the usual office clutter, the pots of pens, the holiday photos, taking refuge in the ordinariness of it all, my hands clenched into fists in the pockets of my jacket. 'And Carly?' I said.

'Terribly anxious and fidgety,' said Philippa. 'She does seem to have taken to me a bit though, which is a big help. I'm dying to start working properly with her – but of course I can't do anything till after the case is heard. It's so frustrating. No one thinks of the child in these cases.'

I nodded, murmured agreement. I wished I could stop feeling so irritated. She was perfectly okay – conscientious and caring and hard-working, and she undoubtedly did a lot of good. I just didn't like her. It was partly that way she had of coming out with ideas that have been around for years as though they were new and stunning insights. To be honest, the sweatshirt didn't help either.

'Who did Carly tell?' I said.

'She told her Mum, and Mum went to the school on the first day of term, and they called in us and the police.'

'And you saw the disclosure?' I said.

'Yeah.'

'D'you believe her?' I said.

'Absolutely,' she said. The smile gone from her face, a little bit shocked that I'd asked. 'And I think she'll come over well in court. Just so long as the defence don't hammer her. These defence lawyers can be absolute bastards – even over the video link. It's like a form of abuse in itself. Well, I don't need to tell you.'

'No,' I said.

I sipped my tasteless coffee. I knew this was the moment. The coffee stuck in my throat like something solid.

'So what's the allegation exactly?' I said, very casual, but my heart beating so hard, I thought she might be able to see it, how it made my rib-cage shake.

'Digital penetration of the vagina,' she said, rather formally. She was still quite new to all this, still a little embarrassed.

'I see,' I said. 'Any physical evidence?'

'Nothing conclusive,' she said. 'She's been examined. The hymen seemed more or less normal. Though there is a bit of redness, and they don't know what to make of it. You can see the report if you like.'

'Thanks,' I said.

She got up and opened her filing cabinet, pulled out Carly's file, flicked through to find the paediatrician's report. She put it down on the desk, turned it so I could see.

I looked down the page. You had to wade through a swamp of double negatives and qualifiers. 'The medical findings do not unequivocally support penetrative sexual abuse . . . The redness might be the result of trauma due to friction . . . It seems unlikely though possible that digital interference would cause the changes seen . . .' Inconclusive as usual: it's rare for medical reports to make things clear.

I took a deep breath, scared that my voice would come out all wrong. 'And does she name him?' I said.

'No,' she said. 'And we didn't want her to have to go through all the trauma of an identity parade. But her description is really quite precise. The police are convinced they've got their man. Though of course these cases can fall apart at any point. It would be heart-breaking.'

I nodded.

'I can't tell you how I feel about that bastard of a psychologist,' she said. 'I mean, he's stolen her childhood from her.'

I made some kind of noncommittal murmur. People always say this and I never quite know what it means. It's a way I suppose of saying that the abuser takes away something profoundly precious that can never be recovered or restored. Which is sometimes true, I think, and sometimes not.

'Actually, as it happens,' she said, 'I've met Daniel Whitmore. At a party, three years ago, before I went on my course. It's rather a weird coincidence, isn't it?'

'I suppose it is,' I said.

'And I have to say,' she went on, 'there *is* something kind of shifty about him. You know how you just get that feeling about somebody? Something about the eyes. He was trying to chat up this friend of mine. Well, Francine's rather gorgeous, it happens a lot.'

I felt a ludicrous little surge of jealousy towards this unknown woman who'd caught Dan's eye.

'She was having none of it, mind,' Philippa went on. 'But it was all rather kind of sexual.'

'Well, chatting up usually is, I guess,' I said. 'You know, kind of sexual.'

She looked at me uneasily, as though not clear if I was taking the piss or not. 'Have you ever met him?' she said.

'I was going out with him,' I said.

It was a cruel thing to do and I immediately regretted it.

She was totally thrown. She went red all over her face and right down her neck.

'Oh my God,' she said.

I put my hand on her arm. 'I'm so sorry,' I said. 'I should have told you before, I've behaved very badly.'

'No, not at all,' she said, stammering a little in her confusion. 'No, I can see it would be difficult to admit to. It's just – well, it kind of makes it all look different, doesn't it? God, I feel dreadful.'

'Please don't,' I said. 'You mustn't, really. It's all my fault. I should have said.'

I patted her arm, said I hadn't told her because I'd wanted her impartial professional opinion, tried to smooth it over, to make it alright. But she was still hotly red when I left. I felt horribly guilty. I realized I'd almost enjoyed having such power to disconcert her, and I hated myself for it. She was new and keen and trying to do her best and she didn't deserve it. She hadn't had a chance with me, really. I'd been angry with her even before I met her.

On my way back to the office, I went to the card index and looked up Carly's address again. 34B Tonbridge Gardens. I'm bad at remembering numbers. I started to copy the address down in my diary, then realized this was probably a very bad idea, so I turned the 3 in my diary into a doodle and wrote the address on a scrap of paper and put it in my pocket.

I had a visit to do that afternoon, to a girl who was due in court on Thursday. Holly Burt, a friendly chatty fifteen-year-old who'd taken part in a nasty robbery in which a younger girl had been tied up with wire. It was only going to be a brief visit: Holly was evasive and unreliable, and I wanted to remind her I'd give her a lift to court and to impress on her the absolute importance of being up and dressed and ready when I called.

It was a grey windy afternoon, the sort of day when the sky seems to come down low and get right into your nostrils, with its smell of soot and petrol and burning PVC. I got in my car and I saw that I was early. I thought I would use up the time by driving past Tonbridge Gardens. It was after all only a little detour, scarcely out of my way.

Tonbridge Gardens is a pretty depressing place. It's not one of those really grim estates where eight-year-olds demand protection money for your car and even the police get edgy. But it certainly has its share of troubles. And it's dreary as anywhere – seventies brick and concrete, weathered and water-streaked, with empty gloomy walkways.

When I got there, I pulled up by the kerb. Normally when I go to places like this I'm there for a reason – visiting someone, my head full of questions, with something to achieve. These purposes act like blinkers, give you a narrow focus, make it all more bearable. But on that grey afternoon, sitting there in my car, I had no purpose – or none that I could articulate – which made me more open than usual to the grotesque unfairness of it all, the arduousness of a life lived amid such bleak vistas.

I was still early for Holly: I had plenty of time. I'll just sit here for a moment, I thought, then I'll drive on and do my visit. But I got out and locked the car.

I walked slowly down the street. Grass grew between the cracks in the paving stones. The flats were set back from the road. There were a few shops – a takeaway, a hairdresser, a newsagent. The street smelt faintly of burning, as though there was a fire some place I couldn't see. It was surprisingly quiet.

At the corner I paused and pretended to look in the window of the little Indian grocer's – but I let my eye rest on the glass, not looking through. The reflection of Tonbridge Gardens filled the entire pane, massive like some great stony outcrop, blocking out the sky. There was something about it that suggested battlements, as though it had been built to withstand siege. The wind licked under the collar of my jacket and I didn't know why I'd come or what I wanted.

This is what lovers do, I thought, at love's beginnings and endings

– before the declaration, after the rejection. Especially fictional lovers, lovers in old musicals, leaning on lamp-posts, self-consciously melancholic, hungry for a glimpse of the loved one. And stalkers do it too, and men in gaberdine raincoats with turned-up collars in spy stories: walking up and down, lurking, peering with studied nonchalance in shop windows, waiting.

A man came out of the grocer's, tucked his lottery tickets in his pocket, gave me a sharp quizzical stare. I turned, went briskly back to my car.

Near where I'd parked there was a kind of open space in front of the flats, with a playground with bark chippings under the swings and a place to play basketball. There were supermarket trolleys lying around, and a dead pigeon. But when I got there I didn't get into my car. I found myself turning away, walking across the open space, heading for the stairway that said '30 to 86'. The sign was only just legible, covered with graffiti in luminous blue paint. The road that led into the estate was bordered with white painted bollards, speckled with yellow-brown marks where the rust was coming through. The windows of the flats had ugly aluminium frames and none of them were open. It was windier here. Little circular flurries of cold air tossed rubbish around and chased their tails like animals.

The stairway was dark and smelt predictably of piss. Three boys who should have been at school were sitting at the turn of the stair smoking. They were young – junior school age.

'Read your palm, miss?' said one of them as I passed. He was freckly and rather appealing, but what he said felt more like a threat than an offer. 'Go on, miss.'

'He's good, miss,' said one of the others, and giggled.

I shook my head.

'You from the social, miss?' Their voices echoed in the stairway.

I went up to the second floor, turned onto the walkway. The concrete barricade came higher than my waist. The windows of 31B were boarded up. Loud music came from 32B. I came to 34B, walked very slowly past. I could hear talk from a television or radio, someone must be in. I glanced through the window, but you couldn't see much. There were crisp net curtains, and on the sill a white vase full of red and purple fabric flowers. There was something rather brave about those flowers, so frivolous and bright: a little defiant gesture, two fingers to all the ugliness outside. You could tell she'd made a haven in there, that you'd go through the door and there'd be colour and comfort and relief from all the bleakness. You could also tell, from the whiteness of the nets, that as Philippa Nicholls had said it would be very clean – much cleaner than my house probably – that the carpet would be hoovered every day and there'd be a peachy pastel smell of air-freshener.

I wondered what would happen if I knocked on the door. I thought of the door opening, Carly's mother standing there on the doorstep, looking puzzled, rather hostile perhaps. I wondered how I would explain myself, what I would say. It would have been so easy: it would only take a simple gesture. All I had to do was to reach out my hand.

I walked on, went down by the next stairway to avoid the boys, and along the road with the rusting bollards and past the dead pigeon and the supermarket trolleys and back to my car, the wind tugging at my sleeve like grief. I got in and sat there for a long time, stared unseeing at the dashboard, still not fully understanding the impulse that had taken me there.

That was the day that Lucy drew her God picture. It was only a little thing, but in some mysterious way it lightened my mood. I eventually got back to the office after a difficult meeting with Holly Burt, who was all smiles and chatter and seemed to slip through my fingers like water. I drove home, dropped off the car, went to pick up Lucy who'd been having tea with Jake. She and Jake had got quite friendly since he'd given up playing kiss chase, and today, said his mother, he'd been trying to impress her by climbing a tree in his rollerblades. We walked home, I started on the chicken casserole. Lucy asked for paper and pencils and glitter glue and scribbled away with total concentration while I cooked. I didn't pay much attention, didn't really look at what she was doing: I was too wrapped up in my thoughts about Carly, what her life was like, what happened behind those clean net curtains. Alice came home, rather pleased with herself because she'd been to Debating Club and they'd debated whether people should have to be licensed if they wanted to be parents – 'I voted against it,' she said, 'but really it was quite hard to decide' – and Lucy just went on scribbling. She'd taken out her scrunchie so her blonde hair fell everywhere, shadowing her page, shimmering when her body shook as she did some filling-in.

At last she put down the pencil with a sigh of satisfaction.

'Look, Mummy,' she said.

'That's nice,' I said.

'Say it as though you mean it,' she said.

I put down the potato peeler, wiped my hands so I wouldn't drip on her picture, went to look at it properly.

'I do mean it. It's a very good drawing,' I said.

He was a genial, solid-looking, authentically Middle Eastern God, clean-shaven, dressed in floor-length robes, with a big grin on his face and splendidly detailed sandals with two straps and proper buckles, smiling down on a landscape that had a horse and a tractor and a swing and a tree with apples. There was a speech bubble coming from his mouth with careful lettering.

'I wanted him to say, "Here is my world",' she said, 'but I only had room for the Here. Look, he's got stars in his hands.'

Stars are tricky to draw, they usually end up bulgy and misshapen, so to get them even she'd drawn two triangles one on top of the other. She was plainly proud of them: the rest was all in pencil, but she'd gone over the stars with yellow glitter glue.

'D'you like the stars?' she said.

'Yes,' I said. 'Very much.'

'You can stick it up if you like,' she said.

So I wrote her name and the date on the bottom and went to put it up. The pinboard was crammed full as usual: I unpinned a lot of stuff – sports fixtures at Alice's school, a reminder to book a smear test, details of a Failure To Thrive workshop I probably wouldn't go on – and I stuck Lucy's God with his grin and his glitter right there in the middle.

2I

I sat with Holly Burt in the waiting room. She was chirpy and full of smiles. We chatted for a bit about her boyfriend, a bouncer called Spider, and this woman she knows in Brixton who does brilliant hair extensions, then she spotted two girls who were friends of hers and went to join them. They sat in a little gaggle in the corner, admiring each other's tattoos.

The magistrates' court where juvenile justice cases are heard is a gloomy Victorian building, quite unlike the aggressively contemporary red-brick and glass of the Crown Court. The waiting room has benches round the walls and shiny cream paint and brown lino, pockmarked under the benches by generations of stubbed-out cigarettes: it's a dreary place to wait. I'd soon read right through my *Guardian*, even the financial pages. I stretched, got up, went to the loo, wandered down the corridor a bit. I read the notices on the noticeboard.

And then I turned and saw him. Felix Floyd. He was right down the other end of the corridor, but quite unmistakable even from that distance: his hair caught the light, so fair it was almost white, like a baby's. He was talking to a woman who was presumably also a lawyer – schoolteacher specs, an expression that would normally I suspected be rather disapproving, a dark suit with lots of right angles, and her arms full of files. Felix was quite straight-faced, but the woman was laughing so much I thought she might drop her papers, shaking with it, her face contorted with pleasure.

Instantly I quite desperately wanted to speak to him. I had a sudden sense of clarity, of ease: like a mathematician who's puzzled over a theorem for weeks and suddenly sees that he must try a new method and that this method will lead him to the solution.

I nearly called out but was too inhibited: everyone would have looked. I turned down the corridor, trying to dodge through the crowd, the lawyers and social workers and frantic parents and drifting children with blank, unreadable faces. In my impatience I somehow couldn't predict people's movements. It was terribly frustrating, like in those dreams of running, where you don't know if you're running towards or away from something, you just know you have to keep moving, though your legs are turning to lead.

I was still several yards away when he left the woman with a touch on her arm, so she stood there hugging the joke to herself, fiddling rather flirtatiously with her very discreet earrings, while he headed off briskly in the opposite direction, weaving his way through the people. He wasn't very tall, but his fair hair shone. I wasn't sure even what I'd ask him or how I'd approach him, still trying to formulate my question as I neared the bend in the corridor that led to Courts 1 and 2.

He disappeared round the corner. I followed, and bumped straight into some poor court official in a voluminous gown. Our bodies actually collided, with a kind of thud. It was very embarrassing.

'Sorry,' we said simultaneously. We brushed ourselves down.

When I turned back to the corridor, it was deserted suddenly. Everyone must have been ushered into Court 1 where the committal for a burglary case with lots of defendants was being heard. There was just a woman with a buggy, a policeman talking into his mobile. No Felix. I couldn't work out where he'd gone: there wasn't anywhere for him to go to. He hadn't had time to get to Court 1 before I turned the corner. I wondered for a crazy moment if I'd hallucinated the whole thing, if he'd never been there at all.

All the rest of the day I kept thinking about Felix: all through Holly's hearing and a brief pub lunch with Jude and a tedious afternoon catching up on my paperwork. I hadn't really given him all that much thought in the two and a half years since we'd had our brief relationship. He'd ended it and I hadn't felt too bad and I'd just got on with my life. But things came back to me now, little things that had annoyed or intrigued me. His evident pleasure in making very sexist or downright rude remarks, especially about my appearance: 'Next time buy a T-shirt in your own size, Chloe' or 'Perhaps you should see a doctor about your hair'. The aftershave he wore, a novelty for me, because men who work for local authorities never seem to wear scent: it was a rather ambiguous kind of scent, too, not as robustly masculine as most aftershave, a bit too sweet for a man. The picture from a girlie magazine he'd stuck up in his downstairs loo, which had really irritated me: a woman dressed as an angel with silvery wings and a halo and wearing a little white top and naked from the waist down, with a shiny black whip pulled tight between her legs. Rather surprisingly, for someone so obsessively neat, he hadn't cut it out, the edges were ragged. But I remembered too the extremely powerful speech he'd made in a case I'd been involved with – that had kept a woman charged with social security fraud out of prison so her three small children wouldn't go into care.

I'd sometimes wondered why he took the cases he did when the pickings were so much richer in other fields of law, whether perhaps through his work he was seeking to put something right, to blunt the edges of old angers, to repair or salvage something. He'd presumably been a victim of the bizarre child-rearing practices of the upper classes – the succession of nannies, boarding-school at seven – but I'd always felt there was more to it than that. It had I think been a cold, cold childhood. The only thing he'd ever let slip when I was with him was that he'd phoned his mother that morning and said, 'It's Felix,' and she'd said, 'Felix who?'

I knew that sooner or later I was going to ring him. There was always the risk that he'd be rude, abrasive, brush me aside, make me feel over-emotional and incompetent – and of course I didn't know how willing he'd be to talk or how much he'd tell me. But I knew he'd been quite fond of me, if briefly, knew too that he wasn't averse to bending the rules a bit if it suited him to do so, and I felt quite sure he would at least agree to see me.

I wondered how best to approach it – whether to ring him at home or in his office. I didn't know how to categorize what I wanted. It wasn't quite work but it wasn't quite personal either. In the end I decided to ring him at home when the girls were in bed.

So late that night I had a large scotch and dialled his number, my heart pounding. He wasn't in: it was his answerphone. I listened to the tape, that very measured level voice he had: I'd never heard him raise it. Answerphones can be unnerving, the voice is so full of the person. I suddenly found the explanation for something that had puzzled me occasionally – why I'd ever had a relationship with him at all. I realized then that he sounded exactly like the cool anonymous controlling men in my less politically correct fantasies. Interesting: but not really enough to base a relationship on. I didn't leave a message.

Friday was Hallowe'en. On the way to pick up Lucy I bought a pumpkin – huge and round and opulent-looking and lushly golden-orange, too big to be put in a carrier bag. I waited outside school, the pumpkin under my arm.

'You don't let them trick-or-treat, do you?' said somebody, noticing the pumpkin.

'I wouldn't dream of it,' I said.

'Me neither,' she said, 'though they always want to. I don't know how people can.' Talking elliptically, as parents will, about the terrors that lurk at the edges of our lives. 'I mean, what can the mothers be thinking of? Anything could happen,' she said.

I nodded agreement, as we shared a picture perhaps – an image so archetypal it was almost like a fairytale – the stranger in a dark doorway luring a child to danger with a promise of apples.

'You never know,' said somebody else. 'You have to be so careful.'

I stood there with my pumpkin under my arm and wondered – not for the first time – What if they knew? I was glad I'd kept my life so private, that no one at school had known about my affair with Dan. There's a kind of safety in the restrictions of these relationships with the mothers of your children's friends, neatly confined as they are to the tea-and-homework slot of our lives, never sprawling out beyond those limits into the messy unpredictability of real intimacy.

After tea I carved up the pumpkin, cut off the top to make a hat, pulled out the insides, the cotton-woolly flesh with its wonderful rich colour and faintly rotten smell. The knife cut cleanly, like carving soap, with a soft shushing sound. I piled up the nicer flesh on a plate: I might do something with it over the weekend. In my more energetic years I make pumpkin pie, though the reality never matches up to the fantasy: pumpkin always looks as though it ought to taste enchanting and sweet like melon or mango, but really it's rather turnipy and you have to add masses of nutmeg to make it work.

Lucy collected the big flat shiny seeds, arranged them to make the letters of her name.

'Do pumpkin seeds make you invisible, Mummy?' she said.

'No – I think it's fern-seeds,' I said.

'Fern-seeds don't *really* though,' she said, a little shiver of doubt in her voice, checking that the world operated according to the laws she'd learned.

'Of course not.'

'Would you like to go invisible, Mummy?'

'Sometimes,' I said.

She wanted to carve the face.

'No – the knife's too sharp,' I said.

'You said last year I could this year. You did. You *said.*'

'No, sweetheart. You can design it though. You can tell me how many teeth.'

'Lots. Lots of teeth.'

'Three – like this?'

'That's not enough,' she said.

I tried to carve out another tooth but the knife slipped and the face went crooked, lop-sided.

'Mum, let's face it, that isn't really one of your best efforts,' said Alice.

'See. You should have let me do it. Or Dan. Dan would have done it right, Mummy,' said Lucy accusingly.

I flinched a little, aware how he was still there for her, vivid in her head. How he'd even been perfected for her in his absence – the man who could solve things, make the world work the way she wanted.

I put the candle inside – one of those squat nightlight candles that can't topple – lit it, turned off the lights. I love this moment, the way the face comes alive as the candle flickers. How with the simplest things, the knife and the candle, like witches with their brooms and salted water, you can make this magic. And every year, the face, carved in so haphazard a way, has its own personality. He looked very knowing, the way I'd done him this year, with his crooked, significant smile. Knowing something I didn't. For a brief crazy moment, perhaps because I was psyching myself up to try and ring him again, the face made me think of Felix.

I studied my daughters in the dark, loving them, the landscape of their faces accentuated by the play of light on dark, their noses, cheekbones, sharply defined, the reflected light of the candle bright in their eyes. Huge shadows danced. With the curtains not yet drawn, you could see the thin moon rising over the garden. I was pleased, it was nicely creepy.

We always tell stories and jokes on Hallowe'en. Alice had first go.

Knock knock who's there. Ammonia. Ammonia who? Ammonia little monster.

Lots of giggles.

'I've got the world's shortest ghost story too,' she said. She cleared her throat. 'Are you sure you're listening?' She made her voice go hollow, lugubrious. '"I put out my hand for the matches. They were *put into* my hand."'

We sat and watched the pumpkin face for a bit. The glimmering light made him almost alive – as though his eyes were swivelling round the room, seeking to focus on something, seeking us out.

'Your turn, Lucy,' I said. 'Tell us a seriously scary joke.'

She said nothing. It was very quiet in the kitchen. A siren blared then faded in the distance. Nearer at hand, down the bottom of my garden or maybe next door, one of the neighbourhood cats started sobbing like a desolate child.

'I don't like it, Mummy.' said Lucy, quite suddenly, in those clear sharp emphatic tones of the child with a high temperature, who, flushed with fever, sits up suddenly in bed and pronounces. 'Take it away.'

I put the light on quickly, wrapped her in my arms. She was trembling.

'No you don't,' said Alice. 'That's not fair. *I* like it. I've got another story I want to tell.'

'Lucy's got herself scared,' I said.

'Well, I suppose she *is* only five,' said Alice, horribly disappointed.

'Come and look, Lucy,' I said. 'It's only a silly old pumpkin face. You saw me carve it.' Reflecting that this is always how we try to soothe them – pointing out the mechanics of the thing. Like at the pantomime. It's not really a witch, just a woman with funny makeup. That spider behind Miss Muffet is painted cardboard: Look, you can see the strings. Briefly evincing some disingenuous faith that the horror is all illusion, that if you go behind, see the thing as it really is, there'll be nothing to fear.

'Come on, sweetheart, let's blow out the candle,' I said.

We blew. The sly face full of knowledge became a hollowed-out pumpkin again, ineptly carved and smelling scorched and unwholesome, as though something had caught fire that wasn't meant for burning.

I turned on the table lamps.

'Look, I've put all the lights on. Now you can see everything,' I said, and pulled the curtains shut to cover the greater dark outside.

First thing on Monday morning, when Jude had gone out on a visit, I looked up Felix's work number, which I couldn't remember any more. I sat staring at the phone for a moment, wondering whether to do it. I hate ringing men about personal things at work. Even with Adam it used to make me uncomfortable. Men in their offices can sound so brisk and self-important, make you feel rather trivial and irrelevant.

I was expecting Jo Hastings, his secretary. But I got straight through to him.

'Felix, it's Chloe,' I said, slightly thrown.

Silence.

'Chloe Langdon.'

'Oh yes. Well, hello, Chloe,' he said politely – as though I was some distant acquaintance.

'Look, I wondered if perhaps we could have lunch sometime,' I said.

'I don't eat lunch,' he said.

'No. Well, perhaps I could come to your office.'

'What for?' he said.

This irritated me. It must have been pretty obvious why I wanted to see him.

'It's about Dan,' I said. 'I want to talk about Dan.'

More silence.

Nat came in, rather late as usual, calling down florid curses on assorted megalomaniac town planners, psychopaths in Ford Sierras and the thought-disordered git who dreamed up the M25 in the first place. I waited till he'd shambled into his office: I didn't want him to hear. At the other end of the line, Felix still said nothing. My face felt hot.

'I hoped you might be willing to talk to me,' I said again.

'Chloe,' said Felix then, 'I'm of course well aware that you've been involved – *deeply* involved, I suppose we should say – with Daniel Whitmore, but he's a client of mine and I couldn't possibly talk to you about him.'

'I don't intend to probe,' I said. 'Really, I wouldn't ask you to tell me anything you didn't want me to know.' I sounded a bit pathetic – almost pleading. 'Of course I wouldn't. We could just talk generally . . .'

'Well, if you don't intend to probe, why exactly are you ringing me?' he said. 'Probing seems to be precisely the word for it.'

'I'm just asking you to agree to talk to me,' I said. 'I don't see that that's such a big deal.'

'Don't you? I suppose it hasn't occurred to you that there are ethical issues here.'

'Of course. But – well,' I faltered, feeling rather desperate, groping around for justification in the face of his absolute refusal to compromise, knowing that as in the corridor at court he was about to disappear into empty air. 'Look, couldn't you ask Dan what he thinks? He wouldn't mind you talking to me. I know he wouldn't.'

An audible sigh. 'No, Chloe,' he said. 'I really don't see the point of any of this . . . Anyway, you're well I hope,' he added in a concession to civility so brief and forced it felt like a further brush-off.

'I'm fine,' I said.

'Look, I'm afraid this is a rather inconvenient time for me,' he said. 'I should have been in court ten minutes ago. We'll speak sometime.'

I gave up, said goodbye, put down the phone.

At first I just felt cross. Then this nasty little thought sneaked into my head. Perhaps he saw it as a come-on. Perhaps he imagined I was using Dan as a pretext, that I wanted to renew our affair. The idea made me squirm. I knew I simply had to see him, I had to explain. Perhaps if I really spelt out what I wanted, made it quite clear this was all about Dan, then he would talk to me.

The need to see him, to set things straight, to make him talk to me, grew all morning. Then at twelve o'clock, surprised by myself, amazed that I should suddenly act so decisively, I signed myself out for an hour and a half and put on my coat and headed for his office.

★　★　★

It was a fresh, wet-smelling day. The wind was blowing the clouds away, and the air had that clarity it often has after recent rain. Against the massed purple clouds you could trace out the actual line of light where the sun was breaking through, like a baroque religious painting, God looking down on a sinning world and pointing his finger.

Felix's office is a little way round the one-way system from Social Services. You pass firms of accountants and insurance brokers and several sandwich bars and one or two small specialist shops that sell fancy dress or accessories for trainsets. The road as always was clogged with traffic, but on foot I got there almost too quickly. On the step outside, I was seized by sudden doubt. I took a deep breath. The wet windy air was somehow invigorating, refreshing me like water: I drank it in. I pushed open the door.

The waiting room is quite modestly furnished, not plush like the waiting rooms of solicitors with a richer clientele. That day it smelt a little of sweat, of unwashed clothes. Jo was at her desk, talking to a young woman: the other secretary must have been on her lunch break. Jo has been with Felix for years, she's utterly devoted to him. She's grey-haired, outwardly rather prim in her tartan skirts and high-necked jumpers, with a kind of unworldly air: you can just imagine her at the Anglican Synod, expounding some obscure theological point. But in spite of appearances, she keeps close tabs on everything, and I didn't know what she'd make of me turning up unannounced after two years.

I waited: she didn't seem to have noticed me.

The young woman leaned towards Jo, saying something about 'my case' that I couldn't quite catch. Her appearance from a distance was conventional enough: but closer up, you could see that her tights had lots of ladders, that her skirt was worn shiny – it was second-hand perhaps – that there was something sad and lost-looking about her dusty holdall. I wondered if she'd just been discharged from a psychiatric ward.

'Mr Floyd knows all about it,' she said. 'I've got to see Mr Floyd.'

Jo murmured something soothing.

As I waited to speak to Jo, a young man came in, let the door bang noisily behind him. He saw Jo was busy, turned to me, immediately started berating me about what had been done to him. They were fucking bastards, he told me, how dare they let his wife take herself off and not tell him where she was, the fuckers, he knew where they lived. He smelt of alcohol. I made sympathetic noises. He grabbed my shoulder. He was bigger than me and quite intimidating.

Jo turned from the lost-looking woman, got up, came briskly over.

'Chloe. How nice,' she said. She put a hand gently on the man's arm. 'Rob, this is Chloe,' she said, like someone at a vicarage tea party.

He let go of me, turned away, muttering.

'Well, we haven't seen you for simply ages,' she said to me.

'No,' I said, smiling, relieved. I remembered how she'd always been warm to me. I think she was usually nice to Felix's girlfriends: she longed to see him married – a motherly urge that would I suspected be for ever frustrated.

'He's still at court, I'm afraid,' she said. There was something slightly reverential about the 'he', the way she didn't name him. 'He's had quite a long list today. D'you want to wait in his office?'

'That would be lovely. Thanks,' I said.

I followed her down the passage. She unlocked the door, took me in. 'So sorry about the unpleasantness,' she said. 'Rob's a real softie, but he does go a bit over the top at times.' It was the way people talk about their pet pit bull terriers. 'Just make yourself at home.'

She went. I sat down on the sofa.

It was all much as I remembered it, comfortable but rather eccentric. There were none of the usual artefacts. No children's drawings, no cheese plants. And of course no family photos proudly displayed on the desk – just a mug stuffed with cheap ballpoint pens and a rather small cactus with lethal-looking spines and three implausible pink flowers: they looked almost as though they'd been stuck on, it seemed so unlikely that something so spiky and unyielding could actually blossom. On a bracket behind the desk there was a big-screen television and video recorder, which he used for playing police videos, and for keeping up with the cricket scores in summer. There was also a large illuminated fishtank on a shelf. Little fish, gold and blue and silver, glimmered through the clear water.

I knew where he kept everything, of course. For those few weeks of our unlikely love affair I'd often sat here on the sofa waiting for him, while he tidied up from the morning's work, for a while paying me no more attention than he paid to his cactus plant. I knew where he kept his Archbold, his gown, his files, his floppy discs. I had a pretty shrewd idea where he'd keep a police video.

I certainly hadn't gone there with any intention of looking through his things. I generally live by the rules: I'm far too nervous to be tempted by delinquency, quite apart from any moral compunction. Those scenes in thrillers where the hero breaks into someone's room and rifles through their secrets always bring my heart to my throat. Yet here I was all alone in his office, and it was just the easiest thing in the world to put out a hand and pull ever so gently on the handle of the middle drawer of his desk. It wasn't locked.

His dictaphone was on top. Underneath the dictaphone there were two videos. One was a Test Match highlights video someone must have lent him. The other had a sticky label on it, with the name of the local constabulary. There was nothing to say it was the right video.

There was the tiniest chink outside the door. I flipped the drawer shut, my body all on alert, my pulse jagged at my wrist. It was Jo with a coffee for me. Without the rattle of the cup I wouldn't have known she was there, the door opened so silently.

'That's sweet of you,' I said.

She put the coffee down on the desk. She looked a little anxious.

'He is expecting you, isn't he, Chloe?' she said, embarrassed.

'Well, yes,' I said. 'Sure.'

I'm a dreadful liar. I was scared that Jo with her priestly air would find me completely transparent.

But she seemed to accept this. 'I hope you don't mind me asking. It's just that there's nothing in his diary.' She must have looked it up. 'But then you know what he's like,' she added smiling.

'Absolutely,' I said, attempting to smile back as though we shared some intimate knowledge.

'He could be quite a while,' she went on. 'At least half an hour, I'd say. I was going to suggest you went off and did some shopping and came back, but it's so wet and dismal out there, isn't it?'

'I'll be quite happy here,' I said. 'Thanks ever so much, Jo,' I added, rather too effusively.

199

The door shut noiselessly behind her.

I sat and sipped my coffee. It was thick with grounds, with just a drop of milk: she'd remembered exactly how I liked it.

It was very quiet in Felix's office, the heavy door an absolute barrier to the clamour of the waiting room. You felt quite cut off from the world in this hushed and separate space. Yet I knew that someone might come at any moment: Jo, popping back to take my dirty coffee cup: Felix's partner, to look in a file: Felix himself, returned earlier than expected from court, because his last case had been yet again adjourned.

The shimmery fish swam in and out and up and down, bright against the dark weeds that waved like hands as the filter stirred the water. I watched them for a moment. Then I opened the drawer again, took the video out. The remote was lying in front of the television. I got up, slipped the video into its slot, took the remote and pressed On, turned the sound down low so Jo couldn't possibly hear, pressed Play.

The screen flickered into life. I sat in Felix's chair where I had the best view of the screen, eased the sound up notch by notch. It was the right video.

22

She was smaller than I'd imagined and very pale. She was naturally fair – white-blonde hair, white eyelashes – but her skin had that additional pallor of the child who isn't always properly fed, who sometimes lives on bread and jam till the giro comes. She was nicely dressed, though – a Disney T-shirt, little frilly ankle socks, her hair done up in a complicated top-knot: her mother had perhaps dressed her with extra care for this special occasion.

It was the sort of room you always find in child psychiatry outpatients or child protection units, as predictable as if it had come in a kit – the cheap low chairs without arms, the fibreboard coffee table, the rubber plant in the corner. The policewoman was sitting to the side of the picture, the little girl full-on to the camera. The woman smiled at the girl.

'Now, Carly, we're at force headquarters in our special video unit. And while we're talking that video's working. And in the other room behind that window there are Annie and Flip. And you know what they're doing, don't you?'

'Listening to us,' said Carly. It was a soft whispery voice – I had to turn up the sound.

'We're going to make a tape, aren't we?'

She was pretty, the policewoman, with wavy blonde hair and an open, innocent face: the sort of face that wins children's trust. She had a pleasant manner too, warm, direct: you could tell at once that she knew what she was doing.

'Lots of children come here to talk to us,' she went on, 'and when we talk we promise each other we'll try and tell each other everything and not leave anything out. And it's important we tell the truth. D'you know what the truth is?'

Carly shook her head.

'D'you know what fibs are?'

'When you're lying and that,' said Carly.

'If I said there was a tiger sitting on that chair beside you, would that be a lie?'

'Yes,' said Carly.

It often follows this pattern with young children: they know about lying, but truth as a concept is altogether more tricky.

She asked Carly her full name, and when her birthday was, and who lived in her house. 'Me and my Mum and Gavin and Lee,' said Carly.

'And d'you know why we're here today?'

''Cos I told my Mum about that man, and then my Mum told you.'

'Could you tell me about this man?'

'He put his hand down my knickers,' she said. Her voice was flat, expressionless, but her hands fluttered like little birds.

The woman asked where Carly knew him from: she said from school, from Northolt: she talked about the Rainbow Room where she'd had her special lessons with this man. I thought of the room that Dan had described to me – the Spot books, the children singing hymns down the corridor.

'What did you call him?' said the woman.

Fear clutched at me like a fist around my lungs.

But Carly merely shrugged. 'Dunno,' she said.

'Shall we just say the man?' said the policewoman.

Carly nodded her head, and a strand of hair fell down from her topknot. The whiteness of her hair and eyelashes gave her an odd look, like the weird paleness of hair and eyes in the negative of a photograph, everything the wrong way round.

'I want you to think of one of those times you told me about,' said the woman. 'Tell me first, what's in this room?'

She obviously knew her stuff – to be very specific, to focus on one particular time and help the child to picture it.

'There's a table and chairs and pencils and everything,' said Carly.

'Could you think of when you were in that classroom? What did he do?' said the woman.

'He put his hand in my knickers, then he washed his hands and gave me two jellybears,' she said.

'Could you tell me what he did with his hand? Did he keep it still or move it about?'

'He moved it,' she said. 'He hurt me.'

'D'you think he knows it hurt?'

'No,' she said, in that whispery rustly voice she had, with a kind of everyday matter-of-fact misery.

And all the time I watched, as I sat there at Felix's desk, gnawing at my fingernails, as Carly talked about the man who'd abused her, I kept asking: Is this Dan? Is this Dan? Trying to see him there in that room with this pale troubled child. But I couldn't do it. Something in me simply refused to picture it. I saw instead some nameless abuser, creepy, self-pitying, with sagging cheeks and a quiet voice with a downward intonation. A TV feature-film paedophile. Not Dan who once I'd love so much, who'd felt like part of my body. Yet for all the way I cut myself off, I found I couldn't stop shaking.

'If you were sitting down on the chair, how did he put his hand inside your knickers?' said the woman.

'He said stand up.'

'Did he stay sitting down?'

'He stayed sitting down.' Still the little hands, moth-like, fluttering in front of her face.

'So were you facing him?'

'I was facing away from him,' she said.

'So where would he put his hand? In front of your knickers or at the back?'

'At the front,' she said.

'And when he touched you, did he touch you on the inside or the outside?'

'Inside,' she said.

I've heard a lot of children's disclosures: they don't upset or repel me so much any more. And I've always felt that this blunting of feeling is not just inevitable but absolutely necessary if you are to be of use. That what is really most compassionate is to use your mind, to think clearly, not to emote: that's what helps the child. Like the pathologist who pores dry-eyed over the body of the murder victim, eager to read the stories told by the wounds. Yet now I found I couldn't do it, couldn't be hard and clear like that. I just sat and heard what Carly said and felt raw and repelled and contaminated, stirred by a fierce anger I hadn't felt for years. But still I couldn't see Dan there.

The policewoman was moving on. 'Did he say anything when he was doing this?'

'He was talking about sex.'

'What's sex?'

'It's dirty.'

'What did he say?'

'Dirty things,' she said. 'About sex and that.'

This seemed to worry the policewoman, maybe because it seemed too general, too theoretical – something Carly had felt was expected, perhaps, not something that happened.

'Can you remember?' she said. 'It's important not to guess and not to lie. You can say things in here and not get told off. You can say words your Mum might tell you off for.'

'He said about sex. I've forgotten the words,' she said. 'Dirty things. About his girlfriend and that.'

I gasped. I stopped the tape, rewound it a bit, replayed it – but she still said the same.

'What did he say about his girlfriend?' said the policewoman.

'He's got a girlfriend,' said Carly.

'Did he use any words that were different – strange words you hadn't heard before?' said the policewoman.

'No,' said Carly.

'How many times did he do that?'

'Every day,' said Carly.

'Monday Tuesday Wednesday Thursday Friday?' said the policewoman.

'Every day,' said Carly again.

'Did you see him every day?'

'Sometimes,' said Carly.

The policewoman nodded but gave up this line of questioning.

'What would he do then?' she went on.

'Wash his hands.'

'Where would he wash them?'

'In the sink.'

'Where was the sink?'

'In the room,' she said. 'He dried his hands and he said I was a good girl and he gave me two jelly bears.'

'What did you do with the jelly bears?'

'I ate one and I put one in my pocket,' she said. 'Jelly bears were my best sweets.'

'Are they still your best sweets?'

'No,' she said.

The policewoman glanced down at her clipboard, uncertain for a moment, wondering where to go next. Carly yawned, as nervous children will.

The woman smiled. 'It looks like you had a late night,' she said. Then she leaned forward a little. 'Now, Carly, there's something that puzzles me. Why didn't you just tell your Mum as soon as it happened?'

'I dunno,' said Carly.

'Did you think she might be cross?'

'I was scared,' she said. 'I was scared of the man.' Her voice was so low I had to rewind, turn it up a little. It was the first time that any emotion had showed in her face: her eyes were wide, she looked so frightened. They'd touched on something that mattered terribly to her. 'He said if I told he would get me sent to divvy school. I'm not a div,' she said. Her eyes were glittery with tears. 'I can't do my letters but I'm not a div.'

'Can you tell me more about this man?' said the policewoman. 'Can you think of anything he used to do or say?'

Carly shook her head.

'Well, did he have a car?'

'Yeah – a blue car.'

'How d'you know he had a blue car?'

''Cos he took me for a drive. He came and picked me up from my house and took me to school,' she said.

'Why did he do that?'

'Dunno,' she said.

There was a little pause, then the woman got up, responding to her ear-piece.

'Carly, we'll just stop there for a minute. Annie and Flip want to tell me something.'

She went out of the picture to go behind the one-way screen where the other women were watching.

Carly rocked in her chair, swung her legs in the frilly ankle socks, fiddled with her hair – for a moment thinking herself unobserved, not conscious of the camera. She was terribly restless, something always moving. I thought again how small she was – it was hard to believe she was eight. Dan had said she looked like she'd never been out in the sun: it was an apt description. She was like a little plant that's kept in a dark corner – that manages to survive, to keep on growing, but whose leaves will be for ever thin and ragged and pale unless somebody puts it out into the light. Then it was like she suddenly remembered the camera: she turned and stared straight at it so her eyes seemed to look into mine.

The policewoman came back in, sat down, glanced at the notes on her clipboard. 'Okay, Carly. Could you tell me some more about the man? I don't know what colour hair he's got.'

'Black,' she said.

'Has he got hair all over his head?'

'Yeah,' she said.

'What colour skin?'

'White.'

'Does he wear glasses?'

'No.'

'Does he have a beard?'

'No.'

And all the time, as the picture became more complete, precise, detailed, the sense of constriction in my chest increasing, till I seemed to be struggling for breath.

'How old d'you think he is? My age, your Nana's age?'

Naff question, I thought. Children like Carly can't do when things happened and how old people are.

'Your age,' said Carly.

'Did he bring anything to the lessons?' said the woman.

'Paper and pens and books and that.'

'What did he carry the paper and pens and books in?'

'He had a bag. A big black bag.'

'Did he bring the books?'

'No. The books were in the room.'

206

'Were they good books?'

'They were baby books,' said Carly. 'They were stupid. About teddies and puppies and that.'

'Okay, Carly,' said the woman. 'I think that's all. Thank you for coming to see us. It didn't hurt, did it?'

Carly said nothing.

'Now, is there anything else you want to say before we go?'

Carly sat there and swung her legs to and fro. 'What do you do with the tapes when you've finished with them?' she said.

The policewoman smiled. 'I keep them locked up nice and safe,' she said. The screen went blank.

It was utterly quiet in Felix's office: no sound but the bubbling of the aquarium filter, the far-off grumble of traffic, my pulse loud in my ears. I leaned forward to press the rewind button. And then I realized. It was the smell I was first aware of, that ambiguous, over-sweet aftershave that he wore. So I knew he was there without looking behind me. But it still made me jump when he spoke.

'Chloe. What a surprise.'

He was leaning on the filing cabinet by the door, sleek and immaculate as ever, with his intense pleasure in having me at such a total disadvantage written all over his face. I had no idea how long he'd been there. I felt myself flush violently.

'Shit,' I said.

'I see your language hasn't improved,' he said, with evident satisfaction. Then he just stood there and looked me over like I was a specimen on a laboratory slide and waited for my justification.

'I'm sorry,' I said. 'I shouldn't have done this.' And then, when he still didn't say anything, 'It was because you refused to see me.'

'Did I?' he said, as though he couldn't remember.

I ignored this. 'I was cross about it,' I said. 'And I came to try and see you, and the tape was in your desk . . .' I knew I sounded completely pathetic.

'Why such faith in me anyway, Chloe? You're the expert, surely,' he said, mocking me. 'You work in child protection. I'm a mere solicitor.'

'You know what the evidence is,' I said.

He came and sat on the desk, quite close beside me. He looked slightly awkward, perching there like that: he was a formal person, the attempt at informality didn't quite come off. I was enveloped in the smell of his aftershave. We sat there quite close, yet somehow poles apart – as though we'd never screwed on the sofa behind us. And I knew there was something significant in the way he'd moved in towards me, realised with a little rush of astonishment and relief that he was going to give me what I wanted: that he would talk to me.

'Tell me what you made of it, then,' he said.

'You mean the video?'

'Of course I mean the video,' he said, infinitely patient, as you talk to a cute but rather irritating child. 'I'm always keen to know what the experts think. Even when their actions are a little irregular.' And when I still didn't say anything, 'I'm waiting.'

I took a deep breath, tried to ignore the sarcasm.

'There are bits that don't make sense,' I said. 'The stuff about seeing him every day, for a start. But I think you'd have to discount anything she said about when things took place – she doesn't yet have a clear concept of time.'

He nodded. 'Right. Go on.'

'Then when she said about going in his car – she seemed confused about that, and I wonder whether it really happened. And if he *had* brought her to school – for some truanting programme, say – then someone at the school would surely know. And the bit about saying dirty things – it was just too vague, it was like she felt it was expected. I'd be dubious about that.'

He nodded slightly, said nothing, gestured me to continue.

'But the core of it,' I said, 'the sequence of what happened, is absolutely coherent and I'm sure it happened to her. The abuse and the handwashing and the sweets. It's got the kind of detail that makes you feel it's true. And there are lots of abusers who behave just like she says – telling her she was a good girl and giving her sweets.'

He nodded. 'Rather a neat analysis, I thought,' he said. It was like being patted on the head. 'I'm with you all the way.' He got up and walked slowly across the room, moving his hands around, putting a point across, perhaps, to the more obtuse members of a jury. 'So he's with her in the Rainbow Room, he abuses her, he washes his hands in the sink, he gives her sweets. Absolutely.' A pregnant pause. He was really enjoying himself. 'Except that there isn't a sink.'

'What?' I said, startled by this, pulled up short.

'There are tiles in that room but no sink,' he said. 'There may have been one years ago. There certainly hasn't been one there since Carly Smithson's been at the school.'

'Dan told you?' I said.

'Dan couldn't really remember. Dan didn't know. I went to look,' he said.

I think that was when I first felt something shift inside me: a little mouse-scurry of uncertainty in the recesses of my brain. But I didn't let it show.

'Children can get muddled,' I said.

'They can,' he said. 'Of course they can. But if she's in fact describing a sequence of things that happened to her – and I'd agree that seems valid . . . If those things did happen, then they can't have happened in the Rainbow Room. The room where Dan saw her.' He stopped suddenly, stared very pointedly at my thighs. 'Chloe, just look at that skirt,' he said in mock horror, as though he'd only just noticed. 'Did you forget to finish dressing or something?'

To my intense irritation, I felt myself flush. 'Oh piss off, Felix,' I said, uncrossing my legs. 'I thought we were having a serious discussion.'

'You did?'

Here we go, I thought. Here comes the lecture. I should have realized I'd been let off far too lightly.

'You sweet-talk your way round Jo,' he went on, 'walk into my office, play a highly confidential video – which, incidentally, is designed to fade after twenty showings, one of which you've just wasted – and then you expect a serious discussion.'

'I know it was wrong of me. I'm really sorry,' I said again.

'So you should be,' he said. 'You should be very sorry indeed. If anyone got to hear about this, you wouldn't be the only one in major trouble.'

'Of course I won't tell anyone,' I said.

'I still don't think you realize what you've done,' he said. 'I ought to have you thrown out bodily. In fact, I'd be quite within my rights to do it myself.' He was absolutely straight-faced, looking me up and down as though I was some sort of object. Sometimes you simply can't tell if he's serious: it's a power ploy at root, I guess, it gives him more room for manoeuvre.

Fuck you, I thought. But I sat there quite demurely. I wasn't going to go till I'd got everything from him that I could.

He turned, went back to that rather deliberate pose he liked, one elbow on the filing cabinet, looking down at me. He was good-looking, really – regular features, sleek hair: better-looking than Dan, but a lot less male somehow. Actually not my type at all. I wanted to ask him more about the Rainbow Room, but I waited quietly to see what he would say.

'Dan tells me you're quite convinced he's guilty,' he said then, in his normal voice again, as though his little outburst had never happened. 'He's completely bemused. Can't understand it.'

'Children usually tell the truth,' I said. 'I don't see why she'd say it if he hadn't done it.'

'You know, Chloe, I don't think that's the reason,' he said. 'I don't think that's why you think he's guilty. I think it's something to do with the nastiness of the crime.'

I didn't understand: I felt stupid, wrong-footed.

'Look,' he said, 'if it was a charge of petty theft and he told you he hadn't done it, I bet you'd have believed him. Wouldn't you?'

I nodded.

'But this is about the nastiest crime you can think of: so if there's the least smidgin of doubt, you feel you have to believe in his guilt,' he said. 'Because it would be so dreadful to get it wrong – to believe in his innocence if he's really guilty. But just because it's nasty doesn't mean he did it.'

'No, of course not,' I said. I didn't want to concede, yet knew there was something in what he said. 'But the man she describes does sound like Dan – the black bag, the blue car . . .'

He ignored this, interrupted me.

'There's something else in the video,' he said. 'I don't know if you noticed. When Carly was talking about the sweets. He gave her jelly bears, she said. "They were my best sweets," she said. D'you remember?'

'Yes,' I said.

'How would Dan have known they were her favourite sweets?' he said.

'Most children like disgusting jelly sweets,' I said. 'All the better if they're full of E numbers or look like worms or eyeballs.'

'The sociology isn't the point,' he said. 'The point is that she said that these particular sweets were her best sweets. She was very specific about that. And maybe the man who abused her knew that. Think about it.' He flicked some fluff from his immaculate sleeve. 'Now, I don't think for a moment she's making the whole thing up. But the fact is – kids do stretch the truth a bit, they do tell tales at times. For whatever reason. I know that, you know that. Don't you?'

'Yes, of course,' I said.

'I mean, I think you've got children, haven't you?' he said, as though he wasn't sure, as though he'd never known me well enough to be sure.

I nodded, trying not to hate him, thinking hard about all the good things he'd done – the poor lost souls with dusty holdalls and skirts worn shiny who think he's Superman in a suit swooshing down to pluck them from the abyss. Thinking very hard indeed.

'So you don't think it was Dan?' I said.

'No,' he said. 'I don't think it was.'

'Felix, tell me,' I said, 'what would you do if you did think he was guilty? Would you still defend someone if you were pretty sure they'd committed a horrible crime?'

'Yes, of course,' he said. 'So long as they didn't admit their guilt to me. Everyone's entitled to a defence.'

'How can you tell?' I said. 'If someone's not being straight with you?'

He shrugged. 'Too much detail. Too little detail. Too much eye-contact. Too little eye-contact.'

'But how can you really be certain?' I said.

'Certain? Who said anything about *certain*?' he said. 'Certainty's not really my field.'

'Really,' I said. 'You make it sound like Zen or something.'

He laughed. 'I'd have thought that was just your kind of thing,' he said.

He turned, went over to his fishtank. He had his back to me, he stood and studied his fish, totally focused on them, as though I wasn't there. Outside, an emergency vehicle screamed round the one-way system, but it seemed very far away.

'My cichlids are new – well, they post-date you, anyway,' he said, after a moment. 'Come and have a look.'

I got up and looked. The cichlids were the silver ones: they had strong black markings like eyes.

'They're pretty,' I said.

'One of them had some nasty tail rot last week,' he said. 'A little bit more missing every morning. But the bactericide seems to be working beautifully.'

The fish must have been able to see us, they swam up to the front of the tank in a sparkly shoal. They were all eyes, the little round goggle-eyes in their faces, the markings like bigger eyes on the bodies of the cichlids. We stood there looking back at them for a bit.

'They've charged him,' Felix said then. 'Did you know that?'

I shook my head.

'Last week,' he said. 'They interviewed him and charged him.'

'How will you defend him?' I said.

He turned back to me. 'There are things we'll pick up, like you did,' he said. 'Things that seem a bit dubious, stuff she might have made up. But clearly the crucial issue is how well he fits the description.'

He opened a drawer in his filing cabinet, took out a pot of fish flakes. He stood with the pot in his hand for a moment, teasing the fish, making them wait. He seemed quite unaware of me. I was scared he'd stop – that he'd suddenly think he shouldn't be doing this, and refuse to take me any further.

'Go on, Felix,' I said. 'Please.' My voice high-pitched and imploring, like a child's.

'The police have narrowed the field to three suspects,' he said. 'The other two are the other male teachers who taught her in that room. The police say Dan's the most likely candidate of the three.'

'He fits the description best?'

He nodded. 'But it might of course be someone else entirely – someone outside the frame. Someone perhaps who abused her and washed his hands in a different room – a room with a sink.'

He shook some fish flakes into his hand, opened the hole in the top of the tank. The fish all shimmered up to the surface of the water. It was rather magical the way they moved, as though he'd drawn them to him.

'How he comes across in court is absolutely crucial, of course,' he said. 'Whether the jury like him. It's all about emotion really.'

It was weird to hear him saying this stuff about feelings. Sometimes I'd wondered whether he had any.

'And will they like him?' I said.

He shrugged. 'There are problems,' he said. 'Dan's domestic situation in particular. There's this guy – nearly fifty – living all on his own in a bedsitter. Pretty sad really.'

'Sad in Alice's sense?'

'Who's Alice?' he said.

'My daughter. You know that,' I said, hating him again.

'Yes – in your daughter's sense,' he said. 'A weirdo. Not at all what you want. It just fits with all those prejudices about quiet men who live alone and are quite unexceptional apart from their unfortunate interest in little girls.' He snapped the top back on the fish flakes. 'At least he doesn't have facial hair and thick glasses.'

'He's been married,' I said.

'Sure – but it's where he's at *now* that worries me,' he said. 'I'll do what I can. His wife and daughter are very loyal, and they'll be in court and we'll point that out to the jury, maybe get them in the witness box.'

I nodded as though this was obvious to me, but wondered about this loyalty of Helena's, wondered with a hot little surge of curiosity just how it was expressed.

He turned towards me then, half his face bright in the light from the aquarium, the other half darkly shadowed. 'I'll tell you what I really need,' he said. 'And, Chloe, look, this mustn't go any further – I mean, this is all thoroughly out of order.' He was standing very close. Sometimes when he looks at you it's like he can see straight through. 'What I really need is someone outside the family who knows him well – someone the court will trust – maybe because of their work or the kind of person they are. Someone to say he's a regular guy with a regular sexuality – that he likes women, likes a screw. Someone who believes in him, Chloe . . .' He let the words hang in the space between us for a moment. Then he moved away from me, went to sit in the chair that I'd vacated, opened the top drawer of his desk. 'Ah well,' he said, 'I guess you can't have everything.'

I stood there in front of the fishtank, said nothing at all.

213

He rifled around for a while in the drawer. 'I've got something for you to hear before you go,' he said.

He found what he was looking for, held it up between finger and thumb with ostentatious delicacy. A tiny cassette.

'From Dan's answerphone,' he said. 'He brought it in to me.' He put it in his own answering machine, pressed the button.

The voice was rough, loud, harsh. 'You fucking pervert. You fucking pervert. You fucking pervert.' The words hit out again and again like a fist in your face. I flinched. It went on and on. I wanted to scream at Felix to make it stop. He switched it off and the silence felt uneasy, all churned up and disturbed like muddied water.

'I don't understand,' I said. 'I mean, who . . .'

'Probably the police,' he said.

'Come off it,' I said.

He shook his head. 'You're such an innocent, Chloe. They do this kind of thing. Anything to make you break down and confess. Believe me,' he said, 'it's not a load of laughs being Dan Whitmore right now.'

He took the tape out of the machine and put it away again. Right on cue, Jo's voice came over the internal phone. Someone was desperate to talk to him.

'Give me two minutes,' he said. 'Right, Chloe. So nice of you to drop in.' Dismissing me.

I didn't move. 'There's a photograph,' I said suddenly.

He nodded. He didn't seem thrown. 'Dan said something about a photograph,' he said.

I took a deep breath. 'It's a photograph of Alice,' I said.

'A dirty photograph?' he said.

'Not exactly. Undressed.'

He shrugged. 'Well, there's nothing about a photograph in the bundle,' he said. 'A single photo's not going to prove anything. I guess they got excited about it for a bit then lost interest. It happens.'

I picked up my bag and turned to go. To my surprise, he suddenly reached out and took my hand. His skin felt cool and dry.

'You are all right, aren't you, Chloe?' he said.

'Yes,' I said, feeling awkward standing there with my hand in his.

'Dan seems to think you're so vulnerable. I told him I couldn't see it myself – I've always thought you were tough as old boots,' he said.

It was Felix's best shot at empathy.

He took his hand away. I went.

Jo was deep in conversation with the man who'd menaced me earlier. She waved warmly at me over his head as I went out into the street.

23

On Tuesday of the next week we had fireworks, though the girls had already been to a firework party given by one of Adam's colleagues at the hospital, a haematologist who had a big house out in Sussex and a garden with lawns and a bit of river. But I still wanted to have some fireworks just for us, though I worried it might all be a bit of a letdown after the haematologist.

I built a little bonfire with the wood that remained from the old shed, lit it with firelighters and matches. It made me think of that night when I'd burnt all my things, I saw it all again, the fire taking my photographs, my diaries, the notebooks about my children, and I pulled my coat more closely around me. Lucy, to my relief, didn't say anything: maybe she'd forgotten, or maybe she was just more interested in the fireworks.

Before Adam left, I'd never lit a firework. Like Christmas tree lights and carving a joint, they remain irreducibly male. And they make me slightly nervous, even now. I always worry that I haven't pushed them deep enough into the earth, that they'll topple over and cause some awful havoc. But I love them too, even the simplest ones, the dazzle in the dark garden, the way the fire spills down in the shapes of fountains or waterfalls, the smell of danger.

It all went fine at first. We had the Jack in the Box and the Retrojet and the Dragon's Crown.

'I like that name,' said Lucy. 'The Dragon's Crown.' She rolled the word round her mouth like a sweet.

It was rather a good firework: it turned the lawn an unwholesome witchy green.

Lucy sighed with pleasure. 'The colour on the grass is the colour of dragons,' she said.

I lit sparklers for them and they waved them around happily, pleasurably nervous, writing their names on the night. A pall of blueish smoke hung over the lawn.

'It's that smell you forget about for the rest of the year,' said Alice, sniffing appreciatively.

Then Lucy chose the Snowstorm. I asked her to bring it over, but she said she couldn't possibly.

'We're not allowed to touch fireworks,' she said piously. 'They said in assembly.'

Alice and I laughed at her a little.

'That's lit ones, duh,' said Alice.

Lucy was upset, full of hurt dignity, on the edge of crying.

'We're *not* allowed,' she said, her voice shrill with outrage. 'Mrs Bennett *said.*'

I hugged her.

'I'm sorry,' I said. 'You're absolutely right. We shouldn't have laughed.'

But her pleasure in the evening was spoilt. She clenched her fists and stamped her foot as we watched the Snowstorm – though it was very pretty, weeping tear-shaped drops of fire onto the grass.

'I hate that firework. It's pathetic,' she said. 'Why don't any of them bang? They're not proper fireworks, Mummy.'

'I got a no-bang box,' I said. 'I thought you didn't like bangs. You didn't like them last year.'

'They all banged when we went to that thing with Daddy,' she said. 'They made Daddy jump. It was cool. *And* we had marshmallows.'

'Well, I'll remember next time,' I said. 'Next year I'll be sure to get noisy ones.'

But I knew just what she meant – I too felt there was something lacking. They were all too gentle, too safe, too domesticated, these fireworks: I longed for one of those rockets that goes way way up and astounds, the fire in the sky.

The girls were cleaning their teeth and I was taking a load of dirty washing into the kitchen when the phone went.

'Chloe.'

'Yes,' I said, my heart lurching.

'It's Dan.'

'I know,' I said.

It was strange how he felt he had to announce his identity – as though he feared that in distancing myself, in pushing him away, I might also somehow have forgotten the sound of his voice.

'How are you?' he said.

'I'm okay,' I said. I kicked the door shut with my foot: I didn't want the girls to hear. 'And you? Are you all right?'

'Well,' he said, 'it's not that easy.'

'No,' I said.

'I'm trying to keep busy.'

'Yes,' I said.

'And the girls?'

'They're fine,' I said. 'Much the same as ever. We just had some fireworks.'

'Good,' he said, rather surprised I think that I was so forthcoming.

A little silence. I didn't know how long we could go on like this, filling in the spaces between us with these platitudes. It was as if he hadn't expected I'd talk to him, so he wasn't prepared, didn't know what to say.

'You saw the disclosure?' he said. Which of course was why he had rung me – because it told him I was still connected, still thinking about him – that I hadn't spun off into some other orbit.

'Yes,' I said.

'Felix told me,' he said. Not asking for my opinion. I sensed how careful he was being with me, as though everything was very fragile and if he made a wrong move something might shatter.

'Felix says the trial will probably be in January or February. That is, if they do go ahead.'

This surprised me. 'Is there a chance they might not go ahead?' I said.

'Only a slim one,' he said. 'Felix thinks it will probably get to court – because the video is so powerful.'

'Yes,' I said.

'I was scared when I saw it,' he said.

'Yes,' I said. 'Me too.'

Another silence. Once we'd been so at ease in the spaces between words – as you are when you're deeply intimate, when you've made love often, and it's like you share a rhythm that pulses on through the pauses in conversation, the moments of not-doing. But now these silences scared me – like little pits I might fall into. Yet I couldn't put the phone down on him any more, couldn't be that decisive: it was something to do with the disclosure, with what Felix had said – these new hopes stirring like animals in the corners of my mind.

I heard his quick inbreath then down the other end of the line.

'Chloe, I must see you,' he said. 'I must talk to you properly.'

I said nothing. I hated this, hated the note of desperation in his voice – hated the power I had over him.

'That's all I'm asking,' he said. 'Just a chance to come and talk to you.'

'No,' I said. 'Not now. No, I can't.'

'Think about it at least,' he said. Not accepting no, not letting me say never. 'Please think about it. It could be any time.'

'I do think about it,' I said.

'I'll ring you again,' he said. A statement, not a request.

'It's best if you ring after nine, when the girls are in bed.'

'Yes, I'll remember, I promise,' he said, his voice softening, a kind of relief in it, breathing more easily, knowing I was giving a kind of permission I'd previously withheld. 'I wasn't thinking,' he said. 'I'm sorry.'

'Never mind,' I said.

'I'll ring you,' he said.

'Yes.'

'Take care, Chloe,' he said, his voice so warm, so gentle, I wanted to get right inside it, to wrap it round me like a blanket.

'And you,' I said. I put down the phone.

And the moment I put it down, it was suddenly like I could smell his skin, the musky smell of it that I'd so loved – like he was there, very close to me, somewhere behind me where I couldn't see him – and with that hallucinatory impulse came such an intensity of desire. I'd been relieved, almost pleased, that I hadn't felt any kind of physical longing during our conversation. Yet now, it seared through me, a sudden, very quick, very focused arousal, as though the intermediate stages of desire – the gentle warmth, the opening up – were somehow left out or overridden, just going straight to this intensity, so it actually hurt me. It was disorienting and upsetting. It was like there were these two different parts of me – the part that just longed to hold him and the part that knew I must push him away – and these parts of me couldn't be brought together, couldn't be reconciled. I stood there, leaning on the windowsill, looking out into the darkness, looking at my apple tree and through it the night sky and the stars, which for a moment seemed magically caught in the nets of its interwoven branches: stood there for a long time and waited for it to pass.

Nothing much happened for a while. I didn't hear any more from Vicky Griggs, which was a huge relief, though I lived in fear of Maureen at the office saying 'Your friend Vicky rang' in that interested, hopeful kind of way – and Vicky coming and giving me some new nugget of appalling information. But the police I imagined had finished with me: they had nothing more to ask.

Outwardly my life followed its usual pattern – crises and grumbles at work, spellings to practise, lunch boxes to fill, companionable walks home from school with Lucy on the days I left work early, stopping perhaps at the Blue Moon for a Mars Bar. Though sometimes my eye would fall on the jelly bears in one of the big transparent sweet-jars behind the Blue Moon counter, and I'd feel a rush of nausea and have to turn away.

There was a short spell of unseasonably warm weather – an airstream from the Azores, apparently. The streets were noisy with birds and we sweated in our winter coats. But the gardens and trees were looking more wintry every day. The silver birch outside the coroner's office had lost almost all its leaves, the bare twigs straggly and crinkled like an old woman's thin hair, and the red crab-apples that had been so lovely in September, gleaming like red glass, were starting to rot. In my own garden only the pansies in my windowboxes were still in flower: the unseasonal sun shone through their petals, the white ones bright and translucent, like parachute silk.

Then it turned cold: low cloud, bitter wind. There was chilly rain that thickened to sleet and came right in under your umbrella: people screwed up their faces as they struggled against it. One morning we woke to a light covering of snow, thrilling the girls but melting even as we walked to school – loose-textured lumps of it sagging off car windscreens, and the streets full of the sound of water and the routine and pointless admonishments of parents as their children made snowballs and got their gloves wet. It was time to turn up the thermostat on the heating, to hunt out the wellingtons and woolly hats. Yet that very same day, just as winter seemed to be really getting a grip, there were suddenly pots of hyacinths in the doorway of the flower shop next to the funeral parlour – just tight green buds, no scent, no colour, nothing much to look at, still lifting up the heart.

I went through it all endlessly in my head: the video, the things that Felix had told me, my conversation with Dan. But I never got anywhere – never reached any kind of conclusion. I thought how Felix had said that certainty wasn't his field. Justice is an inexact science, I guess: it's all about what happened way back in the past, and sometimes of course you can never really know. And maybe uncertainty's okay – if he's a client, and you're a solicitor pleading in his defence: but not if he's your lover, not if he's been that close, as close as your skin, your breathing. So I knew I had to have certainty. Yet for now all I had was doubt and vacillation. For there were now minutes, hours even, when I questioned whether he'd done it: but there were still hours and days when I was convinced he had. And during those times when I felt quite sure of his guilt, I'd think a lot about his childhood, muse fearfully on that great invariable principle of human life, the cruel law whose operation you see every day in the kind of work that I do – that those to whom evil is done do evil in their turn. I thought how he'd been physically and emotionally abused by his father: I wondered how else he might have been abused, that he hadn't told me about. Whether there was some dreadful predisposition, some savage early imprinting, that had led him to assault that little girl.

It was like I had some of the pieces of a jigsaw puzzle in my hand – what I'd learned from Felix, from the video, even from walking past the flat where Carly lived – but they didn't make a totality, there were too many pieces missing, I couldn't see the whole.

And then the idea gradually formed in me that there was some-body else who could help me. Someone who could give me another piece of the picture, fill in those gaps in my knowledge, help me to see. I envisaged our meeting, thought what I'd ask, worked it all out in my head, the questions underlined with bright ball-point pen in my mind. But I simply didn't know if I had the courage.

Then with a decisiveness so sudden it was almost like my body taking over – just taking control and acting, finding the number, moving towards the phone – entirely on impulse, one cold day of harsh wind and white sky at the end of November, I rang her.

24

'Hello.' A pleasant voice, rather deep.

'Is that Helena?'

'Yes.'

'It's Chloe Langdon,' I said.

There was a silence.

'Yes,' she said then. A yes that meant, at the very least, that she wasn't going to put down the phone just yet.

'I wanted to ask if I could talk to you,' I said.

She said nothing.

'It's a lot to ask,' I said.

'It is,' she said.

'Perhaps we could have a coffee somewhere,' I said.

'I don't want you to come to my home,' she said.

'No. Somewhere else then. Anywhere,' I said.

'I'd like it to be today,' she said. 'I don't want to have it hanging over me. Could you do today?'

'Yes,' I said.

'The Arkwright Centre at three. The café at the top.'

'Thank you,' I said.

It was only after I'd put down the phone that I realized we hadn't discussed what we looked like, as you usually do when you're meeting a stranger in a public place, that it hadn't seemed necessary. Maybe we'd thought about each other so often we felt we knew.

The shopping centre is an eighties atrium with three floors and a basement. It's all escalators and glass and metal and mirrors, a place full of reflections and refractions, where you'll suddenly come upon an image that seems familiar and it takes a second to realize it's actually yourself. The café is right at the top under a dome of metal girders and glass, so if you look up you can see the sky. They had the Christmas decorations up already: huge garlands of plastic greenery hanging from the ceiling, and every pillar festooned with purple ribbon and gold tassels, like a stripper in some sleazy nightclub. The 'Skaters' Waltz' was playing over the loudspeaker, briefly interrupted by a measured voice telling us that this shopping centre had been designated a non-smoking area.

I paced up and down like a shopper in the throes of a purchasing decision, stood for a while by Dillons' window with its Christmas display of cheerful yellow angels, pretended to study the fat little snowsuits in Baby Gap, kept turning to look across to the café, feeling furtive, almost delinquent. I was acutely nervous, bitterly regretting the impulse that had made me ring her.

She was exactly on time and I spotted her immediately – Jude had described her well. In her expensive, understated clothes she stood out from the other shoppers, the harassed mothers of toddlers hunched over their buggies, the relaxed middle-aged women in sportsgear treating themselves to chocolate croissants, the older, slower women in colourless raincoats. I watched while she bought her coffee, headed for the table that I would have chosen too – at the edge of the café, next to the banister, looking right down to the fountain in the basement where Alice and Lucy like to throw coins and wish. She put her coffee on the table, cleared away some dirty cups, sat down and straightened her cuffs. She was older than me, but still a good-looking woman. Fine bones, dark hair severely tied back as Jude had described. Skinny and stylish, plainly from quite a privileged background. You could picture her striding through the countryside in a Guernsey jumper and those high green wellingtons the aristocracy wear, calling her dogs.

I went to buy a coffee, took it to her table, concentrating to stop it from spilling. She saw me approach, sat quite still, watching.

'Helena?'

'Yes,' she said.

I put the coffee down: it slopped all over the place. We shook hands briefly, not smiling. I pulled my chair in noisily, scraping along the floor, sat down. I felt huge and clumsy and utterly in the wrong.

'It's very kind of you to see me,' I said.

'It is, isn't it?' she said. 'I thought that too.' She was cool, but not cold. She looked pointedly at my unsteady hands. 'It's alright – I'm not going to tell you how angry I am or any of that stuff,' she said.

'Though I am, of course. Angry, I mean. Well, I was. It's better now.'
She looked down, stirred her coffee with that little white plastic stick they give you, stirred and stirred, staring into the cup.

Her skin, I noticed, was quite lined. Too much sun-bathing, perhaps. In fact she still had the remnants of a tan – acquired in Brittany, with Dan. But she had a strong elegant jawline and rather large dark eyes. I could imagine what a good-looking couple they must have made. Both tall and dark, with just the right difference in height: beautifully matched physically, but with this fascinating discrepancy in class background that would have given the partnership extra glamour somehow.

'I imagine you want to ask me if I think he did it?'

'Yes,' I said.

'Why me?'

'Well, you know him better than anyone,' I said.

'Chloe,' she said, with some difficulty, as though she didn't quite like saying my name, 'it turns out there was a whole side of him I didn't know about.'

I wondered for a moment what she meant. Visions of yellowing newspaper cuttings about previous charges of paedophilia or hidden caches of child porn flashed into my head. It took a second or two to realize she was talking about his affairs.

'You mean you didn't . . .' I couldn't finish the sentence: it seemed to lead inexorably to me.

'I didn't know he had all these other women,' she said.

I flinched, but kept looking steadily at her.

'Of course, I'd wondered sometimes,' she said. 'And actually there *was* one I knew about, several years ago. But mostly you just get on with it, don't you? Our relationship seemed fine, really. You get a bit bored, of course. You can't possibly keep the excitement going with all that parenting stuff, you know, all the spilt yoghurt and clarinet lessons. But it's like that for everyone. No. It was a total shock.'

There was an expression she had that I knew was all about me and how I'd hurt her – a sardonic almost-smile, the corners of her mouth pulled down. I thought how I'd attributed such power to her, at the start of my love affair with Dan, when he'd still been living with her: I'd imagined a perfectly run household, all immaculate and orderly, and Helena presiding over it, a little bit bossy and alarmingly well-organized and absolutely in control. But sitting there at the hard little table with that rueful pretence of a smile, stirring her cappuccino with the white plastic stick, she didn't look in the least powerful.

I didn't know what to say: there are no easy formulae to smooth over such things.

'It's better now,' she said, as though to help me out. 'I've got someone else.'

I nodded, absolutely recognizing the impulse that made her want me to know that.

We sipped our coffee. It was terribly bland, with a thick froth of shiny tasteless bubbles on top and a faint sweet powdering of chocolate. I found I couldn't look at her, so I stared down at the table top, which was made of some shiny metal patterned with crescents that broke up our reflections into hundreds of silver segments. It had been a good choice for our meeting, I thought, this hall of mirrors.

'Quite honestly, it turns out he's been a total rat to me,' she said. 'But child abuse? I've never believed it – never for a moment.'

'Helena,' I said carefully, 'I'd be so grateful if you could tell me why you think that. Why it is you're so sure.'

There was silence for a moment between us. I was afraid she wouldn't answer. I so longed to hear what she had to say that I had a kind of mad fear that she might simply dematerialize: that it was only my will that held her there, and if I let my vigilance lapse she'd vanish like mist or smoke.

She sat quietly for a moment, resting her hand on the coffee cup, running a finger round the rim. Her nails, like mine, were bitten.

'He was such a good father,' she said slowly. 'Always very loving. Very physical, lots of hugs – but there's nothing wrong with that, is there? Children need hugging. There was never anything that worried me.'

'What does Sally think?' I said.

'Sally?' She looked bemused that I knew her daughter's name. 'She's furious about it all. She's absolutely loyal to her father.' She took a paper napkin, wiped some crumbs from the table. 'I think you've got children?' she said.

'Two girls,' I said.

'How lovely,' she said, in that 'I know what it's like' way that mothers have – because really the experience is so similar for us all. 'How nice to have two. We could only have the one, of course.'

I looked at her questioningly.

'After Sally I had an ectopic and nearly died,' she said. 'I didn't want to risk it again.'

'That must have been awful for you,' I said immediately. Yet felt uneasy, sympathizing with her. The normal courtesies felt discourteous here, at this little metal table up under the glass and the sky. It was his responsibility, I kept telling myself – as those whose lovers are married always will, striving for absolution: *I* wasn't responsible for *his* infidelity.

'Really,' she said, 'you'd think he'd invented parenthood. So this abuse thing – I just think it's nonsense. Presumably something's happened to that child. But whoever did it, believe me, it wasn't Dan.'

I waited, hoping for more.

'I had to see the police,' she said then.

'Yes,' I said. 'Me too.'

'That rather prim woman with the trouser-suit? A bit like a Girl Guide?'

'Yes,' I said.

We both laughed a little, enjoying a brief sense of complicity. Our awareness that if we'd met in some other situation we might have liked one another hung in the air between us, a fragile awareness that dissipated rapidly, like the thin scent of early spring flowers.

'I hated it,' I said. 'Didn't you?'

She shrugged. 'I didn't care really. They wanted to know what our sex life was like. Well, quite honestly there wasn't a lot to say.'

I felt a delinquent little surge of pleasure, quickly suppressed.

'And there was stuff about what he'd been like as a father – the stuff I told you just now,' she said.

This was my cue, I thought: my way in to the question that above all I wanted to ask.

'The police showed me a photograph,' I said. 'They'd taken the film from his camera.'

'Just the one?'

'Yes.'

'Are you going to tell me about it?'

'It wouldn't be fair to the person,' I said.

She seemed to accept this: she didn't pursue it. 'Photographs are iffy, of course,' she said. 'The camera can lie and all that.'

'Did Dan ever take photographs of Sally?' I said. 'Kind of dubious photographs?' It sounded terribly clumsy but I didn't know how to put it.

She frowned. This obviously irritated her, perhaps because it seemed to implicate her, too.

'What – Sally in the bath, that kind of thing?'

I nodded.

'No,' she said. 'Not that I can remember. Though people did then. It was just fine to take pictures of your kids with nothing on. Now you can't do it. Boots take them straight to the police, apparently. I certainly wouldn't see taking tacky photos as Dan's scene.'

We were disturbed by the excited yelps of a little boy at the next table: his mother was feeding him chocolate pudding from a jar, he'd got it everywhere, hands, chin, a little in his hair. I was suddenly aware of the world going on around us with all its noises: the tired crying of children, the saccharine Christmas music, the plashing of the fountain in the basement. While we sat there in our little tent of silence and guilt and fraught, contradictory feelings.

Helena pulled a face, watching the little boy and his mother. 'Other people's babies,' she said, 'are never as nice as your own.'

The mother wiped ineffectually at the child's face with a tissue. Helena turned away.

'Quite honestly,' she went on, 'I just don't get why it's gone this far. I do wonder if Dan put someone's back up right at the start of the investigation. Dan . . . has a temper. I don't mean he hit me or anything. But he does have his uncontrollable side. He had a shitty start in life, of course. But then – he's undoubtedly told you about that. Ad nauseam probably,' she added dryly.

I smiled because she smiled, but thought this rather harsh. 'Yes, he's told me.'

'You think I'm being mean,' she said. 'But let's face it, men do love to roll over and expose their weaknesses, don't they? I've always thought all that stuff about men not liking to talk about their feelings is utter crap. They'd be at it all day, given half a chance.'

'Yes, I suppose so,' I said – thinking how I'd loved it when Dan had confided in me, how precious I'd found those confidences. But then he'd been new territory for me, my lover of just a few months, an enticing new landscape for me to wander in, while for Helena he was the flawed, rather vulnerable man who'd fathered her child, who filled her dishwasher. I felt I was starting to develop a whole new sense of what their marriage had been about, the mixture of fondness and irritation with which she viewed him.

'I think that kind of temper is the last thing you need when you're dealing with the police,' she said. 'I mean, they're human too. They're obviously going to take against someone who's stroppy. I've always worried that he'd lose his rag with them – that he'd look guilty. He's got this thing about authority. It's calmed down in the last few years – but it's bound to flare up again when he's really in a corner . . .'

'I heard that they'd done the main interview,' I said.

'Yes.'

'Did he tell you about it?'

She nodded. 'It didn't sound too good,' she said.

I longed to ask more, but I waited patiently. She sat there quietly for a moment, doodling on the tabletop with her finger, tracing out patterns or letters, as children do. But if they were letters, I couldn't see what they said. Then she looked up at me again.

'Look,' she said, 'there are things you could tell me yourself, Chloe. That's why I agreed to see you really.'

'Okay,' I said, wondering what was coming.

'You work in child protection, don't you?'

I nodded.

'I did too, for a while,' she said. 'Years ago. I couldn't stand it, I'm afraid. All those ghastly teenage girls who just couldn't get it together.'

'Well, it can be frustrating,' I said. Seeing just why she'd have hated it – that her empathy had its limits, that she simply wouldn't comprehend how people might be driven to do self-destructive things.

'But you've dealt with cases like this before?'

'Yes.'

'You must know the score then,' she went on. 'Whether he'll go to prison. I want you to tell me what you think.'

'The disclosure's very damaging,' I said. 'But she doesn't actually name him. And I think that's all the evidence they've got. I guess

229

it all hinges on whether the jury think he matches the little girl's description.'

'You're talking as though you've actually seen the disclosure,' she said.

'Yes,' I said.

'So you *are* still involved?' She looked at me sharply, her eyes narrowing.

'No,' I said. 'I shouldn't have seen it, really.'

'So what have you been up to exactly? No, don't tell me. I guess I'd do the same. I'd have moved heaven and earth to hear what that child had to say, in your situation.'

She finished her coffee, put down the cup.

'What will he get if they convict him?' she said.

'Four years, perhaps,' I said.

'Hell,' she said.

There was silence between us for a moment. I didn't know how to finish it, when I should go. The music had changed, to a song about going on a sleigh ride together with you, trailing its baggage of predictable emotion.

'I asked him to come back,' she said. 'Did he tell you that? Not really to pick our relationship up – I mean, we couldn't do that – not after . . .' She gestured in my direction. 'But so he'd look like a family man. Well, that's exactly what he's been, for God's sake: it wouldn't be a lie. He didn't want to. Thought he'd jeopardize his chance of getting you back, I suppose.'

This was unanswerable. I sat and stared into my empty coffee cup, and felt the sense of connection between us, such as it had been, slipping away. And knew there was something I'd come for, wanted from her, that I hadn't got. That I'd wanted her to give me her knowledge of Dan and she couldn't, of course, even if she'd been willing to – because it couldn't be put into words. There was simply too much of it, it was like a great lake of memory, and it couldn't be held, it would run away like water between your fingers.

'Look, Chloe, I think you'd better go,' she said quite suddenly.

I got up quickly. I could sense how she was attempting to protect me from her anger. It confirmed me in the opinion I'd already formed of her – that she was a rather good person.

As I put on my jacket, she got out a cigarette, fumbling, too hasty.

Right on cue, the loudspeaker repeated, 'This shopping centre has been designated a non-smoking area . . .'

'Fuck them,' she said, with extreme bitterness. 'Fuck the lot of them.' She lit up. Her hand was shaking.

'Thank you for seeing me,' I said.

She shrugged, didn't meet my eyes. It was like she'd suddenly run out of goodwill.

'You've been very good to me,' I said. It was some kind of need I had to placate her: stupid really. I should have shut up and gone. 'I don't deserve it,' I said.

'No,' she said. She puffed at her cigarette.

'Thanks anyway,' I said again, and went.

I was several paces from the table when she called me back. I turned, went reluctantly, stood there looking down at her – fearing that her entirely justified bitterness had quite got control of her now.

She looked up at me, her elegant face scrunched up with effort. 'Look, I should have said this before. But I think he really loves you,' she said.

I fled then, fled down the escalator, past the jewellery shops and the kitchenware shops and the Christmas tree lights and the frenetic yellow angels in Dillons' window, right down to the darkness of the car park and the safety of my car. I sat there staring at the dashboard, hugging myself, trying to stop trembling. My meeting with her already felt unreal. I couldn't believe it had happened. I wondered if it had been a huge mistake. If I'd expected too much of her, or given away too much of myself. If it had been embarrassing or preposterous or cruel.

But two days later when Dan rang just as the girls were off for their weekend with their father, and said he wanted to talk, I asked him round.

25

He stood for a moment, looking round, as though registering the familiar things, checking they were still there, like friends. Lucy's God picture was stuck to the pinboard. He went to look at it.

'I like the way she's done the sandals,' he said.

I thought of when he'd first come to my house and stood there with his hair and his shirt soaked through with summer rain, how then too he'd looked at her drawings and asked if I was fierce like she'd drawn me.

'How are the girls?' he said.

'They're okay,' I said. And added, in spite of myself, just because it was true, 'Lucy misses you.'

A little crooked smile. This obviously touched him.

'I didn't bring them anything,' he said. 'I mean, I wanted to. But I thought you'd rather that I didn't.'

'Thanks,' I said.

He went to look out into the garden. It was a cold bright morning. The frost had gone from the middle of the lawn where the sun shone, but under the rose hedge and round the apple tree the ground was still white with it.

'You've re-done your windowboxes,' he said.

'Yes,' I said.

'They're so neat,' he said. 'I liked them better before, when they were all everywhere. They were more you somehow . . . I mean, they're very nice now too.'

I sensed how careful he was being with me – as though afraid that I might evanesce into nothing if he said the wrong thing.

'They looked better before the frost got to them,' I said. 'They get very dry when the soil gets frosted.' But as I looked at my pansies then, each flower drooping and crumpled with the cold, I did feel they were rather ungenerous and conventional and restrained, almost mean perhaps, felt a pang of loss for my alyssum and lobelias, for the sprawling careless abandoned flowers, the scents.

I made him coffee. As I brought him the cup, I caught sight of myself in the mirror over the fireplace, suddenly saw how I'd let myself go, how my hair was all straggly and badly in need of highlighting. We sat opposite each other at the table, as we'd sat so often before. In a weird way, it was his size I was most aware of, how he filled my gaze. He was the biggest person who'd been in my kitchen for ages: usually it was Alice or Lucy in that chair. I thought how strange it was to have him sitting there again after all this time, after all these things happening. I felt a shiver of nervousness on the surface of my skin. Or maybe it was a sexual thing: sometimes it's hard to tell the difference.

'So how are things?' I said. It was the kind of carefully vague question you might address to an acquaintance who's suffered some dreadful trauma, a bereavement perhaps.

'It's been pretty bloody,' he said. 'But it's okay now. The union have been great. They're paying my legal fees. I mean, that's what they're there for, but it's good to know you can rely on them. And Paola's been a tower of strength.' Seeing some expression cross my face, he added, 'You know, Paola Valente, the union rep.'

'Yes, I know,' I said. 'I remember.' As though I'd forget the woman who'd been the occasion of the only quarrel we'd had – before it started happening, before everything fell apart. I felt a surprising, inappropriate frisson of jealousy. I always imagined her as dark, foreign, rather louche: it was something about her name, the way it suggested a glamorously shady parentage and a stern Catholic upbringing full of sexual prohibitions since triumphantly defied: and wonderfully elevated cheekbones.

'Paola's always there for me,' he said. 'I rang her in the middle of the night once, which was pretty unforgivable of me. And she came to watch the disclosure video with me: I really needed her then.'

I felt a little got at by this. In a confused kind of way, I felt I should have been there, that it was my place. It was perhaps how he wanted me to feel.

'It must all be quite exciting for her,' I said bitchily. 'I mean, don't union reps usually deal with disputed travel claims?'

He looked up abruptly. There was a momentary lightening in his face, a hint of a smile. He seemed taken aback by my bitchiness, but kind of pleased too: pleased I still minded.

'Sorry,' I said. 'That was a nasty thing to say.'

'Well, maybe I was laying it on a bit thick,' he said. 'She is good to me, though.'

We sat silent for a moment. I was very aware of the tiniest sounds from outside in the garden, something dripping on the patio as the frost started to shift, the thin sweet pipe of a bird.

'You saw Helena,' he said.

'Yes,' I said.

'She said she'd have liked you if things had been different,' he said.

I couldn't help feeling a little pleased. 'It was really good of her to see me,' I said. 'She's rather brave, I think.'

'I guess so,' he said, with something that was almost pride. 'Shit, what a weird conversation.'

He drank his coffee. I watched. I saw how his hand curved round the coffee cup, how his skin was still a little brown from the summer, how the fine black hairs shaded the backs of his fingers. And I watched the slow graceful arc of his wrist as he lifted his cup to his mouth, and thought how I knew his gestures, knew how his hand had moved when he'd dragged his palm across my face, knew the warm pressure of it and how his skin smelt, tasted. No matter how it all turned out, I couldn't un-know these things.

'Felix says they've charged you,' I said.

'Yeah, they interviewed me. A long time ago now – at the end of October. I blew it,' he said, 'quite honestly.' Suddenly he looked all heavy and drooping, as though gravity pulled very hard on him, tugging him down. It was as though he'd come absolutely determined to be buoyant, a bit defiant, to show he was doing fine, and he couldn't manage it any more.

'I decided I was going to be absolutely straight with them,' he said, 'to tell the truth. I decided that was the only way to do it.'

My quick intake of breath was loud in the still room. I thought for a moment he meant he'd confessed.

'But they can twist anything you say – make it seem like you're lying,' he said. 'They know just how to trap you: you haven't a hope. The harder you try to convince them you're telling the truth,

234

the more they make out you're lying. And of course that gets you angrier – so it's a vicious circle. I mean, I hadn't seen the video then – I went in there still not knowing what the allegation was.'

The sun was fully out now: the light from the window shone through his fingers as he pushed the hair from his face, outlining his hands in translucent red.

'It took five hours,' he said. 'It felt like for ever. It's all taped – so you get these little pauses when they change the tape. And every time they start a new tape, they tell you you're there of your own free will, that you're free to go at any time. And I said to Felix at one point – I was so furious, I thought I might hit someone – I said, "What happens if I just walk out?" And Felix said, "They'll arrest you the minute you get out of the door."'

I waited.

'D'you want to know about it?' he said.

'Yes,' I said. 'Everything.'

'I'll tell you the bits I can remember,' he said. 'It's all a bit of a blur, but there are things they say that stick in your mind for ever – the way they twist your words and try to trap you.'

It had been the usual pair.

'The woman was your mate, that Victoria Griggs woman,' he said.

'She's not my mate,' I said.

The man with gelled hair was called Russell Blake, Dan said, and this time it was the man who did most of the talking. Dan sat facing them, with Felix at his side, in the little grey interview room. 'It's claustrophobic,' he said. 'You sit so close, your knees are almost touching.'

They were relaxed, almost expansive, to start with, he told me. Smiles, leaning back in their chairs. They talked generally about his work. They asked how many children he saw, what kinds of disabilities they had. They asked about his approach to his cases, his preferred way of engaging the children and families he worked with.

'Now, Mr Whitmore, you have an approach that could best be described as informal,' said Russell Blake. 'So you might for instance develop social relationships with your clients – get invited to dinner, that kind of thing?'

'Yes, that's happened,' said Dan. 'Some of my colleagues don't like it, but I think it helps you to be more effective, to win people's trust.'

'Ah yes,' said Russell Blake, as though he'd just made a connection that gave him intense satisfaction. 'To win people's trust. That's important to you in your work?'

'Yes,' said Dan.

There was a little pause, and then Russell Blake said, quite conversationally, running a hand over his sleek, gelled hair, 'I find it surprising that you haven't asked us anything about Carly Smithson.'

'You haven't spoken to me about Carly Smithson,' said Dan.

They told him the allegation then. Felix had only been able to find out a bit. It was the first time Dan had heard in detail what Carly said had been done to her.

Russell Blake had leant forward confidentially, hands spread out in a friendly open gesture. 'I'll be very above board with you,' he said. 'Carly doesn't actually name you. What she says is – it's someone that took her for lessons on her own. That narrows it down to three. Three men who took her for lessons on her own during the year in question. One of them was the teacher who works with bilingual children – and he's black, and Carly said it was a white man. One of them was a support teacher who has glasses and has always worn a beard – and she says the man who abused her doesn't have glasses or a beard. And she also says the man who did it has a blue car.'

He waited. Dan said nothing.

Russell Blake shrugged. 'So it's really quite clear to us,' he said, still in that level, conversational, confiding tone, 'that you are the person who Carly says indecently assaulted her.'

'I didn't assault her,' said Dan.

They didn't respond.

Vicky Griggs took over then. 'Now, I'm aware that you sometimes see disturbed children who come from difficult backgrounds – or children with limited ability – and children that sometimes might lie or fantasize. Now, am I right about that?'

'Yes,' said Dan.

'Do you think Carly was a child who fantasized at all?'

'There's nothing she's ever said to me that would suggest she fantasized,' he said.

236

'What about lying?'

'I can't think of any times she lied when she was with me,' he said.

I gasped when Dan told me this. I thought how this assertion would be used in court, how this was an absolute gift for the prosecution – that in the defendant's own professional opinion, this child doesn't make things up.

Dan responded to the scepticism in my face as I listened. 'Felix thought I was crazy, too,' he told me. 'Afterwards he said I'd been a complete idiot. All children fantasize, he said. But how could I claim she did? If I'd said she did, they'd have asked for examples. They'd have proved I was lying. I mean, they made out I was lying even when I was speaking the truth.'

If it had been me, I'd have said she was capable of fantasizing, I thought.

They talked about his car then. They asked if he'd ever taken Carly in his car. Dan said no, definitely not.

'Mr Whitmore,' said Russell Blake, 'if you *had* taken Carly in your car, are you sure you'd remember?'

'I definitely did not take her in my car,' said Dan.

'Sometimes a psychologist might collect a child from home – if they were truanting. Is that right?'

'It's possible,' said Dan. 'Say the child was phobic about school – you might work on getting them there. But it's more the education welfare officer's job.'

'But it's something you just might do – in exceptional circumstances?'

'It's not really part of my repertoire,' said Dan. 'I suppose maybe if a child was truanting persistently.'

'Now Carly was truanting.' Russell Blake was leaning forward now, his knees sometimes touching Dan's. He was speaking louder, faster, as though somebody had turned up all his controls. Dan could smell his breath. 'So with a child like Carly who was truanting it's possible you might go to the house and take her into school?'

'I suppose it's possible.'

'"I suppose it's possible",' repeated Russell Blake, mockingly. 'First you tell us categorically you did not take Carly into school, now you say there is a possibility. That's different from saying, "I definitely did not", isn't it?'

Dan said nothing.

'Isn't it?'

'I suppose so,' said Dan.

Then they asked how often he'd seen Carly, and he told them three times – that was what he could remember. They'd taken the file notes from his office the day they'd first arrested him, so he hadn't been able to check. Russell Blake said there were six diary entries between January and July that said Northolt Junior. He asked what they meant. Dan said he'd have seen children at Northolt on those dates.

'So,' said Russell Blake, 'I would be right in saying that there are other occasions that you've recorded in your diary when you visited Northolt School when you may have seen Carly, because there aren't any names for the children you've seen.'

'I would certainly have seen other children too,' said Dan. 'But I suppose it's possible.'

'So the statement you started off with – that you only saw Carly three times – is not quite accurate? I would suggest you had far more contact with Carly than you've revealed to us. I would suggest you've been deliberately concealing how much contact you had.'

'I'm not deliberately concealing anything,' said Dan. 'I'm just agreeing I could have seen her more than three times. I can't be sure without the file notes.'

'What concerns me here is that it's happened again, Mr Whitmore. Every time we speak about something that gets a bit near the knuckle you lie to us or change your story.'

'You're playing with words,' said Dan. 'You're twisting what I said.' His words sounded hollow, futile.

Russell Blake had smiled very slightly then, he told me. I thought of the polite and rather narcissistic young man who'd interviewed me, remembered the sliver of steel in his voice when I'd said I didn't want my daughters interviewed.

Dan got up from my kitchen table, went to lean on the windowsill, looking out, the outline of his body dark and precise against the brightness outside.

'There's a point at which you give up,' he told me. 'You stop trying to defend yourself – you know that everything you say is

238

going to be twisted. It's like they've got you all tied up – and you can feel them pulling tighter and tighter . . .'

The police had gone back to the allegation then. That was when they'd told him that Carly had said that after the abuse the man who'd done it had washed his hands.

Russell Blake had asked if he remembered using the sink in the room.

'I certainly didn't wash my hands. I'm not sure there *is* a sink in the room,' said Dan.

'Would you categorically state you didn't wash your hands when you were having a session with Carly?'

'No, I don't think I did. I mean, I haven't touched this child.'

'It's happened again. First you say you're certain you didn't do something – now it's changed to "I don't think I did".'

'But every time I say that I didn't do something, you come up with some reason why I might have done, so I don't know what to say.'

Russell Blake leant back, hands clasped behind his head. He spoke very quietly, his voice silky, savouring his advantage. 'So let me try and understand that little piece of rationale you've just thrown at us,' he said. 'You're saying you can just sit there and lie provided we haven't got any way to disprove what you say.'

'For fuck's sake, I'm not lying to you,' shouted Dan.

Felix stopped the interview, helped him calm down. 'They're only doing it to rile you,' he told Dan. 'Most of it's intimidatory, it couldn't be used in court.'

But I could just imagine it, how Dan would react, how he'd want to hack his way out of this thicket of words, not prise them carefully apart. And I saw how risky this was: how you should keep control, just go on repeating your denial.

'Can I ask,' said Russell Blake then, 'do you often lose your temper like this at work, Mr Whitmore?'

'No.'

'Ah, but we have a witness who says you do. She tells us you sometimes lose your temper quite inappropriately, that you have difficulty establishing working relationships with colleagues.'

Dan knew of course who it was. He'd said nothing, sat there and cursed Fiona Parker in his head, cursed her salaciousness and her bloody hairbands and her air of total righteousness.

239

In my garden the sun was fully out now. Everything glittered and sparkled, the frost briefly bright like blossom on the apple tree, everywhere dazzlingly white, a whiteness that made the everyday colours, like the colours of Lucy's sand toys left out on the lawn, look dusty and dull. Dan stood there looking out for a moment, then he came and sat at my table again, sat quietly as though wondering what to say.

'There was one thing I'd absolutely decided before I went in,' he said. 'That your name wouldn't be mentioned.' He wasn't looking at me. His head was bowed, his hair fell into his eyes, he didn't push it back. 'I wanted so much to keep you out of it. I didn't want you to be there in their notes or on their tapes. But they did speak about you,' he said. 'I'm sorry.'

Russell Blake had said, 'Now, during these sessions you had with Carly, did you ever talk to her about anything other than school work?'

'I might talk to a child about her friends and family,' said Dan. 'It would be part of the assessment – to see how well she could express herself. You might talk about a child's family or her pets.'

'When you're speaking about her family, would you perhaps refer to your own family situation?'

'No.'

'Is that "definitely not" or "I don't think I did"?'

'Definitely not.'

'Because Carly says you talked to her about your girlfriend.'

'No.'

'But you did have a girlfriend towards the end of the time period we're talking about, didn't you?'

'I had a wife and a girlfriend, yes,' he'd said.

He sat there at my kitchen table, staring at his hands, looking so unhappy and defeated.

'They asked your name – as though they didn't know it – and about our sex life,' he told me.

'What about our sex life?' I said.

'I said it was good,' he said dully. 'That was all.'

They'd twisted it all again of course, he told me.

'And you're sure you'd never talk about personal things with a child like Carly?'

'Never.'

'Are there situations in which it's possible that a psychologist might talk about his own personal life? Is it possible that's something you might do?'

'I don't think I ever would. I suppose it's possible.'

'So you think that there's a possibility – just a small possibility – that you might do that.'

'Well, I suppose you might.'

Now it was Vicky Griggs' turn. She leant forward, hands neatly clasped in front of her, in that rather pious pose she did so well, spoke in her virtuous head girl voice. 'I haven't worked with children for as long as you have, Mr Whitmore, but I've worked with children for quite a number of years, and if you asked me that question, whether I've ever talked to a child I've worked with about my personal life, I would say no, I've never done that. I *know* I've not. I wouldn't say "I suppose it's possible" because I *know* I've not.'

'I got angry again then,' Dan told me, 'which of course was just what she wanted. But it had been five hours, and I was hungry and exhausted and I couldn't think straight any more. It's a shame I couldn't have kept a grip for a bit longer – because it was about over then.'

'That was it?' I said, surprised.

'More or less. Like I said, it's all a bit of a haze now. But those were the points where they really went on and on, weaselling away.'

'Did they say anything about Alice and Lucy?' I said.

'No,' he said. 'No, absolutely nothing. I promise. Well, why would they?'

So I assumed – unless he was lying to me – that they hadn't talked about the photograph.

'I walked out of the police station and I knew I'd blown it,' he said. 'I started thinking about prison then. I realized that till that moment I'd never really believed it would go to trial. Let alone that I could be found guilty.'

'Yes,' I said. I could see that was how you'd do it – live it one step at a time.

'But I knew I'd absolutely played into their hands,' he said. 'That they could make me out to be a liar – that I'd been angry and out of control.'

241

He got up, started pacing up and down, his hands clenched into fists, so you could see the whiteness of the bone.

'They charged me a week later,' he said. 'I had to go back to the station. They do your fingerprints, a photo, look for scars and tattoos. You know you're a criminal then.'

He was full of nervous energy. With my intense physical sensitivity to him, I could sense the charge of it, like static in the air.

'I don't know what I'll get if I do go down,' he said. 'Felix reckons four years. Is that what you think? I mean – you've been involved in lots of these cases.'

'Yes, it could be four years,' I said.

'But I might get more because of being in a professional position?'

'It's possible,' I said.

'I'll tell you something, Chloe,' he said. 'If I do go to prison, I'm not going to go on Rule 43. I'm not going to go as a sex offender. I'll just be an ordinary prisoner, take my chances.'

A little impulse of fear ran down my spine.

'You're crazy,' I said, hearing how my voice was suddenly sharp, thin, high. 'You could get beaten up – you could get killed, for Christ's sake.'

'I couldn't go in with the sex offenders,' he said.

'Dan, please don't say that.' I was pleading, my voice choked with the tears I kept swallowing down. 'Jesus – you want to come out alive, don't you?'

He didn't seem to hear me. 'I might be able to do something worthwhile,' he said. 'I could get into prison education perhaps, teach other prisoners. Teach languages or psychology or something.'

'You're so fucking romantic,' I said. 'Prisons are savage places. You have to think about *you* – you just have to get through it somehow, you just have to survive. You don't go to prison to do *good*, for God's sake.'

He sat down, reached across the space between us so the skin of my forearm prickled, expecting his touch, then pulled his hand back. 'Chloe, I don't think you understand,' he said, very gently. 'It might be my way of surviving.'

'I'm sorry,' I said. 'It scares me.'

'Yes,' he said.

I asked what he'd been doing, how he filled his time. He said he'd been seeing people from the office again. 'There's still this rule that we mustn't make contact,' he said. 'But quite honestly I can't see that the Civic Centre are going to check up on it. So I don't feel quite such a leper now . . . And I get bits of news – like about my old cases.' He looked across at me then, his face lightening suddenly. 'I know what I wanted to tell you,' he said. 'That little Downs boy, Nicky, d'you remember?'

'Of course.'

'Fiona Parker did chuck him out. God, I hate that woman. But St Saviour's said they'd have him – d'you know it?'

I shook my head.

'It's another mainstream school. Very dynamic headmistress. And he's getting on fine – they think he's great there, they really appreciate him. Paola told me.' There was genuine pleasure in his face.

'I'm so glad,' I said.

He said he'd been doing odd jobs for people, laying a patio, putting up a wall, knocking down an old air-raid shelter. 'I still see Monica – she's one of the literacy teachers,' he said. 'I painted her whole house for her. Made rather a good job of it, too. Come to think of it, your hallway could do with a coat of paint,' he added, not very hopefully.

I shook my head. He smiled in that way I'd always loved, self-deprecating, like a little boy's. Like when he'd first turned up, late, on my doorstep, after Lucy's party.

'Dan,' I said, 'isn't there anyone who can help? Give you advice or counselling or something?'

'Well, there's PAIN,' he said.

I nodded. It's the self-help organization for people wrongly accused of child abuse.

'I rang them,' he said. 'I thought they might at least put me in touch with other people in the same position. But it was very depressing. They said it was all about damage limitation – that whatever happened there was no way I'd get my job back. Even if I was found not guilty. Even if it never got to court.'

'Yes,' I said.

'That was one of the worst bits,' he said. 'The sense that it couldn't be undone.' He was speaking more slowly now, as though the words

243

were hard to say. 'I got in my car and I drove down to the river. There's a car park where people have picnics in summer.'

'Yes, I know it,' I said. When the girls were tiny, I'd sometimes taken them there to feed the ducks.

'I went for a walk along the towpath,' he said. 'There was no one about. I stood there for ages looking down at the water.'

He waited, as though wondering what to tell me. He turned away a little.

'I just stood there and thought how easy it would be,' he said.

I shivered. It's so cold, the river in winter. It was as though I could feel the coldness of the water, as though the water was on my skin. I wanted so much to reach out and touch him, to lend him some of my warmth. As you'd surely feel towards anyone, whoever they might be, who'd been in that dark lonely place, looking into the water, trying to decide. But I didn't move.

'When I set off back home,' he said, 'and I looked at my watch, I found an hour had passed. A whole hour that I'd just stood there staring into the river.

'That was the worst time,' he said again. 'But I won't do that. I know now I won't do that, whatever happens.'

I couldn't say anything.

Then it had all got a little better, he said. He'd been to Italy for a week.

'I can go abroad as long as I'm back to renew my bail,' he said. 'I went to Florence. I'd always wanted to go and never been – Helena never wanted to travel that far. I went to the Uffizi and the Duomo and Santa Croce.' He sat and looked at his hands clasped in front of him on the table. 'I'd hoped to take you there sometime,' he said. 'I tried to picture you on the steps of Santa Croce. The light's extraordinary there even in winter, kind of warmer, yellower than anywhere else: you'd look amazing with that light washing over you, the way it would catch in your hair. But this weird thing happened. I couldn't see your face at all, couldn't picture it. It was like you'd really left me then, gone from me.'

He saw how I turned from him, hid my face with my hand.

'Chloe, I'm sorry. You don't want any of this, do you? I'll shut up in a minute. Just let me say this once – I won't say it again, I promise. I miss you terribly, I want to touch you so much.'

244

'Perhaps you'd better go,' I said.

'Yes,' he said. But he didn't get up. He leaned across the table towards me. In the sharpness of the gesture as he moved his hand towards me along the table between us, in the intensity of his gaze as he looked at me, his eyes dark, shadowed, the irises absolutely black, I read the anger he felt towards me, that he'd always sought to shield me from.

'I'll go,' he said. 'But please listen for one moment more. I can't, can't understand why you think I did this thing. Nothing's changed. A little girl, a stranger, has said something. Something that isn't true – or that certainly isn't all true – or isn't true as she tells it. That isn't anything to do with me, with us. Nothing's changed between us. It's just you and me here like it always was.'

'No, it isn't,' I said. 'How can it be?'

He followed me to the door. We stood on the doorstep, looking at one another, not knowing what to say. He just kept looking at me and not going and I didn't know what to do. Then he shrugged and turned and left me.

26

I had a complicated violent dream that night, a dream with lots of shooting and running around, and high walls spiky with shards of broken glass, and dogs with big red open mouths full of teeth. I quite often have dreams of this kind, that almost seem to make sense when I wake, to have a thread of plot I can recall. I guess it's because of the Cold War thrillers I read to get me to sleep. Sometimes I revisit these dreams on waking, taking pleasure in their narrative drive and their drama, in the lavish inventiveness of my unconscious: but that night it had been too savage to enjoy, the pursuit closing in with ferocious inevitability, the climax a bloody annihilation in some grim East European ghetto, and the quarry or victim seemed to have been myself.

My clock said 3.14. I got up, shivering. My cotton curtains are pretty but they don't keep out the cold. I put on my frumpy towelling dressing gown. There was frost on the outside of the landing window, whitely feathering the pane.

I paused by the door of Lucy's room, sensing the emptiness inside. The house always feels so quiet without the girls. When they're there you're not really conscious of their breathing, but when they're away you notice the absence of that subliminal rise and fall of breath, even outside the door. And that winter it had started to get to me a bit: I'd taken to drawing the curtains in their bedrooms and putting on their nightlights even when they weren't there. Pathetic, really. I wouldn't ever have admitted it, even to Jude. It just made the house feel less empty, softened the edges of their absence, brought them a little nearer. I didn't like the look of their rooms the next morning either: there was something slightly deathly about them, everything just as it had been the night before, no tumbled beds warm from their bodies.

I pushed open Lucy's door. Her duvet was turned back, her hot-water bottle poking out from under her pillow. It had a cheerful

Gromit cover in brown and yellow fleece. I took it, went downstairs. I fried an egg and ate it, poured myself a scotch, filled the hot-water bottle. I went back to bed, sat there sipping my scotch and clasping the hot-water bottle tightly to myself, trying to warm up a little.

And it was then, at half past three in the morning, as I sat in bed hugging the Gromit hot-water bottle and spelling out all the arguments again and again, as I weighed up the things I'd learnt from the people I'd talked to – Helena who was intelligent and shrewd and very angry with him and still thought he hadn't done it, Philippa who'd told me about Carly's troubled family and the suspicion of past abuse, Felix who'd said how readily we believe someone to be guilty if the crime of which they're accused is particularly vile, Dan himself, with his crazy male bravado, his yearning to do something good if he did get sent to prison: as I walked the entangled pathways of my mind, everything around me all overhanging and murky and shadowed and overgrown, lost much of the time, and doubling back on myself, and confused and unable to find a straight path and not knowing which way to go: it was then that I let myself think, for the first time since Vicky had shown me the photograph, that Dan was probably innocent.

I didn't experience this as a certainty, a road-to-Damascus flash of enlightenment. I knew that in these cases hunches weren't to be trusted. There was still the chorus in my head that warned me to be wary, that knowledge I had from all the cases I'd worked with: the men in smart suits, the respectable fathers of families, who'd turned out to be abusers. There was still the photograph. So there wasn't any sudden shock of instinctive knowing. It was more an intellectual thing, a new recognition that the evidence was really pretty thin, that in some very profound sense the case against him didn't hold together.

And it didn't bring me any comfort, this new understanding. The probability of his innocence had awful implications for me. It meant that I had to act: and that scared me so.

I thought of all the hints, the threats, in the things people had said to me: all veiled in polite language, carefully hidden in the sub-text, but I knew quite well they were there. Like monsters in a child's story, lurking beneath the weedy brim of a lake, hiding between the struts of a rickety bridge, if anything even more frightening for not being made explicit. It's a good thing we caught up with Daniel Whitmore when we did . . . You should take this into consideration in any decisions you may make about your children . . . Simone and I are absolutely agreed that if there was any risk of the girls having even the briefest contact with him . . .

I tried to tell myself my fears were nonsense – that no one was going to take my children away. Yet if Dan were found guilty and I had a relationship with him at any time in my life once he'd served his sentence, a social worker with the flimsiest of suspicions could get my children taken into care. There'd be case conferences and planning meetings and Emergency Protection Orders, the thing would be set in motion, start to wash over us, to sweep us away, and all those things that seemed to fence me in and protect me, the battlements I'd built – my middle-classness, my beautiful house, my daughters' closeness to me, my Certificate of Qualification in Social Work – they'd be about as much use as walls of sand before the rush of the tide. And even if he was found not guilty, the taint would still be there: it never goes. If I then had him to live with me – or even continued to see him – Adam and Simone would surely walk it if they chose to contest custody. I saw the danger so clearly, sitting there with the frost scratching at the window, listening to the harsh rather hostile little noises the city makes at night, a car alarm set off somewhere, the scream of a siren, and behind and through it all the silence, and I clutched the hot-water bottle more closely to me.

But I thought about Dan too that night, thought about prison, what that might mean for him. I didn't have to distance myself any more, I could put myself in his place, and I realized then that, like Dan himself, I hadn't thought it through. So far it had all been words, unreal in a way: the balancing of probabilities, the weighing up of evidence, the speculation on things that might have been. Yet I saw then that this was just a temporary thing, this rather literary phase of argument and abstraction. That these plays on words might be suddenly, brutally, terminated – the door closing, the key turning, the footsteps fading down the walkway.

I thought too about things that happen in prison. In the middle of the night, when you wake from dreams which are of course all image and feeling, the mind, close to dreaming, still tends to work in pictures, in sensations, so you actually see, feel the thing happening.

So I knew these things in a visceral way, as though they were being done to me. I knew boots and fists and the stabbing of screwdrivers stolen from work-benches, knew the crack of the impact on my jaw, the searing of punctured skin, the warm blood tasting of iron in my mouth.

I went on drinking. Eventually, soothed by the whisky and heavy with sleep, the hot-water bottle warming my skin, the wounds I'd imagined staunched and healing, I started to drift off, still sitting up, my head falling heavily, awkwardly, forward, so it woke me – and I slid down under the duvet onto my pillow, curling up to keep the heat in, and was suddenly overcome by my longing for him, all the old hungers triggered again, the longing for the feel of his skin, his smell, for his weight and his warmth with my arms around him, a hunger to hold him that was somehow deeper than desire, more like a yearning for a lost part of oneself – like the longing of a child for a lost parent, a parent for a child.

27

The girls came back at six o'clock on Sunday, with their books and their toys and their dirty washing, and their tales of their visit to Laser Quest and the pizza with pineapple on they'd had for lunch. Hugging me, their bodies warm and solid, the house filling up with their noise and quarrels and laughter like a fruit tree suddenly chattering with starlings. As I made their tea, got Lucy ready for bed, I looked back to the fears I'd had on Saturday night, and decided I'd been paranoid. There were no monsters under the bridge after all. Well, maybe just the tiniest ripple, a faint glossy track in the waterweed. It was impossible to imagine that anything could happen to break up this routine, this essential prosaic dailiness of our lives, all the lost socks and wobbly teeth and chocolate bars from the Blue Moon store and pages of long division. Women like me, I told myself, don't lose their children in custody battles, certainly don't have their children taken away by Social Services. It was unthinkable.

I sat on the corner of Lucy's bed and read her her bedtime story. We were nearly at the end of one of her true life vet books: they were her favourites then – they seemed perfect for her, full of animals with interesting injuries and heroic vets who performed lots of elaborate and slightly gruesome veterinary procedures. This one was the tale of a rabbit called Thumper who had a chest infection, and we'd nearly finished it. And in the penultimate chapter he started breathing in little gasps, with a faraway look in his eyes, and I saw with some trepidation where it all seemed to be heading, and then he died.

'Poor old Thumper,' I said, gently closing the book. 'Still, he was well looked after, wasn't he? They did everything they could. And I expect he was quite old anyway.' Trying to smooth it over, to make it all alright.

But Lucy was outraged. She sat up in bed, all stiff and formal, her forehead creased by a stern frown. 'He can't die, Mummy. It's a *children's* book.'

It was what I'd always told them when they couldn't find the courage to finish a story, when they wanted to be assured before we read another word that it would all turn out for the best, that there'd be some fabulous reversal, an eleventh-hour escape from the belly of the wolf: I'd always said that children's books have happy endings. I've tried so hard to protect them. Maybe too hard. I'm still not sure. Even after everything that's happened, I still don't know what's right.

But now Lucy was adamant.

'Thumper didn't die, Mummy. It's not true.'

And I had to tell the last few pages again, with Thumper still lustily alive at the end of the final sentence.

I gave her a hug, tucked her up.

'So you had a good time with Daddy?' I said, as I turned off her overhead light.

'Mmm,' she said, wriggling down under the duvet, her face full and pink with sleepiness.

'Lucy,' I said, ever so casual, 'd'you like Simone any better now?'

'She's got a new sofa,' said Lucy, yawning.

'A nice sofa?'

She shook her head. 'It's all black and shiny. Alice says it's made from an animal.'

'Oh,' I said. 'Very smart.'

'No, it's not,' said Lucy.

'I just wondered how you felt about Simone now,' I said. I knew it was wrong to probe like this, but I needed so badly to know. 'You used to say sometimes that you didn't much like her.'

'I don't,' said Lucy. I felt instantly consoled. She put her comforter to her lips so her words were a bit muffled. 'But she did take us to Laser Quest. The gumball machine was brilliant,' she said. '*You* never take us to Laser Quest, Mummy.'

'We'll go together sometime,' I said. 'You and me and Alice. And you can have more gumballs. I promise.'

All day Monday, I struggled with it. As I sat through a tedious team-meeting, supervised another painful session with Kyle and his mother, tried to get Trish and Amber talking again, I spelled out all the arguments in my head, on one side and then on the other. And at last I thought, Yes. Yes I will do this: I will start seeing Dan again. Not to have him in my bed – I didn't feel that was possible till we saw how things would turn out – but for friendship, just to sit and talk at my kitchen table, to give him a little support, a little comfort. Where could be the harm in that? I would only see him on those weekends when Alice and Lucy were at Adam's, and before I rang Dan, before I fixed it up, I'd tell Adam exactly what I was planning – so no one could accuse me of being secretive or underhand about it. So I would be quite beyond criticism. For surely if I told the truth, if I made the limits quite clear, it would all be okay. I just had to be very open, very direct.

I rang Adam. He listened in silence to my carefully rehearsed little speech.

'If you do this, Chloe,' he said, when I'd finished, 'I have to warn you, there'll be no second chances.' It was his most intimidating voice, the one he used to lay down the law to inept hospital managers and recalcitrant medical students. 'If I find my girls have been anywhere near that man, I'll take immediate action.'

'Of course they won't be going anywhere near him,' I said. 'That's why I'm ringing – so you would know exactly what's going to happen. I just wanted it all to be totally above board. I mean, I didn't *have* to ring you.'

He seemed to see the logic in that. 'Well, I can't stop you,' he said. 'What you do when the girls aren't there is up to you, I guess. Though quite why you ever got so besotted with that bloody man beats me completely,' he added, with a sudden little spurt of jealous irritation. 'Still, it's your life, I suppose.'

'Yes,' I said.

'I have to say, I don't know what Simone will say about it though,' he went on. I thought I heard a small sigh down the line, but maybe it was my imagination.

'She won't approve,' I said. 'Obviously. She never does.'

'There's no need to get all catty about her,' he said. 'She has a deep and genuine concern for Alice and Lucy.'

Stuff that, I thought. But I said goodbye quite politely.

I rang Dan straight away. He wasn't there.

I listened to the tape of his voice, felt something knot and twist in my stomach, a little kick of desire. I didn't leave a message, though: I decided to wait and try again on Tuesday. Answerphones aren't for lovers. It's so easy to say the wrong thing, and it can't be undone.

On Tuesday it was a struggle getting ready for school, one of those messy chaotic mornings full of grumbling and lost keys and spilt cereal. I'd forgotten to take the loaf out of the freezer so I had to make Lucy's sandwiches with frozen bread: they'd have thawed by lunchtime but I couldn't cut the crusts off, so I knew she wouldn't eat them. Alice remembered at the last moment that she needed her PE kit, and it wasn't clean, and I had to sponge the mud off with a flannel. Then Lucy complained I'd done her plait all wrong.

'It's not in the middle,' she said. 'It makes me feel all lopsided.'

Alice had just set off, grumpily, the dirty kit in her bag, and I'd attempted to placate Lucy with some crisps to eat in front of the *Big Breakfast* while I hunted for my keys, when the doorbell rang. I swore under my breath.

It was Vicky. I hadn't seen her for ages. She was dressed in a smart navy coat and looked rather severe and unsmiling.

My mouth went dry as I greeted her.

'I need to talk to you,' she said.

'Okay,' I said. 'But not now. I've got to get Lucy to school.'

'I think I should come in now, Chloe, actually,' she said. 'I won't keep you long.'

She stepped uninvited into my hall, bringing the cold air from the street in with her.

I took her into the kitchen. The table was littered with breakfast things, a bowl of soggy Frosties, half a cup of tepid coffee. I was very aware of that clean rather antiseptic smell she had: whatever made the smell, it was something she'd just put on.

'Chloe, I'm told you're seeing Dan again.'

I stared at her.

'Dr Langdon rang me,' she said.

'I don't understand,' I said. 'I don't see why he would ring you. I don't see why he would think it concerned you in any way.'

'Chloe, he did the right thing,' she said.

I had to sit down. I leaned forward, spreading my hands on

253

the table, needing to feel the hard heavy oak all solid under my palms.

'But he was alright about it,' I said. 'I told him exactly what I was going to do. I wanted to be completely above board about it.'

'When he spoke to me yesterday afternoon, he certainly wasn't alright about it,' she said.

Shit, I thought. Bloody Simone.

Vicky was frowning, rather flushed. I could tell that beneath her brisk shiny surface she was acutely uncomfortable. She'd become a little too friendly with me, perhaps, felt ill-at-ease in this disciplinary role. I recognized the discomfort: it happens to social workers all the time. You befriend some poor struggling mother, sort out her social security, listen sympathetically when she tells you about her own cruel childhood – how her father held her head down the loo or raped her or beat her up – but the children still seem accident prone, there are fractures that don't make sense, black eyes, the baby has a torn frenum where someone has cruelly snatched his bottle from his mouth – and in the end you take her children away. You, who were her friend.

Vicky sat down facing me, rested her fingertips together. I saw her throat ripple as she swallowed.

'You're putting yourself in a terribly difficult position,' she said. 'You must see that. There's a child protection issue here, Chloe. You're surely aware of the risks – given your line of work.'

She spoke in a perfectly level reasonable way, but there was an edge of threat to everything she said. It scared me.

'But the girls weren't going to see him,' I said, my voice high, protesting, tipping over into anger. 'That wasn't the plan: that wasn't what I told Adam. I was only going to see him when they weren't here – when they were with Adam. That was the whole point of ringing him – to reassure him on that.'

'Maybe that's how it would have started,' she said.

I said nothing.

'We all know that one thing leads to another,' she said. 'You've got to make a clean break. It's the only way.'

I must have looked frightened, because she reached out towards me in one of those truncated gestures of comfort she often used, her voice emollient as Vaseline.

'Look, no one's thinking of taking any action on your children at present. Please don't think that.'

I knew it was an attempt at reassurance, but I didn't feel reassured.

'I have to be straight with you, though, Chloe,' she went on. 'Things could change if they were felt to be at risk. This man has been charged with a serious sex offence against a child: you must know what view Social Services would take if it was thought your children were in any way in danger.'

I said nothing. I knew there was no choice to be made any more, that I didn't have a choice. It was like being trapped in some virtual world where someone had touched a key and changed the dimensions of everything, and the walls of my kitchen were closing in, and the most familiar things, the plants and photos and coffee cups, seemed suddenly huge and menacing.

'I really would advise you most strongly not to do this,' she said again.

'I won't do it then,' I said. 'I won't see him.'

'Good,' she said. 'I knew you'd see reason.'

She got up to go. 'I won't keep you any longer – I know you've got to get that little one of yours to school.'

She went briskly out into the cold street. We didn't say goodbye. She pulled the door shut behind her with a small but significant click like the breaking of a bone.

It was ten to nine. We'd never make it to school in time. I considered taking the car, but the traffic was awful – I could see the tailback from my front door – and it would probably be just as quick to walk.

Lucy was in a foul mood: I had to drag her along.

'Mummy, Mummy, my plait. You've got to do it again. I'm not going to school like this.'

'For God's sake, will you just shut up about it, Lucy,' I said. 'Jesus, the fuss you girls make about absolutely nothing. I am *not* going to do it again. You know there isn't time.'

She was very cross and rather pious.

'It's really annoying when people do things for you and they do them all wrong and you have to suffer,' she said.

All along the road motorists were scraping the ice off their wind-screens, and there were white clouds of evil-smelling exhaust as they ran their engines on full choke to warm them up. It made me mad that we had to breathe in all this benzene and lead, that they were so selfish, polluting the world. I glared at them as we passed. And the driver who stopped halfway across the pedestrian crossing made me furious too, in his stupid swanky Subaru with those horrible bull bars that ought to be banned, that can kill a child at five miles an hour, and the two obnoxious lads in Adidas tracksuits who dawdled selfishly on the pavement in front of us, using up far too much space, and the man running for a bus who didn't give a damn about the people in his path, and just missed banging his briefcase into Lucy. I wanted to hit them all, to push them out of the way. I felt this helpless pointless overwhelming rage with everyone we passed.

Something else happened that week. Something that upset me in a way that was quite out of proportion – because it didn't really change anything, even though it hurt like hell. It was perhaps the lowest point for me – the point when I finally gave up.

I got home at lunchtime on Friday and my answerphone was flashing: there were three messages. Adam, about his next weekend with the girls, the sound of his voice making me briefly furious again, no mention of Dan. My mother, with news of an organic Christmas pudding she'd heard about on *Woman's Hour*. We were staying with her over Christmas: it's what we usually do, I take most of the food and do all the cooking, but already she was getting quite worked up about the potential health risks of Christmas dinner.

And another message, surprising me.

'This is Sally Whitmore.' A warm rather husky voice, with fashionably dropped consonants. 'I'd like to talk to you. I'm doing a placement at City Talk over Christmas.' It was the local radio station. 'You can get me on this number . . .'

I was surprised, pleased, intrigued. I remembered the photo that Dan had shown me – the sweet-faced girl with the nose-stud and strong eyebrows just like his. How Dan had said, I'd love you to meet her: how I'd felt that was impossible. Yet now perhaps it had suddenly become possible.

I was touched that she'd bothered to ring me. In my permanently over-emotional state, it felt like a gift, like a card from a long-lost friend or some flowers thrust into your hand: that at last something good was going to happen to me. I played her message again, drinking in her voice thirstily, listening out for hints or traces of Dan – as lovers will cling to anything that has his mark on or that hints of him, an envelope with his writing scrawled across it, a mutual friend who mentions him casually in conversation. And for a brief manic moment I even imagined that through her I might reach out to Dan again in spite of everything, that through her I might be able to explain.

Before I picked up the phone, I thought very carefully about what I'd say to her. There were so many things I'd like to ask her. Yet it wouldn't be fair, perhaps, to quiz her, to keep firing lots of questions. I decided I'd just approach it with a quite open mind, see what she had to say.

I rang the number, asked for the extension.

'Hello,' said a voice. A woman: it sounded like the voice on my answerphone, but I couldn't be sure.

'Could I speak to Sally Whitmore? It's Chloe Langdon,' I said.

'Right,' said the voice. 'Chloe Langdon.' And then, without introducing herself, without any preamble or warning, 'Yeah. Well, I just wanted to say to your face how incredibly angry I am about what you've done to my father. I'm deeply deeply disgusted with the way you've used him, Chloe Langdon.'

It was like being hit, it winded me like a punch in the stomach.

'If there's one thing I despise more than anything else,' she said, 'it's frustrated menopausal women who go round wrecking other people's marriages. I can't think of a word for the kind of woman you are.' Her voice was harsh, abrasive, her loudness distorted by the line. 'There isn't a word for it. The only words I can think of are too good for you.'

She paused for breath. But I couldn't say anything, I was rigid with shock.

'They were happy, you know,' she went on. 'You may not want to hear this, but they were good together, my Mum and Dad. Then you come along – and there we are, twenty-three years of marriage down the pan.'

She was shouting now, her words banged around in my head, I had to hold the phone away from my face.

'So – you destroy my parents' marriage, Chloe Langdon, you

get my Dad just where you want him – and then what happens? Suddenly, quite out of the blue, you tell him to go stuff himself.' Her voice scraped at my ears. 'He's not what you want anymore. You lose interest. You make out that you believe this lunatic allegation. Just when he has these terrible things to face, you push him away. He's been suicidal, you know. Well, maybe you don't care. I guess you don't give a fuck. But if he kills himself, believe me, you'll have blood on your hands,' she said.

She shut up for a moment. I heard her talk to someone. 'Okay, yeah,' she said. I could tell her head was turned away from the phone. 'Black, two sugars. Cheers. Just stick it there.'

There was a pause. I heard a door shut.

She started up again. 'I'll tell you something else,' she said. 'I'll tell you this for free. You may think you knew him, you may kid yourself you had some kind of cheap intimacy with him. But you never ever knew him at all. You don't know the first bloody thing about my Dad if you think he could do this vile thing,' she said. 'But then I don't suppose that bothers you in the least, does it? Women like you – they use people and spit them out,' she said. 'You're a user, Chloe Langdon. I wish to God my Dad had never met you.'

Then there was silence. She'd finally dried up.

'Are you still there?' she said. Suddenly a little unsure, sounding much younger, a girl scarcely out of her teens, who'd done what she felt she had to do and didn't know where to go next.

'Yes,' I said. 'But I'm going now.'

I put down the phone.

It was cold outside Lucy's school: the frost hadn't thawed all day. Our breath was white as we waited.

'Are you okay?' said Jake's mother.

'Not really,' I said. 'I think I must be getting some sort of bug.'

'You look ever so pale,' she said.

The bell went. Lucy came rushing out, clutching a rather lugubrious reindeer she'd made from the inside of a loo roll. She gave me a huge urgent hug, squashing the reindeer. I hugged her back, needing her warmth so badly.

'How many days, Mummy?' she said.

'Only ten,' I said.

'Counting Christmas Eve?'

'Yes.'

'It's nine then. Christmas Eve *is* Christmas. Really, Mummy, you ought to know that by now.'

'Okay, nine,' I said.

We drove on to Alice's school. Most of the children seemed to have gone, but Alice wasn't there. We waited for several minutes then went in to find her.

The grounds of Connington House are sleekly groomed in summer but today they looked rather bleak. The lawn in front of the school had been trampled in the wet weather, and now was all frozen.

Lucy skipped across the grass. 'You can walk on the muddy bits and your shoes don't get dirty,' she said.

The little fish pond in the rockery by the entrance was iced over, and someone had lifted out some of the ice and left it on the ground: it had a dangerous look like broken glass. A few black pods hung from the laburnum. Two girls straggled past, smiled shyly at me: they were from Alice's class and I guessed her teacher had kept them all in for a few minutes after school, perhaps for some misdemeanour.

As we got to the main entrance, Alice emerged, looking harassed. She thrust a Christmas card she'd made at me: the greeting was in Latin.

'I hate that woman,' she said. 'She kept us in because someone had lost a protractor. Just before Christmas, too. I ask you. There ought to be a law against it.'

'Never mind,' I said. 'We'll soon be home.'

I turned to go back to the car.

She grabbed my arm. 'Wait, Mum,' she said. 'There's something I want to show you.'

'Alice, we really need to be getting back,' I said.

'No,' she said. 'You've got to see this. It'll only take a minute.'

'What is it?' I said.

'Wait and see,' she said.

'Is it a growing thing?' said Lucy.

'Sort of,' said Alice.

She took us round the side of the school past the science block.

259

A solitary trumpeter in a distant classroom was playing 'Hark the Herald Angels' badly out of tune.

'Where exactly are we going?' I said.

'Just follow me,' she said.

We turned a corner round the back of the science rooms.

It was a piece of waste ground really, a part of the school that parents and visitors never saw. Once there had been a kitchen garden there: perhaps long ago, before the National Curriculum laid down what was to be taught, they'd had a gardening project for some of the less able children. Now it was all scruffy and uncared-for. There were a few dilapidated sheds, cabbage stumps, a clump of dying pampas grass, its feathery fronds bent and broken, a lot of weeds. It was an in-between place, on the edges of things, forgotten, unloved. The frosted grass crunched icily under our feet: you could feel its harsh lumpiness through the soles of your shoes.

'I'm cold,' said Lucy. 'I want to go back to the car.'

'*Please*,' said Alice. She was very eager, very insistent.

We turned a corner round a broken-down outhouse. Then we saw why she'd brought us there, why she'd been so implacable. A great old ivy grew right over the back of the outhouse and down to the ground in front of us, and it was completely iced over where water had fallen through the leaves and frozen as it fell, every leaf frosted, and huge white icicles hanging from every twist and turn of the twigs and branches. A waterfall of ice, at once massive and exquisite, the crystalline shapes all in harmony yet infinitely various, as snowflakes are, or blossoms on a tree.

There was a sound of running water.

'It's a burst pipe,' said Alice.

'It's beautiful,' I said.

We stood and stared at it, this miraculous thing, sculpted by water and cold and the shapes of leaves, and the water went on escaping and the ice sculpture slowly grew, moment by moment, with that special heart-stopping beauty of things that you know won't stay that way for long – elaborate sandcastles right at the edge of the sea, and little children, and flowers in the desert that only bloom for a day.

Lucy put out a finger, tapped an icicle with her fingernail. There was the faintest resonance, like a tiny gong.

'Be careful,' said Alice. 'It's terribly fragile. It's better not to touch.'

We stood quietly there for a moment, shivering in the shabby forgotten garden. Then, our feet and hands aching with cold, we went quickly back to the car.

'Suzie found it,' said Alice as we drove home. 'We've only shown it to Sophie and Clarissa, and Mrs Evans because we thought she'd like it, and now I've shown it to you.'

She took off her gloves. Her fingers were purple, she blew on them to warm them.

'It's very very secret,' she said. 'We're only going to show it to people we can trust.'

28

I was very busy in the days leading up to Christmas: as usual I'd left everything till the last minute. It was my busyness, I think, that kept me sane. I made the lists, bought the presents. For Lucy there was a Polly Pocket Dream Castle I'd have killed for as a child, and a Pet Doctor Barbie with lots of pink accessories, but I did draw the line at the rapping Santa from Homebase that she'd really set her heart on. I found Alice the latest CD from her favourite boy band, and rings for the piercings in her ears, and lots of spangly cosmetics. I wept at Lucy's nativity play in which she appeared as a very fetching shepherd.

We were going to my mother's the day before Christmas Eve and staying till the day after Boxing Day. She's too frail to travel by train or coach, and it's easier than driving down there and bringing her back. Adam and Simone had wanted to have the girls for Christmas – Simone apparently saying with extravagant solicitousness that it must be *so* dreary for those lively girls with Chloe's mother, and really next Christmas we simply must come to some other arrangement. This made me cross, of course, and scared too, shivering with that little chill of apprehension I always felt when she criticized or tried to change our visiting arrangements. And anyway she'd got it all wrong: the girls love the New Forest. They see it with quite different eyes from me: the gloomy garden that so depresses me is perfect for hide-and-seek, and they love the cattle on the common, and the chaffinches and bluetits with their feathers full of colours, so different from London birds. But we agreed that after Christmas they'd spend several days with Adam and Simone.

There was the usual round of work parties. They were mostly tedious lunchtime affairs, where we'd drink Cabernet Sauvignon and munch mince pies and moan about management, standing round in furtive little groups like witches round a cauldron, usually it seemed with Nat as chief warlock, stirring away and uttering an occasional imprecation. Not my idea of a good time, really: I avoided these events whenever I could.

But there was to be at least one proper party, given by Gina Reece, Philippa Nicholls's team leader – an evening party with dancing, though you had to take something for the buffet. Jude and Nat and I had all been invited. I didn't much feel like it but I thought I'd make the effort. It was a long time since I'd been out anywhere, except to the pub with Jude.

The party was the night before Christmas Eve. I took plenty of time to get ready, did all the right things: eyeliner, eyebrow pencil, blusher, the works. I even dug out a dress I'd bought in the summer when I was with Dan: it was made of yellow silk, and I was amazed by its brightness, the colour singing out in the winter room. But when I put it on I found it hung from me far too loosely: I was shocked to see how much weight I'd lost since the summer. So instead I put on my usual short black dress, dressed it up with my highest heels, put up my hair. When I looked in the mirror I could see I'd done rather well. I seemed to have sharper edges, to be more clearly defined. But, perhaps because it was months since I'd put on that much makeup, I also had the weirdest sense that this woman smiling back uncertainly out of the mirror wasn't actually me.

The house was in Kipling Avenue, a rather classy tree-lined street. Gina herself opened the door.

'*Chloe*. I'm *so* glad you could come,' she said, with slightly too much emphasis. I knew that Philippa would have told her all about me – that they'd have had a cosy little chat about my emotional state, gossip in the guise of caring.

Enticing smells washed over me – cigarettes, women's scent, mulled wine. There was a lot of noise from the living room: a surge of talk, laughter, jazz playing. I took off my coat.

It was a very elegant house with pale blinds and bleached pine floors – the sort of floors you would only choose if you didn't have children and weren't for ever on your knees being a fierce lion or scrabbling under the sofa for mislaid bits of bacon sandwich. The decorations were terribly grown-up too, no vulgar red or tartan or tinsel or holly berries, just lots of elegant bare branches, some discreetly touched with silver, lovely to look at, perhaps a trifle chilly. In the corner of the hall there was a tree decorated in the best possible taste with subtle blue ornaments – quite unlike my own, which was as usual heaped with bright fuzzy things the girls had made out of cottonwool and glitter glue.

I went into the party room, clutching my tuna mousse to me like a talisman, wove my way through the milling people, the glittery women in black with shiny bits, the immaculately shaved men laughing loudly. It was like everyone had been turned up a notch: voices higher and louder, eyes brighter, swivelling round the room, smiles showing lots of teeth. There was a big mirror over the mantelpiece, so the room seemed very full. I felt a surprising little glow of anticipation: there were lots of people here that I knew, quite a few that I liked: it might all be okay.

The food table, as usual on these occasions, made up for the rather astringent healthiness of the savoury things – all tofu and lentils – with the extravagance of the puddings, mostly covered in cream and meringue and exuberant curls of chocolate. I tucked my bowl away at the back behind a splendidly garnished dish of tabbouleh: cooking isn't really one of my things.

Nat greeted me as I went to get a drink.

'You're looking well, Chloe,' he said appreciatively. Today's code for 'Like that dress'.

'Thanks,' I said.

I took a glass of mulled wine, sipped at it. It wasn't terribly nice: she hadn't used whole spices, so the cinnamon was powdery like talcum on your tongue, and I suspected she hadn't heated it all up for long enough, the tastes were distinct – orange, nutmeg, brandy – they hadn't had time to blend together. Still, it's hard to get mulled wine just right, and at least it had a warm rich Chistmassy smell.

I stood on the edge of the room, sipping my drink, looking round very deliberately. For once, I thought, I would follow Jude's advice and pick somebody up. It would do me good, I told myself – aware, even as the notion formed in me, that it sounded more like a week at a health farm or a bracing walk after a heavy lunch than an erotic experience.

Jude came up – in a silvery knitted dress, demure in front but with most of the back missing – clutching a mince pie.

'You look amazing,' I said.

She shrugged modestly, and the dress threatened to fall off. 'You're looking great yourself,' she said. 'There's a kind of glow in your eye. On the make, perhaps?'

I grinned.

She bit into her mince pie: icing sugar swirled everywhere, sifted down onto her arm. She swore gently.

'Is Helena here?' I said.

'No,' she said. 'Don't worry – I've kept an eye out for her. Anyway, I thought you and she were best buddies now.'

'Not exactly. At least, I wouldn't like to bump into her unexpectedly.'

We were both glancing round the room as though expecting the wives of our former lovers to rise up out of the woodwork and upbraid us.

'Hey,' she said, lowering her voice, 'there's the guy from Fostering and Adoption I'm always going on about.'

I looked. He was Nat Mark Two. Taller and younger than Nat, but the same lived-in look, and, I suspected, equally self-deprecating.

I shook my head. 'Depressive,' I said. 'I can tell at fifty yards.'

'Chloe, I'm really surprised at you,' she said. 'I'd have thought he was just your type. Well, moving right along, we have Andy from Probation.'

'The clean cut one by the window?' I was starting to enjoy this.

She nodded. 'He's recently separated. No big complications. Great sense of style, don't you think?'

I shook my head again. He was too straight, I thought. Blazer, club tie. The sort of man who'd like women with tons of makeup and complicated underwear.

'Chloe,' said Jude severely, 'life's all about compromise. Didn't anyone ever tell you that?'

Then something caught my eye in the mirror above the mantelpiece – a man pushing his shirt cuffs back from his wrists, rolling up his sleeves. I could only see his hands and forearms. It was the gesture that got through to me: it's so quintessentially male. Then the man stepped back, laughing, moved into view. Jude looked too.

'He's cute,' she said, wiping a light encrustation of sugar from her mouth.

I didn't recognize him: if I'd seen him before I'd certainly have remembered. He was dark, slim, with an expensive shirt, perhaps a little too lean for my liking, but definitely a possibility.

'D'you know him?'

'No.'

'Did he come with anyone?'

'I don't think so. He's been talking to that guy Roger from Housing for ages.'

'He looks younger than me,' I said uncertainly.

'What the fuck,' said Jude. 'Mature women are definitely in. What grown man really wants a submissive little anorexic without a thought in her head?'

'Almost all of them, surely,' I said.

'Chloe, you have a serious attitude problem,' she said, and slipped off tactfully to get some banoffi pie.

I moved towards them, not too obviously. Then as I approached, Roger from Housing drifted off towards the drinks table, leaving the dark slim expensive man with no one to talk to.

It was all very easy. We smiled at one another, I moved in. I had a sudden slightly manic sense that tonight I was blessed, that everything would flow.

We chatted briefly about the deceptively high alcohol content of mulled wine. He had a light pleasant voice, with expensively educated vowels.

I told him I didn't much like Christmas and I'd decided to come out about it.

'In that case you must have children,' he said. 'Women who can't stand Christmas always have young children.' Hinting at vast experience with women's feelings.

So I told him a little about my children, mentioned lightly in passing that I was divorced, just to open up the possibility. Then we moved on to how nice Gina's house was and a nasty experience he'd once had rag-rolling and how women rather than men still tend to choose colour schemes – which led inexorably on to whether the women's movement which is of course a very good thing in its way has really gone too far – an opinion which Jude and I decided years ago to tolerate in men who are getting off with us but not in any other circumstances. As we talked he bent in to me, moved his hand towards me, stopping just short of my skin. He told me pretty quickly

266

that his girlfriend, a journalist, was on assignment in Budapest over Christmas.

He had a perfectly proportioned, rather immobile face, the sort of face that can seem a little inexpressive but looks good in photographs. There was something about this slightly unapproachable one-dimensional beauty that made me think of a programme the girls had once watched, an animated version of Hamlet, beautifully done in dull melancholic colours, browns and ochres, the animation technique a series of paintings on sheets of glass. He was the sort of man of whom you say to yourself, Lots of women must fancy him – rather than actually wanting to reach out and touch. But at one point he brushed my bare shoulder with his fingertips, very lightly, but in a gesture that was entirely superfluous to the conversation – and I felt a distinct little stirring, a flicker of desire.

He went to refill his glass and took mine too, which seemed promising.

Gina had changed the music, I noticed: it had simpler rhythms and lots of bass. One or two couples were dancing down the end of the room where the lights had been turned off. It was all getting warmer, darker, more intimate. Soon we'd be dancing too.

'By the way,' he said, when he came back, his fingers resting on mine as he handed me the glass, sex hanging in the air like scent or smoke, 'I'm Jonathan Peters.'

'I'm Chloe Langdon,' I said.

He flushed to the roots of his dark hair, took a slight but distinct step back.

I was appalled. 'What is it? What on earth have I said?'

'I'm sorry,' he said. 'I didn't mean to . . .' He moved back in to me, patted my arm, a touch that was conciliatory, not sexual, trying to make it all right again. 'I'm an educational psychologist.'

'Oh,' I said.

He was watching me warily, like an unpredictable animal that might suddenly turn on him or shy away. 'I worked with Dan Whitmore. Before it all happened. You were Dan's . . . You were involved with him, weren't you?'

'Yes,' I said. I had a sudden sense of vertigo, like standing on the edge of a pit. I was scared I would lose my balance, go plummeting down.

'I hope you don't mind me knowing.'

'Why should I mind? It wasn't a secret,' I said. But I did mind, quite a lot.

He pulled a face, as though something tasted bad. 'It was a lousy business,' he said.

I nodded, couldn't speak. The powdery sediment from the mulled wine had caught in my throat.

'How is he?' he said. 'I mean, do you still . . . Sorry, it's not my place really, is it?'

'No, I don't see him now,' I said. And when he said nothing, 'Do you?'

He shook his head. 'I did send him a Christmas card, though, poor bastard,' he said. 'I mean, you must feel like some kind of leper.'

It was presumably just an illusion, something to do with the hyper-sensitivity of my nervous system, but I felt exposed, felt there was a sudden hush, that people had turned to us slightly, that everyone was listening, everyone could hear.

'We're all bloody careful now, I can tell you,' he went on. 'When I see a kid on their own I always make damn sure there's someone who'll come and look in a few times during the session . . . You've got to protect yourself. It could happen to anyone.'

'I guess so,' I said. Everything I said, I had to wrench the words out of me. I knew I was drinking too fast, kept raising my glass to my mouth, needing something to hold there so he couldn't read my feelings in my face.

'It was unbelievable, the way it happened,' he said. 'It was like he had the Ebola virus or something.' It was rather a studied image: I could tell he'd told this story before. 'Dan just disappeared, and the police cleared out his room. And there was this directive from on high, and we were told he'd been suspended, and we were forbidden to have any contact with him or talk to anyone about him.'

'Yes,' I said. 'He told me about that. Well, I guess it's the way it's usually done.'

We were standing much farther apart now, he was no longer bending in, no longer reaching towards me, the space between us that had seemed to fizz with sex now empty and unbridgeable.

'Some people paid no attention, of course,' he said. 'I know he still sees Monica a lot – and Paola, of course. She's the union rep. She's great, Paola.'

'Yes, I've heard she's very good,' I said.

'When does it go to court?' he said.

'Pretty soon now, I guess,' I said. 'Some time in January probably.' Drinking too quickly, the wine and brandy skidding into my veins.

There was silence between us for a moment. He put down his glass, he was turned a little away, apparently preoccupied with the hedgerow garland on Gina's mantelshelf.

'I took over one of his groups,' he said then. 'For the brothers and sisters of children with severe learning difficulties. They'd obviously adored him – he was very good with children.'

'Is,' I said.

'I'm sorry?' he said.

'*Is* good with children.'

'Oh.' He blushed.

He picked up his glass and drank, rather fast like me. I looked round the room, wondered if I should go and find someone else to talk to. I spotted Jude, who was at quite an advanced stage of foreplay on the dance floor, draped all over the probation officer, who'd taken off his blazer. Their bodies seemed to blend together, pelvises angled inward, so you really felt you shouldn't look for too long. Jude always knows what she wants: I envy her that, she's very different from me. Half the time I get so far, then I suddenly feel unsure.

Jonathan was still standing there, rather pink and embarrassed. And I didn't know what to do, didn't know whether to seek to revive whatever had been going on between us, didn't know if it was worthwhile or even possible. I guess he was wondering the same, because then he moved an inch or two nearer to me, touched my shoulder.

'I'm sorry,' he said. 'I've gone on a bit, haven't I? I guess this isn't at all what you came for. You came to have a good time and a bit of a break from all this.'

We both knew it was a question.

'Yes,' I said, trying to smile, swallowing down all the complicated feelings that knotted in my throat. 'That's what I came for,' I said. And believed it, and told myself I was starting over and putting the past behind me. With plenty of alcohol swilling around inside you, the most ambitious projects can start to seem quite plausible.

'Perhaps we could dance,' he said. 'Would you like to dance?'

We danced. It was music I liked, and I tried to lose myself in it, to shake off the shame and anger. And then there was a slow dance, so he held me, quite decorously at first, then easing the palm of his hand slowly down my spine, pulling me in to him so I could feel his erection pressing promisingly against me, and it was very hot and dark there at the end of the room, with the music pulsing seductively, and my body all loosened and softened with the alcohol. Okay, so it wasn't an overwhelming feeling, but this wasn't the most sexual part of my cycle and it all felt very pleasant and very simple, and I decided that I would, after all, invite him back for coffee. Just for a good time and a bit of a break from all this.

I drove, which I shouldn't have done as I must have been near the limit. Hannah was curt and monosyllabic, and I had the distinct impression she didn't approve at all – or maybe it was just that she'd wanted to watch to the end of *ER*.

We drank our coffee and I went meticulously to check that the children were asleep. Lucy had her felt Christmas stocking out on top of the duvet, clasping it even in sleep, so she wouldn't forget it tomorrow. She knew Father Christmas didn't really exist, but she still thought she might not get her presents if she put out the wrong receptacle. Then I took him to my bedroom.

We were both quite drunk, which usually helps with the getting into bed bit, but I still found the undressing awkward. It was the kind of encounter where, like on a windy beach, you struggle with your clothes, and he undoes your dress and lets it sift to the floor with a sexy whisper of silk, and all you can think is how silly you look with that band of elastic round the top of your tights and your stomach sticking out. He looked good with his clothes off, though: everything about him seemed to fit together, his body all of a piece, his penis rather long and slender like the rest of him. I liked looking at him.

We kept the duvet on: it was so cold. He kissed me with an exploratory tongue, he tasted of mulled wine. We moved our hands over each other a bit, then he went to work on my breasts. He had various clever ways of moving his palms and his fingers, tracing circles, teasing, flicking: it should have felt good, but to be honest it irritated me rather. It's some weird legacy of those months of feeding babies that I don't quite like having my breasts touched unless I'm very turned on – and really I wasn't that evening. I think I started to withdraw a little then, to hold something back. He must have sensed how I felt: it's the sort of thing you know straight away when you touch somebody – how welcome you are, how close you can get. And from then on there was something tentative about his touching: like he only skimmed the surface of me, as though he didn't quite have the right.

He was a good lover, though, attentive, courteous. What do you want? Tell me. Show me. He did all the right things. He used his mouth on me and it felt good of course as it always does, but I didn't reciprocate, which I know was rather impolite: I just couldn't quite manage it somehow.

I concentrated hard, lost myself in a little fantasy of compulsion and constraint, and the whips, the velvet gags, the intransigent men with obscure but explicit desires all worked just as well as ever, and I actually came quite quickly. He'd waited for me: he came soon afterwards, and I lay for a bit with my head on his shoulder as our breathing slowed. His hair smelt of other people's smoke. I felt rather empty and troubled, like I'd lost or broken something.

I started to wonder, as he did too perhaps, how long we should stay like that, for politeness, before we moved apart. For the first time in years, I yearned for a cigarette, for the way it structured these ill-focused, undefined moments. I tried to think of something to talk about, searched my mind for appropriate trivial chat, and found nothing: my head felt completely empty, as though now we'd made love there was nothing left to say.

I stirred a little, and he responded.

'I'd better go, I guess,' he said.

'It's probably best,' I said. 'I don't really want the girls to know.'

'No, of course not,' he said.

I watched as he got dressed, as he did up his zip with a deft flick of the wrist – that little gesture, inherently comic, that draws a line under every casual sexual encounter.

I got up and put on my dressing-gown. My eye makeup had left greyish smudges on the pillow.

We thanked each other politely at the front door under the grape ivies, smiled a bit too much. The glass panels beside my door reflected the hall, the velvet curtains and books and the Christmas paper chains the girls had made: our reflected shapes as we stood near the glass were dark against the illuminated background, faceless but precise, like Javanese shadow puppets.

'Hang on, you don't have my number,' he said. He thumbed through his wallet, gave me his card. 'Give me a ring sometime,' he said, but we both knew I wouldn't.

'Thanks,' I said.

There was another little silence.

'Look,' he said awkwardly then. 'I hope it works out okay – with Dan, I mean.' He moved one hand in a gesture that could have meant anything. 'Well, you know. Whatever you want.'

I touched his arm. 'It's nice of you,' I said.

He went off into the dark.

I closed the door with a slight sense of relief. I remembered how Dan had made love to me there that first time, remembered the hot night that smelt of flowers and how when he'd touched me I'd felt I was going to fall apart. I went through to the kitchen. I still had the card in my hand. It seemed kind of ungracious to put it straight in the paper recycling bin, but I did it anyway.

I sat at my table for a long time. It would be very cold outside. Little sounds scratched at the edges of the silence – the thin high bark of a distant fox, a train. I started imagining I could actually hear the frost, its metallic whisperings as it settled in the garden, its tiny siftings and creakings and enclosures. I thought about it taking over everything, whitely stippling the bare branches of my apple tree, encasing every blade of grass in a separate steely sheath, silvering the edges of the leaves and the tracery of veins on the leaves. And I thought of the brittle extravagance of the icicle that would hang from my garden tap and the clear dark glazing over of the puddles on my patio and Alice's frozen waterfall and how fragile everything is.

29

Next morning I packed the car, checked and double-checked my list – the usual going-away things, and the girls' presents, the stocking presents, the turkey in a cool bag and all the other things for Christmas dinner it was hard for my mother to buy. Going away for Christmas with children is incredibly complicated.

The car was ready and waiting and the girls just poised to get in – Alice wearing her most decorous skirt and a cheerful orange top in deference to my mother, who thinks clothing should be colourful, Lucy clutching her stocking to make quite sure it wouldn't be forgotten – when the florist came with flowers for me.

There were lilies and carnations and a mist of tiny white flowers whose names I didn't know. The cellophane made an expensive rustling sound. I thought at first they were from Jonathan, that he'd got up early and made this rather nice gesture to smooth things over, so if we met again there wouldn't be too much discomfort between us.

There was a little card in an envelope stuck to the cellophane. I opened the envelope. To Chloe, Happy Christmas, All my love, Dan. The words were in the florist's handwriting, carefully rounded and neat, the way an infant teacher writes. It was weird to see Dan's love sent in the writing of a stranger. I stood and stared at the words for a moment, giddy with a sense of dislocation. But I didn't want the girls to see who the flowers were from, so I tucked the card in my pocket.

He'd never sent or given me flowers before: it wasn't quite his style, perhaps not quite mine either, it suggested something rather traditional – engagement rings, expensive dinners, that sort of relationship. More like the kind of relationship I'd had with Adam. Yet they were so lovely to receive, speaking of summer, so delicate and fragrant.

273

'Ah, cool,' said Alice. 'Who're they from?'

'You wouldn't know him,' I said evasively.

Lucy touched one of the petals yearningly. 'Will you give me some flowers one day, Mummy? *Please?*'

The blooms had been picked with care, they were at the precise moment of their opening, the petals unfurling as though a warm sun was shining down on them, gentling them, easing them apart. The lilies were pink, the edges of the petals so pale they were almost white, the hearts of them darker and lavishly daubed with red. I buried my face in them for a moment, breathing them in. The scents, subtle from a distance, were shockingly intense when you got in close, the carnations spicy like cinnamon, the petals so soft, like skin.

But I knew it would be pointless to take them with us – they'd undoubtedly wilt on the journey. The traffic was always awful on Christmas Eve: we'd probably get stuck in some ghastly tail-back at the M3/M27 junction and they'd be dead when we got there. So I took them round to Dorothy, my neighbour, who was staying home for Christmas and was very happy to have them. As I handed them over, I felt a sudden sharp snakebite of psychic pain, so intense and precise I could locate it precisely in my body, here, under my sternum, next to my heart. I almost put out a hand and grabbed them back, almost told her I'd changed my mind. But of course I knew I couldn't.

We got in the car. Alice chose the tape and I put it on. As always I set out for my mother's with a slight sinking of the heart.

Lucy sucked at her stocking, briefly mistaking it for her comforter, and got a mouthful of felt. She spat it out.

'Where did you put the flowers?' she said suddenly.

'I gave them to Dorothy,' I said. Tentatively, sensing trouble.

'You didn't, Mummy,' said Lucy, her voice shrill, edgy. 'You can't have.'

'We couldn't have brought them with us. It's far too hot in the car,' I said. 'And if we'd put them in the boot, they'd have got squashed because of all the presents.' Trying to placate her, reminding her of all the Christmas packages.

'*I* would have looked after them,' she said. She was appalled, near to tears. 'Mummy, I *hate* you. They were so beautiful.'

We drove out of London and down the motorway, through the Surrey landscape with its gorse and thin conifers that's like an outpost of the Forest already, taking me back to childhood, and all the time she sat there, silent and unrelenting. I saw her whenever I glanced in the rearview mirror, her fierce unchanging face, the stern frown stitched to her forehead.

My mother heard the car crunching up the track and came and waited for us in front of the house in the shadow of the trees, a tiny stooped figure in her Marks & Spencer's tartan. She's quite frail now, every time I see her a little more hunched, but she manages. She sleeps downstairs, and she has good neighbours – people who shop for her, people who come to play bridge. Sometimes I worry I ought to move nearer her – but I don't really see how I could, because the girls need to be within easy reach of Adam. Anyway, to be honest, she and I find each other's company an effort. Around her I feel both tenderness and irritation in precisely equal proportions – and she, I suspect, feels much the same about me.

That Christmas she started out in a particularly sour mood, because Adam had rather stupidly sent her a Christmas card – and not just any old card, but one that could be read as a gesture of reconciliation, with 'Peace' and a dove on it, and she'd elaborated this little fantasy about him and me working it through and getting together again. Men never look at what's on the card they send – never think how it might be interpreted by someone with too much time on their hands. And when I said, 'No way,' she was rather cross. She'd liked everything about Adam – his job, money, status, the reassuring Aran sweaters he wore for country weekends, above all that air of dependability which doctors cultivate – and which in his case had proved to be largely illusory.

'Well, you're on the shelf for good now, of course,' she said to me, her lips pursed, thin with disappointment. 'Especially if you will wear all that black.'

I can never sleep well at my mother's. Since Adam went off, the girls get put in the two single beds in the spare room, and I go in my childhood bedroom, which is crammed with boxes of things my mother can't bear to throw out that seem to use up all the air, and which isn't in the least conducive to sleep, with the light from the refinery seeping in through the curtains. That night I dropped off quickly enough – I was tired and a bit hungover from the party –

but I woke at two to hear one of the children coughing, I couldn't tell which. I got up, went to their room. It was Alice. She didn't seem to be properly awake, her eyes would open as she coughed, then they'd close again and she'd go straight back to sleep. She hadn't had any cold symptoms that I'd noticed: I wondered if she was developing an allergy to my mother's woollen blankets. Lucy didn't seem to be disturbed by it, thank goodness; she had the blankets pulled right up to her eyebrows, her hair on the pillow warmly gold like mustard-fields in the light from the little lamp on the dressing-table. The stockings full of presents that I'd laid across the girls' beds creaked and rustled a little as they stirred. I went back to bed but I couldn't sleep for hours. I'd keep drifting off, then the coughing would start again.

But Christmas Day went fine really, against all my expectations. Even the dinner went well. I didn't know what my mother would make of Alice's emergent vegetarianism, but in fact she was quite approving, and the two of them had an excited conversation about the perils of fattening turkeys with oestrogen. And the organic pudding was delicious, and the girls enjoyed their presents, all new and shiny and beautiful in their boxes, and with plenty of sherry inside her my mother mellowed a lot and sat and reminisced quite happily, and it was all okay.

On the day after Boxing Day my mother said she wanted to go to my father's grave. It's in a quiet little churchyard with a view of the Solent. We stopped at a shop on the way, to buy flowers. The girls came in with me: my mother sat in the car.

'Do we have to do this?' hissed Alice. 'God, Mum, it's so morbid. I mean, we're talking ancient history here. Like when dinosaurs walked the earth.'

I placated her with a copy of *Sugar* which I hid in my bag so my mother wouldn't see. I knew she wouldn't approve of Alice's magazines – they have far too much sex advice and the clothing is all so skimpy. Lucy chose the flowers, a bunch of red anemones.

The church is quite high up: on that winter day, with the leaves off the trees, you could see right down to the narrow blue streak of the Solent in the distance, and part of Southampton on the opposite bank, a cityscape of factories and cranes and blocks of flats, far off and still and silent. Nearer at hand, the other side of the perimeter wall, there was a shabby bungalow, a churned-up field with a horse eating hay from a bale, a caravan, a fence of corrugated iron. The countryside always looks tatty in winter, there are so many bits of rusting metal lying around. But the churchyard itself felt very old and friendly and peaceful. The grass was crisp with frost, but the sun was bright. Above us, a seagull soared through the clear air, the shadow of its flight flicking across the white ground.

My mother sat in the church porch, her hands crossed neatly on the top of her stick. It's a gesture that Lucy has inherited: she sometimes folds her hands in precisely that way. I remembered how she'd gone into the study to sit between Vicky and Bernadette, putting her hands together just so, quite primly in her lap. They're intriguing, these little genetic markers, telling us, even when we might prefer to forget, just how connected we are.

In spite of the sun, it was cold. I took my mother a rug from the car. Alice found a comfortable gravestone out of sight and settled down with her magazine, sucking her hair abstractedly, and Lucy and I went to get a jam jar from the church porch, and filled it with water at the churchyard tap, and put the anemones in it, and placed it carefully on my father's grave.

'There,' said Lucy contentedly, 'he'll like those.'

The present tense charmed me: that poignant uncertainty that children have about death, what it means, if it lasts.

She found an interesting bendy twig and decided she'd make a catapult from it with a blade of grass. We picked a blade that wasn't frosted and we tried to tie the ends of the blade of grass to the twig, but the grass was rather flimsy and split when you knotted it and she soon got frustrated. So she went off to sit with Alice, using her twig to scrape at the stone, flaking off bits of lichen, and they had a gruesome conversation about worms and whether eyeballs rot.

I sat on a bench by my father's stone and thought about my father – what kind of a man he'd been, how he'd looked at life. It was a train of thought triggered perhaps by Lucy's present tense – the way she'd talked as though he was still alive, still here. I thought about his depressions – that kind of upward frown he'd had, his eyes a little too full. I thought about his tenderness to me and how much I'd loved him. And in that quiet graveyard on that cold bright midwinter day, I realized for the first time and with startling clarity just what his legacy to me had been. His belief that hope was irrational: that the ground of our being, the truest thing, is the sadness: that depressives see the world as it really is. That you were somehow in tune with the universe, moving to the deepest rhythm of things, when you gave up hope. That the illness is always terminal, that sooner or later the blow will fall.

And I thought how I'd carried these beliefs of his around with me for so many years, hugged them to me, cradled them close in memory of him because that was all that was left of him. How this had been his memorial in me, raised up in his memory as surely as this nicely polished stone of grey speckled marble with its tastefully restrained lettering. So when the bad moments came – the moments of awful revelation, my illusions peeled away like sticking plasters – Adam sipping wine in the summer garden and telling me he was leaving, or the photograph pushed inexorably towards me across the blank acres of my kitchen table: in those moments I'd think, Yes, of course, this was inevitable, how deluded I was ever to have imagined otherwise.

Then, in that moment in the graveyard, the strangest thing happened. It was like my father was there with me: not exactly a physical presence, yet I could understand how other people who had such an experience might talk as though they'd actually seen the person, might speak of ghosts or spirits. For a moment, he seemed quite real to me – as real as when he'd been alive, as real as in those dreams when he sits at the kitchen table drinking tea from the green-rimmed china, and tells me death isn't what people imagine, that he hasn't actually died. It was like I could hear his voice, like he came towards me. And I knew what I had to do, knew I had to say no to him. To push him away, to turn from him, to tell him I didn't need him now after all these years and would he please just leave me alone. Yet it seemed so harsh, I couldn't manage it somehow. Not then, not yet. So I just sat there on the bench by his gravestone, poised between one thing and the other, not wanting to keep him always by me but also somehow unable to tell him to go: sat there quite quietly while Lucy played with her bendy twig and sang a little song about worms and Alice stretched out her slender limbs on the gravestone and flicked through an article about vegetarian vampires and my mother sat in the church porch, musing on the past. It wasn't exactly a spiritual experience, but maybe it was the closest I can come – that long long moment of absolute stillness, and knowing there was a decision that had to be made. Knowing that one day I'd make it.

But then Lucy called to me: she'd spotted a huge cargo ship piled high with blue and orange containers, easing slowly down the Solent and out to sea. She came running up and slipped her hand in mine and we watched it together for a moment, its slow inexorable progress through the quiet water, the dailiness of things restored. I blinked hard, rubbed my eyes. I knew it was time to go: Alice was coughing again, we needed to get out of the cold. I went to fetch my mother, helped her back to the car, left the little churchyard to its silence and its presences, and the jar of anemones that would so soon wither and fall, red petals bleeding onto the whitened ground.

Part IV

30

On a cold bitter day in the second week of January, Felix rang.

'So, Chloe. How about that lunch we were going to have some-time?'

'You told me you never ate lunch,' I said, startled.

'Did I?' he said. 'Some weeks are worse than others – I guess it was a bad one. How about tomorrow?'

'Why exactly?' I said. 'Why now?'

He laughed. He didn't seem perturbed. 'It wasn't so long ago you were so keen to see me you broke into my office,' he said. 'Look, I'm making you an offer you can't refuse. I'm going to treat you. At an establishment of your choice. You can't possibly turn me down.'

And I couldn't, of course. I was far too curious. I simply had to know what he wanted to say.

'I could do tomorrow, as it happens,' I said. 'But I really don't want a massive meal – I've got to get some work done in the afternoon.'

'I suppose we could go to that Café Picasso place,' he said. 'That's your kind of thing I imagine.'

Next day he picked me up from work. He was sleek and immacu-late as ever, smelling of bergamot. It was, as he'd surmised, a café I liked, rather self-consciously casual, with lots of dark panelling, and floorboards so stylish they hadn't been stripped but were still coated with battered old brown varnish, and starched white tablecloths and classical music. A Brahms piano concerto was playing when we got there, turned up rather loud, the harmonies a bit too rich and lavish, somehow, for lunchtime. It was all very relaxed, a place where women felt comfortable flicking through a newspaper and waiting for their friends. Felix, I suspected, would have preferred somewhere more luxurious.

We ordered mussels, and he chose the best white wine on the list, the Pouilly-Fumé, which was quite delicious. I knew I'd have to be careful: it was the kind of wine you can drink an awful lot of and not feel drunk, just get more and more elaborately articulate, till you find yourself lost in the labyrinth of your own subordinate clauses. The mussels came quickly, strangely satisfying to look at, those big rattling heaps of grainy blue-black shells.

He spent a long time on quite general conversation, enquiring politely about my work, like a friend of a friend whom you bump into unexpectedly at a bus stop.

'You're still working in child protection, I take it?' he said.

'Yes,' I said. 'It has its painful moments, but it's what I know about.'

'I seem to recall that's been your field for quite some time now,' he said, lifting a mussel to his mouth, delicately ripping away some flesh with his regular, very white teeth. The white teeth, the black shell: it was probably some perverse effect of the alcohol on an empty stomach, but I found myself thinking of the picture in his loo, the pornographic angel, her soft white skin, the thin black shiny whip.

'It's nearly fifteen years,' I said. 'But I don't terribly much like adding it up.'

'And you're still dealing with child sex abuse cases?'

I nodded. 'I've got several at the moment,' I said.

'Good,' he said. 'Excellent.' With the impartial enthusiasm of a doctor who's just extracted a fat syringe-full of blood from the tender vein in the crook of your arm.

It wasn't his usual style, this rather anodyne small talk. I didn't understand for a bit, didn't know why we were there. I did briefly wonder – just for the sake of completeness really – whether it was some kind of sexual ploy. He'd often wrong-footed me in the past because he gave so little away: when he'd been seeking to seduce me, he was sometimes so insouciant, so impassive, that I simply hadn't got it – like the time when, sitting at a café table much like this one, he'd suddenly said, 'What's the best way for you to come?' and a neat little tube map had popped up in my head, precise in every detail, all the lines in their right colours and a restricted service through Chigwell. But whatever he was up to now, I was sure it wasn't a seduction. His body language was absolutely all wrong, for one thing. He was studying me with considerable interest, but

284

it didn't feel in the least like sex, more like an entomologist eyeing up a rather intriguing earwig.

Surprisingly, he even asked after my children.

'They're fine,' I said.

'They must have got very used to having you all to themselves,' he said, wiping a shred of orange flesh from his lip with the crisp white napkin. 'I suppose when Dan came along and became almost part of the household it was all a bit tricky – getting them to accept their mother's new boyfriend.'

A waitress walked past with the remnants of people's lunches. Someone had had lobster, one plate was piled with bits of exoskeleton and rather large pink claws. I waited till the woman had gone, didn't want her to overhear.

'It wasn't so difficult. In fact Lucy got very attached to him,' I said. And then, seeing how his eyes gleamed, that intense look of interest that belied the casualness of his questioning – 'Felix,' I said, 'why do I suddenly have this feeling I'm being *used*?'

He laughed. 'Chloe, you are *so* astute,' he said. He pushed his plate to the side, folded his arms on the table, looked straight into my eyes. Setting out his stall.

'Let me explain,' he said. 'Dan's case is in the warned list for next week.'

'Yes,' I said, my heart banging at my ribs.

'We won't know the actual date till the day before.'

I nodded.

'I think we've got a very strong case,' he said. 'I think we can cast doubt on much of the prosecution evidence. I could go through it item by item if you like. I'd be very happy to take you through it in detail.'

'Not now,' I said. 'Just get to the point.' But I knew what that point was, of course, and fear came at me, clawlike, digging in, getting a good firm grip.

'I need a character witness, Chloe,' he said. 'To be blunt, I need *you*.'

'Why me? What do I have to contribute?' I said. '*I* can't tell them whether he did it or not.'

'That's not what a character witness is, Chloe,' he said, the epitome of sweet patience, a teacher explaining some very simple arithmetic to a rather obtuse child. 'That's not what you'd be there for. You wouldn't be asked any questions about the case. You'd be there to – well – be yourself.' He uttered this rather New Agey phrase with some reluctance: I guessed he was trying to speak what he imagined to be my language, though it grated on him.

'Think about it,' he went on. 'You work in child protection. You have vast experience of child sex abuse cases. All your working life has been about kids, about protecting them, you're patently on their side.' Kids: it sounded rather studied and deliberate coming from him, he was trying too hard to seem casual. 'You look right. You have an innocent face. And you know Dan intimately: you have – to put it crudely – screwed him. The court would believe you, Chloe. If you can show you believe in Dan Whitmore's integrity, then I think the court will too.'

'What would I be asked?' I said, fear rising like bile in my throat.

'Just the basic facts about you and Dan: you wouldn't have to say very much. You're worried of course that it might all get horribly intimate?'

I nodded.

'It's possible we might want to ask something about your sex life. How might we put it – Was there anything unusual about Mr Whitmore's sexual behaviour? That kind of thing. To which you would answer . . .' He spread his clean white hands, waiting for my reply.

'Well . . . no,' I said.

'See? It's easy. And I promise you our side wouldn't get any more intimate than that. Probably just that one question that might be a bit embarrassing. Obviously I can't predict what the prosecution might ask.'

'No, of course not,' I said.

He looked down for a moment, ran his finger round the rim of his glass. To my surprise, he seemed for a moment a little bit uncertain. Some expression I couldn't read briefly creased his face, like a sudden wind crinkling water. 'There is of course the additional complication that you and I had that fling,' he said.

'Oh,' I said. 'Does that matter?'

He raised his eyebrows very slightly, as though to say, What an innocent woman you are. 'They'd make mincemeat of me if they knew I'd had a relationship with a witness,' he said.

'Well, how could they possibly know?' I said.

'Let's hope they don't,' he said.

'You think it's important,' I said. 'You think it's worth that risk.'

He nodded, refilled my glass. I drank quickly.

'Frankly, it could decide the thing,' he said. 'Whether Dan walks free or goes to prison for a crime he didn't commit. Just think of it, Chloe, this idiot scheme he has for not going on Rule 43 if he goes down. He's told you about that?'

I nodded.

'I'm really not sure that he can be dissuaded,' he said. 'Dan Whitmore is stubborn as a mule. And it doesn't end when he comes out, of course. In today's climate, it's a life sentence.'

He paused to let this sink in. He's good at pausing for effect: he does it often in court. I looked away, fighting his hold on me and the power of what he said. But he leaned across the table towards me, fixed me with his steady blue gaze, pulled me back to him. 'I don't want to lay it on too thick,' he said, 'but I do think that your testimony could clinch it.'

'Felix,' I said, 'if that's not laying it on thick, just what would be exactly?'

I tried to keep my tone light. Yet sitting there at that café table, with its starched napkins and tablecloth and heaps of blue-black shells, everything clear and crisp and black and white between us, facing that stark choice, I was seized by a sudden helpless rage. Rage with Felix: but rage too with Dan, that he was putting me through this. Didn't he know, didn't he understand, that there were things at stake for me too? Though even then I hadn't registered quite how much he was asking or what the cost might be. Yet even as I felt so angry with Dan, I could also understand why he was making this demand of me. Drowning you'd clutch at anything – a coat-hem, ankle, bit of sleeve – whatever you could reach, even if it meant pulling the other person under with you. And that was what Dan and Felix were doing – they were pulling me under. I knew I had to shake them off if I possibly could, to put a stop to this here and now and for good.

'Could you *make* me do it?' I said.

'Well, yes – in theory. But what would be the point? No. If you do it, it has to be because you want to. Because you believe in Dan.'

I nodded, relief flooding through me. I took a deep breath, quite determined.

'Look, Felix,' I said, 'I can see just why you'd like me to do this, but . . .'

He interrupted me. 'Ssh,' he said. He put a finger on his lips, a playful childlike gesture, yet peremptory too, impossible to disobey. 'Don't say anything,' he said. 'The last thing I want is for you to say anything now. I don't want a decision. I appreciate it's extremely difficult for you. Just think about it for a bit, that's all I'm asking. Let it simmer away.'

'No, Felix,' I said. 'I think I've decided, I think . . .'

He cut me off again, quite rudely this time, wouldn't let me finish. 'There's something else you should know,' he said. 'This is absolutely my own idea. It didn't come from Dan.'

'Oh,' I said, disconcerted. I had that unnerving feeling he'd given me sometimes before – that he could see straight into me with those baby-blue eyes of his – especially the more shameful bits of me, the cowardice, weakness, pointless childish rages. But then the shameful bits of people were what he traded in.

'He didn't want you involved in any of this, didn't want me even to raise it with you,' he said. 'But I told him I intended to ask you unless he actually instructed me not to. That man is incurably romantic,' he went on. 'He'd much rather keep you out of it altogether, doesn't want you sullied by any of it at all.'

He left a little pause, watched me for a moment, gauging the effect of what he'd told me. I sat there and didn't say anything, refusing to respond. It was Mozart over the sound system now, that piano concerto slow movement they used years ago in some sentimental film or other: it's oversweet and repetitive and you hear it everywhere, and I hate it for the way it masters me, always brings this massive lump to my throat, fills my eyes with stupid embarrassing tears.

He was watching me thoughtfully, all sympathy and concern, but with the very faintest smile playing around his eyes. 'He's even said he doesn't want your name mentioned in court,' he went on. 'I've told him I don't see how we can avoid that. From where I stand it's simply not a priority, quite frankly.'

'Well, at least that's refreshingly honest,' I said, trying to be dry and cool, which was hard because of the lump that threatened to clog up my voice.

He refilled my glass.

'Just think about it,' he said. 'Ring me if you want. Any time. If you wake in the middle of the night – I seem to remember you do that sometimes – and it's all getting to you and you want to talk it over, just give me a call. I'd be more than happy to hear from you.'

And I saw how much he wanted this. Which meant he thought it was absolutely crucial to the case. And I thought how Jude had said, Felix usually gets what he wants.

That was it, really. He'd said what he'd needed to say. There was a bit of wine left, and we drank it, and he talked about his fish, his new black swordtails and his silver lyre-tail mollies, and his plans to start a saltwater tank and the extreme viciousness and exquisite beauty of the undulated triggerfish he intended to keep in it. But it was almost like he was talking to himself, no longer interested in engaging me. Felix was always like this, in court, in bed, everywhere: he'd do what he was there for and instantly lose interest.

He offered me coffee, but I could tell he was itching to get back to his office, so I said no.

'I can walk,' I said. 'The fresh air will do me good.'

'If you're sure,' he said.

On the pavement outside, he kissed me on the cheek, his mouth cool, decorous. The scent of his aftershave brushed briefly against me.

'Remember,' he said. 'Any time. Think about it.'

We set off in opposite directions. When I reached the pedestrian crossing and looked back down the street to where he'd left his car, he'd completely disappeared.

I walked back to the office through the bitter afternoon. I'd left my gloves on my desk and the cold reddened my hands. I felt light-headed from the wine, decided at least three times in the course of that brief walk that I'd do what Felix wanted, and three times changed my mind.

Jude was on her way out, off to see her least favourite family, the Ruddocks.

289

'Jesus, I'm dreading this,' she said. 'That ghastly mother and granny whose teeth keep falling out and that damn labrador that tries to fuck your foot.' She buttoned up her coat, flipped her hair out from under the collar. 'So tell me, how was the psycho? What's the current virgin count?'

'Felix is okay,' I said, refusing to smile. 'He's just a bit eccentric, that's all.'

'You're upset,' said Jude, changing register abruptly. 'What's happened? What did he say, that bastard? It's about Dan, isn't it?'

'The court case is listed for next week,' I said.

'Right,' she said. 'But you knew it would be soon. So what's upset you so much?'

'It would take too long to explain,' I said. Then, seeing the concern in her face, 'Look, Jude, I'm fine, really. It was a very nice lunch.'

'I don't think it was,' she said. 'Hell. I have to go this minute. Just don't keep it all in, Chloe. Call me tonight. Promise me.'

'Okay,' I said. But I didn't want to, I knew this was something I needed to think through for myself.

In spite of the wine, I couldn't warm up. The cold had penetrated even into the office, the central heating wasn't really up to it. I remembered I'd seen a couple of fan heaters in a cupboard in the secretaries' room: perhaps they'd let me borrow one. But I couldn't quite be bothered to go and ask, so I put on my coat instead. Raggety puffed-up pigeons huddled on the ledge outside my window, trying perhaps to filch some warmth from the glass, and the heavy sky pressed down.

I hoped to make up for the long lunch hour by working late: Lucy was going to tea with Jake, and Alice had a key and could let herself in. I made some very strong coffee and spread out my notes on my desk. But just as I was sitting down, ready to get stuck into the first report I had to write, the phone went.

'Mrs Langdon?' A woman's voice, a little hesitant and very posh. People with voices like that don't ring Social Services.

'Speaking,' I said.

'This is Connington House. Look, there's absolutely nothing to worry about . . .' It's what schools always say when they ring: meaning, Your child isn't dead. 'It's just that we feel that Alice needs to be at home. She has a very nasty cough and really she's quite poorly. She's in the medical room.'

'I'll come and get her,' I said. I felt I didn't have a choice. I was irritated, though. Schools always seem so ready to send children home – and half the time they worry unnecessarily because they use those strip thermometers you press on the child's forehead which give inaccurately high readings.

I went to see Nat, explained, told him I'd write the reports at home. He was sweet as ever and promised to sign some letters I needed to send that day.

I drove carefully to the school through the grey afternoon, aware that I was perilously near the limit. She was sitting on the edge of the bed in the medical room, waiting for me. I put a hand on her forehead – it was slightly damp but not abnormally hot: if she had a temperature, it was only a very mild one. But her face was white as wax, and her hair looked funny – lifeless, flopping lankly round her ears as though it hadn't been washed for weeks.

'I've *got* to be back by Friday, Mum, we've doing our rainforest thing in music and I'm doing the glockenspiel bit and I can't let them down,' she said, her face scrunched up with worry. I made comforting noises, but it seemed very unlikely to me that she'd be back by Friday. There was something about her that unnerved me.

She sat quite quiet in the car all the way home. I was worried enough to wonder whether I should ring Adam to ask his advice. Yet really there was nothing to discuss. She didn't have any rashes or pains. It was just a feeling.

I tucked her up in bed with some Lemsip and a pile of her favourite magazines. Then I went down to the kitchen to make myself the coffee I hadn't had time to drink at work.

With Lucy at school and Alice in bed, the house was very quiet, felt almost cloister-like, secluded and set apart. I sat at the kitchen table, moulded my hands round the coffee mug to warm them, hugged the silence to me. The reports could wait, I thought: I would use this time to sit very still and think, to muse on this thing that Felix was asking me to do.

Outside, my garden seemed barren and dreary under the pallid sky. The flowerbeds and fruiting trees were all black and grey and lifeless, all entangled bare branches, the honeysuckle round my kitchen window just a fragile tracery of tiny bare twigs. Even my pansies had finally succumbed to the frost. It was harsh and bleak and cold out there, and threatening to get still colder: it was strange to think we were well past the solstice, the days were lengthening, every morning and evening a little more light. It's the time of year when you feel it will all drag on for ever, the grey cold days, the wolf-bite of winter air, you don't really believe in spring – yet deep inside those dead-looking trees and bushes, already things are happening, little urgings and stirrings, the inexorable slow swelling of glossy brown buds at the tips of the bare branches, the sweet sap rising.

I sat at the table in my cold kitchen looking out into my garden, and sipped at my coffee and went back over everything that Felix had said, heard his voice again, his clipped precise seductive voice, and wondered what the hell I should do. And I couldn't see a way forward, just couldn't see what was right.

I thought about Carly then, saw her very clearly as I'd seen her on the video, the neat topknot, the frilly socks, the hands fluttering like little birds, the edge of fear in her voice when she talked about the threats made by the man who'd abused her – for this child, I knew, had undoubtedly been abused. I thought about the grim estate where she lived, and the haven her mother had made, the clean net curtains in the window, the defiantly bright fabric flowers. I wondered what had been done to her and who the abuser had been and whether we would ever find out for sure. And I wondered why she'd told the story the way she had – why she'd seemed to blame Dan if Dan hadn't done it. Yet of course we would probably never know. In my line of work, you soon learn that 'why' is the dumbest question, the question to which you never get a useful answer. You learn that people don't have the faintest idea why they do what they do – why they choose these particular clumsy, tentative, even self-destructive steps to try and put something right in their lives, especially if they're powerless or scared. The 'why' is always a mystery.

I thought about Carly for a long time that afternoon: wondering what it was like to be her, and how the world looked to her, and how it could possibly be right to do what Felix was asking of me, to seem to take sides against this frightened troubled child.

It was getting dark already in my kitchen, shadows reaching out from the corners. I turned on the lamp on the dresser. The light fell on Lucy's God picture – that splendidly omniscient God in his beautifully detailed sandals, smiling down on his world, the glitter glue still sparkly. It made me think of all those things I'd learnt as a child – what Lucy once called 'that religious stuff and advice from God' – the instructions and commandments. It had seemed so simple then: not cheating at algebra, being nice to your guinea-pig. And right through my teens and twenties it had gone on seeming simple – the useful work, the political enthusiasms, snipping the wire at Greenham, taking children away from cruel parents.

Yet here I was just into my forties and utterly perplexed, absolutely not knowing which way to go. I sat and looked at Lucy's picture and asked myself what it meant to be good – to do the right thing, to take the right path. And I found I really didn't know, maybe hadn't known for a long long time. Certainly I'd felt little sexual guilt for years, and no guilt at all about my relationship to Dan – though plenty of people would surely have thought it wrong. Like Sally, who'd called me a user. Yet to me it had felt, for those first weeks, somehow deeply inevitable and right. Which didn't mean it *was* right, of course: desire pleads its case with such eloquence. Maybe something had happened to my moral sense, I thought. Maybe it was like an unused muscle that had atrophied somewhere along the way.

I was still sitting there at my kitchen table, sipping my coffee and musing on what it means to be good, when I heard Alice starting to cough. And there was something about the cough, the strangulated gasping sound of it, that had me straight on my feet and leaping up the stairs two at a time. I got to her bedroom door just in time to see her vomit spectacularly all over her duvet. But even the vomiting didn't stop the coughing. I held her shoulders, kept telling her it was alright, everything was alright. Eventually she quietened. I wiped her face with a tissue. She was trembling: dark purple shadows smudged her eyes.

'Poor love, how horrid for you,' I said.

'Sorry, Mum,' she said hoarsely, as I carefully rolled off the duvet cover.

I got her a sick bowl and lots of pillows.

'Does it hurt when you cough?' I said.

'Yes,' she said. 'My chest goes right in.'

I put on a new duvet cover, washed her face, tied back her hair.

'I couldn't breathe,' she said, her voice thick, croaky. 'You don't think I'll die, do you Mum?'

This was melodramatic for Alice, normally so rational, so sensible, teasing me for my own anxieties.

'Of course not, my love,' I said. 'It's just a horrible cough.'

I went downstairs, went straight to the bookcase, pulled out Penelope Leach. I looked up Coughs. It directed me to Chest Infections, Croup, Whooping Cough. I knew it wasn't croup, and with a chest infection you'd expect to have a temperature. With a sinking heart, I looked up whooping cough. It said that it starts like a cold, that it develops into the typical cough with spasms of barking coughs on the outbreath, that each coughing spasm may end with vomiting, that a serious attack of whooping cough is one of the lengthiest and most daunting illnesses to nurse. I cursed Penelope Leach and all her works.

The doctor came quickly, a brisk little woman with wire-rimmed specs. She couldn't make a definite diagnosis, but agreed it might be whooping cough when I told her I hadn't had Alice immunized. 'Older children don't whoop, so it's harder to tell,' she said. 'But we'd better keep a close eye on her. She's obviously quite poorly.'

I rang Adam. He was helpful and soothing, didn't seem too concerned, never once said, I told you so, which I thought was pretty good of him. But it sort of hung there in the spaces between the words. He said to feed her little and often, to cut out milk because it made mucus, told me how to hold her upright when she coughed so she could breathe more easily.

I took the television and video up to Alice's room, put on the *Narnia* video she'd loved when she was younger. I rang Ellen, the child-minder who'd had them both when they were little: she said she could help me out at least to the end of the week. I rang Jake's mother, asked if she could bring Lucy round as I couldn't leave. I made Alice a small nutritious milk-free meal, which she instantly brought up. I changed her duvet cover again, stroked her back, wiped her face with a warm flannel.

And as I rushed around doing all these useful busy things, I felt in the midst of the worry a kind of precarious peace. Life was simple again. The voices in my head urging me first one way and then the other were stilled. At least for now I knew what I had to do.

31

I left Alice reluctantly next morning, after getting up twice in the night to nurse her through exhausting bouts of coughing and vomiting. Ellen had come early, soothing and sensible as ever, making both Alice and me feel instantly better, but had then alarmed me by saying she wouldn't be available the next week: she was going to stay with her daughter in Hartlepool. I wondered how on earth we were going to get through this, whether in fact I'd have to take lots of sick leave myself. It reminded me of the early days of parenting, the labyrinth of child care and the struggle to find your way through, all those complexities you hope you've left behind for ever when your youngest starts school.

Just as I was leaving with Lucy a letter came from Felix's office. There was a typewritten sheet and a note in Felix's handwriting: 'This doesn't commit you to anything. If you do testify – as I hope you will – it gives us something to work from. I reckon the trial will last three or four days and you'd probably be needed on day three.' I glanced down the sheet. It summarized what I'd told him at the Café Picasso, all about my work and my relationship with Dan, and he'd added the date the relationship had ended. It seemed accurate enough. I signed it and put it in the stamped addressed envelope and Lucy slipped it in the letterbox.

The sun was coming through as we walked to the car, a low bright winter sun. Our shadows were immensely tall, with tiny heads and great big boots, stretching out on the ground in front of us. The light dazzled me as I dropped Lucy off at school and drove in to work, outlining the buildings with brightness, but it was still very cold.

Jude got in just after me.

'You didn't call,' she said.

'I'm sorry, I forgot,' I said. And then, without preamble, 'Alice has whooping cough.'

'Oh Chloe.' She put her arm round me. 'What the hell are you doing here? Go home this minute. Tell me what needs to be done and I'll take care of it.'

I shook my head. 'Ellen's coming in this week. I need to save up my leave. Alice could be off for twelve weeks.'

'Jesus,' said Jude. 'Ever felt someone up there has it in for you?'

'It's my own bloody fault,' I said. 'That's what's so awful. Because I didn't have her immunized.'

'Don't do this to yourself,' said Jude. 'You were absolutely right to be worried. I mean, look at Gulf War syndrome and all those nasty flesh-eating bugs. Half the time, doctors don't know what the fuck they're doing.'

But she was almost too emphatic, and I knew she was only saying it to try and make me feel better.

I had a supervision session with Nat first thing that morning, and I felt I needed it. Several of my cases were reaching crisis point; there's often a weird synchronicity about this – the way things go all wrong for clients when you're most under pressure yourself. Amber was living at home again, but she and Trish were having lengthy slanging matches, and I knew it was only a matter of time before she ran off and started soliciting in car parks. And one of my foster placements was threatening to break down in a particularly painful way. Lydia and Craig Donahue, brother and sister, placed of course together when they'd been taken into care away from their violent father. Lydia was a quiet child with silky hair falling over her face and enigmatic eyes and her misery all locked up inside her, Craig a wild and driven little boy who kicked and hit when gripped by one of his rages. And now the foster mother was saying she wanted only Lydia, with whom she'd formed a very close bond, that she couldn't handle Craig and wanted him out. I knew that sooner or later I'd have to help Lydia choose between one kind of grief and another. No one should have to make such a choice – least of all a fragile eight-year-old who scarcely knows what love is.

Nat's office is a narrow, poky place, always messy, the walls crammed with political posters that shout their slogans at you, the wastebin mysteriously already overflowing even at the start of the day, but with a window from which there's a rather lovely view out over the city, the factories and warehouses and steeples and gas holders and long long lines of rooftops, pulling the eye out into the distance and away. That day it was all bright and shiny under the low sun, windows and chimneys and fire-escapes catching the light.

I told him about Alice first, and he was sweetly sympathetic and said he'd had whooping cough himself when he was a kid and it had been vile and to be sure to let him know if there was anything he could do. Then I went through my cases, and he slouched back in his chair, his feet on the desk, all loose-limbed and sprawling as if his body was fixed together with string, and listened in his usual thoughtful way to all my plans, occasionally nodding, or asking a brief, pithy question. His frayed shirt-cuffs were pushed up to his elbows, a faint smell of Camels clung to him, he waved his hands around a lot as he talked, the nicotine stains like scorch marks on his skin. He never gave me much advice: mostly then, as now, he'd let me get on with it. Yet I'd always leave his scruffy disordered office feeling clearer, more intelligent, more purposeful than when I'd gone in.

We'd decided on some work on self-esteem for Amber, and a despairing last-ditch attempt to hold the Donahue placement together, and he'd agreed with my plans for most of my other cases, and I'd thanked him, and was already halfway out the door, my heap of files clutched to my chest, when he said, 'Chloe, tell me, what's happening with Dan? I gather the case is listed for next week.'

'Yes,' I said, my pulse careering off in my wrists, my throat. 'Felix reckons they'll probably go ahead then.' I stopped in the doorway, let the door swing back, went to sit on the edge of his desk. 'Nat,' I said, 'I don't know what to do.'

He said nothing, motioned me to continue.

'Felix wants me to testify,' I said.

'What about?'

'As a character witness. You know, to say Dan's a good guy – that kind of thing.'

He took his feet off the desk, sat abruptly upright. He had a sharp, wary air suddenly, like an animal that's just scented something that shouldn't be there.

'What did you tell him?' he said.

'I said I'd think about it.'

'Chloe, I can't let you do this,' he said. When he frowned, the

lines that trenched his forehead seemed extraordinarily deep, like
lines drawn with black felt tip in a child's caricature.

'Well, it isn't really up to you, is it, Nat?' I said gently.

'Maybe it is,' he said. 'Maybe it is up to me. I'm your line manager,
for God's sake.' He got up, started pacing up and down the room,
past the bookshelves crammed with obscure social work theory, the
strident posters. 'Jesus, there's your career to think of, for a start.
Have you given any thought at all to the possible implications for
your future?'

I shook my head, I think I shrugged a little, I didn't understand.

He paused in front of the window, leaned back against the
windowsill, darkly in profile against the gold-streaked city outside.
He was quiet for a moment, working out what to say. Far below us,
the traffic growled round the one-way system. A phone shrilled in
the office behind us, but neither of us moved.

'Listen then, Chloe,' he said. 'At the risk of embarrassing you,
I've always thought you bloody good at your job.' He was looking
away from me, out into the city, a little embarrassed himself. 'Quite
honestly, you're one of the best I've had. But I feel you've never
really stretched yourself, never really given everything you could.'

I felt accused. 'I've got children,' I said.

'Sure,' he said. 'Sure. That's why I haven't pushed it. I know how
involved you are with those daughters of yours, the original earth
mother and all that, and that's lovely of course. But I'd always
imagined, always hoped, that when they were a little bit older, you'd
want to start climbing the ladder, looking for a promotion.'

He made an expansive gesture, opening his hands out sideways,
standing there in front of the window, as though in some way he
was offering me all this – this bright, cold, glittery city, these towers
and cranes and factory chimneys all touched with gold by the sun,
these limitless vistas, paths, possibilities.

'I'd love to see you managing, Chloe,' he said. 'God knows, we
need good managers in this department, hands-on managers, with
that kind of really solid grass-roots experience you could bring to
the job.'

'Well, thanks,' I said. Speaking lightly but inevitably feeling rather
flattered.

He was leaning forward now, his eyes burning. 'We've made so many wrong choices over the years,' he said. 'Anyone ought to be able to see that. Turning away from children's needs. It's all bloody budgets and audits and "Needs not Wants" and how we can justify pushing people away. Staying within budget – that's the sole mark of good management nowadays.'

I nodded but knew not to interrupt. It was one of Nat's big themes. And really I thought he was right: I just didn't feel it all with quite his fervour.

His sense of conviction transformed him: he was vivid and taut and ferocious. 'We need managers with hearts,' he went on. 'Managers who'll put children first again, who'll commit themselves to prevention, to getting into families before it's too late, before it all falls apart. People who know what this work is really about, who don't try to run the place like it's a factory churning out fucking silicon chips.'

There was something rather intoxicating about his passion. And I sat there and listened, and a picture started to take shape inside me, elaborate, exact, seductive: a case conference with me in the chair, the manager with a heart, being compassionate and clever and putting children first and committed to prevention and dressed in a rather severe linen trouser suit ever so subtly feminized by some strappy suede sandals and everyone deferring to what I said.

Nat came towards me then, lowered his voice slightly. 'I wasn't going to tell you this yet,' he said. 'But in view of all this I think you ought to know. There's a job share coming up in the Brideshill Team. The team leader post. This is inside information at the moment, so for Christ's sake don't repeat it. It's only temporary – maternity leave – but it would give you a toehold, get you past that Catch 22 of not being able to apply for a management job till you've got management experience. I can just see you in that job, Chloe.'

'Come off it, Nat,' I said. 'I wouldn't get it anyway. There are other people in this department who'd be in with a much better chance than me.'

'You do yourself down all the time,' he said. 'Really, I want to shake you sometimes. You'd be a very attractive candidate, very attractive indeed. You're known here, you have an excellent track record, and I could give you an embarrassingly effusive reference.'

He turned away, went back to his place by the window, looking out. He rested his hands on the windowsill, he was kind of sagging again, all the fire seemed gone from him.

'But if you're planning to pop up in the witness box during the defence of Dan Whitmore – well, quite honestly, Chloe, you can forget it,' he said. 'You take that step – and you'd just be chucking your future away.'

I was appalled. 'Nat, you're surely not saying that if I testified you wouldn't give me a reference?'

To my relief, he looked pained. 'Shit, Chloe, of course not,' he said. 'That's not the point. The point is how others would see it – how you'd be seen for ever afterwards, quite honestly.'

'I can't believe you're saying these things,' I said. 'I've never felt you thought Dan did it anyway.'

'Jesus, you still don't get it, do you?' he said. 'I'm not saying for a moment I think he did it. He's just one hell of an unlucky guy. It could have been any of us. And it's terrible for him. But why should he bring you down with him?'

He rubbed a hand across his lined brow.

'You're getting me quite upset, Chloe,' he said. 'I don't want to see one of my best-ever workers just throwing away all her chances of promotion.'

'He might get acquitted,' I said. 'Felix seems quite hopeful.'

'Sure, he might get acquitted,' he said. 'Let's hope to God he does, poor bastard. But there's still the shadow. Whatever happens, the shadow'll always be there.'

I took my files and went.

32

By Friday I still hadn't found a childminder to replace Ellen while she was away. I'd tried various mothers I knew at school, but none of them could help, they were all too worried about infecting their own children, and really I couldn't blame them. I knew I'd have to take the next week off – claiming sick leave for myself, as mothers of ill children so often do.

Friday lunchtime, Jude burst into the office and slammed her bag down with a very disgruntled air. She'd spent the morning with her favourite and most infuriating client – Jamie Simmons, who was fourteen and set fires. She'd had to take him back to the secure unit he kept absconding from.

'Why do I get this feeling it didn't go well?' I said.

'Disaster,' she said. 'Total disaster. The little twit left before I did. I mean, deep down I knew I shouldn't have stayed to coffee. I should have had more will-power, then I might have left first. But he'd done a runner before I'd finished my second custard cream.' She collapsed into her chair, all crumpled and defeated. 'Sometimes you wonder why you care,' she said.

'I bought you a sandwich,' I said. 'Chicken and avocado.'

'Ooh,' she said. 'With herb mayo?'

I nodded. 'I thought you might need cheering up.'

'Chloe, you're something special,' she said.

We sat down together and ate.

'So it's next week?' she said then, quite casually.

I nodded.

'Will you be there?'

I shook my head.

She spread her fingers out in front of her, as though examining her pristine nails for blemishes. They were a rather doleful purple today: she'd used one of those trendy varnishes she loves, probably with a stylishly inner-cityish name like Concrete or Shelter.

'Chloe,' she said gently, 'that doesn't mean you've decided to do what Felix wants, does it?'

It was one way of reading it – because of course if I was going to be a witness I wouldn't be able to watch the trial till after I'd testified.

But it was a question I couldn't answer even for myself. So I shrugged and lied a little.

'I don't suppose so,' I said. 'Anyway, I need to be with Alice.'

Jude looked at me almost flirtatiously from under her lusciously mascara-ed lashes, like a little girl with a secret she's itching to tell.

'As it happens, I've got some leave I need to use up,' she said. 'If it's the early part of the week, I might go myself. Then I could fill you in on all the details.'

Her generosity brought a lump to my throat.

'Jude, you don't have to do this,' I said.

'But I want to,' she said. 'Fact is, I'm rabid with curiosity. How long do you think it will last?'

'Felix reckons three or four days,' I said.

She nodded. 'Should be okay,' she said.

'You're so sweet to me,' I said.

'Well, think how you cared for me when I found Greg Rosen under my duvet with that trashy Kleinian therapist,' she said.

And when I got home that evening, there was a message on my answerphone from Felix to say Dan's trial was scheduled for Monday, and I rang Jude and it was all fixed up and she said she'd come round on Monday evening and tell me about it.

The weekend passed incredibly slowly. I didn't go out at all: it was like when the girls were babies – that sense of being in an enclosed space, separate, sequestered – as though the outside world, the world of people and pavements and trains and busyness and important public things was infinitely far away and utterly irrelevant. It might have been tedious but I didn't find it so – it was like I got into a different rhythm: I didn't try to do anything for myself, not even to read the newspaper, I was just there for the girls, and it was all very simple.

Nursing Alice became almost routine. I started to find the coughing fits more predictable: they seemed to come roughly every two hours, though getting out of bed to go to the loo could set her off sooner. I learnt to hold her and talk her through the coughing and vomiting. I still hated to see how she panicked and struggled for breath – but I also knew it would end, that she'd sink back into her pillows, her eyes smudged with black, but able to breathe again.

It was terribly cold, the sky a desolate grey, puffed-up starlings like round brown fruit in the bare branches of my apple tree. Lucy and I virtually lived in the kitchen: the living room with its patio doors is hard to heat in the winter. But even the kitchen was on the cold side. I thought I'd light a fire in the pretty Victorian grate but it wouldn't take, each firelighter burned merrily then went out with a dismal little phut without the coalite catching, and in the end I gave up. I guessed the chimney needed sweeping, or some bird perhaps had rashly made its nest in the chimney pot.

Lucy spent most of Saturday playing with her Barbies. She made them a hospital under the kitchen table and nursed them through a series of horrific lung complaints, their gory and highly productive coughs described for me in lavish detail as I tried to eat my lunch. But when I brought down Alice's duvet cover to wash, she hid in the study till it was safely stashed in the machine.

By Sunday morning she was thoroughly bored. I ran through the usual list of things she could do – drawing, painting, playing with her Sylvanians. Each was greeted with a petulant shake of the head. I found myself wishing I had one of those books of a thousand things to do on a rainy day – though I'd never had one in the house for fear of being co-opted into something horribly fiddly, requiring amazing reserves of Pritt Stick and patience.

'What about some clay? Or making a Valentine card? Or a story book?' I said.

Her face brightened. She liked the book idea.

'It could be a book of tests, Mummy,' she said.

'Yes, it could,' I said, though I didn't quite understand at first.

We got some sheets of paper, folded them and punched holes for the string, tied them together to make a little pamphlet. She wrote 'Lucy's Tests' on the cover. Inside on each page she drew three sets of squiggles, with space for a fourth. She worked hard at it, and it kept her busy for a long time, so I had a chance to flick through the Sunday paper, though I was far too tired to read anything more demanding than the captions to the photographs.

'Right, Mummy,' she said then, 'it's time to do your test.'

I had to sit beside her and draw squiggles that looked like hers in all the spaces.

'That's great,' she said, as I finished each drawing. 'Well done.'

Then she said she needed to work out my score, and she got her calculator and pretended to do some elaborate computation, wrinkling up her brow in a deliciously studious way. She ran up the biggest number she could make, a number with eight digits.

'That's your score, Mummy,' she said. 'You were brilliant.'

She asked me to show her how to spell 'brilliant', and copied it out at the bottom of the final page.

She leaned back, admired the work she'd done.

'D'you think my writing looks like Dan's?' she said.

'Maybe it does,' I said, turning a little away.

'Not "maybe", Mummy. It does. It's just like his.'

On Sunday Adam rang to see how Alice was. We talked for a bit about the illness and its possible complications, then he started to quiz me about my childcare arrangements.

'We've been wondering how you're managing,' he said. 'With your job and everything.'

'It's okay,' I said. 'I'm taking this coming week off, with Ellen away. I'm not sure after that. It depends when Ellen gets back.'

'We could always have Alice over here, you know,' he said. 'Simone's offered to take unpaid leave to look after her.'

'Oh,' I said, with a little thrill of unease at the thought of Simone yet again flaunting her credentials as a mother to my children. 'Well, I really don't think she needs to do that. We're managing fine.'

'She *is* a nurse, of course,' he said. 'She's very highly regarded on the Intensive Care Unit.'

'Naturally,' I said, rather bitchily.

'There's no need to get so uptight about it,' he said, responding to the sarcasm in my voice. 'I thought it was very good of her to offer, actually. The fact is, we're not quite happy about you using a childminder when Alice is so ill.'

I could just see Simone saying this – how she'd toss her expensive hair around and talk about 'the childminder' as though the very word tasted rather nasty, conjuring up visions of women with cigarettes hanging out of their mouths and garages full of neglected babies in prams.

'Come off it, Adam,' I said. 'Ellen's great, you know that. She's brought up four of her own and they're all lovely.'

'Okay, okay,' he said, all sweet reasonableness. 'We're only trying to help. It's just that we do feel you've been under an awful lot of strain recently.'

That irritated me intensely – the thought of my ex-husband and his mistress sitting on their tacky new leather sofa and having urgent and compassionate discussions about my mental state.

'Perhaps Simone needs a baby of her own,' I said.

It was tactless and intrusive and I thought he'd be really annoyed. But to my surprise, he sighed a little. 'It isn't always that easy,' he said.

'Well, I guess it isn't,' I said vaguely, not knowing quite how to respond, wishing I hadn't said it. 'Anyway,' I went on briskly, 'Alice is staying here. I'm sure that's best for her.'

'Yeah, well, you've made your position quite clear,' he said. In a way I think he was relieved. I suspected he'd been told what to say by Simone – and now he'd said it he'd discharged his duty and he wasn't really all that bothered about the outcome. 'Okay. Well, I just wanted you to know that Simone would be more than happy to help.'

I wondered what Simone would think if she knew what Felix was asking me to do.

33

On Monday evening Jude came round as she'd promised.

'Did you go?' I said.

'Sure,' she said. 'Can't you tell?' She was wearing the outfit she always wears when she has to go to court, a grey flannel suit so severe she sometimes quips that it's quite capable of giving expert evidence all on its own.

I took her up to see Alice.

'You poor thing,' said Jude, and ruffled Alice's hair.

Alice smiled wanly.

Jude had brought her a present, a video of Alice's favourite boy band on tour. They grinned out at us from the video case, fetchingly clad in leather and very discreetly pierced against a mellow gold backdrop. I put the video on, plumped up Alice's pillows, took Jude back to the kitchen.

I offered her wine, she said she'd rather have coffee. I switched on the kettle, we chatted inconsequentially. I was sick with curiosity, but it was as though we'd tacitly agreed that what she had to say must wait till I could give it my full attention.

I heaped coffee into my cup to help me concentrate, sat opposite her at the table, clutching the cup. It was hot, it hurt my hands.

'So tell me,' I said.

'It was mesmerizing stuff,' she said.

'Did you see the video?'

'Yes,' she said. 'We had the prosecution's opening speech and Carly's disclosure, and then they questioned her over the video link.'

'What did you make of her?'

'She's such a poor little waif,' she said. 'Tiny. A bit undernourished, I guess. All dressed up for court, her hair in a top-knot, like on the video.'

'Yes,' I said.

'And she's obviously been abused. I mean, you think that too, don't you?'

I nodded.

'Yeah,' she said. 'That child's talking about something that happened to her.' She stared into her coffee cup, the little lines deepening at the corners of her mouth. 'There are certainly holes in what she says – though I guess there often are. It's clear it can't have happened exactly like that – not the way she tells it. Not on those days – I mean, she said it was every day – and maybe not in that room . . .' She looked across at me then, a miserable, resigned sort of look. 'But Chloe, I'm sorry, but I have to say that the description she gives seems absolutely clear. I mean, who else could it have been?'

I said nothing, I think I flushed, felt a kind of shame – as though it was my own guilt that was being discussed. As though I'd done it.

'I did a double-take when I was watching,' she said. 'I know Sandy Willis who interviewed her. I did an interview with Sandy once myself. She's sweet with kids. Well, you can tell that from how she talked to Carly, I guess.'

'Yes,' I said.

'I can't say I'm sure about Felix's choice of barrister,' she went on. 'Samuel Allerdyce . . . I'm sorry, but I just don't like the guy.'

I felt a little rush of panic. 'Why ever not?' I said. 'I mean, Felix knows what he's doing, doesn't he?'

'Maybe it's just physical. He's really big and bony, got this massive jaw like a thighbone. And he made Carly cry,' she said, frowning. 'He kept asking her stuff – and she kept saying she couldn't remember. And he said, There wasn't really a sink, was there? And she said, They've blocked it up. And he said, It didn't *really* happen, did it? A man didn't *really* put his hand down your knickers. And she asked to go to the toilet and she was crying. It was awful. All the women in the jury were kind of flinching.'

'Oh God,' I said. I stared down into my coffee-cup, thought of the troubled little girl I'd seen on the video, the way her hands had fluttered when she was scared. I had a feeling that was more like grief than anything, the fear and terrible restlessness of grief. I felt my eyes fill up, but I didn't know who my tears were for.

I blinked hard, took a deep breath, didn't look at Jude. 'How did Dan seem?' I said.

'Older than when I knew him. You know, when we ran that group together,' she said. 'Well, that was several years ago now. But he's kind of older and thinner than I'd remembered. I guess he's not the kind of guy who looks his best in a suit.'

I couldn't picture him at all, couldn't see his face. I wanted her to describe him, to draw him in careful detail for me, like those artists who sketch defendants in trials for the Nine O'Clock News – every frown-line, eyelash, bit of stubble, the angle of his head, the way he held his hands: to flesh him out, make him real for me.

'Please tell me properly,' I said. Sensing she was being evasive with me, seeking perhaps to protect me.

She shrugged a little. 'What the hell d'you expect, Chloe?' she said. 'He looks damn awful.'

'Yes,' I said. 'Well, I suppose he would.'

And then quite unbidden, as I struggled to see him and absolutely couldn't, I had one of those hallucinatory flashes I'd sometimes had when we were first together. It must have been the stress, the lack of sleep – but it was as though I could feel his hand on mine, the firm dry touch of his palm, the warmth of it moving through me. Absolutely real, as though he was there, as though it was happening. I'm going mad, I thought.

Jude reached across the table to pat my arm.

'Chloe, are you okay?' she said.

'Sort of,' I said. 'It just feels so unreal.'

'It's pretty damn unreal even if you're there,' she said. 'The whole thing's so bizarre – the gowns and wigs and all this ridiculous language – I mean, they keep addressing the issue of whether impropriety occurred, for God's sake – and Daniel Whitmore sitting in the dock. It's a weird, weird thing.'

'Was Helena there?' I said.

'Yes,' she said. 'Looking very elegant – I guess she's good at that.'

Ludicrously, I minded this, as I sat there dressed in my oldest clothes, with that faint sour smell of vomit I could never quite wash from my hands.

'She always goes up to Dan in the breaks,' said Jude. 'He's bailed when the court rises, so he can come down and chat. His daughter's there too, and people from his office, and he talks to them for a bit, then he goes off into this little room with Felix and Paola and Jaws.'

'And the jury?' I said.

'Five men, seven women,' she said. 'Wearing their best tailored clothes. Blouses with bows at the collar are really big with jurors.'

After the disclosure video and the questioning of Carly, she said, they'd called Carly's mother.

'Now that was all very interesting,' she went on. 'The mother said Carly had lots of behaviour problems last year – truanting and not eating and wetting the bed. Which was all by implication being blamed on the abuse, on Dan. But then it came out that she'd taken Carly to the doctor two years ago with all those things – and they had the doctor's records to prove it.'

I felt a sudden little surge of hope. 'That's way back before Dan ever saw her,' I said.

'Exactly,' said Jude. 'Poor little kid. You do wonder what the hell's been going on.'

She drained her coffee cup, put it down with an energetic click.

'Look, Chloe, I have to go,' she said. 'I'm seeing Elliot tonight.'

'Perhaps he'll finally buy you a metropolitan,' I said.

'I'll believe that when it happens.' She got up, poked out her tongue at herself in my overmantel mirror, turned to go. 'I'll be back tomorrow night with the next instalment,' she said.

'Jude,' I said, 'you don't have to.' It was a huge effort to get the words out, but I knew I had to say it. 'You could be spending your leave in Harvey Nichols or something. You mustn't feel you have to go for me.'

'I don't,' she said. 'You couldn't keep me away now – I'm hooked. I've simply got to see how it turns out. It'll be all the other prosecution witnesses tomorrow – I wouldn't miss it for the world. D'you know who they'll call?'

'No,' I said.

'The judge said right at the beginning that he regarded the video as the evidence in chief,' she said. 'Which suggests they haven't got anything else on him. No kiddie porn in his airing cupboard. No other poor little child to say he did something he shouldn't – and God knows they must have looked hard enough for that. So really it's all going to hang on whether the jury think that Carly's account makes sense.'

I went to the door with her.

'And will they?' I said.

'I'd say it's wide wide open,' she said.

A thin bitter rain was falling, the sort of rain that insinuates itself everywhere, into the parting of your hair, under the collar of your coat. I lent her my umbrella. She hugged me and went off into the night.

Alice got worse that evening, her skin grey, almost translucent, so you felt you could see right through to the veins underneath, a thin milky film of sweat on her forehead, the shadows dark like bruises round her eyes. The coughing bouts left her so exhausted she scarcely had the strength to speak, and I had to wrap her arm round mine and walk her to the loo.

At eight o'clock I rang the doctor again. They have an answering service and I had to leave a message.

Ten minutes later the phone rang. I rushed to pick it up, relieved she'd rung back so quickly.

'Chloe?' A woman who sounded familiar, but definitely not the doctor, who always calls me Mrs.

'Speaking,' I said.

'This is Jo Hastings,' she said. 'You know, Felix's secretary.'

'Oh,' I said.

'Felix just asked if I'd give you a quick call – to say the Dan Whitmore case went ahead today.'

'Yes,' I said. 'I heard about it.'

'You did? That's great,' she said. 'Look, Felix says if you do want to testify, you'll probably be needed on Wednesday. But I'll give you a ring tomorrow, just to let you know. I hope that's alright?'

'Yes,' I said. She was so pleasant, so reasonable, with her Anglican Synod air, I felt I couldn't possibly explain I probably wasn't going to go, that Alice was worse and I couldn't possibly leave her, that it was all impossible. Which, I guess, was exactly why Felix had got her to make the call.

'That's all then, Chloe,' she said. 'So sorry to trouble you. 'Bye.'

I put down the phone, heard Alice coughing, went wearily up the stairs again.

34

On Tuesday morning I took Alice to outpatients. The doctor wanted to have her X-rayed to see if she was developing pneumonia.

The whole thing was vile – getting Alice dressed and into the car: walking her across the hospital car park, where she had a bad coughing fit, clinging desperately to someone's Ford Mondeo: the hour-long wait for the X-ray. But they said her lungs were clear, which was a huge relief. All the effort tired her out, and that afternoon she slept for nearly three hours without coughing. The sleep seemed to heal her a little: she woke looking rather less ethereal, and ate some toast and kept it down, and laughed at something I said.

At seven o'clock Jude came. She dumped her handbag on the kitchen table, pulled out the local paper, folded it over and held it out to me.

It wasn't too bad. It wasn't a very big piece, and it wasn't on the front and it didn't name him. The headline was MAN DENIES SEX ASSAULT ON SCHOOLGIRL.

> An education psychologist indecently assaulted a young girl at a junior school during one-to-one lessons, a jury has heard. Sex assaults on the girl, who had special needs, happened on several occasions when the pair were on their own together in a room, it was alleged. After assaulting the child, the man told her not to tell anyone, claimed Mr Graham, prosecuting. Mr Graham said, 'If the prosecution is right he strayed very far from his responsibility and breached the trust placed in him. Far from assisting the child he used her for his own gratification. They had a number of private sessions alone in a room and impropriety occurred.'

'There's nothing in the nationals,' said Jude. 'I had a good look.'

'Thanks,' I said.

This time she wanted wine. I opened some Chardonnay.

'Tell me,' I said.

'It was mainly prosecution witnesses today,' she said. 'First they called these other two male teachers who could have taken Carly for one-to-one lessons. The other ones who might have been "the man".'

'Yes,' I said.

This was the bit of the trial I'd been waiting for – I had a wild hope that there might be some new evidence, that some crucial fact might be revealed to incriminate somebody else. But I could tell it hadn't happened: Jude was quite relaxed, quite matter-of-fact, I knew she wasn't telling a story that had a dramatic conclusion.

'There was this guy Krishna Chauhan who worked most of the time in the Rainbow Room helping bilingual kids with their English,' she said. 'I think he was mainly called so the jury could see him, because Carly had said the man who abused her was a white man. Allerdyce asked him about the sink, and he said there had never been a sink. He thought perhaps the building had been built as a factory but there had never been a sink in that room since he'd been there – he said his desk was in front of where the tiles were.'

'Yes,' I said.

'Then they called this support teacher, Philip Bradley, who'd also taken some of the kids for lessons on their own, so he was definitely in the frame – and he had a beard and glasses. And Graham said, Without being offensive, can I ask whether your appearance last year was the same as it is now? And Philip Bradley said yes. So he couldn't have been the man.

'Then,' she said, 'they called the headmistress, Fiona Parker.'

'Hell,' I said.

'Why? D'you know her?'

'No,' I said. 'Well, only what Dan told me. He didn't like her.'

'He'll not like her even more now,' she said. 'She was a dream witness – all brass buttons and very confident. There was lots of stuff about the layout of the school and whether there was a sink in a room just down the hall. I guess they were trying to find some other sink for Dan to have washed his hands in.

And there were photos and plans of the school for the jury to see.'

She leaned back, drained her glass.

'There are things I still don't get about the justice system over here,' she said. 'I mean – think how much that trial must be costing. Yet when there were photostats for the jurors to see, they had to share one between two. Can you believe it?'

I shrugged, nodded. I poured more wine. It was going to my head too fast. My body felt thin, light, out of proportion, not quite my own: the feeling made me think of the earliest days of parenting, when you never get enough sleep – how eventually you don't feel tired any more, just utterly unreal, and you flinch when your hair falls over your face and hear things that aren't there.

'Then they got her to talk about some slanging match she'd had with Dan,' said Jude.

'Shit,' I said.

'You know?'

I nodded.

'She was kind of pious about it,' said Jude. 'Like, "We had a difference of opinion over how a particular child's needs might best be met, and I'm afraid Mr Whitmore lost his temper." And the barrister said, "And how was this resolved?" And she said, "I'm afraid I had to ask Mr Whitmore to leave." It was this picture of Dan as someone who's impulsive and not very professional. Not what you really want,' she added dryly.

I thought of that long-ago summer evening when Dan had told me about it: how we'd drunk wine after making love, how I'd shivered when the chilled wine had spilt on my skin. And I thought how Dan had been full of regret and afraid, how he'd known he'd made an enemy.

'No,' I said. 'No, it's not what you want.'

'And then they called this policewoman so she could say they'd searched Dan's flat, and about the interview with him. Victoria Griggs, with very neat hair. Is that the Vicky you saw?'

'Yes,' I said.

'She read part of the transcript of the interview with Dan,' said Jude. 'It was like a drama class – Vicky Griggs did the police part and the barrister was Dan. He kept denying it, she said.'

'He told me about it,' I said.

'Chloe,' she said then. She looked round, lowered her voice a little, though there was no one to hear. 'They did read out the bit where he'd said that you and he were lovers.'

'Well, they would of course,' I said.

'It was just very brief,' she said, 'just the facts. That he'd said you'd been lovers since June of last year, that your sexual relationship was normal and good – I think those were the words. And he'd said that prior to leaving his wife their sexual relationship was alright but it had ceased some months before he left her. That was all, I promise. Your name was only mentioned twice. But it made me so angry. I mean, why the fuck do they need to know all this stuff?'

I shrugged. I was hardened, I guess – I was used to this kind of exposure. The thing that really got to me was that no new evidence had emerged, nothing to inculpate anyone else. Little cold waves of disappointment seeped into me – that nothing had come out that I didn't know already, nothing to make it clear. And I realized how crazy my fantasy had been – that inarticulate hope I'd had, that there'd be a startling twist in the course of the trial, like at the end of a television drama, the credits starting to roll, the scattered pieces fitted together, the smiling villain exposed.

She stayed for a long time that night, and we drank, talked about other things – her orthodontist and his unusual sexual preferences, and the pros and cons of liposuction, and the threatened restructuring at work – they were always threatening restructuring at work – and where she was going for her summer holidays – Umbria with the orthodontist, but don't hold your breath.

At nine o'clock the phone rang. I went to answer it in the study. It was Jo again.

'Just to say the defence case starts tomorrow,' she said. 'Felix says if you do want to come you should say who you are at the security desk, and they'll get one of the ushers to take you through. That's all. 'Bye then.'

I put the phone down, went back to the kitchen. I didn't tell Jude what the call had been about.

Jude did most of the talking that evening – I was almost too tired to talk. Towards the bottom of her third glass of Chardonnay she started to reminisce about her childhood: dreary wet winter days in

London can fill her with a transient yearning for Chicago, where the winters are white from October through to March, and in April you think spring's finally come, but there's always another snowfall. We finished the wine, and in the end she said, 'I'd better go. You look shattered, Chloe.'

'I guess I am,' I said.

We went to the front door. I opened it.

But she didn't leave, just stood there looking away from me, the lines in her face deepening.

'What's wrong?' I said.

'Chloe, I don't think I can go tomorrow,' she said unhappily. 'I'm so so sorry.'

'Oh well,' I said, trying to shrug it off. But really I felt utterly adrift. It was like I'd been torn away from Dan all over again, that the only link that still held us together was broken or wrenched away. Tomorrow I knew might well be the verdict, Dan's future being decided, and without Jude there I'd never know exactly how it all happened.

She was flushed with discomfort. 'I couldn't face telling you,' she said. 'I haven't got any leave left.'

'For God's sake, you mustn't apologize,' I said.

'It wasn't meant to happen,' she said. 'I was going to take time in lieu. Hell, they owe me enough. But Nat rang tonight, said there's a conference on Jamie Simmons, I've got to be there. I hate it, I really feel I'm letting you down.'

'That's total crap,' I said. 'You've done so much for me.'

'You could speak to Flip Nicholls,' she said. 'I'm sure she'll go tomorrow. She'd probably love to talk to you – she likes to feel important. I could get her home number from Gina if you like.'

'Don't worry,' I said. 'I'd really rather not. It would just be too embarrassing, talking to her.'

The street was full of night, the stars covered in cloud. We said goodbye, I went back to the kitchen.

I sat at the table, read the report of the trial in the newspaper again, noting those strange, rather pompous statements. Used her for his own gratification . . . Breached the trust placed in him . . . With Jude gone, in the silence after her noise and certainty and laughter, the room seemed oddly empty, shadows reaching in from the corners like the shadows of branches, like trees pressing down, shutting out all the starlight. I felt terribly lost and alone, filled up with darkness.

The door crashed open, made me jump, and Lucy came stumbling in, looking very little in her over-sized new Hercules nightshirt, clutching her comforter, cross and clear and definite but only just awake, her hair falling everywhere.

'Those people woke me,' she said grumpily. 'With their noisy cars in the street. Some people are very very selfish.'

'Never mind,' I said. I guessed it had been Jude in her dreadful old Alfa Romeo, driving off rather ferociously because she felt upset.

I pulled Lucy onto my lap.

'I *ran* past Alice's room,' she said. 'She might have been sick. I hate it when she's sick.'

'Poor old Alice,' I said.

'Poor me too, Mummy,' she said.

'Poor you too,' I said.

She yawned a luxurious yawn.

I played with her hair, lifted a bit of it into the light, looked at all the shifting colours in it, tawny colours and mud colours like wet sand streaked with sunlight, let the strands fall heavy like sand between my fingers. Her breathing slowed, her warm head pressed down languorously on my upper arm. I held her close to me, kept her there for a long time after she'd gone to sleep, comforted a little by her warmth, sat there at the table, holding her close and reading the report in the newspaper again and again till the words stopped making sense, staring at it as though there was some secret code to it, as though the letters were hieroglyphs or runes or yarrow sticks fallen into significant patterns, and if only I could interpret them aright I would finally understand.

35

It rained heavily in the night: I heard it tipping down when I got up to see to Alice. By the morning the storm had stopped, but it was still dark and overcast and everywhere was wet, the lawn drenched, the patio covered in puddles, and every twig on my apple tree had a single clear drop of rainwater hanging from the end of it, like a tear.

I got Lucy ready for school and Jake's mother came to walk her in. I put on the nine o'clock news, ate some muesli. I made some toast for Alice, took it up to her, put in a video for her. I changed her duvet cover, wiped her face and hands. I took the dirty duvet cover down to the washing machine, made coffee.

I kept arguing with someone in my head, kept telling this person how impossible it all was. You can't expect me to do this thing, I said. There's so much I'd put at risk, my job, my custody of my children. These are my priorities, they have to be, not a man I once loved, however much I loved him. These things have to come first: surely you see that, I told the person, my voice so clear and emphatic in my head, it was almost as though I was speaking aloud, I could hear the tone of it, petulant, shrill with self-justification. Anyway, I said, shifting my ground a little, I'm still not sure enough, not absolutely one hundred per cent certain. Not sure enough to take this irrevocable step.

I felt it was a woman I was arguing with, Jo perhaps, in her role as Felix's mediator. I appealed to her motherliness, to the womanly feeling in her. Here I am with one of the most daunting illnesses to nurse – Penelope Leach says so – and yet you're making all these demands of me. I don't think you quite realize what you're asking, I don't think you've thought it through. You don't know what it's like for me, up all night, all the worry, all these troubles, I said, the voice in my head whining with self-pity. I'm sorry but my child comes first. You surely can't expect me to leave my sick child. I can't possibly do what you're asking me to do. Whenever Dan's image came into my head – in the dock, in his formal clothes, as Jude had described him, his head in his hands, or staring down at the floor – it was like I flinched away, as you flinch from touching some part of your body that's bruised or broken.

I made a coffee, thought I'd drink it with Alice. I knew she wouldn't want to talk much, so I took the newspaper Jude had brought under my arm, thought I'd look through the classified ads. There might be a violin for sale that I could get for Lucy, she'd been saying she wanted to learn. I sat on the floor by Alice's bed, drank my coffee, flicked through the ads. Alice lay back, watching her video. The boy band were singing something plangent in a soulful ecclesiastical setting, candles glittering everywhere, and some of their shirt buttons sexily undone.

The phone went. I rushed downstairs, expecting I don't know what – some news, some sign perhaps. But it was only a rather perplexed stranger, wanting to speak to Hayley. I went slowly back up to Alice's room, my pulse gradually quietening, my body so heavy I had to drag myself up each step.

Alice was sitting up straight, not leaning against the pillow, more alert now, tense almost. She had the newspaper spread out on the bed in front of her. It was opened at the account of the trial.

'Mum, this is Dan, isn't it?' she said, pointing, her voice hoarse, husky, from all the coughing.

'Yes,' I said.

'What will happen to him?' she said.

'I don't know,' I said. 'It's still going on today. The trial is still going on.'

'Now?' she said. She tried to clear her throat. 'Is it happening now – at this minute?'

'Yes,' I said.

'Does he have to sit in that wooden box thing, like on the telly?' she said.

'Yes,' I said.

She said nothing. She pushed the paper away, turned back to her video. It was such a relief that she didn't pursue it. I wondered if she was too ill for it to register, too exhausted to really think it through.

It was almost eleven o'clock when I went back downstairs. I tidied up a little, put on the radio, sponged off some cupboard doors I hadn't cleaned for ages. This, I thought, is one way to make a decision – wiping down a cupboard, listening to a consumer programme, trying not to think. Going through the motions, as sleep-walkers do, who, quite unconscious, embark on some everyday sequence of activity and can't be made to stop. Pushing your thoughts away as you push at insistent children who pluck at you when you're trying to sleep. Perhaps this is even how most decisions get made – because this not-doing, this waking sleep, is in itself a decision. And soon, I thought, the uncertainty will all be over: soon it will be too late.

At half past twelve I took Alice some scrambled egg for lunch, but she screwed up her face and said she couldn't eat it. I took the plate back downstairs, put the dishwasher on. I dusted the crockery on the dresser and sorted my kitchen cupboards. I watered the geraniums on my windowsill but they didn't really need it, the water stood in the saucers, so I tipped it out again.

I heard the floorboards creak above me. She must be getting out of bed. Going to the loo perhaps. The effort of walking down the passage usually brought on a spasm of coughing, and she needed me there to help her. I went to see if she was alright.

But she hadn't gone to the bathroom, she was still in her room. She had her back to me. She was poking around in the top drawer of her dressing table – a drawer Lucy isn't allowed in on pain of death: it's where she keeps her favourite things, her fruit soaps and velvet chokers and merit notes from school and a grain of rice with her name written on it in wonderfully fine lettering which she bought from a New Age stall at Camden Market. It's all very carefully arranged. Other mothers moan about their adolescent daughters' sluttish habits, how they're always finding toffees stuck to the radiators and bubblegum under the bed, but Alice is almost obsessional. The things other girls might keep mostly get thrown away – even back numbers of her magazines.

'Alice, you shouldn't be out of bed,' I said. 'You'll only start coughing again.'

She paid no attention, pulled the drawer a little further open, so I thought it might fall out, went on hunting around in it. I wondered if her illness had made her deaf, or perhaps a little confused, like children can sometimes be with very high temperatures – saying things that don't make sense, cringing from spiders that no one else can see. But she didn't have a temperature.

'Alice, sweetheart, listen to me,' I said. 'You're really not fit to get up. Alice, please.'

She turned to me.

'It's all right, Mum, I've found it,' she said. She was rather wobbly and frail, but seemed perfectly rational. She had something in her hand. She held it out to me. 'Look, it's so pretty,' she said.

It was the little paper bird that Dan had made on that long-ago summer evening when they'd pored over the origami book together, and she'd chosen the crane, and he'd groaned that it was the hardest one in the book, but he'd made it for her, perfectly.

'It was for luck,' she said. 'That's what it said in the book.'

I was amazed she'd kept it, when she always throws everything out. It was such an ephemeral thing, never meant to last very long, transitory like a joke or a phrase of music, the sort of thing that's soon lost or crushed or forgotten. Yet here it was, still white and precise and immaculate, like he'd only just made the final crease and put it into her hand.

'Mum,' she said, 'I want you to do something for me. I want you to give this to Dan. I think he needs it more than me.'

When I didn't move, she said, 'Go on, take it. I'm sure you can manage that, Mum.'

I took it. She got back into bed, collapsed against her pillows, her head lolling to the side, as though she was too tired to hold it straight. The bird lay on my palm, its delicate white wings uplifted as though it was poised for flight. And I thought how Alice hadn't even liked Dan – how she'd been suspicious of him and resented his presence in her life and the way he'd seemed to take my attention away from her: yet she'd loved this fragile thing he'd made for her and she'd found a special place for it and stored it with infinite care and kept it safe.

'Mum, you look funny,' she said. 'What's the matter? You're not going to cry again, are you?'

'No,' I said. 'That's not what I'm going to do.'

I sat beside her on the bed, the little white bird in my lap. I put my hand on top of hers. Her skin was clammy, you could tell she was ill from the feel of it.

'Alice,' I said, 'I want to ask you something.'

'Yeah, okay,' she said, rather wearily.

'There's a photograph,' I said. 'A photograph somebody took of you. Some time in the summer. My guess is it was that day Dan came round and showed you how to use his camera.'

She was watching me very intently, her eyes huge blue pools fringed with shadow.

'It's you in the bathroom mirror,' I said. 'Just your top half, with nothing on. D'you know who took that photo?'

She took her hand away from under mine, but she went on looking at me.

'I thought it wouldn't come out,' she said. 'It was the end of the film, so I hoped perhaps it wouldn't come out.'

'Who took it?' I said.

She looked so terribly tired. 'I promised I wouldn't tell,' she said.

'You must tell me,' I said.

'Is it important?'

'Yes,' I said. 'It's important.'

She said nothing, weighing it up, trying to decide.

'Alice,' I said again, 'who took it?' Then realized I knew what she was going to say before she said it.

Her mouth was twisted down: she still didn't want to tell. Then she gave a resigned little shrug.

'It was Lucy, Mum,' she said. 'She sneaked up behind me. She can be such a brat. She was ever so quiet, but the film started winding back and it made this whirring sound and it gave her away.'

'Yes,' I said.

'I was really mad, I was going to come and find you. But she thought she'd get into big big trouble because she'd taken Dan's camera. I mean, you know what she's like.'

'Yes,' I said.

'So I said I wouldn't tell, and we took it back downstairs and put it on the table in the hall.'

'Yes,' I said.

'I think she was jealous,' she said. 'Because Dan showed me all that stuff with the camera. She had this thing about Dan.'

'Yes, she did,' I said.

'I thought it hadn't come out,' she said again. 'Because nobody said anything.'

'It did come out,' I said.

She nodded vaguely. She rested her head back on the pillows, worn out. With the bruise-coloured smudges around her eyes, she looked like she'd been beaten up.

'Alice,' I said, 'will you be okay if I get Dorothy to come and sit with you? She's quite old and she may not be able to do very much. But you'll be okay won't you?'

She nodded.

I got up. I had the bird in my hand.

'Are you going to take it to him?' she said.

'Yes,' I said.

She sighed, sank back in the pillows, shut her eyes.

I went to get Dorothy, who was in, thank God, and quite happy to come and watch Alice's videos with her. I put out some bread and jam for Alice's tea – it was all I could think of. I grabbed a jacket, picked some of the fluff off it, ran wet hands through my hair, picked up my bag. And I put Alice's bird in the pocket of the jacket and went out to my car.

36

'You are Chloe Langdon?'

'Yes,' I said.

The defence barrister was just as Jude had described him, tall and thin and cerebral, his bones too big for his body.

'I'm going to ask you some questions,' he said. 'Could I ask you please to address your answers to the ladies and gentlemen over there?'

I turned to face them. Twelve faces, unsmiling, intent, all staring straight at me. They seemed very far away. After several days spent mostly in Alice's bedroom, the court felt vast, the space between me and the jury a huge abyss to fall into, a great big mouth that threatened to suck me in. The proportions of things were all wrong – like in the earliest preoccupied days of motherhood, when your baby fills your gaze, so adult faces seem gross, threatening.

I tried to focus on the twelve faces, tried to ignore all the others, all the people behind me in this big crowded court – Helena, Vicky, Russell Blake, union people, hangers-on, people from Dan's office, and a woman I thought must be Carly's mother sitting with Philippa Nicholls. But I could sense the eyes of those people on me, boring into my back, could sense the intensity of their curiosity. Felix was sitting behind the barrister, all cool and controlled, but allowing himself just a very discreet little smile. Dan was off to the side of me, in the dock at the back of the court, a black and white blur on the edge of my vision, distracting me, the sight of him pulling at me like a magnet. No matter how I turned my head he was always there, I couldn't help seeing him.

'I want to ask you some questions about your employment,' said the barrister. 'I believe you are a social worker working in child protection.'

'Yes,' I said. I felt surprisingly calm. But the heating was turned up too high for the day and the air felt dry and dense and it was hard to breathe.

'And that employment includes work with children who have been sexually abused?' He spoke very precisely, the consonants crisply articulated.

'Yes,' I said.

The jurors were all still staring at me, the strip lighting leaching the colour from their faces. I looked past them, concentrated on the thin purple stripes on the wallpaper behind them. It was a bland eighties interior, with a pale blue synthetic carpet and padded tip-up seats like in the cinema – yet still hugely imposing, as courts always are, where so much is in the balance and every word is weighed.

'And I believe you have worked in this area for approximately twenty years – at first full-time and latterly part-time?'

'Yes,' I said. He had been briefed by Felix, of course: Felix had given him the statement I'd signed. Yet the way this stranger knew all about me made me feel dreamlike, unreal.

'Could you give us some idea how many cases involving child sex abuse you have worked with over that time?'

I gulped, had a moment of panic – I wasn't sure how to answer. 'It's hard to say. But at present I have fifteen cases on my caseload and six are child sex abuse cases.'

'And does your work involve contact with both the children and the perpetrators?'

'Yes,' I said. 'Though the main focus is the children.'

'Now, I believe you are divorced?'

'Yes,' I said.

'And you have two daughters of your own?'

'Yes,' I said. 'They're twelve and five.'

'And your daughters live with you?'

'Yes.'

He left a little pause then, looked down briefly. I followed his gaze, focused on the things on the desk in front of him, the water carafes, ring binders, bundles tied with ribbon, pink highlighter pens. I realized I was holding myself quite rigid, like when you're about to be hit.

'Now, Mrs Langdon, could you tell us please whether you know Mr Whitmore?'

'Yes,' I said.

'And have you known him long?'

'I've known him since last summer,' I said.

'And could you tell us how well you know Mr Whitmore?'

'We had a relationship,' I said. Then, recognizing the ambiguousness of this, 'We were lovers.'

'When did your sexual relationship start?'

I told him.

'And was your relationship an intimate one from the beginning?'

'Yes,' I said, my words falling, small but heavy like stones, into the absolute silence of the court. I had my hand in my pocket, clutched the origami bird.

'And could you please tell the court what your sexual relationship was like?'

'It was very good,' I said.

'Mrs Langdon, could you speak up please,' said the judge in his gravelly, ponderous voice, making me jump.

'It was a good relationship,' I repeated. 'We had a very good, very normal sexual relationship.'

'In your experience, was there ever anything unusual about Mr Whitmore's sexual behaviour?' the barrister went on.

'No,' I said. 'Nothing at all.' I saw Felix at the Café Picasso, preparing me for this, nibbling at the mussels with his regular very white teeth. He was right, it was easy. Except that somehow the air was too hot and thick to breathe. I had to struggle to get it into my lungs, my chest ached with the effort.

'Mrs Langdon, could you tell us, did this relationship continue as an intimate relationship?'

'No,' I said. 'It ended in September.'

'And whose decision was it that it should end?'

'I ended it,' I said. 'It became too difficult with all this happening – with the allegation.' I couldn't think of the right cliché.

'The allegation put a stress on your relationship?'

'Yes,' I said. 'But in December I decided I wanted to start seeing him again.'

I could see Dan out of the corner of my eye, my peripheral vision keen, like a hunted animal's. I knew he'd looked up when I said that, knew he was looking at me.

'Did you contact him then?'

What to say? It was all so complex, so intricate. Just tell the truth, I thought.

'I saw him once,' I said.

The barrister glanced down at his notes, slightly uncertain: I could see him wondering whether or not to pursue this.

'During the period of time when your intimate relationship was ongoing, did Mr Whitmore come to your house at all?'

'Yes,' I said. 'We saw each other several times a week. He spent a lot of time at my home.'

'And were your two daughters present on these occasions?'

'Yes,' I said. 'They got to know him well. I was never worried in any way by his relationship with my children – it seemed very comfortable and natural.'

'Did you ever leave your daughters alone in his presence?'

'Yes, that happened quite often. I was perfectly happy with that.'

'And how did your daughters react to the ending of the relationship?'

'My younger daughter in particular was very fond of him,' I said. 'She misses him a lot.'

'Could you tell us how you know she misses him?'

'She cried when she was told he wouldn't come round any more,' I said. 'And she still sometimes says she wants to see him.'

'Thank you, Mrs Langdon,' he said. 'No further questions, Your Honour.' He sat down.

I could see Felix more clearly now over the barrister's shoulder, could see the rather smug little smile that crinkled the skin round his eyes.

The prosecuting barrister stood up. He was round and smooth, with a shiny good-humoured face that made the wig look kind of ironic. He smiled at me with great charm. My heart started beating very fast.

'Ms Langdon, you told us you had a relationship with the defendant which started in June of last year. Is that correct?'

'Yes.'

'And the defendant was in fact living with his wife of twenty-three years at the time your relationship with him – your *intimate* relationship – started?' It was all quite subtle, just the slightest emphasis, nothing too obvious. I could hear my heart, its hard dull thuds.

'Yes,' I said.

'Would it be fair to say that your relationship with the defendant was a very passionate one?'

'Yes,' I said.

'Would I be correct in saying that you were indeed somewhat infatuated with the defendant?'

I knew this needed care: infatuation instantly implies impaired judgement. 'We were very close,' I said.

'But in September you ended it. As you said, there was a lot of stress on the relationship.' He was very gentle, his head on one side, his voice all hushed and empathic. 'Is that correct?'

'Yes,' I said.

'And then at the beginning of December, you had a change of heart?'

'Yes.'

'You decided that you wished your relationship with the defendant to resume. Is that correct?'

'Yes.'

'So you contacted Mr Whitmore in December – and yet as you told us you saw him only once. Am I right?'

'Yes.'

'So you were, as you put it, very close to this man. You had, as you have agreed, a very passionate relationship. Yet you broke the relationship off until December, when you saw him again – but only once. This was rather strange behaviour, surely, given the intense nature of the relationship. Would you agree?'

'Well – you could see it like that,' I said.

'Something perhaps was stopping you from taking further steps to patch up your relationship,' he said. 'Am I correct?'

'Yes,' I said.

'Would it be true to say you were in a state of inner conflict about whether or not to continue your relationship with him?'

I didn't know how to answer this. I knew he was building up to something, that he was going to catch me out or disconcert me. I felt incredibly tired suddenly. I just wanted it all to stop, wanted to go away and hide somewhere and sleep for weeks and weeks. 'It was a difficult time for me, yes,' I said.

'Ms Langdon, I would suggest you didn't renew your relationship with the defendant because deep down you had some terrible doubts about him. For yourself you were still deeply attracted to him – yet you knew you didn't want him in the same house as your children. Isn't that right?'

'I didn't know what to do for the best,' I said. 'It was very difficult.'

His bland round face was suddenly fierce and stern. 'You have much experience in these matters, and, to put it bluntly, you feared your children might not be safe with him, didn't you?' he said.

In some weird way, his aggressiveness made me feel stronger: I had something to oppose. I took a deep breath.

'No,' I said. 'I would trust him completely with my children.'

'If that wasn't the reason for all this vacillation, all these changes of heart,' he said, 'could you tell the court exactly what was the reason?'

'I didn't contact him because the police advised me not to contact him,' I said.

A tiny shiver went round the court, like a quick intake of breath. On the edge of my gaze, I saw the white blur that was Dan's face, how he stared at me. And I thought as I said it how extraordinary it was that I should be telling him this now – in this very public theatre, in the glare of these lights, in front of all these people.

'Thank you, Ms Langdon.' The 'Ms' came out with a little hiss, very deliberate, hinting at untold depths of feminist depravity. His parting shot. It was I suppose the best he could do in the circumstances. 'No further questions, Your Honour.' He sat down rapidly, in that neat almost elegant way that plump people sometimes will, making themselves seem smaller than they are.

The defence barrister stood again. 'If I may ask just one or two questions arising from what you've just said to my learned friend . . .'

The judge nodded.

'When the police advised you not to contact Mr Whitmore, how did you react?' said the barrister.

'I knew I had to do as they'd advised,' I said.

'Did their advice affect how you felt about Mr Whitmore in any way?'

'No,' I said. 'I trusted him. I wanted to see him, but I knew I couldn't.'

He thanked me and sat down.

The judge took off his glasses. 'Thank you, Mrs Langdon,' he said, shaking out his big purple cuffs. 'You are free to stay in court or to go about your business.'

I nodded. A great wave of relief washed over me. It had been pretty unpleasant, but I knew I'd done okay, and now it was over, thank God. I felt a little drunk, as though I was important, as though I'd achieved something significant, perhaps even something good. I guess it was the adrenalin high and the drama of it all.

There were three rows of public seats at the side of the court, opposite the jury. Most were filled. I went to an empty seat at the end of the second row. Everyone seemed to be looking at me – Vicky, rather serious and dejected, and Helena, and Sally, who was sitting next to Helena. I recognized her from the photo Dan had shown me. She was gazing at me with wide, inquisitive eyes, her forceful eyebrows arched, as though she was perplexed or startled by something I'd said. The tip-up seat let out a little scream as I pushed it down.

I felt huge, hot, my face burning, twice my natural size. After all that public exposure, it was like I had to make myself small and insignificant again. I sat there very still, trying to look inconspicuous, studying the back of the woman in front of me. It was a rather nondescript back: one of those ubiquitous navy jackets that women choose when they aren't quite sure what to wear, and very fine grey-streaked hair which was caught in the collar of the jacket. The back of a woman who was too self-confident, serious-minded or simply wrapped up in other things to bother too much what she looked like.

The woman turned, smiled a conspiratorial smile, reached out to shake hands. 'Hi, I'm Paola,' she whispered.

'Hello,' I whispered back.

She was quite nice-looking in a friendly, wholesome way: round metal-framed glasses, rather plump, no earrings or frivolous lipstick, by no means the sultry beauty I'd always envisaged. With all the adrenalin swilling around in my veins, this struck me as funny – I laughed a little inside to think how I'd feared her power.

I turned to look at Dan but he wasn't looking at me any more. He sat there in the dock with a Group 4 woman in a navy suit beside him. I knew she was there as a warder, really: technically he was in custody. He was staring down at his hands, everything about him sunken, gravity pulling him down. Jude was right: he was older, he'd aged even in the month or so since I'd seen him. I so longed to put my arms round him, to give him some of my strength, to explain everything.

The defence barrister said he had no more witnesses to call: I realized I'd only just got there in time. There was a flurry of activity in the seats where the legal people sat, papers were rifled through, water was poured into tumblers. Then the prosecuting barrister rose to make his closing speech.

'Members of the jury,' he said, 'this is a case that is all about two people, and two very different people at that, whose lives are poles apart. One is a middle-aged professional man – the other a little girl. A little girl, moreover, who had particular problems, in that she was assessed as having special needs. This was why she was referred to the defendant: he was seeing her to assist her with these difficulties she had. Yet we have heard evidence that he strayed very far from his responsibility: that he abused the trust placed in him and used her for his own gratification.'

He spoke with passion, rolling the words round his mouth like fine wine. Paola was scribbling away, trying to write it all down: I could see over her shoulder, she had rounded loopy handwriting, like a child's. Everyone else sat absolutely still.

He went through what Carly had said had been done to her, and how she'd called the perpetrator, 'the man'. 'Who was the man? the police asked her. But Carly couldn't remember. She is, as we know, a child who can't always remember dates and names and times. But she's been totally consistent in what she's said about the man – he saw her for one-to-one sessions, he had dark hair, a blue car.

'So what we've done,' he said, 'has been to set up a coconut shy and knock away every other candidate.' He liked these little metaphors, striving for the common touch. 'We've asked the other two men who might have seen her for one-to-one sessions to appear as witnesses. Mr Chauhan, whose room it was – but she said it was a white man. Mr Bradley, who might also have taught her there – but his appearance is entirely different from the description she gave. That leaves one man – and the Crown says he matches the child's description in every detail.'

He talked about Dan then. 'You have heard that Mr Whitmore's marriage has ended and that he now lives alone,' he said. It was that image of the solitary paedophile that Felix had been so anxious to dispel. He made much of Fiona Parker's evidence. 'Mrs Parker has described to you how Mr Whitmore lost his temper and acted impulsively and inappropriately in a professional situation.' He spoke rather sadly as though this revelation caused him genuine pain. And then he analysed what Carly had said. 'There are certain problems with the account she gives,' he said. 'One of the problems is that time doesn't seem to mean the same to her as it does to us – which doesn't mean she's any less capable than the rest of us of telling the truth. Indeed,' he said, his voice soft and slow and full of significance, 'I would remind you that the defendant himself says she was not a girl given to fantasizing.'

I thought how Dan had told me this, as we'd sat at my kitchen table on that silent December day, with my flowers all crumpled up in the cold garden and the frost just starting to thaw. How I'd known at once what a gift this was for the prosecution.

The barrister skimmed lightly over the issue of the sink. 'Maybe he went to the staff cloakroom down the corridor to wash his hands. It's possible. For Carly, the fact that the abuse happened would be the thing that mattered,' he said. He suggested that Carly's failure to name the man who'd abused her actually made her a better witness. 'Assume for a moment that this was a malicious complaint by the girl. You might expect someone who makes a malicious complaint to name the person from the start – but she doesn't name Mr Whitmore, and has never named him. We say that this doesn't detract from the case, but rather adds validity to it.' And he appealed to the jury to accept what Carly Smithson said and find Daniel Whitmore guilty.

He sat down, in that neat, rapid way he had. I looked at Dan. He was bent over, his elbows on his knees. The tubular lighting took all the colour from him, the lines of his frown were cut sharply into his face. I wished I could reach out and comfort him.

Then it was the defence's turn. The defence barrister stood, all skin and bone and big frontal lobes. I noticed again the clipped way he spoke, the precise articulation.

The charge, he said, was a very serious one – this terrible abuse of trust. The victim was young and fragile and grievously wronged – a child who had undoubtedly at some time, in some situation, suffered the abuse that she had described so poignantly to us on the video.

'And I would absolutely agree with my learned friend,' he went on, 'that what the child says is the heart and soul of the case. There is no corroborating evidence – no injury, no torn underclothing, no screams. Her complaint about indecency stands or falls on its own.'

He went on to list the problems with the prosecution case. His voice was flat, measured: he didn't seek to beguile you. He reminded us that Carly hadn't named the perpetrator, that she'd given a terribly vague description. He said that the frequency with which she said it had happened – every day – couldn't be squared with this defendant. 'Mr Whitmore wouldn't have had any opportunity to see her without other people knowing – let alone on consecutive days,' he said. 'And it doesn't make the prosecution case stronger,' he added sternly, 'to say she has a poor concept of time.' And her description of the sink in the room could not be squared with the room in which Mr Whitmore saw her. He dwelt on this, of course. 'She describes the room where it happened as one where he washed his hands – she wasn't describing a man washing his hands in some room down the corridor. It's no good for the prosecution to move the goalposts and claim he went off down the corridor. You must decide this case on the evidence, not on speculation by my learned friend. And there *is* no sink in the Rainbow Room. We have affirmative evidence from Mr Chauhan – his desk was in the very corner where the tiles were.'

Then there were Carly's behavioural problems, he said, the sleep-walking, the refusal to eat. 'The prosecution has claimed that these problems were caused by the abuse,' he said. 'Yet it's quite clear from her GP's records that there were behavioural problems well before Mr Whitmore was called in.' It was the point that had made even Jude pause a little – in spite of her unrelenting conviction that Dan was guilty.

And he talked about Dan. 'This is a man whose wife and daughter are in court today to give him their whole-hearted support,' he said. 'A man who is dedicated to his work. A man who has indeed on one occasion lost his temper at work in a way that was undoubtedly inappropriate – but why? Because of his intense concerns for a child who was a client of his, a child whose needs he felt weren't being properly met.' So I knew that Dan's own account of the row with Fiona Parker must have come out in court.

'We have also heard,' said the barrister, 'from a woman who has known him intimately.' The palms of my hands clasped together in my lap were suddenly wet. I kept my head down. 'A woman,' he went on, 'who says she has trusted him with her children – and whose judgement I would suggest we might do well to respect, because of her professional experience in this very area, in the protection of children from abuse.'

He reminded the jury they only had to have reasonable doubt. He asked how they could possibly fail to have reasonable doubt – given the inherent improbabilities in the prosecution case. He sat down.

The court was very quiet. The judge summed up, went through all the facts again. The jurors listened, their mouths turned down with the effort of concentration. When the judge poured himself a tumbler of water, two of the jurors did the same. It seemed to go on for ages, and quite honestly I can't remember most of it: the court was so hot and stuffy and I was so tired. Finally he told the jury they were to reach a unanimous verdict, that they mustn't feel under any pressure of time, and the jury bailiffs were sworn in and the jury picked up all their stuff, their handbags and jackets and notes, and were ushered out.

I looked towards Dan. He didn't look at me, he was talking to the warder. I wished he'd look at me. Then the judge got up and left the court, and Dan and the warder went out through the swing doors at the back of the dock. He'd be closeted with Felix, I guessed, reliving it all again, trying somehow to get though the endless minutes or hours until the verdict.

There was a restrained noise of conversation, as people turned to one another, talked fast and urgently, yet with lowered voices like people in church. No one talked to me. I expected a nod, at least, from Helena, but she was deep in conversation with Sally and Paola and a man I didn't know.

37

I went out into the corridor and down to the floor below to go to the loo. The flooring was all of tile or brick, built to withstand hard wear. There was no daylight anywhere, just lots of little spotlights in the ceiling, so my hand when I raised it to my face cast many shadows. There were variegated plants in troughs, and sepia prints of local battlefields, and cigarette stubs on the floor.

I passed the café, which was rather whimsically called Rumpole's. People would be whiling away time in there, eating snacks they didn't need from little segmented trays. A smell of chips and vinegar hung around outside. The door swung open as I passed and a court official came out and greeted a colleague in the corridor.

'How're you doing? Okay?'

'Yeah, well. Struggling through. You know how it is.'

The loo was round the corner. It was empty, quiet. I had a pee, went to wash my hands. As I turned on the tap I looked randomly at myself in the mirror, noting without much interest what a mess I looked. My skin was blotchy because I hadn't put on any makeup before I'd come out; my hair had frizzed in the rain, my jacket was creased. Not at all how I'd have looked if it hadn't been such a last-minute thing. Well, it didn't really matter. I pressed the lever on the soap dispenser: the soap had that institutional antiseptic smell, and a little wave of desolation I couldn't quite explain washed over me.

The door creaked open behind me, stayed that way for a moment, noise from the corridor seeping through. I couldn't see the door from the basin, couldn't see who was coming in. The person was standing in the doorway, talking to someone outside. I felt a quick rush of fear. There were people here I very much didn't want to meet. Carly's mother, Philippa Nicholls, Vicky, Sally. It could be any of them. Everyone except the jury presumably used this loo.

But I needn't have worried, there was nothing to be afraid of,

334

it was only Paola Valente. She came in, the door banging behind her, her lips already stretched in a smile as though she'd known I was there.

'Hello again,' she said.

'Hi,' I said.

She stood there smiling, in her predictable jacket, her modest knee-length skirt. I thought again how ironic it was that I'd had this image of her as some kind of Mediterranean siren. How I always expected the worst.

'I want to say that it was a very brave thing you did in there,' she said.

I appreciated her saying that: I felt this rather childlike need to be told I'd done all right.

I shrugged. 'I don't know,' I said.

'No, really. I'm sure Dan must be terribly grateful. I can only guess what it took to do it – to sort of expose yourself like that,' she said.

'Well,' I said, noncommittally. I dried my hands on the grey-green paper towel, got out my comb.

She stood leaning back against the basin, didn't go to pee: I wondered why she was there. 'Felix had been quite desperately hoping you'd come,' she said, with the rather self-satisfied air of the insider, the one who knows. 'He never felt you were quite in the bag, as it were.'

She started to wash her hands, soaping them all over with elaborate thoroughness, though she hadn't been to the loo. She had long pink fingernails filed into points, manicured with a care that didn't quite fit with the rest of her.

'Yesterday was grim,' she went on. 'I think Dan was very depressed. He tries to keep it inside: but when you get to know him, you can always tell when he's down.' A faint flush of colour across her face, as she showed me how well she knew him.

'I heard about it,' I said. 'I gather that Fiona Parker said some damning things.'

'Too right,' she said. 'If you'll excuse the term – she's a total b . . ., that woman.' She lowered her voice as she said it, as though this was really rather daring. 'We've had trouble with her before, as it happens – refusing to work with certain psychologists, that sort of thing. Some head teachers are foul. They rule their little empires, it breeds this kind of megalomania. It was great that you popped up, to put the other side as it were.'

'It wasn't such a big deal,' I said, starting to find all this effusiveness a bit hard to respond to.

'Don't do yourself down, Chloe,' she said. She dried her hands briskly on a paper towel, and took off her glasses and polished them on her skirt. 'I think what you said could just swing it. Sam Allerdyce made it virtually the climax of his closing speech, after all.'

She put the glasses back on. They made her eyes look smaller, as glasses for short sight do: made her gaze narrow, sharp, almost a little predatory. She took a comb out of her bag, turned to the mirror. We stood there side by side, looking in the mirror, combing.

'Your hair's so pretty,' she said. 'I wish I had hair like that. Mine goes all lank in the rain. Is it natural, or do you give nature a bit of a helping hand?'

'It's pretty much natural,' I said. This flattery made me uncomfortable, when any disinterested observer could see my hair was a total mess.

'It's lovely,' she said again. 'Aren't you lucky?'

I shrugged, wishing she wouldn't keep on about it, wanting to change the subject.

'You've been here right through, haven't you?' I said.

'Absolutely,' she said.

'What do you think will happen?'

'The prosecution case is obviously quite iffy,' she said. 'I mean, Carly's description is really very vague. Overall, Felix is optimistic, I'd say. But the opera isn't over till the fat lady sings.'

'No, of course not,' I said.

'And even if Dan does get off, I'm afraid he'll certainly lose his job: when it comes to dismissing employees, a different standard of proof applies – it's balance of probabilities. My guess is there's no way they'll have him back. We're going to have to give him an awful lot of support,' she said, rather fervently. 'We could take it to tribunal, of course, but even if we won that wouldn't mean reinstatement – just a cash pay-out. A damn sight better than nothing, though.'

'I guess so,' I said. I thought of Jude saying, 'He's done for,' Felix saying, 'It's a life sentence,' Nat who'd said, 'There'll always be the shadow.' Now, with my absolute certainty about Dan's innocence, it seemed so shocking. But I knew it would probably all happen just as Paola predicted, she'd lived with this for months, she knew what she was talking about.

'That's our next battle,' she said. She turned her head a little, apparently studying her reflection. The harsh light glinted on the wire frames of her glasses. 'Still – let's win this one first.'

'Yes,' I said.

'But whatever happens, it certainly doesn't end here.'

'No,' I said.

I took out my lipstick, started to stroke it on. The antiseptic smell of liquid soap on my hands.

'Look,' she said, 'you do know about Dan and Helena, don't you?'

'What?' I said.

'That it rather looks like they're getting together again?'

I said nothing. I couldn't speak.

'It's very recent,' she said. 'Just the night before last – the first night of the trial. He took her out for a meal, he told me they talked all night, just sat there and talked. Trying to find a way through, to connect again. Well, you can imagine. After everything.'

I told myself that what I had to do was very simple: to keep my face absolutely still, just hold it in place like a mask, absolutely unmoving. But I couldn't do it, my lips simply wouldn't stop trembling.

'We're all so hoping they'll work it out,' she said. 'It would really be rather touching, don't you think? After everything that's happened?'

She paused for a moment. She was watching me with her narrow, eager eyes. She didn't seem bothered that I didn't respond to her question.

'And you've got to admire her,' she went on, 'the way she's stood by him – through everything, in spite of everything. I mean, we all know men can go a bit batty in their forties – but to have all this to cope with too. And yet it could be this whole ghastly business will actually bring them together again. Kind of a silver lining.'

She played with her comb, pinging it, running her fingernail along the teeth.

'I've got to know Helena rather well during all this,' she said. 'And

337

really she's quite a woman. And absolutely loyal – I mean, talk about unconditional love.'

She dropped her comb back in her bag.

'There'd be a rightness about it, I feel,' she said. 'Dan looks so much better now, it's like a weight's been lifted from him, in spite of everything.' She touched my arm. 'Sorry,' she said. 'You obviously hadn't heard. Sorry if it's a bit of a shock. I just wanted to warn you, so you'd know – I hope that was okay.'

I managed to nod.

'You do look rather pale, Chloe,' she said, turning towards me. 'Are you *sure* you're all right?'

I tried to murmur some kind of assent. But my mouth had gone absolutely dry, it was stuck together, I actually couldn't open it.

'I just worried you didn't know,' she said. 'And I was obviously right.'

She did up the zip on her bag with a neat finality.

'Look, I'm sorry if I've upset you. I just felt you needed to be warned. I hope I did the right thing.'

She went.

I stood there, looked at the woman in the mirror, saw how her face seemed to crack and break and fall apart, stood there in front of the grey-green paper towels and the liquid soap dispenser, like so long ago in that little room off the casualty ward where they'd told us, my mother and me, that really we mustn't torture ourselves, that it had certainly all been over very quickly. And I thought how stupid and blinkered I'd been that I hadn't seen this coming. Because it was all so obvious: Helena was a good person, and loyal, and she'd forgiven him – which is the hardest thing for anyone to do – and they had all that life they'd shared to bind them together, and she was his *wife*, for God's sake. I felt ugly and greedy and blind. And I felt a kind of shame, too. I'd been so pleased with myself. I'd convinced myself that I'd come here to tell the truth, that this was a good act that was required of me, to offer my own little bit of knowledge to the court, to help justice be done – and now I saw my motives in such crude relief: saw that it had all been about what I wanted for me, about getting Dan back, and now that he wasn't there for me any more I felt it was unfair. As though I believed he owed me something because I had told the truth. As though my testifying had been a favour, for which I should be paid with his continuing love. And I was appalled at what this seemed to say about me.

And I saw too, with absolutely shocking force, how I had brought this on myself. How he had waited and waited for me, reached out, never been angry – or, at least, had shielded me from the anger I knew he'd felt with me – because he had not done this thing, and therefore he could not understand why it should come between us. And I had kept on pushing him away – and never really asked the questions that mattered, because I had been too scared. And now it was too late. Whatever happened back in court, it was too late for Dan and me. It was over.

I studied my reflection, to see if anyone could read my shame and grief in my face. I looked rather odd. I saw I'd stopped dead halfway through putting on my lipstick, and my top lip was shiny red and my bottom lip kind of purple. But I couldn't do anything about it, my hands were shaking too much. If I tried to finish it off, I'd probably miss my mouth, scrawl scarlet all over my face.

I would go and get some fresh air, I thought, take some deep breaths outside, try and get myself together. Because I was quite determined I would go back into court when the time came. There was nothing admirable about this: it was simply pride. I didn't want anyone to know how upset I was. Especially Paola. I recognized the pleasure she'd taken in what she'd told me, and I couldn't bear her to know quite how much she'd hurt me.

But when I went out into the corridor, turned towards the stairs, I found there was lots of purposeful activity outside Court 4, people being ushered back inside, a sense of expectation. The jury it seemed had reached their decision very quickly. I didn't know if this was good or bad for Dan. I followed.

And the jury came back, and the judge, and we all sat down and Dan was told to stand, and the foreman of the jury stood there in her blouse with the bow at the collar, clearing her throat, weighed down by a sense of significance, the paper in her hand shaking just very slightly, and nobody breathed.

'Members of the jury, have you reached a verdict?' said the judge.

'Yes,' she said.

'And are you all agreed?'

'Yes,' she said.

'Do you find the defendant guilty or not guilty?' said the judge.

'Not guilty,' she said.

A sigh went round the room, then a murmur of voices, excited but contained. I looked at Dan. He seemed quite impassive: I guess you school your face to be still in that moment, as your future is given back or taken away. Then he rubbed his hands across his face, like you do when just waking from sleep, pushed his hair back with his fingers. I saw how his body relaxed, how his shoulders dropped, how the tension started to leave him, as muscles begin to relax in the warmth of the sun.

'You are free to go,' said the judge. He rose, we all rose, he left the court.

It was suddenly noisy. The warder pushed open the door of the dock. Dan stepped out, blinking, loosened his tie. People rushed up to him, not exactly congratulating him, perhaps not really knowing what the convention was for such occasions. Yet it all had a very celebratory air, all smiles, men slapping him on the back, saying Thank God for that, and It's all over, women hugging him. Helena hugging him.

I watched how she embraced him, the arm round his shoulders, the smile, the few whispered words, saw how the others hung back a bit for a moment, giving them space, an instant or two of privacy in the crowded court. I was acutely conscious of how she moved, of the assurance with which she touched him. It was the embrace of a woman who knew she owned him: an embrace that claimed him. It seemed to tell me everything.

Then I sensed Dan looking over towards me, and I couldn't stand it, couldn't bear to catch his eye. The court seemed suddenly crowded, all these people gathering round, moving up to Dan, talking together, going through it again, happy, expansive, taking up so much space. There were so many people between me and the door. I struggled through, I was desperate to reach that door, everything in me was focused on getting out. I excused myself, pushed past people a little roughly, just wanting so desperately to be out of the courtroom before I started crying.

Paola was busy organizing some kind of celebration. She turned to me as I elbowed my way past her. 'I thought we could all go to this great sushi place I know,' she said. 'D'you want to . . . ? No, I guess not.'

I reached the door, almost fell on it, pushed against it with all my strength. I walked briskly through the bland brick corridor and past the plant troughs and the pictures of battlefields and down the first flight of stairs, holding tight to the rail like a child or a frail old person because I couldn't see the edges of the steps, I was blinded by tears. I passed the café with its buzz of chatter and smell of chips and coffee, came to the top of the next flight of stairs, walked on into the future. And as I went I talked to myself, kept up a busy chatter, a list of useful imperatives, things that had to be done. I would go straight home, I told myself, and make Alice a nutritious dairy-free meal, and I'd ask Jake's mother who was picking up Lucy if she could stop off at Blockbuster and get a new video for Alice, and I'd ring a homeopath that I'd heard of, that everyone at the school gate said was good, see if he could give her some clever alternative remedy, and next week I'd take time off, really be there for Alice, look after her and hold her through her coughing and help her get well again.

Because this is now my future, I thought: me and my daughters together, in my house with its yellow walls and its flowered china and hanging baskets, like a child's picture, and my useful work and my friends and my garden with the mulberry and the apple tree and the window boxes, and sitting quietly in my kitchen and gradually getting older, each morning a little greyer, my hands a bit more wrinkled, a little stiffness, a gradual drying out, the almost imperceptible daily shifts and changes, the slow accretions of age. And that's not such a bad way of living, I told myself through the tears. I have so much, I should cherish what I have, I said to myself, as the tears fell, shaming, uncontrollable.

A court usher turned, stared at me.

'Are you alright, madam?' he said, uncertain, rather formal.

I nodded, walked on.

And I am alright, I told myself. Or at least I *will* be alright. Soon. Next month, next year, I'll be alright. For it is all over now, this whole strange chapter in my life. The Dan and Carly chapter, the chapter about those two very different people, poles apart, as the barrister said, yet bound together, and pulled under almost by what has been done to them, and pulling me with them. And one day, I told myself, I'll look back and see it like that. One day I'll really be able to see it was just a chapter. The part of my life when I was in love with Dan. When all those things happened.

I came to the bottom of the stairs and went past the Incident Control desk and the security desk and the guard in her navy jumper who'd checked me over for weapons when I'd arrived, and out through the automatic doors. The rain was tipping down again, fat raindrops bouncing high on the brick paving outside the courthouse, and I was instantly soaked because I'd lent my umbrella to Jude, my legs splashed through my tights, and my hair and the arms and shoulders of my jacket all wet. But in a way I welcomed the downpour, in its extremity it seemed to match my mood, as I walked away from that sombre place, all humbled and dishevelled, and the water fell everywhere, washing away my tears.

38

I thanked Dorothy profusely and showed her out and held the front door open just long enough to be polite then shut it firmly on everything. The kitchen seemed airless and stale. I opened the window, letting in smells of wet earth and leaves, and something unexpected too, a sudden polleny sweetness. In one of the leafless grey gardens round about, though not as yet in mine, something must be flowering, a witch-hazel or mahonia perhaps. I stood there for a moment, breathing it in.

Alice was propped up against the pillows, watching a video, half-asleep, eyelids drooping. But she heard me come into her room and opened her eyes.

'Did you give it to him?' she said, her voice rather thin and far away.

'No, sweetheart. I'm sorry. It was too difficult. All these people wanted to talk to him.'

She frowned. 'But he'd have wanted to talk to you too, Mum, wouldn't he?'

'I don't know,' I said.

'He didn't go to prison, did he?'

'No,' I said. 'He didn't go to prison. He got off.'

'Will he get his job back?'

I shook my head. 'He'll probably be sacked. That's what usually happens.'

'Even though he got off?'

'Yes, even though he got off.'

'He won't like that, Mum,' she said.

'No, I guess not,' I said.

'I wish you'd given the bird to him. I really wanted him to have it.' She yawned, eased herself down in the bed. 'You're always saying you'll do things and then you don't,' she said through the yawn.

I pulled the duvet over her shoulders and left her to sleep.

Later Jude rang, of course, and we talked for ages and I told her everything and cried a bit. She made me go over all the stuff about Helena in great detail.

'But I thought you said Helena had someone else,' she said, puzzled.

'Well, that's over presumably,' I said.

'Oh Chloe,' said Jude. 'You poor thing. I guess some things just aren't meant to be.'

I kept going somehow, that night, the next day. It helped that Alice needed me so much. I'd sit down and cry, then I'd hear her starting to cough, and I'd have to go and hold the sick bowl and rub her back and soothe her. And Lucy was quite demanding, jealous perhaps of the attention Alice was getting, and wanted me to join in all her games: and there was always the washing, cleaning, tidying. Plenty to do, but nothing at all in any of it to occupy my mind. I moved slowly from one task to another and just kept reliving everything, all my mistakes and failures playing out in my head with almost hallucinatory vividness, the things I'd got wrong that couldn't be undone.

On Thursday afternoon I was tidying up before Lucy got back from school when I came on the jacket I'd worn to court: I'd flung it down on a chair when I'd come in and not yet hung it up. The paper bird was still in the pocket. I took it out. It was all scrunched up where I'd clutched at it when I was giving evidence. I was about to put it in the bin when something stopped me – the thought that here was one thing at least that I could put right. A small and insignificant thing, but still perhaps worth doing.

I smoothed out the creases in the paper as well as I could, and folded the wings down flat. I wrote Dan's name on an envelope and slipped the bird inside, and I put in a note that said, 'Alice wanted to give you this.' There was part of me that thought this was all rather foolish and embarassing, but I did it anyway. And when Jake's mother came to drop Lucy off on the way home from school, I asked if she'd mind sitting with the girls for twenty minutes while I went to the shops, and I got in my car and drove round to Dan's flat.

I parked a few yards down the road where a cherry tree in some-body's front garden leaned out across the pavement. I didn't get out, just sat there for a while. It was pouring still, it never seemed to stop. I could hear the rush-hour traffic building up on the main road, that swishy sound tyres make in the wet, the banging of a lorry going over a man-hole cover, but the only sound in this quiet street was the drumming of the rain.

If I craned my neck, I could see into the front part of Dan's living room through the big bay window. It all looked much as before, his books still on the shelves, the sash window a few inches open at the top, as he always left it. This surprised me. I'd imagined he'd have wanted to go straight back to Wimpole Avenue. In fact, I'd half expected to come on him right in the middle of moving out, kicking open the communal front door, struggling along the pavement with boxes of books and suitcases. Moving back to the elegant house with the Smallbone kitchen, the familiar orderly routine, the wardrobes full of Helena's expensive understated clothes, the desultory bed where so often she'd turned from his touch. But the street was empty, no one came.

I sat and stared at the door with its four doorbells and wondered whether I was actually going to do what Alice wanted. Just for now I couldn't move, my body felt heavy like in dreams, weighed down and burdened by everything that had happened. It seemed to require such a huge feat of will – to go and lift the letterbox flap and push my envelope through: it seemed impossible. Yet, I told myself, it was really the simplest thing, something I'd done so often and so happily in the summertime of our love affair, when I'd left him all those letters, the little notes about the ways he'd touched me and how it had made me feel. I thought how bold I'd been then, able to do things and say things I hadn't before and wouldn't, I guessed, again. The audacity of it all astounded me now. And I thought of the empathy between us which had made it possible, that sense of being seen into and understood: and the tenderness too. I'd loved him so very much: still did, in spite of everything. I tried so hard to hope he would be happy.

I took the envelope out of my bag and opened it and slipped out the note I'd written and looked at it. Alice wanted to give you this. It seemed a little cold, I thought. I scrabbled in my bag for a pen, found one of the children's red felt tips, wrote, 'All my love, Chloe', at the bottom of the note. The smudgy red ink didn't match the rest of the writing, the letters seemed to leap out at you, bigger and brighter than I'd intended. I tucked the note back in with the paper bird. The envelope looked so scrappy, the woman who lived in the downstairs flat would probably think it was rubbish and throw it away. That didn't matter: at least I'd still have done what Alice wanted. I got out and went to the door and slipped the envelope through.

Jake's mother was itching to go when I got back: I realized I'd been much longer than I'd planned. Alice was fast asleep: Lucy was in the living room, curled up with her comforter, watching television. I emptied the dishwasher, tidied up the kitchen. Lucy came to join me when her programme was over, and we went through some spellings she had to learn for school. Then I put out the Sylvanians for her to play with and got the pastry-making stuff together and mixed up the butter and flour to make a chicken pie for supper. It was one of their favourite meals: Lucy I knew would be pleased and Alice I hoped might manage to eat a little.

The phone went and I swore under my breath. My hands were covered in pastry, I was right at the stickiest part, kneading in the water before you roll it out, when it clings to you.

'Could you answer that, Lucy?' I said. 'Just while I wash my hands.'

Lucy was pleased: she likes doing this. She went to pick up the handset. It was far too big for her, she held it carefully to her ear like something precious. She recited our number, very precisely, listened for a moment.

'Oh,' she said, a little flushed. She looked at me uncertainly.

I rinsed the dough off my hands.

'I'm afraid she's terribly busy at the moment,' said Lucy into the phone. Her grown-up voice, polite but rather formal: it made me feel like laughing, it sounded just like me.

I shook the water from my hands and went to take the call.

'Who is it?' I said to Lucy.

She put the handset behind her back.

'Guess,' she said.

'Oh Lucy, honestly.' I reached for it but she stepped neatly to one side. I knew I couldn't get it without a tussle and one of us might drop it and the call might get cut off.

'Go on, guess, Mummy.'

'Jude,' I said, playing safe.

'Nope.'

'Jake's Mum.'

She shook her head, blonde plait skittering. She turned, spoke into the phone. 'She got it wrong,' she said. 'She's a really hopeless guesser,' and giggled at something the other person said.

And then I couldn't bear this game one moment more.

'Lucy, for goodness sake, just tell me who it is.'

'It's Dan,' she said. 'And he says you've got it *all* wrong and he wants to come and see us. He says, is that alright?' Watching me slightly anxiously to see what I would say.

I couldn't speak. *Was that alright?*

Lucy held the phone with both hands, spoke cheerfully into the mouthpiece. 'It's okay, she's smiling,' she said.

Man Guilty on Child Porn Charge

A man who was arrested during a concerted police action across the borough has pleaded guilty to two charges of possession of child pornography. Darren Smithson, 22, unemployed, of 105A Tonbridge Gardens, had pleaded not guilty to the charges at a previous hearing, but he changed his plea to guilty at a hearing presided over by Mr Justice Browning. Smithson was warned that he would almost certainly be facing a gaol sentence. Proceedings were adjourned for four weeks so that pre-sentencing reports could be prepared by the probation service and Smithson was remanded on conditional bail.

Surrey Comet, 4 May